STROKE OF LOVE

LILAH LANCE

TITAN SECURITY BOOK VII

To the girl who stopped believing in love

MISSION BRIEFING

Welcome to Titan

Seven years ago, former CIA operative Gabriel Monroe lost his wife.

He spent the last seven years searching for any sign of her.

The first half of his story is the beginning.
The second half is how his mystery unfolds.

Good luck on your <u>final</u> assignment at Titan Security

PART ONE | THE SUN GOD

SEVEN YEARS AGO

CHAPTER 1
ISOBEL

I WAS DYING.

It was another nightmare. I knew it was.

But I was dying in it again.

The shadows swallowed me whole. Hungry and dark and looking for blood. Someone was screaming, throwing me somewhere—I saw my father's eyes, my sister was shouting.

And then I was falling into a pool. Sinking into water. I was drowning. Again. Pale blue in front of my eyes and someone blurry was swimming to me.

Someone. A man. I began to panic.

Over the last few months I'd had dreams of drowning. A man swimming to me in the water.

Come find me. Where are you?

Why did you let me go?

Why haven't you come for me yet?

I gasped for air but none came and my lungs began to burn with the pressure.

The hands were rough again shaking me now. Calling my name.

Isobel.

Isa. Wake up.

Wake up.

"Isobel!"

I woke up with *someone* shaking me.

The way I recognized them I knew who it was.

Bright green eyes met mine. *Liam.*

Liam's eyes were creased with worry, his frown in place now as he shook me and when I did wake up I was in his arms.

"Isa."

I blinked into his eyes looking around uncomfortable.

The sun was blinding and then he was thankfully so close it blocked it out. I burrowed into the nook of his neck inhaling his clean scent and the hint of sweat as I grumbled.

"Where are we?"

Rubbing my eyes I sat up straighter in the car, as his hands went around to my neck massaging the crick in it.

I groaned at the sensation.

"Gas station. Outside Quantico. I need to go get gas, shortcake. I think you fell asleep but I pulled over when I heard you making that sound again."

He held me closer to him and Liam lifted a bottle of water to my lips I gratefully chugged. I knew what he was talking about.

The one where he knew I was having nightmares again.

Liam always knew.

"I hate sleeping in the car."

He made a softer noise. "I know. But you looked so tired, I just let you."

I rubbed my eyes feeling fifty instead of twenty-two as my brother rubbed my neck and hair. "It's okay, shortcake. Just breathe, I gotcha."

"How far are we?"

Quantico.

"I think thirty minutes, but I don't give a fuck if we're late." Liam never did.

"This is the CIA, Liam. Not college. We cannot be late."

"Isa," he pulled back a little not stopping as he gripped the back of my head now. His eyes twinkled with mischief. "Everyone's late." He motioned around the gas station. "See."

I slowly looked and saw other people out age holding maps. "Bet you solid money they're all trainees."

I smiled a little. "You are sneaky."

"Hell yeah." I looked back at Liam still smiling at me from the driver's seat.

His smile softened out his too handsome features. One of his earring cuffs on the shell of his ear glinted in the sunlight.

He had taken out some of them for training but left one.

I had gotten him that one for Christmas.

"What? I gotta keep an eye out. You looked tired when you left." He was always looking out for me. All the time. "I need to get gas though before that lineup of six go in. Fucker's look hungry too. I need snacks, sis. You good?"

I nodded and felt his lips against my temple brushing light enough. "Hold tight. I'll be back."

He quickly left to get gas as I breathed and sipped water slowly.

I had met Liam when I was twelve.

He had helped me at school with the bullies making fun of my accent. I remembered Liam clearly still. He had been so tall, his clothes, dirty, and he had bruises under his jacket.

But he had stepped in, and I remembered those little things about him.

When I shared my lunch with him that day, it started being a pattern.

The next day, I sat next to him sharing breakfast and lunch with him all day.

Liam at first, was a little proud, but too hungry to refuse. But my father noticed. William Santos noticed everything.

In a few days my father sat me down and asked me why I was smuggling sandwiches like a thief. Caught, I told him about Liam.

That day my father came to school with me. I didn't even have to show him. He already knew. One look at Liam?

My father brought Liam home with us where I don't remember the conversation at my kitchen table. Just Liam looking nervous.

His parents never reported him missing and I didn't know what happened to them.

One day Liam was my friend—the next day he was sleeping in my bed all clean and tidied up with new shoes. All of a sudden I had a brother.

My father gave him our name.

And Liam gave me his whole heart with interest. My entire life he had become my protector.

Right now he was going into the gas station, a woman eyeing him up and down and I grinned.

Liam had grown into a lean six-four with messy inky hair and tattoos spread out on his arm and he walked into the shop with confidence.

I turned back to my phone, my wallpaper flashing with a photo of the three of us last Christmas.

The three of us—my family smiling into the camera at the selfie Liam took.

I sat back and looked around at the horizon. The sun was bright on me but I felt the shadows in my mind practically writhing in hunger.

I couldn't shake it.

My nightmares had been a common thing. Liam knew about them for years. He held me through them.

Right now as I leaned back breathing in and out, I felt the shadows rushing to me in waves.

Bringing me back to a world I didn't understand. My father had left Mexico when I was twelve.

A life I didn't remember save for the nightmares.

I breathed out slow and long deep breaths that Liam taught me whenever I was panicking at home. Over things I didn't understand.

My father never talked about Mexico.

About Mama and Evie. My biological sister. I just knew we had left them. Now, Isobel Tanja Santos was a soon-to-be CIA operative.

Now? Liam had convinced me to join the CIA for their new cyber-intelligence programs.

Think about it, shortcake. We're good at this shit. We can get paid for it. A stupid desk job? With a security clearance?

It would open so many doors, Isa.

We had applied our senior year and got accepted graduating in the top ten percent of our class.

Liam and I were both computer nerds.

More him than me, I knew what he was doing because I spoke several languages and for me—computers were just another language. Syntax and grammar in code when you really thought about it.

Liam had convinced me to do it and I trusted his judgement. For money. For my family.

For everything we wanted in the future at our fingertips if we worked for the CIA. It meant we got to take care of our father and he could retire from his construction job. It meant everything we wanted was right there.

We just had to pass through so many weeks of training.

And then? Freedom.

I blew out another breath the sky above me so pale blue it was blinding.

I leaned back in my seat waiting for Liam to come back.

This world was temporary.

Eventually, I would have Liam, my father, and my little family would be back to peace.

This was just a simple temporary stop in my life.

I had no plans of ever letting the CIA become my whole world.

Liam was walking back to me now a grin on his face holding a bag of snacks as I rolled down my window. "Shortcake, they didn't have the cupcakes you liked so I got these instead, is that okay?"

I smiled up at him, the sun blinding against his head as he grinned ear to ear when he saw me. His eyes looked eerily bright on his face but he was so beautiful.

He opened the passenger side door for me and knelt.

"Here."

"Oh, I love these. This is strawberry?"

"It is," he looked proud of himself. "I elbowed a bitch for these so I hope you like 'em."

I giggled as his eyes twinkled with mirth, and our laughter mingled as he passed me my drinks.

"You know what's crazy?" He mused as he got around to the driver's seat. "We haven't even started and I'm already done with these fuckers."

I laughed outright then. "I feel the same."

He held out his pinky. "A few years. We get ourselves set up. And then we're free."

"And then we are free." I linked my pinky with his. "Promise."

His smile was wide, his eyes twinkling. "Promise."

We were a team.

CHAPTER 2
GABRIEL

"GET YOUR FUCKING ASS IN LINE, AND FILL OUT THE FUCKING paperwork."

I groaned internally at David Young yelling. He was always fucking yelling. At five-four with a shaved head and mixed race, he had classic short man short dick syndrome.

At best.

I knew guys like Young. Former Air Force something or another.

It always the guys fucking idiots out of the Air Force who thought they were on their high horse.

You never caught a Marine in here screaming his fucking head off—because they didn't have to. They knew how to carry themselves. Overcompensation was short man syndrome in full force.

Short man. Short dick.

A disaster waiting to happen.

He was the only one in the flight I didn't like.

Always making jabs and comments and shitting on other people. But I was tolerating it.

Tolerating. Being the key word.

I blew out a breath. The quieter instructors were the ones I liked being around.

Yet, today something was off. I slept like shit. I kept waking up to the sensations of someone in bed with me. But nobody lived with me. Sometimes over the last year I had seen this woman.

In the mist. In my sleep. She would get closer and closer and then laugh and drift away. It was maddening. I overslept today because last night in particular she had decided to dart so close I swore I saw her. But that was impossible.

I rushed to work to the harsh glow of a gymnasium instead of my usual office.

It was too fucking early in the morning for me to even look at some of these people. I chugged my coffee. I didn't believe in... dreams. I believed in hard work. Dedication. Loyalty.

That's it.

I was here for training.

For boot-camp.

Into the fucking Central Intelligence Agency.

I prayed to the fucking Universe to hear me. But then again, the Universe had never been on my side. Ever.

So why would it start now?

New recruits were still trickling in, their face is a mixture of excitement and apprehension, and something else.

They were a little afraid.

I got that the directions to the training facility had been a little unclear even for us, and we had to make last-minute changes, but even I had to roll my eyes at the sight of the people sitting in the large gym.

Scrawny. Awkward. Under-developed.

I was a former SEAL. Probably why pussies like David Young pissed me the fuck off.

And now the agency wanted to advance its cyber-intelligence and so here I was— doing baby-sitter duty. At best.

The agency had decided to hand select some of the top college students across the States that wanted to come and join a program where they could hopefully become the next generation of cyber intelligence experts.

Hopefully.

I wasn't one of them, but I was good at being a trainer.

It was annoying as fuck being here when I was doing it for the credits.

For a 'well-rounded' portfolio. I'd rather be out on the field in Special Activities or anywhere shooting anyone other than this.

This wasn't my thing.

7

But I gotta admit, I got to wear sweats to work now so there was a bonus.

You ain't gonna be director in a few years if you don't kiss some ass, kid.

My mentor Jim Koller's voice was in my ear as I walked around the place looking at the idiots I had to whip into a shape fit to protect my ass.

It didn't matter if none of these guys were in any kind of shape to defend me, somehow I had to get them there.

And I didn't have enough faith in myself to do so.

I stalked along the sidelines of the training facility already irritated by everything.

The whole point of introducing them the way that we were, on the first day, almost like a military Boot Camp, was so that they would understand that this wasn't college.

They couldn't just fuck each other over and sleep with each other, because in this world, they were consequences with that.

We didn't need 'good enough.'

Koller always taught me good enough got people killed.

And weakness couldn't be taught.

That was a fact.

Twelve weeks? Not nearly enough time to mold them into anything useful. But enough to get me out and into a better position. This gig looked good on paper.

And that's all it was. I lived and I breathed the rules. The discipline.

So here I was, babysitting a bunch of guppies. Bored out of my goddamn mind.

I was so out of it I almost didn't hear her.

"*Hola, is this the right place for training?*" A beautifully accented, low feminine voice cut through *everything.*

One that I could only describe as something that made me shiver for a nanosecond, closing my eyes as I turned my head. And swallowed. *Hard.*

Standing in the archway to the training area, dressed in jeans that must've been painted on her hourglass body.

Her white tank top, if you could even call it that, had a robe buttons that strained against a more than ample pair of lush breasts. Olive skin peeking out under it.

The top was short enough to let me see her belly button .

That isn't even a tank top. I can see her belly button.

My mouth went dry.

A faint strip of skin exposed where the fabric met, and it was the golden color of her skin.

"I'm looking for the training hall." She held up a letter, caramel eyes sparkling a little with something akin to amusement.

Her accent was thick but it was...so fucking attractive.

The musical lilt of her voice was almost soothing.

What? I heard nothing. Nothing.

I took her in, long dark inky hair cascading just past her breasts, and bright, caramel eyes looked at me with her wide-eyed question.

I blinked as though she might've been a mirage. A dream. Conjured up from the mist of my nightmares.

Lush, pink full lips, her button nose, the heart-shaped face, and her big, dark eyes with long lashes—I exhaled, unaware I was holding a breath.

She blinked again at me. *"Hola?"*

My mouth stopped working, my brain didn't know how to process this...creature.

Had we been out I would've fought anyone to take her home, I wouldn't have to because she'd come to me.

Recognize me as hers.

What the fuck was I saying?

She was saying something, her dark eyes glittering as she took me in then her eyes curious as she took a step forward.

I could smell her as she drew closer to me, and then she was a foot away from me.

Say something.

What? Let me take you home?

"Hola, hablas espanol?"

I blinked at the letter in her hand.

"Are you all right?"

She got so fucking close to me for a moment I had to blink back. I lost my breath.

Up close she was breathtaking. Soft, inviting eyes and a hint of worry in them. She was saying something and I didn't hear it.

Those eyes had flecks of gold in them, they shimmered in the light.

There was a hint of mischief in them that sent heat to my already throbbing cock.

"I'm here for training."

My brain registered one thing at that moment.

This woman. *This woman in front of me.*

Who looked *nothing* like the rest of the lazy fucks in there? Was here for *training*.

As in she's about to be a student and I was a fucking trainer.

Holy—

They'd eat her sweet eyes alive.

That was the entire point. But her? Not this girl.

She didn't belong here. Not among these idiots. I could tell.

Before I could open my mouth a dark haired man jogged up next to her with bright green eyes.

"Shortcake, I thought I told you to wait!"

She turned saying something to him while motioning to me and then she pointed at her map.

He was saying something in Spanish to her shaking his jet black hair, skin paler than hers, making his bright green eyes stand out. I clocked him quickly.

Band tee. Ripped jeans. I didn't like the way he touched her waist.

At all. *Get off her.* I heard nothing that he said.

She said something to him in Spanish and then he saw me.

And his green eyes widened.

"Shit." And then he said. "He doesn't speak at all?" He looked at me. "Can you help us get to the training hall? We got lost."

What? She didn't notice me staring down her little friend. *That's all he was, right?*

If he was hers he would've kissed her or something or spanked her for running off without him.

Besides, it's not like he called her *baby*.

They were friends. Except his hand stayed on her waist.

Not her. She doesn't belong here.

"Liam, I don't think he speaks." What the fuck was that accent? Where was she from? *Liam.*

"You're *late*," I said, my voice cutting through the air. They fell silent, her eyes widening. "Get in there."

Her lips parted. Breath hitched. Hers or mine?

She was a trainee. Off-limits.

Absolutely the fuck not. I broke the rules for no woman.

Let alone this one. Even if I had never seen anyone who looked like her in real life.

Even if girls like her only existed in a dream or a magazine. Her lush lips tipped up in a smile on me. A shy look in her eyes.

"Did I stutter?"

I didn't need to yell. My reputation preceded me.

But instead of being cowed her lips tipped up wider. "No."

"Then why aren't you two heading in there where everyone else is?"

"We are standing here with you," she said as a matter-of-fact. "So we cannot go."

Smart-ass.

"I can see that," I said to her, crossing my arms over my chest not missing the way her eyes roved over my biceps. Should I have felt the heat in my body flare from that alone?

We didn't get supermodels in the Agency cyber unit.

"You are keeping us here," she said softly, like I was the reason she was there. "We ask you for directions. You did not hear me."

I heard her. I heard loud and clear. So did my dick.

The guy next to her grinned wider and wider like a demented rock star. He muttered something in Spanish and she fucking giggled.

She said something back quietly her eyes warm on me.

Both of them grinned at me.

"What are you smiling at?" Is she laughing at me? I bristled at that determined to regain composure. She was a fucking trainee.

I eyed the idiot at her side. He was as tall as my six-five.

"Nothing," he grinned wider. "You gonna let us go?"

Before I could open my mouth she cut me off.

"Where do we go? The space is big. Directions?" Oh. My. Fucking. God. She knew exactly what she was doing. There was nothing but mischief in her eyes.

Trouble.

"Do you not see the space?" I jerked my chin.

"Si, I see it."

"Then get inside."

"But where?"

"Can you tell us how?" The guy next to her said. Both of them looked like two devious kids.

11

"Directions." She said again.

I pinched the bridge of my nose trying to maintain my composure and I caught the guy snicker.

"Both of you. Inside. Now. To the right, follow the steps, and sign in."

Both of them shared a smirk and those honey eyes darted back to me. Her smile was wide on me as he grinned and they both walked past me.

As she did, I caught a whiff of something, candy. Toffee? What the fuck was that scent?

Why did she smell like a *dessert*?

But more important?

Why wasn't she afraid?

I didn't miss the way she took me in as she did, that little smile on her face.

Just like I had stood like a fucking idiot too stupid to say a thing to her.

"*Gracias.*" Her lips tipped up as she turned her head, her hair over her shoulder and she went with...*whoever* the fuck he was.

And when she did walk away, I realized, I hadn't gotten her name.

But his name was Liam.

I didn't know hers.

But I was about to.

I didn't even fucking hesitate to head back over to the instructor pool so I could find her.

CHAPTER 3
ISOBEL

"I don't know why I listen to you."

First day at the CIA training facility and Liam and I were already causing trouble. Of course.

Next to me Liam smirked.

"Because you love me." He frowned then. "Don't run off like that. I don't want to lose you on our first day here."

"I don't want to lose you at all."

My English was good, but my brain didn't always understand certain things. Not everything. So I got a little lost and I found that man.

The blue-eyed man with the shorter hair and mean expression. Well, I think he was trying to be mean, but I just found him funny.

"I cannot believe I'm doing this." My accent sounded thicker even to me. "This is a little silly. Everyone is so serious."

He laughed easily at my expression. "Chill, it'll be fun. You're going to be fine. I think it's called bearing? You know? When everyone has to look like someone put a baseball bat up their ass but—"

"Liam!" I laughed as he chuckled.

"What? They look so fucking serious. It's just fucking paper-work." He grinned at me. "Look even the guy who stopped us looks too damn mean for his own good."

"Si, but he was funny."

"He was fucking hilarious." Liam rolled his eyes.

I noticed many eyes turning toward us, and I glanced at Liam uneasily. I hated this. I hated people staring. As we signed in, Liam found our names.

Santos. Check. Check.

"I'm so happy you changed your name," I commented.

"Yeah me too, Santos sounds way better than Sullivan." Liam pretended to shudder. "I don't like it here already. We do this. We leave here. You get your dance studio. I get my martial arts studio. We live happily-ever-after."

I laughed easily. "Yes, you reminded me in the car ride here several times."

"And I'm gonna keep reminding you too," Liam teased me often. But I loved him.

So I was here entertaining this idea he had. When I told Liam I wanted to own my own dance studio and teach girls—Liam said I needed money and we had to be better than what we were.

Not poor.

Not living in a one-bedroom apartment.

But better.

So here I was. My eyes drifted around the room. *"Todos están mirando."*

Everyone is staring.

"At you," Liam snorted looking at his beat up sneakers he had for years. "Nobody's staring at me."

"They are staring at you." I frowned at him. *"Quién es el?"* *Who was that man?* "He is staring at me too."

The one who moved quietly, his blonde hair short and eyes like ice blue. Cold.

He looked like he needed to laugh more. He was so pretty it hurt a little to stare at him. He was taller than Liam and I didn't know *that* was possible.

His eyes had stood there taking me in like he had never seen a woman before.

Liam was watching me with a careful expression in his eyes. "I don't know, but I'll find out by the end of the day."

Liam was an information gatherer, and I was a problem solver.

Because I didn't speak the same language as him most of the time? And I thought differently, we discovered we were stronger together.

As a family. Since we were kids.

I saw the blonde man walk up to the pad where we signed our names in.

Someone else spoke. "All right, you'll be breaking up into teams by last name."

Liam and I shared a look. "Thank God I'm a Santos," he muttered.

"We'll be your trainers..." I didn't listen to them. Instead, my eyes drifted.

The blonde man was staring again at me. I looked away.

I saw Liam watching him with a shrewd look in his eyes.

He only did that when he was trying to solve a complicated problem.

"Qué pasa?" I looked at Liam. *What is it?*

Liam didn't speak much Spanish when he came to live with me but he learned over the years.

He shook his head, motioning for me to pay attention. I did.

"Santos."

"Sí."

Both Liam and I stood. When we did, he shook his head.

"Only one of you at a time."

My heart flipped a little as Liam looked at me. "I'll go."

"No, I'm not afraid," I shook my head. "I can go first."

I walked across the gymnasium, crossing the length of it to meet the blonde man head on.

I reached for the paperwork from him as he explained it off to me.

"Let me know if I lose you..." And then he began to explain to me what he needed from me.

I looked at the paper, trying to ignore some of the stares from people. I got that a lot.

Was he coming closer? I could smell his cologne from here and felt his heat. He was enormous compared to my five-four and bigger.

I wasn't around too many men. Not since college. But now?

I felt something in my stomach for him. Which was...not right. So I ignored it.

"Do you understand it?"

I nodded. I wasn't stupid.

Sometimes people don't because I had an accent, but I didn't understand what they were saying. But I understood everything. I had a hard time speaking.

Did he think I was stupid?

"You realize you're going to have to speak English here, right?"

The moment the words left his mouth, my head snapped to him and I felt a burning sensation in my chest.

In my throat. I heard a few students snickering behind me and suddenly, a bucket of ice water fell over my desire for him.

It was gone.

Because in that moment he did not remind me of the man I met in the front of the gym looking lost and a little sad.

He looked like the people who bullied me for coming to America.

Years ago I remember the humiliation I felt, that Papi felt.

Liam had helped him understand paperwork and documents where I could not. Liam helped us both.

I stiffened but didn't back down. I met him eye to eye, cool to warm. "Do you think because I do not sound like you, I do not understand you?"

"I never said that."

"You just did. I am allowed to speak any language I want, as long as I speak English when do work. Si?" I put some steel into my voice.

"Easy, sweetheart," a short man who looked mixed race smirked my way. "He's just saying for you to speak English here."

I blinked as the blonde man next to me stiffened at the sight of the shorter man who was even shorter than me. He looked gross.

"You know, you'd be prettier if you smiled—"

Or you can fuck off, you short—

"Young." The blonde man next to me cut him off with his voice laced with iron, and what he was about to say because I felt my blood boil now.

"I speak English," I said, my eyes meeting the blonde's icy blue eyes. "It's not like yours, but I understand perfectly. You can continue."

The man named Young did not back down. "What, Monroe? Just saying she comes in here with all that attitude, *who the fuck do you think is gonna—*"

"I swear to fucking God." Monroe the blonde with icy blue eyes raised his voice. "Your trainee is eating his pen. Can you go and

16

manage your kids? One of them started crying at the waiver section. You don't have to worry about me or mine."

The way he said the last part made me realize…this might be my trainer. Of course I would meet him first.

I saw the other man roll his eyes and leave.

"Fucking pussies. I don't see why I gotta be here…" I did not catch what he said. Only that Monroe turned to me.

"Where were we?"

"You were insulting me."

He blinked surprised by me and I swore I saw a hint of amusement in his eyes.

My father always said my mouth would get me into some trouble.

I told him not some. Just *enough*. Enough for me to feel good at the end of the day about standing up for myself.

I despised the other man with his dark beady eyes and nasty comments immediately.

And now I was starting to despise *Monroe*.

Under the lights, his short blonde hair glowed and his eyes even more so as he watched me.

"I speak English. It is good enough to be here, so it will have to be good enough for you. *Entiendes?*"

And then I took it.

He blinked slowly and tipped his head. His eyes never left mine.

"Where are you from?" He asked me low.

"*America.*" I shot back. "Finished?" I held up the folder. "Or would you like me to sign something else?"

He paused and handed me a pen and blank paper.

"Write your name on this."

I didn't even think. I reached for the pen, our fingers brushing for a second as I scribbled my name in cursive across the paper he gave me.

"There." I handed it to him. *Why did he want my name?*

Monroe looked down at my name. "Isobel Adrianna Santos."

Why did he make my name sound like that?

His deep voice rumbled my name as he said it, his eyes flickering up to me.

"*Si.*" I felt nervous now and I didn't know why, and I tugged my shirt down a little. His throat worked as he watched me but I turned away. I didn't care.

And went back to Liam, telling myself not to cry. I had my father at home and Liam by my side, and it didn't matter who he was.

Kiss him?

I wanted to murder him.

I looked at Liam, who was looking at the ice man with his eyes on him. "Santos, *Liam.*"

Liam smirked. "Well, he *definitely* knows me."

I watched Monroe's conversation with Liam. He was much colder, his eyes narrowed on my brother.

I saw Liam grimace and remove his earring and pocket it.

He didn't ask Liam to write his name.

Instead, Liam came back with a scowl.

"That motherfucker is frostier than ice," Liam said casually. "But I know who he is. I caught his name on his water bottle. *Gabriel Monroe.* Agency's up-and-coming golden boy. I heard someone talking about him in the hallway. He's doing this as a mentor to show he can train anyone and climb up the ranks. Douchebag."

"Gabriel?" I said quietly. "That's his name?"

Liam nodded. "But I'm down to call him Frosty, since it can't get colder than him."

"Frosty sounds good."

Liam and I had given everyone nicknames since we knew each other as kids.

He smirked again, his eyes glinting under the lights. "He thinks he can rattle me? He's got another thing coming. I'm not scared no white-collar golden boy. I don't give a fuck whose ass he kissed. I'm not backing down from him ever."

Me too. *"Yo también."*

Liam's brighter green eyes met mine and he smiled easily. "Mucho amo." He held up his pinky finger. I laughed now.

Something Papi did with him to teach him but Liam got Spanish phrases confused in the beginning and he came up with this.

"Mucho amo." I linked my finger with his.

He was trying to tell me he loved me lots.

I didn't care. I had Liam.

You realize we speak English here, right?

I hated him.

I hated Gabriel Monroe.

18

CHAPTER 4
ISOBEL
SIX WEEKS LATER

"I HATE HIM!"

I hated Gabriel Monroe.

I woke up, and I hated him.

I went to sleep, and I hated him.

I told Liam, and he laughed and *laughed.* "Few more weeks, yeah?"

Huffing and puffing on my run, I shook my head. I wanted to cry. Weeks of this.

Sometimes I noticed him watching me like he liked watching me suffer.

Or when I was struggling and another trainee that wasn't Liam helped me—Jeremy Bradford.

Jeremy was a sweet younger looking boy. About my height and a little round and red-faced but he helped me up and Gabriel all but barked after him.

Jeremy all terrified ran off.

Gabriel's head had snapped to me all angry winter blue. I scowled right back before running off. Or trying to, he'd promptly caught me by the back of my hoodie and dragged me back.

He shoved a water bottle at me. His voice was ice. "You haven't drank water all day. Take it before you die out on me."

I frowned as I chugged aware of his eyes on me.

A shiver chased down my spine.

After I'd finished I'd torn off my hoodie too hot in it and my white tank top today stretched tighter across my bra. His eyes watched me the entire session.

I caught up to Jeremy with an easy smile. He was sweet faced but he looked nervous as he talked to me.

Whenever I paired with Jeremy or anyone who wasn't Liam for some reason—Gabriel hovered. Close. He went off on them. Criticizing every single thing about them until nobody but Liam partnered with me.

I hated Gabriel Monroe. With everything in my soul.

I had weeks of this stupid training course. I had been accepted into the agency, but they wanted us to be...better? *Why?*

"We sit at a desk all day, looking at photos and videos," I said, hating how thick my accent got. "All day long and he wants to train me like I am a soldier. I am not a soldier."

I kicked a rock and yelped. Liam rushed over to me then all but picking me up.

"Why do we have to do this for twelve weeks? This is the longest twelve weeks of my life!"

"Whoa, whoa, whoa." Liam soothed me effortlessly, the wind blew his inky hair to the side and his eyes softened on me, the usual harder shade of green becoming lighter. Brighter. "Easy, look at me, shortcake, look at me. There you go. That's my girl. No hurting yourself. Okay?"

"Okay."

He took my face in his hands and smushed my cheeks together.

"I'm not good at this," I whimpered. I could keep up physically, but mentally? Emotionally? I hated this. *"I'm not a spy."*

"You don't have to be." He looked around, and seeing that it was clear, he dropped his head to me. "Look, in a few weeks? We never have to see Frosty the Snowman. Ever. Again."

We started calling Gabriel Monroe "Frosty the Snowman" because it was easier than calling him the rude, ignorant dick that he was. He was awful.

A good trainer but awful to deal with. Awful to be around. He was heartless. At best.

At worst?

He was the devil.

Breathing down my neck, correcting my stance, barking orders at everyone. His hands lingered on my back, my waist, my arms correcting my form all the fucking time!

Or that one time, I had candy in my mouth after lunch and his eyes had locked on me. He'd made me all but spit it out into his hand. I didn't do that. I just walked over and pretended to throw it out.

"I hate him," I muttered. "Who does he think he is? Always like a ghost! Everywhere I look Gabriel Monroe is there. He is everywhere!"

Liam chuckled at my expression. "It's his job to make sure we don't die."

"Whose side are you on?"

"Easy, shortcake. I'm always on your side." He smushed my face more. "But he has to be a hard-ass. Remember? It's his thing. Besides, the icicle up his ass makes it harder for him to concentrate on being a nice guy."

I shook my head at the ridiculous image he painted.

"This is temporary." Liam always reminded me of why we were here. "We do this shit. We get paid swell. We have government jobs. A security clearance. We get out of here? We can do whatever we want. You and me. I'll open my martial arts studio, you'll do the damn studio, just think, in a few years, we'll be having lunch instead of being worried about Frosty. Fuck that guy. He's temporary. He isn't your long lost love or anything—he's just some guy. Gabriel Monroe is just some guy." He smushed my cheeks tighter. "Say it."

"He is just some guy," I repeated. "After this we can go home and see Papi. We can take care of him."

But even as I said it I imagined Gabriel's winter ice eyes. The way they watched me. His expression not hard at all, but something softer. If he saw me looking he'd look away with a grimace.

Six weeks of this! Ahhhhhh!

Liam smiled, his green eyes twinkling in his all black on as usual. "Exactly. And I get to pierce whatever the fuck I want in my body."

I giggled making Liam laugh.

We were just walking now on a break.

I was in black, which I hated; I preferred wearing white and brighter colors, not this drab darkness.

But over the last few weeks, when we have moved here, I noticed that everybody here wore different clothing. And I didn't wanna stand out anymore than I did.

21

So I was borrowing some of Liam's clothing sometimes, but I mostly just wore black now.

"*Who's my brave girl?*" Liam asked dropping his voice and suggestively wiggling his eyebrows, making me laugh despite my mood.

I raised my hand. "Me."

"Who's gonna show these fuckers who's the best?" Liam's grin was infectiously wicked.

"*Me.*"

He was squeezing my face. "*See,* you got this." I felt my neck prickle, but there was no one else out here but us.

"Come on, shortcake. I'll race you back."

I slapped his arm, cursing at him as he ran off, tugging my clip off. *"Liam!"*

As he ran off with it, I huffed my hair out, shaking it out. I didn't mind how my hair blew in the breeze though.

My neck prickled, and I rubbed it, not liking that I felt like I was being watched. The only thing in the distance were the offices of the instructors, and nobody should've been in the office at this hour.

It was getting late.

Liam and I rarely walked outside this late but today I had been upset.

I followed Liam out of the woods, jogging after him as the back of my neck continued bothering me.

Like someone was watching.

I turned back one last time to see nothing.

Even as I ran I kept thinking about the weird dreams I had ever since this whole thing started.

Who cares? You're twenty-two.

Nobody is coming to save you, Isa. Keep running.

Frosty was a tyrant, pushing us to our limits and then some.

My muscles ached constantly, and no matter how hard I tried, it seemed like he was always singling me out, driving me insane.

I vented to Liam in Spanish as we jogged.

"*Why is he making us work harder?*" I huffed, pumping my arms. "*He's always driving me insane!*"

Liam glanced around nervously, as if expecting Gabriel to materialize out of thin air. *"A ti y a todos los demás, Isa."*

You and everybody else.

I couldn't understand it.

When I first laid eyes on Gabriel, I thought he was an angel.

Sculpted features, wheat-blond hair, and eyes that had seen too much. Those icy blue depths had lingered on me that first day, taking in my curves, and for a moment, I thought I saw interest.

But now? He was cold, harsh, and unrelenting.

He was colder than ice.

"He used to be a SEAL," Liam explained jogging next to me. "People talk, they say he's in line to climb the ranks quickly. He's good, *and* he's young, maybe twenty-four, Isa. That's *scary* young, which means he's willing to do whatever it takes to climb up. And if I didn't know any better? If he keeps going, he might even want to be the next director. And that's a ruthless climb to the top. That's probably why they're grooming him."

Grooming Gabriel? To be who?

He was only twenty-four. Military. Now this. He was... superhuman.

I was twenty-two.

But it felt like he was a *decade* older than me.

He'd been doing this for a long time.

Liam kept going. "If I did the math correctly? He enlisted at eighteen, deployed to dangerous places, the Agency got a hold of him and now he's one of their best. He's doing this to boost his resume. Once he's done here? He's gone. Moving up to better things. And we won't ever remember you or me. Got it?"

I nodded. But when I looked at Gabriel Monroe I didn't see his success. I saw sadness.

I saw pain.

He reminded me of Papi, who I knew had seen darkness his entire life. My father was Brazilian and my Mom Mexican, but they met in Brazil when she had been visiting.

They had me and Evie. My little sister I hadn't seen in years when they separated. I didn't remember much or how.

That part of my life was a blank.

The only thing I remembered most was Liam.

But Gabriel's eyes? Were my father's eyes. I saw the same

23

calluses on his hand my father had on his. Something about his hands told me his story.

It made my heart ache because I imagined how much Gabriel Monroe had been through, and I felt my throat tighten at how his eyes looked like that at such a young age.

My father was much older but I understood some nights he sat at the kitchen table until three am and Liam would sometimes find me crying about it.

I barely heard Liam now, my mind stuck on that first encounter.

The sadness in Gabriel's eyes, the way he looked trapped. I'd been rooted to the spot, unable to look away.

"Isa!" Liam's shout snapped me out of my thoughts, but it was too late. I tripped, tumbling to the ground in a heap. Liam tried to catch me, but I hit the dirt hard.

"¿Ta bien?" he asked, helping me up.

"Si, no enfocada," I muttered, brushing myself off. "¡No entiendo! ¿Por qué es tan horrible? ¿Por qué tiene tanto frío?"

I couldn't understand why Gabriel was so awful, so cold.

As we walked, I confided in Liam about the challenges of being the only one who looked like me, the way some of the girls treated me.

He understood, having seen it firsthand in college.

"Yeah, but it's just like college," he reassured me. "I got your back, and I'm not going to pretend I understand or minimize your suffering. But I know you're the best person here for this. Besides, you're going to make Papi so proud."

I smiled at the thought of our father. Liam was my brother. I didn't care what anyone said.

He was.

"He would hate the cold, but that's true."

Liam reminded me. "But you made it through college, and now you'll make it through this."

He held my hand briefly, then his expression turned serious.

"Isa, I think you need to talk to him. There's a part of training I've heard about. It involves being underwater. They're going to tie your hands together and dunk you, and you have to escape. From the bottom."

My stomach churned at the thought. I hated being tied down, feeling trapped. But I had heard rumors of it.

24

In intelligence, even though we worked at a desk all day, it still required us to maintain our composure in crisis.

All of these exams that we were taking tested specifically for fear responses in panic management.

They were critical skills that anybody needed with access to sensitive information.

Because we were still vulnerable and at any point in time, we could've been kidnapped or attacked.

And we needed to be strong about it.

It was a little surreal. For me especially. But I was terrified of being held down.

I couldn't remember why, but the idea scared me.

The shadows and darkness of my past came back interrupting all rational thoughts.

Sometimes I had nightmares when Liam and I would share a room.

Whenever I did still, he was there.

I felt sick already at the sensation.

Once in high school one of the guys in the school had picked me up with my arms held down and I lost it.

Liam had destroyed him getting into a fight so bad, my father hadn't known what to do with him so he put Liam into martial arts where he'd honed his skills more.

"No quiero preguntarle," I whispered. *I don't want to ask Gabriel.*

But he was our instructor. Unfortunately.

We caught his eyes day one.

"It's okay," Liam smiled cryptically. "I think he'd be okay with it."

I doubted that. Gabriel seemed okay with nothing but making people suffer.

As we emerged from the clearing, I spotted Gabriel leaning against his car.

His face, usually impassive, turned cold when he saw Liam.

"Did you do something to make him angry?" I asked. "Or does he look at everyone like that?"

Because even I didn't know why he was like that with Liam.

He never went after him. But he did not like him.

Liam smirked. "I think so. Ask him, Isa."

CHAPTER 5
GABRIEL

SHE WAS FUCKING *GORGEOUS*.

And a student. A *trainee*.

I couldn't stop watching her either way because I had never seen anyone who looked like that running wild.

Women like her were usually married or someone's girl. Someone not me.

Every so often I'd catch the way her inky hair cascaded down her back in soft waves, catching the sunlight and revealing subtle hints of blue. She'd toss it back over her shoulder effortlessly and say something sassy to Liam.

She had a habit of tucking her hair behind her ear when she was concentrating, her tongue peeking out just a little while she worked through problems.

Not that I noticed.

I just looked in passing.

Especially when she fired back a response to someone who dared to say anything stupid to her.

Or when she helped fucking Jeremy Bradford with his form. Bradford was about five-six and built like a pear.

The weakest link on the team.

Mentally he was sharp, but physically he was about as fit as a baked potato.

And he stared at Isobel with these fucking heart-eyes. Irritated the shit out of me.

She was always early, always left after everyone with Liam at her side. She always double checked her gear and Jeremy's who was slowly latching onto her.

I rolled my eyes. "Bradford!" I barked. "Get your ass over here."

I let out a breath pinching the bridge of my nose as his portly red-faced self walked over.

God, if he wasn't fucking CIA he might as well be a giant marshmallow. He was gonna get people killed.

I bit back a sigh. "Bradford, do you think Santos is going to be there when you're in a fire fight? Do you think she can adjust your gear all the fucking time?"

"N-no, no, sir." He looked like he was going to pee himself.

I bit back my sigh again. Again. I held it back so hard. "Then why does she adjust your fucking vest every single fucking day?" *Are her hands soft? Do you like them on her?*

"I'm sorry, sir. It won't happen again."

"See to it. Get lost."

"Yes, sir."

When he jogged back to Isobel she frowned at me. God, she was hot as fuck. But I resisted.

Because this girl had a fucking heart of gold.

Picking up for others. Cleaning up after people to make sure the cafeteria staff didn't have more work.

Her and Sullivan helping out Jeremy fucking Bradford with translations.

Or when someone made fun of him, the way she threw it right back.

I looked the other way when she did. I didn't not like Bradford. He was a good kid.

If he stopped looking at Isobel's boobs? He'd be even better. Especially the days she wore a white tank top.

Those days I went home and shamelessly groaned in the shower while palming my iron hard cock over my one wet dream of a student.

Who I absolutely shouldn't have fucking wanted.

Isobel was an absolute fucking spit-fire.

Not that I noticed it.

Or when she turned her head, her bright honey eyes sparkled with a mix of intelligence and mischief.

Always with a smile on her face. Always giving credit where it was due. Always fixing someone's clothes or adjusting herself quietly. Discreetly.

Isobel was a fan favorite. As much as Liam was with women. Because that motherfucker got women. The girls in the class lost their fucking mind over him.

And Isobel would laugh about it. That one smile that got me every time.

The one that made her nose wrinkle at the bridge and her canine flash.

It was infectious when she tossed something at her brother thinking I wasn't going to notice.

I had to fight back my grin, hiding it in a cough when she did that shit. Because Liam didn't see it coming.

She looked like she had secrets. And I wanted to know all of them. Wanted to taste her. Feel her walls clenching around my tongue while I slid it deep into her feeling her inner thighs shiver around my ears.

Her golden skin seemed to shimmer, and I found myself wondering if it was as soft as it looked. If she glowed as soft and pink everywhere else.

I was going to hell for wanting a student. But she was only two years younger than me.

But it wasn't just physical.

Isobel Santos was fucking intelligent.

Over the course of the last six weeks, I learned she was also brilliant. Solving puzzles nobody else could quietly, backwards, and with a wit I didn't forsee coming.

She got excited about cracking a code, her eyes lighting up when she did. She lived for it.

Isobel finished everything with pride in her eyes and gave it her all.

She caught on fast, ran long, trained hard, and did everything with a smile on her face. With her entire fucking heart. I saw it.

And it made me want to protect her.

When everyone else complained, she laughed, and I heard her from where I sat. Liam's joining hers.

The two of them drew attention easily, but they also didn't look alike so most people didn't realize he was her brother.

Older by a year.

But he hadn't *always* been her brother.

No. The Agency had a file on him. Adopted. Abusive parents. The first thing I'd fucking done is deep dive into both of them.

He'd come from a shit home and been adopted by her father.

Liam Sullivan parents were drug-addicts. Poor.

His brother had been murdered in jail after drunk driving and hitting a couple.

Isobel was from Mexico, but her father was from Brazil. Dark hair, bright eyes, flush skin, she was like a fucking wet dream.

But Liam wasn't really her brother.

Which meant...they were close but would it be possible something was between them?

I didn't know, and it was none of my business—but it felt like it was.

I glanced over at Isobel.

I bit my tongue, finding her utterly infectious, and I wanted to...laugh with her.

She took out something from her pocket.

Over the course of the last few weeks I had fucking noticed wrappers turning up on her desk.

Did I steal one? No.

It fell on the floor and I'd picked it up at the end of class.

Butterscotch.

That's what she smells like. And suddenly I had this vision of kissing Isobel Santos. Her tasting like candy.

Nothing phased her.

Not even when she shot marksman, having a natural affinity for finding the target. She did this tiny little dance. A wiggle. Liam rolled his eyes and threw something at her as he adjusted his glasses.

I covered my face and hid it with my clipboard so nobody would see me grinning at her.

She was excelling.

And if there's anything people loved more than someone who excelled, it was someone who excelled *happily*.

The same things men were praised for, women got shit on for doing. And I knew it was only about time.

~

Week 7. That's how long it took.

29

A bunch of the trainees always—they always did this shit—broke off into different cliques.

Only Liam and Isobel were together, and Liam, for all his watchful eyes, wouldn't have seen it coming.

I only knew because I was a wraith.

Nobody knew I was there, even for my size. I learned to be silent from a young age. Survival meant the world to me. It was all I knew.

And I heard it.

Kourtney Young was David Young's sister. I realized why they let him into the program was because his father was set to be a congressman. Turns out sucking enough dick to the top was a thing.

Not that I would know.

But he did.

I'd gotten Young kicked out easily in Week 2 after he almost spit at another trainee. I discreetly dropped it to Koller who handled it.

This wasn't the fucking military. We didn't need POS's like him. But his sister was in the program.

And she was an absolute fucking spoiled cunt like her brother.

"Who does she think she is?"

God, I couldn't fucking stand girls like this.

Every so often once in a blue moon, we had someone come in with connections, annoying, privileged and spoiled.

No reality checks ever until now. And judging by her brother they were cut from the same cloth.

Girls like Kourtney got people killed if she wasn't eliminated from the program.

"She thinks she's hot shit, flaunting her relationship with him. Aren't they brother and sister? I smell incest."

I wanted to tear Kourtney limb from limb. Watch her scream that shit in a CIA black site. See how well she did then.

Look at how loud she laughs, she's so fucking annoying. I bet she's a fucking slut with that fat ass of hers.

Who has tits like that?

I'm just saying they can't be real.

I took deep steady breaths. Women and men could be cruel. Bullies. But women in the military and in the Agency were the worst to each other.

And so it began.

Everything that was Isobel's strength would be used against her.

Everything. The girls in the unit would start tearing it down, and they'd get some idiots in on it. I fucking knew.

I could hear it from the locker rooms.

I was always paying attention because I couldn't stand bullies. I fucking hated them.

And I liked Isobel.

She was...a breath of fresh air.

Every fucking day, I inhaled the scent of butterscotch, soft vanilla, and something just her.

It was...different. I'd gone home and imagined her lips parting the way she did and sinking into her tight little—and I shook myself out of it.

Really? In front of her? Snap the fuck out of it.

Oh, but she fucking *hated* me.

I could tell. I wasn't nice to her.

I couldn't be, not if I wanted to stand a chance to take care of her. Or watching out for her when she ran around with those fucking tank tops on and the idiotic guys in the back argued about how big her breasts were.

That had been a fucking flaming riot to put out.

I couldn't assess threats to her more objectively if I was the one staring at her tits too.

Plus, they'd know I liked her, use it against me or her.

And that shit...that shit was dangerous.

Keep lying to yourself, punk bitch.

Those big, fuck-me doe eyes, mischievous and adorable at the same time? I was gone.

She'd look up at me with those eyes soft-half curious, half defiant.

She'd shoot back someone with her fiery tongue. When she cursed out Liam and ran after him.

She was life.

Something in her eyes spoke to me. Like she knew me. Which was fucking impossible.

Insta-lust. That's all it was. She was hot. I needed pussy. And I hadn't gotten laid in a while. That's all it was.

If I was her friend?

I knew I couldn't watch out for her. No. *Like* attracted *like.*

And I'd already heard shit that made me want to protect her.

I heard it daily.

And Isobel? Does she know?

Did she know she was being bullied? She didn't do anything.

She existed. She just breathed, and I heard.

"Look at her, who does she think she is?"

This fucking Kourtney bitch is gonna get everyone killed in the field.

I resisted the urge to scowl.

My eyes drifted to Isobel briefly, several times, but I made sure to look around and make it look natural.

She was on her phone with Liam, and he said something that made her grimace and shoot him a dirty look.

Even then, she looked attractive.

Did she have a bad angle?

Isobel caught me for one fucking reason more than anything. More than it all.

She fucking loved solving problems, specifically puzzles.

The first time I'd introduced cryptography to the class, she'd devoured it.

Her mind, because she didn't think like everyone else, excelled in out-of-the-box thinking.

But she didn't speak English like I did, so she wasn't limited by the restrictions my brain had.

She spoke Portuguese and Spanish.

I was willing to bet a few more. A polyglot.

And now I realized why they'd picked her up.

People like Santos...*Isobel* would lead us in a different direction.

And then I heard. "I have a plan on how to fuck her over. That stupid Mexican bitch—"

I rolled my eyes at Kourtney thinking she was slick.

I sat up straighter, listening.

I don't think people realized how sharp my hearing was.

A lifetime of listening for danger led me here. I sighed. *Here we fucking go.*

I saw Liam nudge her while I listened, and then she seemed to shake her head.

I refocused my attention on the girls in the corner who didn't think they were being loud. Idiots.

I heard everything.

And then I turned in my perch on the bleachers. I saw Isobel moving. She began walking.

Is she...she's coming here...

I can't help but notice the way her waist dips in her workout gear.

Her shirt is always a little too tight around her breasts, which I fucking loved.

And I wasn't the only one.

People watched her. Stared. Coveted.

Even as she sometimes hides next to Liam, who always keeps her by his side. But never touching.

She's coming to me.

No, don't. Isobel. Not here. I have to be straight.

Don't come to me, pretty baby. If you come to me, I'll hurt you just now. Just for now. I'm sorry if I do.

As she steps closer, her hair all around her, she looked so adorably young.

I want to pull on her hair, reveal her soft throat, and bite down while I—

She was walking towards me, her hourglass figure prominent, her waist tucked in neatly, her hips shapely, and I want to— *Stop.*

I inhale her scent, something with roses, and it smelled incredible.

"Hola," She tipped her head, sending curls and waves tumbling in every which was. *Beautiful.*

She doesn't give a shit. And I love that about her.

"You have a second?"

For you? I have hours.

I tipped my head, not trusting myself to speak.

The voices below us have gone quiet, which means they're listening.

I have to get her out of this situation.

"I had a question about the exam at the end," she began, but I couldn't be nice.

"You need to put on something decent," I cut her off, watching as her eyes widen and blink back in surprise. "You're distracting people."

My stomach churned as the words left my lips, the bitter taste of cruelty lingering on my tongue. Isobel couldn't protect herself the way I could protect her.

It was my job to take care of her.

"This is a training facility, not college. You know that right? So where's your hoodie again? You can't be showing skin like that." I raked my eyes on purpose down her lush curves, bigger breasts that heaved, and I swore I saw the outline of her nipples. Fuck. I swallowed finishing at her hips, her pants curving around them. Jesus. Christ.

The Universe was not listening to me sending me a student like this. But the moment I looked back at her eyes?

Caramel that had gone molten dark?

I knew I've fucked up.

Big time.

I watched as her eyes change from sleepy and warm to wide with feminine rage.

Unholy rage. I fucked up.

I said the wrong fucking thing.

She's about to destroy me.

Big time.

I heard the snickers below me because Kourtney's girl gang was listening. I saw Isobel's spine stiffen. I swallowed hard as she opened her mouth.

I'm about to get my ass handed to me.

"I don't give a fuck if the entire world thinks you're their golden boy." Utter sass and feminine rage emanate from her. "You are not shit to me."

Oh. Shit.

Isobel leaned into me and I had to look up into a fucking gorgeous sun-warmed goddess.

Hair shimmering in those waves as she glared down at me inches away from my face, her breasts heaving, the scene of caramel in my lungs. My dick practically grew to steel with how gorgeous she was.

Please get mad more often, beautiful.

"I will not be putting on anything. In fact, *tomorrow* I'm coming naked."

She's fuming, and my brain is too ashamed of myself, and my dick is too hard to see anything else.

Oh Jeez. If she came in naked I'd cry.

And then I'd eat that pussy like a motherfucker.

"I'm not here to ever attract anyone. Not even you—"

"Liam—" my mouth forms the words like the pathetic sack of shit I am.

An astounded laugh escapes her.

"*Liam?*"

The look on her face confirms what I'd suspected all along.

Just siblings. *Got it.*

And then Isobel did me a solid.

She went off in Spanish. I didn't know what she said, I just knew sitting there with my straight face? She was going off on me. Hard.

"I thought the stories about you being made of ice were just a story. But you really are just a *pendejo.*"

That shit sounds awful.

Her face is twisted with disgust.

"For the rest of my time stay away from me, and if I find out you do anything to stop my performance or anything—" she hissed her eyes flashing at me and for a moment I wanted to kiss her so fucking badly. "I will never hesitate to stand up for myself."

I know. That's what I fucking love about you.

Deep down inside, I recognized it.

Isobel was the kind of woman who would've protected me as a kid. She would.

She always positioned herself between me and whoever I was going off on. Looking out for Liam. Herself. Jeremy.

The way she diffused situations. The way she handled herself with sensitivity.

In a heartbeat.

As she turned I watched her hips and lower and I looked away. I was so fucked. Because over the last six weeks I had recognized Isobel Adrianna Santos as something other than a woman.

But as someone who matched me step for step. She was intelligent, bright, vivacious, kind, and everything I could've asked for in a partner. In a woman.

On paper? She hit every single check mark I had.

The only one she didn't hit?

The fucking fact that she was my fucking student.

She whirled around, that hair in my face for a second, and my inner being knew I had fucked beyond repair.

Why had I said those awful things to her?

Her words echoed in my head as I watched her walk away.

A part of me demanded I run after her, pull her into my arms, and then what? Apologize? Kiss her? Tell her she was perfect and that for six weeks? I fucking analyzed her down to the two dimples on her lower back I fantasized about?

What else did I tell her?

I knew when she was angry because her chest heaved up and down faster. Or that she was beautifully expressive and I knew behind those soft eyes she was crazy intelligent?

How did I tell her I wanted her?

Without losing my job? Risking my life? Risking her future?

And our fucking careers?

She was everything I couldn't have.

Everything I shouldn't have wanted.

And every single fucking thing that felt more right than breathing.

Another part of me warred with that. I saw Liam's features cloud over, as she walked away.

I can't let her in. How?

Tell her you want to fuck her until she moans your name and can't think?

What if she hates you?

And the truth was she probably did.

And another part of me knew it was better she hated me than knew what I really felt.

This way neither one of us could get hurt.

And even as I said it I knew it was a lie.

Besides, I already knew Kourtney's next steps. She was following Isobel with her girl gang.

I huffed out a breath.

I had to go and save my girl again.

No. She wasn't my girl.

I had to go and save Isobel.

CHAPTER 6
ISOBEL

He isn't Frosty.

He's the devil.

Evil. Awful. Idiot. Monster. Ice.

He was a horrible man. I hated Gabriel Monroe.

I hated him so much.

Golden boy of the CIA my ass.

I scrubbed at my skin a little bit harder than necessary, trying to get his words off of me.

Even through the scrubbing, the humiliation, the laughter of the other girls, his cold voice it seeped into my skin.

It wasn't even Gabriel that made me cry. It was the fact that for me?

Life had always felt like an uphill battle. It didn't matter I did. They were always going to find something wrong with me. I would always be the other.

I would always be competing with myself.

Every time I reached a goal, they would move the goal post.

It wasn't fair.

It wasn't okay.

It broke me. That's what broke me.

When I first came to America, I was made fun of for a few weeks until I met Liam.

I saw Liam had been made fun of as well. When he'd shown up

to my house it had been with ripped up clothes and bruises. He had been hungry.

Papi had fed both of us. And Liam had eaten everything. I had cried a lot unable to stop myself.

He had stayed over at our house that night. And he had never gone home. I remembered that night as I felt my eyes burning.

Gabriel's words echoed in my mind, each one a sharp blade cutting deeper into my heart.

How could he think so little of me?

Did he not see the effort I put into my training, the dedication I poured into every task?

He was the golden boy, the one everyone respected and admired.

And I? I was just a girl from a different world, struggling to find my place in this unforgiving environment.

Who's my brave girl?

I heard Liam's voice in my head.

I am brave.

But I'm also human.

I stepped out of the shower. Still crying, the tears mixing with the droplets cascading down my face. I wiped my eyes, trying to compose myself, but the hurt and humiliation were overwhelming.

I don't belong here. I just want to go home.

Liam was wrong.

We don't need the CIA. We can just take out a loan and open my studio. I'll make money. I will.

I don't need this life.

I won't pass the final exam.

And the whole point of going up to him was to ask him for help. And we both know that he was never going to give it.

As I reached for my towel, my hand grasped at empty air.

Confused, I looked around, expecting to find it hanging nearby, but it was nowhere to be seen.

A strange unease settled in my stomach as I realized that not only was my towel missing, but all of my belongings were gone as well.

"Hello?"

I called out, my voice echoing in the empty locker room.

Silence greeted me in return, amplifying the growing sense of dread that crept up my spine.

I stood there, dripping wet and completely exposed, covering myself as best I could with my arms

The cool air raised goosebumps on my skin, and I shivered, feeling vulnerable and alone. My mind raced, trying to make sense of the situation.

I knew I had brought my towel and clothes with me into the shower area.

I distinctly remembered placing them on the bench just outside the stall.

As I scanned the locker room, desperately searching for any sign of my belongings, I heard the sound of footsteps approaching.

My heart leaped into my throat, and I instinctively tried to make myself smaller, hoping whoever it was would pass by without noticing me.

Luck was not on my side.

I recognized the two girls who rounded the corner and stopped dead in their tracks when they saw me.

A brunette, her lips curled into a smirk. "Parading around naked?" Kourtney Young. She was a mixed race girl with a fake accent that made her sound like she was in a rap music video. Liam said it was called a blaccent. When people who grew up in privileged environment's mimicked a black accent to sound cool.

It did not make sense to me.

I did not fake my accent. Why would anyone fake it?

"Have you seen my things?"

I felt my cheeks burn with humiliation as they stared at my naked form, their gazes filled with contempt and judgment. I covered my body with my hands tighter feeling the goosebumps skate higher.

I wanted nothing more than to disappear, to sink into the ground and escape their scrutiny.

"Is this what's normal where you come from?" Kourtney asked, her dark hair a cloud around her head. "Flaunting yourself like this? This is what happens when you let trash into America I guess."

"I'm an American citizen," I shot back. "What the fuck does that have to do with my towel?"

I hated girls like her. I hated girls that found nothing out of thin air and tried to make it a problem all the time.

It was like that in high school when people had a crush on Liam and they thought I was his girlfriend, so they would be mean to me every chance they got.

Except I didn't understand why she was being mean to me. I didn't have anyone in my life that she wanted.

She never spoke to Liam so I know she didn't want him.

"You just walk around naked like you own the place?"

I opened my mouth to defend myself, but no words came out. I felt utterly helpless, trapped under their malicious gazes.

"What are you talking about? What did you do with my stuff?" *Liam. I need Liam.*

"*We'll tell Monroe—*" Kourtney smirked. "Maybe then he'll see what a filthy fucking loser, you are." "And we'll see what he does about you being a whore then?"

"A whore?" I snapped. "Are you crazy, you stupid girl. Give me back my stuff!"

"We'll see how you fare once we let Monroe know all about your kind." Kourtney said. "She won't make it here another day." Her two friends snickered eyeing me up and down like hungry wolves and I felt a sliver of fear.

What were they going to do?

Liam wasn't here to save me, to stand up for me as he always did. I was alone, vulnerable, and at the mercy of these vicious bullies.

But then, a deep, silken voice cut through the panic.

"*And what would he do?*"

Gabriel.

I froze, my heart pounding in my chest.

"I'm invested," his voice was deep, like velvet cutting through the air. "I didn't know you guys were mind-readers."

My heart pounded in my chest so hard, I couldn't breathe then.

Both girls' eyes rounded, their faces paling as they realized who had overheard their conversation. Kourtney's dark eyes went wide as I heard footsteps behind me.

And I was naked.

I was shaking now, wildly, as I closed my eyes and curled into myself covering myself.

I felt my eyes pooling over. I was terrified. I didn't know what to expect, what Gabriel would do or say.

He's going to humiliate me here.

I cried harder but I pressed my lips together, turning away. Trying to cover myself and feeling myself shrinking.

If the world could swallow me now I would appreciate it.

The universe was not listening to me right now.

But instead, he spoke softly, his voice filled with a quiet menace as something landed on my shoulder. His jacket...

I had a second to think before I grabbed it wrapping it around myself turning away to not look at anyone.

"Finish your sentence," he said. "I dare you Miss Young. I'd love to see you say it to Agent Koller. After all, he fired your brother a few weeks ago. I'm sure you can join him for sexually harassing a female student in your first few weeks here."

I turned over my head and saw Gabriel holding his phone up.

He hit play and my jaw dropped as it played it from me saying 'hello' and then the entire conversation.

I didn't hear him move, but suddenly he was standing next to me, his presence a solid wall.

"You three can pack your things."

They paled even further, their bravado crumbling under the weight of his stare.

I could see the fear in their eyes, the realization that they had crossed a line they could not uncross. I heard the sound of a zipper.

"Sir, we didn't know—"

"Pack. Your. Fucking. Things."

I dug my toes into the floor as he moved around me, his back blocking my view of them.

What was he doing?

I was pretty sure I felt my abdomen cramping like crazy now with the stress.

"We're sorry."

"We can get her clothes."

I had never noticed how cold he sounded. "Don't bother, I have them."

"How—" Kourtney began looking annoyed with him but also she bat her long fake lashes at him.

"I'm not going to repeat myself." Gabriel's voice was hard as iron. *"Get the fuck out."*

If I thought he was scary before? This is terrifying.

Wait a second—

She—Gabriel. Even in my state I was processing the look in her eyes. Not Liam. Never Liam. Him? But Gabriel was our instructor. I had nothing to do with him. Why would she ever think I would be into him or be her competition?

What? Did he have the power...he's their golden boy, he's going to climb the ranks and fast, they like him.

He did. He had power.

The silence after the girls left was deafening.

I looked down at my toes, feeling vulnerable and exposed.

The room fell silent as the girls left, their footsteps echoing in the empty locker room. He was standing guard in front of me, broad shoulders stretched out in a hoodie, all black and sexy.

His dark sweats on his frame as I clung to his jacket swallowing me whole.

When the door shut, I couldn't look at him. I didn't understand him.

I was grateful, but I didn't like hot and cold men.

I liked people who knew what they wanted. *Not this...*

He let out a breath.

"I heard them when you came up to the bleachers." He said softly. "I didn't think they'd be this fucking stupid. It doesn't matter where you go, there are shitheads everywhere." He didn't turn. "I'll go get your towels."

I didn't move as he moved around me, not looking at me.

But as he turned, he looked at my legs, his head tipping a little, and then up at my face. My abdomen cramped a little at that.

His eyes, usually cold, were full of emotions.

"Why are you—" He looked murderous, his eyes darting to the door. "Did they—did they hurt you?"

What? I looked down and saw—I gasped. *"Dio."*

I had gotten my period. And I saw a trickle of blood leaking down my legs. If this day couldn't get ANY worse. It just did. No wonder I was so emotional. No wonder all I want was a gigantic candy bar and to cry in my bed.

His eyes went wide, and he looked away immediately, searching for another towel.

"Which one of them did that to you?"

"What?" What was he talking about?

I was shaking. I had been so stressed that I did get my period.

And in front of—I wanted to be swallowed by the ground.

The universe hates me.

"Isobel, who did this to you?"

"Dio mio!" Was he stupid? What was wrong with him?

I was so upset I didn't even realize he said my name for the first time in forever.

This was scary for me. Too much, too fast, I felt trapped. I wanted to run.

I stumbled back, hitting the lockers, and he turned his eyes on the jacket.

His eyes looked at me handing me a towel, and I was wide-eyed as I stared at him.

Something unspoken passed between us.

"I have...pads..." I looked away, turning so red I didn't know what to do. "In my bag. You said you know where they are. My pads are in my bag!"

His eyes went wide like I had three heads. *"What?"*

"Get my bag!"

Did nobody tell this man about a woman's body?

He moved, heading to a set of lockers out of sight.

When he returned, he was red in the face, unable to look at me, and I realized his jacket was unzipped halfway down.

I huffed. I had my priorities and right now, getting my period in front of this man, naked, cold, and alone? Was not how I wanted today to go.

My eyes burned again.

I was so sensitive on my period. Both Liam and Papi gave me space. I didn't like Liam unless he brought me smores and a heated blanket.

Pads first, then clothes.

He turned away as I yanked them out stripping his jacket and feeling my eyes burn. A noise left me as I cramped. "I got my period, you idiot."

I moaned low, my cramps losing their mind after that scare. My heart was racing.

I whimpered. "Why? Why does everyone hate me?" I sniffled unable to stop myself as a sob left me. I went off in Spanish about the universe not liking me. Everything being a struggle. I cried a little as I cleaned up, put a pad on, clean underwear and sweats. Thankfully I had that.

Quickly, I took care of myself, grateful for the momentary privacy.

"What?" He whispered.

"Did nobody tell you what a woman's period is?"

He paused. "I mean—"

"No, don't answer that. I might kill you."

I wanted to murder this man even though he saved me.

My hands were still shaking, but I managed to get everything in place. I zipped up his jacket, relishing the warmth and the scent of him that surrounded me. His cologne. Even if it was damp? It was warm and I forgot my t-shirt.

"How are you a twenty-four-year-old man, and you can't even figure out what a period is! Who has raised you! Wolves! I can't even be grateful because you are an idiot!"

"Did you just call me an idiot after I saved your ass?"

"Yes!" Call me emotional or whatever, I was so upset right now at what just happened. "How do you not understand I just got my period? *I was so scared. And you scared me, and then they scared me.* And now? I ask you for pads and you have no idea!"

I threw the first thing I saw, my stupid notepad, at him, hitting his back, and he scowled his beautiful features contorting as he looked over his shoulder to find me fully dressed. *"Dammit, woman! I just helped you!"*

I threw a scrunchie at him. "You insulted me. You have done nothing but attack me—"

"I'm trying to protect you!"

"How?!" I shouted. "How are you protecting me? You insult me. You shame me. You are—" I was struggling to talk to him in English as I felt my eyes water.

"Look—"

"You look!" I was livid closing the distance between us even with cramps. "Ever since you met me, you insult me, my English, you stare me down every single time you see me, and you do one nice thing for me, and you think I'm supposed to be like—" I changed my voice to a high-pitched, annoying voice that other women used on him in my fake American accent. *"Oh my God, thanks so much."*

His eyes gleamed as I did that, and I came back to my normal accent.

"No, this happened because of you—"

"What?" His eyes widened.

"This happened because of you!" I shouted at him. Feeling my eyes water as he watched me stunned. He looked at me in disbelief. "This is your fault! I'm done. I don't want to do you or your stupid program, your stupid women who try to ruin my life since I come here, and I'm not going to do this—Not anymore! I quit your stupid program!"

His mouth opened and closed on me.

"I quit. I'm not going to pass this program. I am done. I cannot do this. And I give your jacket back later. I don't have a shirt."

I stormed past him, my bag slung over my shoulder, his jacket hanging on my body.

I could feel his eyes on me as I left, but I didn't dare look back.

My heart was pounding, and my blood was boiling with a mix of anger, embarrassment, and something else I couldn't quite put my finger on.

But it didn't matter. Liam was right. I couldn't pass the program without help. And I wasn't getting it, so I wasn't going to pass.

I was done.

Before I even began.

I couldn't stop myself from crying harder as I stepped outside to the parking lot where Liam stood in front of his blacked out Charger.

Liam saved every penny he could to buy that used car and he was good at fixing things so it was now pristine condition as he said. It was his baby.

The moment his head tipped up and he saw me those eyes of his went wide and he ran to me closing the distance between us, running his hands over my body, holding me tighter.

"What happened? Who was it? Tell me everything." He held my face in his hands asking me in Spanish.

I broke down in his arms. I couldn't hold back my sobs as I brokenly told him.

His face fell as I continued and when I got to Gabriel, my brother's expression changed with confusion.

And then became unreadable.

I cried in his arms as he hugged me tight to him.

"I quit," I croaked as Liam's lips found my temple. "I'm finished. I don't want to do this. I don't feel safe here."

I would figure out another way to make my father happy.

Liam held me so tight it was the only place I felt safe right now. "We'll see about that, shortcake."

CHAPTER 7
GABRIEL

"IS THERE A REASON YOU DON'T ASK TO WALK INTO MY OFFICE?"

Nor did he knock.

Liam Santos was brazen. At best.

He was every superior worsts nightmare because he would spit in the devil's eye if it suited him.

I fucking knew Liam Santos would be the one walking into my office that night. I fucking knew it.

He was an hour late. I was writing the email to Jim for the next morning.

I knew he'd be threatening me though. In my head I imagined he drove Isobel to their apartment a few minutes away and came right back to kick my fucking ass for making his sister cry.

Unlike other trainees who came to my room nervous, Liam walked in like it was his fucking office. In his ripped jeans and band tee's like some rockstar from back when.

His signature smirk was in place. So were his earrings and tongue piercing.

No, Liam walked with a confidence that belied his age. Despite being younger than me and about my height, he held his own. I respected that about him.

He didn't let life phase him.

Probably because Liam was just as fucked up as I was. We had the same lives. We did. He just didn't know it.

And he had Isobel.

I had no fucking doubt he was normal because of her. I could see it.

But the words out of his mouth were not the ones I expected him to say.

"You've got a hard-on for my sister."

I almost fell out of my chair. Almost.

I stopped typing to watch him and his smirk as he sat down across from me and dropped his long legs on my desk.

I dropped down to his black sneakers this time.

"You like her. You want her. I got that. I do." He didn't sound impressed with me. In fact, Liam didn't look like he liked me very much. The feeling was mutual.

"I suggest you—"

"You like her, and that's why you're so fucking mean to her. Because you've got the emotional intelligence of a fucking teaspoon. You're an immature man-child who can't express his feelings, is too damn wounded from his fucked up upbringing, and you fucking hate that she's your trainee when you just want to throw her down and fuck her everywhere you see her." He tipped his head back, his hunter green eyes observant and eerily focused on me like a hungry wolf in the wild. "How am I doing so far?"

I didn't move. I didn't even breathe.

"I didn't know they offered PhD's in psych out of trailer parks."

His grin didn't falter. "See *Monroe*, I know *you*. I know guys like you. She's my fucking sister. I grew up with her. I know everything about her. I know exactly what she likes in her coffee, her pizza toppings, how she sleeps—I know everything about her. And I know guys like you." His grin was wicked, canines and all teeth and his eyes held a hint of malice and madness.

I had only seen that smile on men who didn't care if they lived or died. And Liam had come here to fully wage war with me.

"You're gonna do this shit with her for a couple of more weeks. You're gonna lose your mind whenever you see her. You'll go crazy after she's gone, but eventually, you'll realize that you were never enough to handle her and then you'll spend the rest of your life lamenting on why you fucked up so bad. But deep down inside? You're going to end up in one empty relationship after another. Alone. Desperate. Sad. *Pathetic*. Like you are now."

Red hot fury blazed through me with his words. Who the fuck did this little shit think he was?

"You don't think I can take you right now?" Coming into my office. Threatening me.

Liam continued like I wasn't even important.

"Because you can't give her what she wants, what she needs. So you're going to pretend like she pisses you off, stress her out, make her cry—"

I made her cry?

Liam zeroed in on that.

"*See,* and then you're going to realize in maybe two weeks, that she's too good for you. No, she's the best. She's everything a man like you could ever need in a woman. But you're an immature man-child with attachment issues, you think therapy is a waste of time, so you're never truly going to see her or appreciate her." He leaned back in his chair. "How am I doing for the trailer park, *compadre?*"

Liam Santos was...fucking crazy.

"That's enough." It was a growl in my voice.

His green eyes were wild and wicked as he watched me, his tousled black hair falling over his eyes, and he smiled.

I wanted to wipe that smirk off his face.

"*Oh,*" he said softly like I was a puzzle he was figuring out. "*You* didn't realize you had it that bad."

"I said that's fucking enough!" I shot out of my desk, ready to rip into him, but Liam stood his ground, squaring off with me nose to nose. "*Watch your mouth, I'm still your superior.*"

"Is that the bullshit card you're going to whip out?" He scoffed in my face. "*You're a fucking coward.*"

In a flash, I had him by the throat, pinned against the wall.

"*You don't think I could kill you for your insolence? And make you disappear?*"

It wouldn't be hard, considering he didn't have anybody to lean on. I could make him—

"You're not going to do that," he grit out.

"You wanna bet?"

"For her." His words made me pause. "You won't do shit to me because you know it would hurt *her.*"

An unfamiliar emotion spread through my chest as I realized what he was saying.

His eyes held no malice, just something I had never seen before.

"Aren't you supposed to be trained in manipulation and deception and shit? You don't think I know you got it bad for my sister?"

That little shit was still grinning. *Goddamn it.*

I released my grip on him.

He brushed himself off as if he were shaking me off him.

Then, he moved.

I didn't even see it coming, my thoughts having drifted to a particular brunette with stunning eyes. Under me.

Gasping my name in that soft accent.

"Think fast, Frosty."

Suddenly, I was crashing down onto my back, one of my legs caught in Liam's grip. I growled in rage.

Okay, now all bets were off. Sparring with a trainee?

Except he wasn't a trainee.

He was a fucking asshole.

I was up and at him in an instant, sending him flying over my head. He hit the couch with a groan.

"*Oh, you fucker—*"

Of course, Liam had conveniently left out the fact that he knew how to fight.

"What the fuck is that?" I growled.

"*Kyokushin, bitch.*" He grinned at me. "*Get like me.*" He laughed and I caught his tongue piercing I told him to remove weeks ago still in. This little fucking shit. No wonder he never opened his mouth around me.

"Do you want to keep going?" Because I could.

"Fuck yeah." Liam laughed. And he came at me. As we circled each other, he mock pouted. "Just don't hit my face, she doesn't like that. Gotta keep myself pretty for the ladies."

This motherfucker.

I growled and lunged at him, the reason for her preference only fueling my anger.

It made him laugh as he jumped out of the way.

We traded blows, grappling and slamming each other into the furniture. Liam was skilled, I'd give him that.

He could take a hit and dish it out just as well. But I had years of experience on him, and I wasn't about to let some punk kid get the best of me.

"Why are you so insufferable?" I panted, wiping sweat from my brow. I was still a fighter.

"This is the most fun I've had all year." Liam was having a blast. "Isobel says the same shit."

That name cut through the haze of adrenaline.

I hesitated, and Liam took advantage, sweeping my legs out from under me.

I hit the ground hard, the air rushing out of my lungs.

"She's scared of...she doesn't like feeling trapped. Long story. I heard about the underwater rope day, I know it lasts for hours. She can't do it. She's going to fail the term. She came to ask your stupid ass a question before you insulted her. Nice save by the way. Did you really not know what pads were? How are you that fucking stupid?"

I could hit him for the grin on his face alone.

"What?" My head reeling. "Why do you talk like a fucking sphinx?"

Liam's grin was wide even if his lip was cut and he was panting. "You don't know what pads are. Isobel needs help. Are you going to do it?"

My head hurt talking to this motherfucker.

I struggled to my feet, my mind reeling. "What do you mean, doesn't like feeling trapped?"

Did someone hurt her? *Who? I would find them—*

"Whoa, easy Frosty, don't look like that. I don't know why. She's never told me."

Frosty? Did they give me a nickname?

"All I know is, she doesn't like it. She runs away from things when she feels trapped or afraid and trust me, she's a good runner."

I knew that much.

She didn't run fast, but she ran long.

"She can swim, but you put her in there with ties? She'll panic. And we both don't want her to die."

No. No, I didn't.

I couldn't even think about that. I saw so many of my friends die and Isobel, she—

"She has to," I had done it, everyone did it. "She won't pass without it."

"Exactly." His eyes locked with mine. Fuck. *She wouldn't make it without it.* "Which is why you're the only one who can help her." He looked at me like I was stupid. "Are you stupid or are you slow, Frosty."

"I will fucking shoot you."

"Meh," he made a noise. "All these fucking threats. Are you

going to help Isobel pass or not? If it's a not? I'm dropping out tonight too. If she doesn't come with me? It's not worth doing."

Then I'd lose two students. Not just one.

Even though she said she quit the program, I wanted to wait twenty-four hours to see if she changed her mind and she had gotten her period.

Between my work and my schedule, my training and paperwork, the slim hour before bed was mine.

Not to mention, what he was asking me for wasn't legal.

I couldn't give a trainee extra hours.

He knew that though.

And he had known I wouldn't have cared. He locked eyes with me again. It occurred to me then.

"Why aren't *you* helping her?"

He rolled his bright eyes. "So no. Got it. I quit—"

"She hates me." After what I'd said to her? She definitely wanted to see me dead.

He gave me that look again. *"Is that what you think?"* He made a noise. "So you're slow and stupid, Frosty."

"How does she tolerate you?"

That grin was back.

"So you'll do it."

Yes. I already knew I would. I tipped my head.

If possible, his grin widened. "You might be the first man I'm willing to tolerate who likes her. Even if you are a moron."

"I will shoot you."

He grinned looking rather smug. "No you won't. I'm hers. I've seen the line up in her life. You'd rather crawl on rocks."

There were others?

Of course there are others.

She's a fucking goddess, and you are an insect compared to her. I was. I was dirt under her feet.

"Don't look like that," Liam cut into my thoughts. "Just try to be nice to her, you'll get more flies with honey? Is that the saying? Well, you'll catch Isobel if you just stop being a dick and start showing up as her friend."

Why was he helping me?

Why was he doing this?

Why did I feel so out of it talking to this kid? He was only a year younger than me but ten degrees smarter.

Koller would love him.

"I gotta get back to her now. She likes s'mores and a heating pad on her period. FYI." He winked and turned to leave my office leaving me standing there dumb-founded.

What the fuck just happened?

Until it sank in that I'd need to apologize to Isobel.

And help her through the next phase of training.

Fucking fantastic.

CHAPTER 8
ISOBEL

"You want your new heated blanket?"

Liam knocked on my bedroom door holding a large stuffed bear wearing a small smile.

I frowned over at him miserable on my period.

I laid under the covers watching *Sabrina the Teenage Witch* on television and eating s'mores.

We did not have class or anything the next morning.

And I had quit so I didn't have anything to think about.

Especially not *that* man. Or his jacket hanging off my closet doors taking up all the space in my room.

I felt like it was staring at me. *Judging* me.

With my period, I was morbidly sad laying there crying a lot and sulking as he would say.

Gabriel's eyes kept flashing in my vision and I wanted to throw something across the room.

Liam's frown was in place as he walked over to me bare-chested wearing only pajama bottoms. It was late for him. For us. But I couldn't sleep.

There were multiple tattoos scattering his chest and arms. He was slowing forming a larger piece.

"Yes."

"Are you watching Sabrina?" His little smile was back as he walked up to my bed and crawled in with me. "You used to love that show."

"I still do."

I moved over so Liam could sneak into my bed. He'd done this since we were kids.

Since he was scared of sleeping alone and he found himself in my bed all the time.

We shared a room for years until college. It had been strange not being around him every second of every day.

Eating lunch with him. Dinner. Spending all my time playing with him. We did everything together.

"I brought my phone so we could listen to music." He held up his headphones as he sat against the headboard his thigh and arm pressed into mine under the covers.

I yawned a little taking his headphones from him as he muted the cartoons playing on TV.

"Something good?"

"Mhm, I found a new band." He put his headphones on my ears and played some nice alternative rock.

I didn't think I'd like the songs he liked, but overtime it grew on me. And Liam blasted reggaeton in his car for me.

"It's an up and coming alternative band called Check Mate. Super cool concept..." he spoke softly as he showed me some music until I yawned some more leaning into his shoulder.

"This room is so you," he said softly. It was. Now that we weren't living with my father and we weren't in college, I picked out a lot of white and gold furniture. Nicer things.

"You haven't moved in yet," I said softly. "You are afraid we will not stay? Just because I quit doesn't meant you have to."

"Uhh, actually," his voice sounded a little nervous. "So Frosty told me he wanted to see you in his office tomorrow."

I sat up, alarm burst through me. "What?"

Liam looked a little nervous as he said it. "He says it's not a big deal." Liam shrugged lightly without looking at me. "Just a little paperwork or something. He had me sign it. He said he was missing your signature."

I blinked. "He...it's not about me leaving?"

Liam shook his head again but he wouldn't look me in the eyes.

"Que pasa?" I asked him. *What is it?*

When did he have time to go and talk to Gabriel?

"When did you talk to him?" I took it from him. "Did you see him last night when you went to the drug-store?"

55

He had taken forever but when he came back it looked like he bought the drugstore.

"No," he looked at my new heating pad. "No, I just went for you. No big deal." His eyes finally met mine a little softer. "Come here." He held his hands out and made grabby hands.

I was helpless as I curled back into his arms, inhaling his scent into my lungs. Liam always smelled different than Gabriel.

While Gabriel smelled like the sea and storms, Liam smelled like the forrest. Like home. Stable. My strength came from him. "I don't want to go."

He rubbed my back holding me closer like I had held him for years.

"I know, shortcake. But I think it'll be fine. Maybe he wants to say sorry."

Yeah, and maybe hell is freezing over with him. I didn't say anything I slowly got drowsier on Liam.

"It feels weird having a separate bedroom from you." I murmured softly. "We always share everything."

"Yeah," he said still rubbing my back. "We still do."

His voice held a faraway quality to it.

Liam could always put me to sleep in the past, I'd always fall asleep on him on the way home.

He was my brother, my best friend, my other half.

I could never imagine anyone replacing him.

THE NEXT NIGHT BEFORE CLASS, I WAS IN FRONT OF GABRIEL'S DOOR.

My heart was pounding right out of my chest, my palms nervous and clammy.

I knocked and stepped into it knowing he'd be there.

Liam said as much.

I will just sign something and then leave. I will leave. It will never even matter.

"You asked for me?" Why was I whispering?

Here, in his domain, the shadows seemed to swallow him whole, but I could still make out his silhouette leaning against the desk, arms crossed.

His eyes glowed in the darkness, set in that striking face of his.

Pale blue. Brighter than the moon. Gabriel was not human. I was sure of it. Too pretty to be real. Too masculine to be anything else.

"Liam said you wanted me to sign something." He stood up in the low lighting but there was nothing in his hands.

Gabriel's face came into view, and I gasped.

"Who did this to you?"

Without thinking, I rushed forward, my hands reaching out to touch him. Heat seared my palms as they made contact with his skin.

"Isobel, I'm all right," he said softly, his hands coming up to grasp my arms.

The sound of my name on his lips was rare, and it sent a thrill through me.

"No," I insisted, taking in the sight of his injured brow.

"Where's your first aid kit?" My voice left no room for argument. "I can leave after."

Gabriel's grip on my arms tightened, and a wave of unease washed over me. "You're still thinking about leaving?"

I suddenly realized how close we were, alone in his office with the door closed. "Thinking?"

"Did something happen?" he asked, his voice low and deep. "Something more than the locker room?"

I shook my head, confused. "I mean, they are always like that. It does not matter." I looked at his expression. "Are you here to kick me out instead of me quitting?"

Surprise flickered across his face, and his eyes lit up, his lips twitching. "You thought because you handed my ass to me, I would be that petty and get you kicked out?"

Now *he* looked upset.

I stumbled over my words, trying to tug out of his grip as panic began to rise in my chest. "W-well, when y-you say it...t-that—"

"You think so little of me?" There was ice in his eyes now. "You think I would ever hurt you like that because you stood up to me?"

"I thought you hated me," I whispered, the words spilling out before I could stop them. The panic was clawing at my throat now, making it hard to breathe.

Gabriel swore softly, closing his eyes for a moment. When he looked at me again, the chill had faded.

"I don't hate you." But he felt something because his jaw was tight. "I'm not going to get you kicked out for standing up to me when I was a prick to you. You stood up to me. I respect that. Only the best do."

I tugged at his grip again, the trapped feeling crawling up my spine.

"You can let go now." I couldn't even speak around him.

Instead, he pulled me closer, my chest pressing against his. A strangled gasp tore from my throat.

He said softly. "Do you have what you need?"

I was confused by his line of questions.

"For your..." He gave me the same look he did when I was on my...I turned pink.

I nodded, confused. *What was happening?* "I can't believe you thought it was snacks."

He turned pink. "I don't exactly have women in my life."

"I could not tell."

That got a twitch of his lips, and I almost wondered what he looked like if he smiled. Heart breaking. Beautiful.

He looked down at me. "Glad to know sarcasm is an international language."

And then he tightened his hold.

My breathing came in short, sharp bursts.

"What are you doing?"

Was he going to hurt me?

No, not Gabriel.

Not him. He protected me.

But I didn't know him.

"Your brother says you won't be passing the course. And you're dropping out because of that." I stiffened. He knew? Liam told him? "It's a requirement."

I struggled in his grip. It wasn't like Liam to tell anyone. But trying to get out of Gabriel's grip was like trying to escape iron.

"I didn't know hurting a woman was a class—"

"It's an art." The words sliced through the air and through me. *Oh God, he was crazy. He was going to kill me.*

I stopped moving, feeling panic crawl up my throat. Was he—

"One I excel at. But I would *never* hurt *you*."

Those eyes of his were hauntingly pale.

What? What was he talking about?

58

"Then let me go."

"I can't, because your brother asked me to help you," he murmured, his lips brushing against my ear. "And for some fucking reason, I can't say no when it comes to you."

But he was too close for my comfort. My breathing was coming out in sharp gasps.

"No, no. Don't freak out. It's just me." His words were meant to soothe, but I could barely hear them over the pounding of my heart.

Tears spilled over, hot tracks down my cheeks, as I twisted against his hold, desperate to escape the suffocating fear.

Gabriel shifted his grip, holding both of my wrists in one hand.

His other hand came up to cup my neck, fingers spanning the column of my throat as he tipped my head back. Gentle but commanding. Strong. Powerful.

In no words Gabriel told me with his body if he wanted to, he could snap me in half and was choosing not to.

"Look at me," he whispered, his eyes filled with sympathy. Or something close to it. The Gabriel I knew wasn't capable of that. He didn't have a heart.

"Focus...there you are, stay on me. Just me...Good girl."

Just like that something happened to me.

The praise hit like lightening, shocking my system—fundamentally shifting.

It was irreversible since I hadn't felt this way about him since I had first seen him. And now that sensation was back.

Something I never imagined would happen with Gabriel Monroe.

It had been weeks of us at each other's throats.

I hated him. The few weeks had been him pushing me to my limits in every way. And now this?

The praise settled somewhere deep inside me, warm and unexpected.

As I stared into his ice-colored eyes, I saw something soften in their depths. He was dangerously addictive.

Foreign and familiar all at once.

His nose dipped closer to me, and for a moment he closed his eyes inhaling lightly.

"What do you have in your mouth all the time?"

Why was he so disarming? "Butterscotch. It's candy. My father gets it for me."

"I know that," he leaned forward like a curious lion. "But why?"

"It tastes good." I found myself saying it and I swore his lips tipped up a little in a ghost of smile.

Gabriel's gaze drifted over my face, lingering on the tears that tracked down my cheeks. And then, in a gesture that stole my breath, he pressed his lips to one of them.

I froze in his arms.

"I'm going to get you through this," he murmured against my skin.

He told me then that he wanted to train me himself, to prepare me for the second half of the class.

I could barely comprehend his words, my mind still reeling from the storm of emotions that had consumed me.

Liam asked him. And he answered.

"Why would you do that?" I asked, my voice hoarse. Why would he help me? Or Liam?

Gabriel didn't answer, his eyes searched mine in a way that every part of my skin was now aware of. Dropping down to my lips.

"It's not always bad," he said softly, his deeper voice dropping enough for me to see the way he watched me now openly. "Being restrained."

Heat bloomed in my core at his words, images of him holding me down as he moved above me flashing through my mind. Gabriel moving over me. Inside of me.

Holding me down like this. His mouth trailing fire across my skin.

Me. I hadn't been with anyone since college.

Not since...that incident happened and Liam had almost killed the guy.

I swallowed hard, suddenly aware of his arousal pressing against my thigh.

"Gabriel."

His eyes closed quickly for a second then, his throat working hard.

"You're not afraid of being trapped," he whispered, his breath ghosting over my skin. "You're not afraid of it at all. You're afraid of the emotions."

He was right. I was terrified of the feelings that threatened to overwhelm me, the intensity of what I felt for him.

"H-how do you know?" I stammered, my heart racing.

Gabriel's jaw clenched, as if he were fighting some internal battle. Those eyes of his were dark. Hungry. On me.

"I know."

He held me like that for long moments, his eyes never leaving mine. I felt like I was suspended in time with his eyes on me. Those eyes. Eerie. Pale. Blue. Brighter than anything I had ever seen.

Slowly, the panic began to recede, replaced by a strange sense of calm.

"When you need to in the future, just focus on me," he murmured, his hands gradually releasing their hold on me. "I'm right here."

I nodded, unable to form words.

As he let me go completely, I felt a rush of relief, but also a pang of loss. His touch had become a lifeline, and part of me didn't want to let it go.

"Did Liam do that to you?" I asked, gesturing to his injured brow. It twisted painfully in my stomach to see it because I knew exactly how Liam got Gabriel to do what he wanted.

Which...shouldn't have surprised me.

He didn't answer, his expression unreadable.

"I'll see you tomorrow at eight. There was no paperwork for you to sign. I think your brother is just clever." Under his breath he muttered. "Too clever."

I turned to leave, my legs shaky beneath me. But before I could reach the door, Gabriel's voice stopped me.

"What did you call me earlier? In Spanish?"

I flushed, remembering the nickname Liam and I had given him. Did he know?

Frosty.

Frosty, the Snowman.

But now it seems wrong to say it.

He isn't cold at all.

I mumbled, avoiding his gaze. "I was just worried about your eye. You should get that bandaged."

I smoothed my hands over my jeans, feeling his eyes track the movement.

Every instinct screamed at me to run, to put as much distance between us as possible.

But another part of me, a part I didn't quite understand, wanted him to chase me, to catch me and never let me go.

I didn't see him coming.

Not once.

Not at all.

CHAPTER 9
GABRIEL

I<small>T TOOK EVERYTHING IN ME TO NOT DRAG HER BACK AND CHASE</small> after her.

The urge to hunt, to claim, clawing at my insides with an intensity that shocked even me.

God I wanted her so bad.

Even now my cock was so painfully hard at the feel of her nipples brushing against my chest.

The realization that Isobel didn't fear being tied down or trapped, she feared someone doing it meaning harm? It shot off so many emotions within me.

The ice I'd spent years cultivating was thawing just a tiny bit around her and I didn't know why.

She'd wriggled her little body against mine and had gasped when I pulled her up. God, what would she do if I held her down and showed her restrained pleasure would drive her insane. Taught her how sweet surrender would be.

Which made me fucked up for even thinking like that—but that's what I was into.

Restraint was my thing.

And I bet Isobel would love if if I moved inside of her, my cock splitting her open until she came and came and came so hard she could only take.

My dick didn't care if I was training her. Or the professional boundaries I needed to have.

It didn't care she was my student and we couldn't do this.

Even now my dick was straining against the zipper of my pants. Damn. I wanted this girl. More than anything else.

I blamed it on not being able to have her.

But after weeks and weeks and weeks of trying to get her out of my system—I fucking knew what Liam was doing.

I just didn't know why.

Because my dick didn't care about anything. Not the rules. Not anyone. Me. The guy who'd never fucking broken the rules unless necessary deemed this moment necessary. For her.

Liam hadn't been wrong.

Nothing would stop me from having her.

Absolutely fucking nothing.

⁓

HELL ON EARTH WAS ISOBEL SANTOS SHOWING UP AT MY OFFICE dressed in comfy clothing, ready to be destroyed by me.

And not sexually. Not in the ways my mind wandered to.

"Are you ready?" I kept my voice low and controlled.

She shook her head, the inky hair swishing this way and that, and I bit back a laugh at her honesty. Least, she was always telling me the truth.

"No?" I pressed my lips together as I walked over to her. *Professional, asshole.*

"Do you want to use a word to let me know when you've hit your limit?"

I didn't say safe word.

This wasn't sex. This was...*oh fucking Hell.*

As soon as she saw the rope, she was backtracking, hitting the door of my office.

"Yes," she thought about it. "*Snowman.*"

I paused, a thought suddenly occurring to me. It clicked into place and I didn't know why I didn't think it before.

"Do you *think* in Spanish?"

She nodded.

"And then you translate it to English before you speak?"

She nodded again.

Good to know.

Anything about her was good to know.

64

"Don't run," I whispered, not moving, like she was a startled animal. In a way she was. But I was bigger. I would chase her if she even thought about running.

I was a hunter on the inside.

And when I found her, she wouldn't like what I did to her.

She would *love* it.

"It's just me." I didn't acknowledge why Isobel had agreed to let me help her with her fears. I only knew she did.

I slowly walked up to her, and she looked like if she could crawl back up the door, she would.

"Look at me." She did. "What did I say?"

"F-focus, on y-you." *That's right, baby.*

"Focus on me, good girl." I tried not to notice when she flushed at the praise. *Professional.* "Let me see your hands."

She bit her lip. No. She shook her head.

"No, Gabriel. I can't do this. I'm too afraid."

I could listen to her talk forever. *Gabri-el.*

I know, baby.

"You have to. You know why?"

She shook her head again. No. I smiled a little.

"Because you're going to be one of the best operatives once you learn to face your fears. Everything you ever wanted is on the other side of what you're afraid of."

She swallowed and looked at me. Really looked at me. "Promise?" She held out her pinky.

Oh hell. I took her pinky. "I promise."

And then I *moved.*

Even as my heart tugged, I just continued to work quickly.

She was no match for me.

I had her bound in record time as she struggled. When I finally pulled her back against me, she was whimpering. Sweet thing she was.

I turned her around and gripped her neck.

"Isobel," I whispered. "Focus."

My heart raced as I held her close, feeling the warmth of her body against mine.

The scent of her, that intoxicating mix of butterscotch and her filled my senses. Her hair in my way. Soft and lush like her. Every inch of her pressed to me.

I wanted to bury my face in her hair, to breathe her in until she was all I knew. But I couldn't.

Not now.

"I've got you," I murmured, my thumb stroking the soft skin of her neck. "I won't let anything happen to you."

I intended to keep that promise.

"Now breathe for me."

AND SO SHE SHOWED UP EVERY SINGLE DAY.

Every single fucking day. Terrified but getting better.

Isobel progressed rapidly through every single thing I gave her almost like even if she was terrified she wanted to keep up with me. She wanted to get better.

"Take it easy," I motioned for her to take a step back.

Not because I needed space—I mean I did—but because I needed to not freak her out completely with my dick hardening from the sheer proximity of her wrapped around me.

Me. The guy nobody touched. I was now holding Isobel Santos close to me like she was the one reason for living. It was insane.

But I did it.

Where we worked on her breathing, her undoing her ties, or even techniques to manage her emotions.

Maybe it was special treatment.

Maybe Liam knew I secretly relaxed when I got in more time with her?

During the day she ran wild on the field and Jeremy ambling behind her like a lovesick bear.

Liam grinning ear to ear at Jeremy struggling but the three of them worked it out.

If Isobel was good to Jeremy so was Liam.

I looked into the latter deeply as a trainee and student and found him disarming since he was the most like me.

Liam Sullivan originally had a life similar to mine.

So similar it was eerie. I hadn't said a word about what was ever done to me.

But the difference between Liam and me?

Was one solid thing.

Her.

I wasn't a fool.

I had seven fucking weeks to live and breathe in the same space as her for almost eight to ten hours a day.

I think I knew her by now.

CHAPTER 10
ISOBEL

IT FELT LIKE THE SWEETEST TORTURE.

Facing my biggest fear with the man who drove me insane with pleasure.

Being held tight to him while I struggled with a sensation I never thought I'd grow to experience.

He pushed me past my limits. He *excelled* at it.

And by the fourth night, I was losing my mind.

When it was over, I was on the floor on my knees, Gabriel curled around me in a way that made me feel smaller. Helpless. But not in a bad way.

"Are you all right?" His gruff whisper pulled me from my reverie, his voice sinking into my skin like warm hot honey.

I nodded, not trusting myself to speak.

The room felt charged with an energy I couldn't quite place, a tension hung heavier with every breath in the air.

Slowly, I curled against him, seeking his warmth, his solid presence. His heat.

I rubbed my eyes so I wouldn't look at him.

"Te odio a veces…" I whispered. *I hate you sometimes.* "But I remember why you're doing this."

"What does that mean?"

He didn't speak Spanish.

I didn't say it. I felt like sugar dissolving in a glass in his presence. And he remained quiet.

His quiet nature a constant reminder of the distance between us.

But even in his silence, I felt the weight of his gaze.

I wanted to stand, my legs feeling weak, and if he sensed that, he helped me up.

I couldn't bring myself to look at him, my eyes instead landing on the clock.

It was late, far later than our usual sessions.

He had stayed an extra hour with me. And we were both exhausted. I could see it on his face.

"What do you do when you go home?" I asked, needing to fill the silence, to distract myself from the way his touch made me feel. "Do you...have dinner or...?"

"I just go back. Sometimes I have dinner. Some nights I just pass out," he replied, his words clipped, his tone distant.

Like ice.

I felt a pang of guilt, realizing how little I knew about him, despite the judgments I had made.

"Do you..." I hesitated, gathering my courage. "Tienes a alguien en casa?" It slipped out quickly and I translated it. "Do you have anyone...at home for you?"

I didn't know why I asked.

"No."

His answer cut through the air, and I nodded, letting out a breath.

The thought of Gabriel going home alone, of him not having anyone to share his life with, tugged at my heart. It always had.

He reminded me of Liam a little. But the Liam I met years ago. The thought hit me like lightening.

That's who he reminded me of. My brother.

But...where Papi helped Liam...*did anyone help Gabriel?*

Maybe you can.

I turned away, wiping my eyes as the ache intensified.

"Sometimes..." I began, and he paused, tuning in to my words. "Do you want to come and have dinner? Liam gets food—"

"You want me to be in the same room as him?"

I blinked, surprised by his reaction. "Why not? He is my brother. My father adopted him. I came to America and I met Liam in school."

The story fell out of me.

69

"Someone tried to hit me in school when I was twelve or something. Liam, he saved me.

I shared my food with him and my father kept asking me who was eating all my lunch and when he met Liam…"

I realized Gabriel probably didn't know about Liam's past and it wasn't my place to say anything.

"We adopted him. But he is my brother and I love him. But I'm sure if he asked you to help me—he trusted you. I do not think he will mind if you eat with us." I shrugged a little. "You are already breaking the rules."

Why not just eat with us?

A corner of his mouth tipped up. "So full send on that, huh?"

"*Como?*"

It wasn't my imagination he was smiling and the sight made my stomach flip. "Means, just go ahead and break them all the way."

I nodded like the answer was that. "Yes."

His lips tipped up higher.

"So you come for dinner, si?"

His eyes went wide, Liam said I did that. Turned it right back around to what I wanted. I smiled and nodded.

I saw his eyes intensify on me, those blues taking me in.

"Dinner."

"Si, Liam gets take out," I told him I cooked most of the time so he did me favors and got take out. "Are you hungry? We can go now. What time do you sleep?"

He looked at the clock. I saw it all over his face. "Now."

I bit my lip, guilt flooding me. "I'm sorry."

He was doing me a favor.

"Don't be. I chose to stay late."

Something in his voice made me shiver. I told myself this was just attraction. That was it. No big deal.

It was just Gabriel.

And because he saved me from those girls.

And because he watched out for me.

That's it. Nothing else.

I nodded, looking away, grabbing my sweater and shrugging it on, unsure of what to say. "It's okay, you don't have to, I just—"

I didn't know how to say anything around him. Not like this.

"If you show up an hour earlier, we have more time."

I looked at him, standing by his desk like a marble statue.

My heart clenched a little at the sight of him. He was too pretty for a man. Pale eyes. Blonde hair. And cute.

Something between a movie star and something otherworldly.

His hair was growing out now and I was tempted all the time to run my fingers through it.

Who am I kidding? I want to kiss him so bad.

"Are you coming then?"

I waited. And then very slowly he tipped his head.

CHAPTER 11
GABRIEL

"I GOT THAI CURRY! I WAS CRAVING THE GREEN ONE WITH EXTRA chilis. Did you mind?"

I heard Liam's voice the moment she walked in with me.

As I stepped into the apartment with Isobel, the aroma of Thai food filled my nostrils, accompanied by the sound of her brother.

I couldn't fucking believe I agreed.

I was either hungry, stupid, or both.

Probably both.

"No! I hope you got extra!" Isobel grinned at me, her soft eyes alight with excitement. "I have a friend with me!" A friend?

It moved something in me. I couldn't explain it.

I wanted her *bad*. I wanted to swallow this woman whole. Eat her for dinner. "You will like it, I promise."

"I always get extra for you, you hippopotamus, who is she? Is she cute?" Liam's voice came through like he was coming closer. "You feel like a hungry hungry hippo tonight again?"

A what?

"Not hungry hungry," Isobel said with a laugh her eyes twinkling. *"Just hungry."*

Isobel rolled her eyes at the insult and laughed at my bemused expression.

Liam walked out of the kitchen, clad in pajama bottoms only, tattoos across his arms and bare chest and a wide grin on his face.

72

That dropped the moment he saw me. " Sweet *Jesus fucking Christ. What the fuck Isa?*"

It immediately morphed into a look of exaggerated shock the moment he laid eyes on me.

He blinked rapidly at me pointing a spoon at me. *"Why is Frosty in our home?"*

Frosty?

Isobel shot off something in Spanish I didn't understand and Liam gaped at her.

He blinked, staring at me in mock disbelief, those eyes brighter than me.

"You invited him for dinner? I took off my clothes because I thought it was a hot friend!" He looked at her like she had committed a federal offense. *"Que?"*

Isobel shot me an apologetic look. "Ignore him. He has no manners. You would think Papi raised you better!"

"He did, he raised me *not* to let a polar bear into my home."

I blinked.

Liam scowled at me eyeing me up and down like I wasn't *his* fucking instructor too.

She turned to Liam, and a burst of words shot from her mouth like sparks, her quiet demeanor from the car ride gone as she squared off in front of me.

She said *'something something polar bear'* which I take meant me. And Liam shot me a grimace.

I couldn't understand a word, but the way Liam's eyes sparkled with mischief told me all I needed to know.

He was fucking with her.

"So you brought him home? I'm not taking in refugees now from the Arctic."

Isobel kept shouting at him until he groaned.

Her little body blocked me from him the best she could as she waved her hands.

I didn't know what she said just that she was frowning adorably, her brows knit tight as she put her arms around me like she was protecting me from Liam.

Liam groaned dramatically and left swearing in Spanish.

"There isn't enough for him!"

"Yes, there is, pendejo. He can have mine!" She looked at me and I felt a niggle of unease by all of it. "Come on, Gabriel."

I didn't…go home to anything.

And suddenly my microwaved meals sounded better than this. I didn't wanna cause problems.

"I don't wanna cause any problems." An uglier part of me reared up at the sight of it. "I don't think he likes me—"

"Don't worry Gabriel," Isobel said easily taking my arm. "Liam loves problems. They're his favorite to solve. Come. Take off your shoes. We don't wear outside shoes in our house. You are the same size maybe as Liam's slippers—"

"He cannot have my slippers! Isa—"

"Yes he can!" She screamed into the apartment. "Gabriel, put them on."

She motioned to the slippers in question lowering her voice again. "You can use those, hm? And then we will eat dinner."

There was no room for questions as she took off her shoes and slid into her slippers. Red flip flops. Liam had several pairs shoes in the entryway.

She hung up her sweater and then padded inside the apartment so fast. Like it was a rhythm for her.

I heard Isobel screaming at Liam and he groaned again dramatically.

I didn't know whether to laugh or be afraid.

This was nothing like the girl at training.

She was replaced with a wilder woman who ripped into Liam without hesitation. Like she'd ripped into me weeks ago.

She was waited for me in the entryway when I put on Liam's slippers feeling out of place in this setting.

My all black sweats and hoodie looked out of place in this colorful eclectic home filled with colors and photos all clearly hers.

"I'm sorry," she apologized, looking a little flustered. "He isn't usually this bad—"

"I'm way worse—" he shouted. *"Go back to the Arctic, Frosty!"*

She screamed something that even I translated as "be fucking quiet" and I blinked feeling a little afraid.

I had *never* seen this version of her.

"He always get's like this when I have someone over."

She rolled her eyes as she said it.

But it occurred to me that Isobel, as attractive as she was, probably did have men over. In the past.

The thought made my stomach churn and something ugly rear up inside of me as she led me into their small kitchen.

"You brought someone home?" I murmured.

"It was one time," she shook her head her eyes a little far away and darker now. "Liam didn't like him."

Good. Good riddance.

"He hurt you?"

Isobel looked uncomfortable as I asked that.

What was his name? I could find out his Social Security number in nine seconds. And he would be dead.

"Gabriel," she turned around, but I saw the answer in her eyes.

"What did he do?" I pressed, moving closer to her, not sure what I was doing or why I felt comfortable doing it.

We stopped before we even hit the kitchen where Liam was grumbling about having to *share* for dinner.

But Isobel wasn't wrong. It was like a family feast on the table.

She smiled up at me. "Told you, we have enough."

She reached out, tugging me into the house by my sleeve, her touch gentle.

Her hands burning my arm wherever she touched me. My earlier thoughts forgotten with the promise of food.

My stomach growled at the aroma of Thai food and tea with what looked like dark jelly inside, and the sight of Isobel moving about the kitchen, placing food around me.

"Gabriel, you want Thai tea with boba?" She passed me one of the drinks. There was four.

"Isa, that one was mine," Liam whined a little. Isobel growled at him as she handed it to me.

I waited until she handed me a plate and utensils before settling next to her on the island while Liam stood across from us glancing at me like I was expired milk.

"What are you doing here?" He mock whispered. "I said train her, not let her bring you home. I live here. Do you think I can exist in peace knowing you've sat in *my* seat. With *my* sister?"

"*I swear to God—*" Isobel went off on him again and he rolled his eyes groaning.

She said something in Spanish, rapidfire, her words like sparks, and he grumbled focusing on his pad Thai.

Clearly one of the Santos siblings did not want me here.

"Go on," she motioned to me. "It's okay, Liam won't do anything." She growled at her brother as he rolled her eyes.

"Isa, he's the size of a polar bear. He doesn't need you to protect him."

"You will stop talking!" She took off her shoe, and flung it at him so fast I didn't even see it coming. My hand drifted to my chest a little stunned at how fast she moved.

Oh my god, this woman was terrifying.

And I liked it.

Liam ducked, laughing, and I bit my lip, stunned as they went back and forth. "Monroe, she's abusing me because of you—"

Isobel shouted something at him in Spanish again throwing her other shoe.

Liam hit the ground laughing harder and she sat back down primly apologizing to me as she took another bite of her noodles.

When Liam did come up, he was grinning red-faced.

This was the same guy who took me down in my office.

He could easily stop the slipper.

So why didn't he? I didn't know this side of Liam or her existed.

I had never seen this side of her in class. She was a ninja with her slipper, and it was...all for me?

Something unfamiliar kept blooming inside of my chest at this. At all this.

I was overwhelmed.

She's protecting me. Why?

"Eat, Gabriel. It's okay."

Her caramel eyes were kind as she smiled at me softly. Warm. Inviting. Lush.

She took a bite of her satay, and I followed suit, biting back another smile as I dug in.

It tasted better than anything I had. But this was unfamiliar to me. This...dynamic.

This was different than what it felt like when I was in the military. Or when people inviting me out to dinner for business.

This felt different with the two of them.

Liam grumbled, his eyes balefully meeting mine like a cat. "Don't get used to this, Monroe."

"Get used to it!" Isobel shot back. *"He is having dinner with us from now on!"*

I blinked.

I didn't even get a say.

This woman was going to ruin my fucking schedule.

My solitude.

Carefully constructed as I thought it was? It was crumbling like a sandcastle with every warm smile she shot me.

And I didn't give a damn because I wanted to keep her by my side forever. Take her in spades and take in everything about her.

Even when she was angry.

"Eat Gabriel. We have plenty for you. *And none for the demon in the corner!*"

"You replace me and have the audacity—"

"I replaced you?!"

"Yes, you replaced me—you don't even care about me—"

"*Dio Mio estás siendo ridículo—*" *You are so ridiculous.*

"*¿Oh, estoy siendo ridículo?*" *Oh, I'm being ridiculous?*

The two of them went at it, at each other's throat until Isobel found a paper towel roll and threw it at him.

I winced as it hit his shoulder.

"It's okay, Gabriel," she turned to me a total one-eighty. "Don't be afraid, Liam will not make it through his sleep tonight."

Scary.

And hot.

I bit back my laughter and failed watching them interact like the most human thing in the world.

Except...I had no intention of replacing Liam.

He was her brother. *Clearly.*

I didn't want...I didn't know what I wanted with Isobel.

But I sure as fuck wasn't her brother.

CHAPTER 12
ISOBEL

"Why are you so jealous?"

I walked into Liam's room finding him reading on his e-reader.

His room still looked like he was still moving in. Liam always kept his place neat.

He only had a photo of me and Papi and himself on his dresser.

We were both smiling while Liam looked angry at the photographer for taking forever.

He threw his e-reader down making room for me to crawl into the other side.

"I'm not jealous."

Yes, he was.

"Why?" I crawled over to him and bumped his shoulder with mine sitting next to him. "You are my family. Do you think if Gabriel comes over he will be my family?"

Liam paused and his eyes met mine then with a strange look in them. "Is that what you want?"

It hurt me he asked. "You think I will replace you?"

He shook his head looking away. I never thought Liam would think that. It had always been us. Just the two of us. Through everything.

"Hey," I pushed at his shoulder despite him being bigger than me. "You are my brother. How will I forget you?"

He looked a little angry as I said it. I knew Liam didn't have romantic feelings for me.

We talked about it the one time he'd fought that other guy in high school for me. He loved me, but not romantically. And I knew he didn't because Liam secretly slept with anything that walked.

But he was jealous of Gabriel.

"Do you think if he comes to our home, one day I will leave you and forget about you?"

Liam was silent. Was that was this was about?

Liam was adopted. I knew that. But that made no difference to me. Had it made a difference to him.

"Hey," I pushed him gently. "*Mirame.*" When those lighter green eyes met mine, I said it to him in our language the one he understood. Liam spoke better Spanish now but I knew English would not be sufficient for him. "*It's you and me. Always. Even if I am with Gabriel, I would never forget you. Just because Papi adopted you and brought you into our family, does not make you temporary. A one time thing. You are a Santos. You're one of us. You're my heart. My love. My brother. My protector. Nothing else will replace that. Even if I end up loving him? I would never forget about you. I wouldn't let him forget you. Understood?*"

Liam blinked a few times. He held up his pinky. "Promise?"

I linked it. "Mucho amo," I teased him with his broken Spanish phrase.

Liam smiled a little but I saw something in his eyes I hadn't seen before. Liam had been the one to ask Gabriel to help me.

But now?

Now I saw something new in them. A fear.

"I will never let you go," I whispered. "Doesn't matter what happens. You are my family too."

"Even if he ever becomes yours?"

My heart beat louder. Gabriel was barely my boyfriend. Why did Liam even worry? He didn't...he wasn't...no. Sometimes I forgot even if Liam was twenty-three—he was still as Papi called him, a baby. *Pobrecito. He's still a baby.*

I shook my head.

"If he's my family—he's your family too then. Remember?"

He shuddered a little playfully like he didn't want that. But it was true. Anyone who was a part of my life had me and Liam.

"Somehow I can't imagine being brothers with Monroe. He's a polar bear and I'm hardly like him. I'm like..."

"A grizzly bear?"

He nodded seriously.

I giggled like they weren't the same person. In Spanish I told him that meant they were technically the same but from different climates.

I grinned at his shock and laughed louder as he shoved me down into the bed and pretended to roll away from me.

"I don't wanna be related to a bear."

"So then be a dragon or something."

"Isa, dragons aren't real."

"Neither is Frosty the Snowman but you call Gabriel that."

Liam growled. "Isa."

I couldn't stop laughing at him grumbling about ever being related to Gabriel Monroe.

Like it would ever happen.

~

HE JOINED US FOR DINNER EVERY NIGHT. LIKE HE BELONGED THERE. Like he'd always been there. And for the next week? Every single day—Gabriel was there.

I offered for him to stay in the living room, but wondered if he'd fit.

My bed would accommodate him better, though I didn't want to propose that.

Dio Mio. I wanted to. But I shouldn't.

Each evening after training I brought him home.

Liam stopped being oblivious, ensuring we had ample food or cooking for us some nights, aware we'd be out late.

When we got back one night he'd left us alone having eaten before us.

And he stopped complaining about Gabriel taking his spot.

"He doesn't care anymore?" Gabriel asked, his pale blue eyes studying me.

"No," I shrugged. "He's not going to be a jealous idiot anymore."

"I can hear you." He shouted.

"You were supposed to!" I snapped back.

I turned to Gabriel with a smile, and he blinked, surprised by my shift. "It's okay, I have to act this way with Liam, or he goes crazy."

"You brought Frosty home," Liam yelled back. "I can be crazy."

"Don't call him that," I chided, resting my hand on Gabriel's arm without thinking.

Liam popped back into the kitchen. "Isa, he sits in my seat every night—"

"We can get you another chair!"

"But I like that one!"

"Then take mine and sit next to him so I will stand."

"No, are you insane?" He looked at her offended. "You can't stand."

"I will stand now!" I shouted back getting up and dragging the chair over to him so I could go back to Gabriel's to stand and he immediately stood to offer me his seat.

"*Gabriel sit down.* You don't have to listen to this demon." I growled at Liam. "Stop being mean to him. He has done nothing to you."

Liam grumbled something about stealing his sister.

I blinked up apologetic at Gabriel. "He is very protective."

Gabriel looked uneasily at Liam and then me. There was something in his eyes. Something foreign. A hint of uncertainty.

I wanted to stab my brother then.

I pushed at Gabriel gently. "Please, sit."

He stiffened at my touch, and I apologized as he blinked a few times at my hands.

Liam focused intently on Gabriel then as I motioned for him to sit down.

Liam's greener eyes took on that crazed look he got when solving a problem. What was he seeing now that I wasn't?

Something...I glanced at Gabriel, who looked down at his food with that expression. "I should go."

No. I glared at him who dared to turn away then rolling his eyes at me and leaving the room.

"No, stay. You're here so late anyway. Liam—" I pleaded with him. "It's late—You can stay in my room if you'd like. I can sleep on the couch—"

"No—" came my brother's voice from the hall where he clearly was.

I was going to murder Liam. Slowly. Painfully. He would die.

I had enough. Enough. I didn't think. I just moved. Sliding myself into Gabriel's lap not even thinking twice about it.

"There, now I have a seat. And you cannot leave."

I picked at his food, popping a sushi-roll into my mouth.

Even as heat flared through me, even as I felt his shock, even as his arms banded around me like he couldn't help himself.

I forced myself to speak. "Don't listen to Liam, he's just upset."

"I didn't do anything to him."

"No," I shook my head. "But he isn't used to sharing me with anyone. And even you." Liam would be listening and I didn't care. "But he doesn't know he doesn't have anything to worry about."

Gabriel's arms banded around me as though bringing me tighter to him, flush against his chest until I looked over my shoulder and he was right there.

Cheeks slightly red from our proximity. Winter blue eyes on me.

"Should I get off you?" My throat was working. "I can bring the chair back." His arm tightened around my waist at that.

He shook his head, the tiny movement speaking volumes as my heart pounded. I felt a smile curling my lips.

"You can stay here tonight," I whispered.

Liam said nothing. And Gabriel went back to eating not letting me go.

~

THE NEXT NIGHT GABRIEL AND I SPEND LONGER TRAINING together.

Every single day he made it more challenging. I struggled but he covered my lips with his larger hand. "Don't scream, don't panic. The more you panic, the more your hearts going to race. You'll run out of air."

I knew this. But I couldn't stop panicking. Not once.

It's just Gabriel. It's just Gabriel. It's just Gabriel.

I told myself this over and over and yet. I didn't see him. Not once.

I saw someone else. A dark specter. Shadows in my vision. The darkness flooding my sight.

Murkier images flooded my brain like a damn breaking.

Gabriel had moved us away from his office to one of the spare training rooms. This way we could be alone.

He kept the lights dimmed lower and once it was fully darker and the sun had set it created an eerie feeling to the room.

Now? It amplified my memories. Of a past I thought I had forgotten.

"Isobel!" I heard Gabriel far away. I screamed a little at the sound tearing from my throat as I dropped into darkness.

In my memories, I was a doll, dragged and tossed around. Someone was screaming. Women. Someone was laughing.

Hands were grabbing at me and I couldn't stop screaming as I felt iron bands of arms tightening around me.

Someone was throwing me into something.

I was screaming for my father. Only he could help me.

My mother was in my vision. She was shrieking.

Evie was in her arms. Evie. My *sister*.

I remembered her.

I couldn't move. My hands banded at my sides.

"Help me!" I was shrieking.

"Isobel!" Papi was running to me. He had a gun in his hand.

I was screaming louder as someone closed in my vision. My father was shouting, grabbing for me. I couldn't stop crying and then I woke up.

It was like snapping awake. Winter blue eyes in my vision now.

"Baby," he was panting harder. "Baby, please. I'm so sorry—" he broke off looking distraught. "Shitshitshit, come back. I'm so sorry, I didn't meant to push you so hard. I'm sorry, baby." His lips were at my cheek and I didn't realize I was crying.

"Evie," I gasped. "Evie was there."

"Who's Evie?" Gabriel asked, his brow furrowed. "She's not in your file."

"I *saw* something." A memory. The past.

Something darker in my brain.

Shadows. They lived there.

"I need you to do that again." I looked at Gabriel and realized we were on the floor. Me in his arms.

"No." He shook his head. "Absolutely not."

"But I saw it—I saw something—" I was gasping but I gripped his hoodie tighter. "I need to know. You have to push me through it." He always pushed me to my limits.

"Gabriel. Mi unica oportunidad, Gabriel. Necesito, por favor."

He held my face in his hands then his eyes frowning. "I don't understand."

"It's my only chance. You are. I need this."

"Tell me what you saw."

A memory. I told him. And as I did he frowned. Listening carefully. "Evie is your baby sister?"

I nodded. "But..." I told him how Mama and Evie were gone from our lives. Mama had left and gone somewhere else in the States and Papi had split up. I didn't remember a divorce. I remember them saying goodbye tearfully, Evie in her arms as she ran off to a bus.

My sister had no idea what was happening and neither did I. I just remember Mama crying as she left us.

I told Gabriel. "I always wanted to find her. But I never knew what happened."

He shook his head looking like he wanted to do anything else other than this. I grabbed his hoodie tighter. "*Gabriel.*"

Those winter blue eyes hit mine. "I say no and you just hit me with those eyes and I'm supposed to give in?"

"Yes." I nodded.

His lips tipped up in what I knew was a reluctant smile. It took him a long moment of consideration and finally he nodded. "Fine. One. Just one. If you freak out? We stop."

I nodded. "Promise."

He held out his pinky. I took it without hesitation. And we started again. This time it was like falling through the trap door. Once it was unlocked—not even Gabriel could stop it.

I fell into the shadows of my worst nightmares now.

The past coming to meet me head-on. Sharp and clear like broken glass in my senses.

The restraints, the darkness, unlocked something darker, in some sealed part of my memories.

It took me through a series of emotions. Sequences of memories that I didn't know I had.

That told me why I hated this sensation.

Why I was who I was. Why my family had been torn apart. Why I was here.

Gabriel's touch was what brought me right back.

Right into his arms slamming into the present with gasping breaths. Shaking. Crying. His lips against my temple urging me to breathe.

His hands stroked my hair and I had to process what I knew now. What I learned today.

"I know what happened. I remember everything."

CHAPTER 13
GABRIEL

I was fucked.

She wasn't my girlfriend.

She was my student.

But she sat on my lap, cried in my arms, hugged me like she couldn't let me go and I was *invested*.

I had three weeks with this girl left to go. And time seemed to be flying by.

Isobel been kidnapped by the cartel at twelve.

This wasn't on her file. None of this was. It was painted like she moved. She didn't move. She was uprooted violently.

Her father rescued her and her family. His wife. Himself.

Their *two* daughters.

Evie was her little sister, six years apart from her, *roughly*.

Her mother Adrianna Santos and Evie were somewhere in the States. Somewhere Isobel had no clue. Because her father kept his secret.

She didn't know if they changed their names or if they were still alive. But she said her father split them up to protect them that night.

They left Mexico with nothing. Were granted asylum in the States. And they became citizens while Isobel was in school.

It was the middle of the day and I needed a second to see if I could find anything on Evie Santos at all.

Eva.

Evie was what her family called her. She might be thirteen, fourteen right now? I could find her with my resources if I tried right?

Except who could I ask besides Koller?

I hadn't even spoken to him too much since starting this fucking program.

The fact that I was even considering using agency resources for a personal issue went against everything that I believed in. Everything he taught me.

Sure, I broke some rules.

But this was blatant. Me looking for a civilian. That wasn't even my family but a female trainees? Danger.

She wasn't mine, and I had no right to interfere in her life. No right to do anything for her.

But I wanted to.

Finding Evie, meddling in Isobel's life would have reverberating professional consequences.

Ones I couldn't risk for a not girlfriend. Not that I ever considered having one anyway.

My phone rang then. I looked at the caller ID. Koller. *Speak of the devil.*

"Sir." I answered without hesitation.

"Listen kid," Koller wasted no time, his voice gravel and I knew he was sitting at his desk buildings away hating everyone around him.

I liked Koller. He was retired military and he had a give no shit about nothing attitude. "You done in a few weeks, huh?"

I was. "Yes, sir."

"I got good news and bad news, you want the bad news first?"

Yeah. He always knew me. I just wanted to take a hit up front.

He let out a breath. "Listen, I had no problem with taking Young out of the program. The older one. He was a nasty son of a bitch and nobody liked him. But we got a problem."

"Like what?" My stomach turned a little at the sound of his voice. I already had a bad feeling now.

"Like you kicking out the younger one, Kourtney. She griped to daddy dearest and he's been kicking up a storm the last few weeks over his daughter." Of course he fucking was.

"Don't fucking tell me." I knew exactly where he was going with this. "She attacked a trainee in the bathroom."

She attacked Isobel. My Isobel.

"I know, I've seen the Santos siblings and their track record. Solid kids. I heard the girl is whiplash smart."

She was. She was also turning into my *baby. My girl.*

"But you know young's father is about to be a congressman, turns out it's got some pull."

"Of course it does," but my voice was steel not hiding the rage building underneath. Bubbling to the surface violently.

Koller didn't sound happy. We both despised this shit.

"She's been brought back to the program on a warning. She so much as looks as the Santos's siblings wrong or anyone—she's out then. Hr father begged for a second chance."

Irritation flared through me hot and bright. "You told me mediocrity and good enough gets people killed. You don't think she'll do that?"

"It doesn't' matter what I think Gabriel," Koller sounded remorseful. "Higher-ups are saying why not, see if she can be mentored into being better."

Just the way he said it I knew he didn't fucking mean it. He fucking hated this as much as I did.

"That's bullshit—"

"I know. You don't think I know? No such thing as training weakness."

Weakness could never be trained.

I let out a breath. "I gotta tell them." Both Liam and Isobel.

Koller paused. "Do you want the good news or not?"

Hit me. "Nothing's gonna help this shit. I gotta juggle that fucking cunt with everyone else."

Koller chuckled. "I got an assignment for you already lined up." I sat up straighter at the prospect. Fucking finally I'd be out of here. *But...Isobel...*"Details will follow. But it's a good one."

"Bigger catch than this?"

Koller chuckled now breaking the tension even though the unease sat in my gut. "Solid."

I nodded even though he couldn't see me.

"Just think, in a few weeks, you'll never have to deal with those fucking trainees again. You'll be free. Back at it. Chin up, Gabriel. You'll never see those people again."

These people.

Isobel. Like she was just another trainee.

Like she wasn't turning into my heart just a tiny bit thawing me out from the inside out.

Five foot nothing of a spitfire with a penchant for standing up for me like I needed it all because I helped her overcome her fears.

Nine weeks ago when I start this program, all I wanted to do was get out, but now I was wishing it would never end.

That was supposed to be good news.

I was gonna go onto bigger things. I had plans.

But none of my plans could've foreseen her.

And now I didn't know how I was supposed to let her go.

CHAPTER 14
ISOBEL

"WE HAVE TWO AND HALF WEEKS LEFT."

Gabriel's winter blue eyes watched me glittering in the midnight light of the pool.

Tonight he had driven us even farther away from the apartment to a place with an indoor pool.

An apartment complex that hummed with quiet luxury vibes from what it looked like.

I didn't know how to ask if it was his.

I couldn't imagine Gabriel sleeping like a normal person. Or doing *normal* things. But I know he did.

With me he did.

Right now—he looked anything but normal.

Bare-chested. Golden skin. Standing in front of me like a sun god that stepped out of a myth. Like Apollo.

I stood across from him in my white swim suit cover up.

"I know it's fast, but this is the last step. If you can get this? You'll pass. I promise."

His voice was softer and more intimate in the quiet space making my stomach jump a little.

I nodded feeling nervous as his eyes darted to my coverup. "Ready?"

I shook my head. No. I was not ready.

I was too nervous to think straight.

It was strangely intimate being here with him. More than my home. More than anywhere.

It was just the glow of the pool and us.

Slowly, I reached for my coverup untying it and feeling tremendously shy under his gaze.

He didn't look away and I didn't want him to, but the last time I had been undressed with a man—he'd told the entire campus about it. Or tried to. Liam got a hold of him and nearly broke his arms.

I knew Gabriel wasn't like that.

But my fingers trembled nonetheless.

What if he didn't like the way I looked? What if it was too much?

Tugging and dropping the coverup on a bench nearby I tucked my hair behind my hair blinking up at a little at him. Gauging his reaction.

I had worn an inexpensive white bikini. Simple.

It was one of the few I had.

Gabriel who looked like he'd been molded from clay and brought to life was staring at me like I was...like him. I wasn't.

His chiseled pecs, broader shoulders, tapered waistline that led to his swim shorts were beautiful.

But he stared at me like I was something precious. Rare. His eyes went eerily bright in the light as he watched me.

I looked at him apprehensively watching his hands clench and unclench.

"Did you think I was going to tie you up and throw you in?" I nodded, and he smiled disarmingly. "No, I won't. Get in the pool, baby."

I felt that telltale hitch in my breathing whenever he called me that in private, like he couldn't help himself.

Slowly, I moved forward, dipping my toes in first.

The water was warm and inviting, and a delighted noise escaped my lips as I sank into it, swimming a few lengths feeling like a free mermaid.

I forgot how good this felt.

I loved swimming and had memories teaching Evie, while my mother photographed us. I knew we had photos somewhere.

I needed to ask Papi one day.

Except those blissful times never involved the man who now dove in after me.

I gasped, retreating against the pool's wall as Gabriel cornered me, rising like a god from the ocean depths. Droplets down his chest, his face, his usual wheat colored hair darker now.

He pushed back his wet hair, eyes bright with something I rarely saw. Amusement. A playfulness to them.

And he looked *infinitely* more handsome.

"Where'd you learn to swim?" he asked.

"Mexico," I replied, motioning him closer. His lips quirked upwards.

"At the YMCA?" He studied me intently. "You have trouble with idioms?"

"Some," I admitted warmth flooding me as we circled each other curiously. "I like 'couch potato'."

He pressed his lips together, clearly fighting laughter.

My chest tightened painfully at his suppressed mirth.

Before he could speak, I did something I'd always wanted—I splashed him boldly.

The glittering water splashed across his perfect face and my laughter echoed off the walls at his stunned expression.

And then he did something I never expected—Gabriel's face split into a breathtaking grin.

Dio, he's handsome.

He cannot be real.

My own laughter died as I took in his unguarded smile.

His easy laugh, flashing canines, flushed cheeks—I was gone. Lost to this version of this beautiful man I had never seen.

Every time I was with him, I unraveled a new layer. A different side of him.

God, he's so beautiful.

I like this man.

I didn't know him for very long, but I felt like he had seen me at my vulnerable moments. Seen me through a lot of my training.

With Gabriel I felt safe enough to be vulnerable again.

I didn't just like him for who he was, but how he made me feel.

Safe.

Complete.

Stable.

A lot of these new experiences for me—and in turn it brought me closer to him.

So I splashed him again, peals of laughter escaping me as I delighted in drawing out more of his bright smiles.

I swam away, some of me part of me knowing he would give chase me.

Though an excellent swimmer, I was no match for Gabriel's speed.

He nearly let me believe I'd evaded him successfully before catching my ankle underwater.

I squealed as he surfaced, pulling me into his arms and pinning me against the pool's edge.

Against all of him, his body a wall of strength and heat and I was helpless.

I helped push his damp hair back as it fell over his eyes, momentarily giving him a boyishly young look. Beautiful.

Human.

Our bodies were mere inches apart in the warm water.

He was panting softly, his brilliant blue eyes locked onto mine with an intense yet tender expression.

Slowly, he reached out and traced the string of my bikini top with one finger leaving fire wherever he touched.

"Tell me you've never worn this in front of anyone else," he murmured, his voice low.

I considered teasing him for a moment, but the open vulnerability in his gaze stopped me. Holding his stare, I shook my head. "No. Only today."

Gabriel closed his eyes briefly, hanging his head as if overwhelmed by my admission.

When he looked at me again, his eyes shone with an emotion I couldn't quite name. "For me."

"Para ti," I affirmed quietly.

He swallowed hard, seeming to understand the Spanish phrasing.

"For me," he repeated, tasting the words.

"For you," I echoed clearly.

In that heated moment, suspended in the water's embrace, something pivotal shifted between us.

I don't know who moved closer or if the water helped us a little bit more inching us closer, but he never took his eyes off me.

When our mouths sealed together after months of whatever *this*

was, the moment I touched him, my entire body sighed, like I was...
home.

It felt inevitable after months of circling him that this is what I
had needed. This moment.

My entire being sighed as Gabriel's arms wrapped around me. It
was recognizing that I had been missing something that I hadn't
even known or understood clearly.

I moaned softly, pulling him closer until there was no space left
between us.

It started tenderly, our mouths tangling tentatively. Softly.
Softer than I imagined.

But it quickly deepened into a hungry, passionate exchange as I
granted him complete access, nipping at his full lower lip before
sucking on his velvet tongue.

Consuming him, being consumed in return, was a revelation.

One of Gabriel's hands cradled the back of my head while the
other drifted lower, grazing the top of my bikini strap with trembling fingers.

I whimpered at his featherlight touch, and he shushed me
soothingly.

"Shhh, I've got you," he murmured against my lips. "I have you."

He did. He did have me.

He was tugging at my bikini top, my breasts still in the wet
fabric as he untied the knot at my back.

I was gasping against his mouth as he plunged his tongue inside
claiming me with a hunger I didn't know he could have but it
matched my own.

I didn't even realize I was squirming until his other hand
gripped my hip tighter.

Wrapping around me until I was flush against him.

The pools light was playing across his features. Just enough for
me to see everything in my face reflected back in his. Want. Need.
Fear. Lust.

All of it that I had in me.

"Hold still," he thrust his tongue back into my mouth. "You
always smell like candy."

"I can give you some tomorrow," I whispered.

His grin was wicked and wide as he licked my lips. He looked
delighted and it sent a thrill through me as he kept kissing me.

I was completely blissed out on his taste.

Desperate sounds escaped me, as I felt his mouth skating down my neck, sucking my pulse, and then I felt his hands working behind me hauling the strings around my wrists.

I stopped as he continued to work and his mouth dragged along my skin.

The dual sensation of pleasure along with the thrill of being tied up.

I didn't know *what* I felt. He raised his head up lazily and his lips moved over my mouth again.

"Easy," he whispered. "I have you."

I was kissing him despite feeling the tight binding of my hands and the way he'd had to exposed my breasts while he used my bikini top to tie up my hands behind my back.

In the water.

Like a fantasy I didn't know I had.

"I have you." He tugged on his knot and I gasped as he looked at me then with those eyes. "Is that too tight?"

"No."

His smile was fierce and proud of me.

He leaned in again and kissed me softly. I moaned at the sensation of being held down as he moved his body with mine. He was panting as he trailed his lips down my neck again.

"*Gabriel.*"

"Fuck, you're so beautiful like this." He was whispering across my flesh. "I knew you'd fucking love it if I showed you there was so much more to your fear."

He kept going, his tongue licking fire down my skin.

"If you only knew."

He was right between my breasts, bobbing in the water, his tongue licking at the column of my throat. I moaned as he kept going lower.

"I don't have any self control around you."

My breasts were right there. My nipples achingly hard and I panted.

For long moments he stayed though as though calming himself down.

Suck on me.

It was my only thought as he held me, my breasts almost arching up to him.

His eyes met mine as he rose up.

He was struggling with himself. With me. With this.

"This is what you'll be like? If I don't give you what you want you'll give me those eyes and arch your back for me?"

I wanted to sob as I inhaled air into my lungs.

He dipped his head, opening his mouth around my nipple.

I moaned wishing I could hold him closer.

But if anything it made the pleasure course through me harder.

And then a shrill noise cut through the silence.

I would've screamed had he not risen his eyes floating up to me and I focused on him as lights flashed around me.

Raw panic rose through me at the sensations.

"Fire alarm." He said, covering my ears. Those winter blue eyes met mine. "Focus on me."

CHAPTER 15

GABRIEL

"That's fine. We'll head back in now."

I grumbled to the fireman keeping my voice clipped. Professional.

Like he hadn't just interrupted my fucking night in the middle of me tasting my candy covered girl.

I was grateful it was a false alarm and there wasn't a real fire.

But if he looked at Isobel's legs one more time in my hoodie draped over her—I would shoot him.

She looked so young and vulnerable shaking a little tucked into my side for my heat.

His eyes darted between us knowing exactly what he'd interrupted.

Idiot.

As I bid them goodbye, I had her in my arms. "You good, baby?"

"C-cold," she curled her hands into mine and she was freezing. It was only Autumn but at night? By the water? It was frigid.

I needed to get gloves for her. A scarf. Something to tuck her into.

A bigger sweater. I was planning it like she intended to stick around after she passed the final exams.

I rubbed her hands together.

"You are not cold, amor?" She asked me with her teeth chattering as I got us to my grey truck, helping her into the passenger seat before getting in myself and turning on the heat for her.

"No, I burn pretty hot."

I always had. But now I was grateful I let Koller talk me into buying a pricier car just to be warm.

She was shivering as I gave her my jacket. We'd both barely dried off and I'd helped her the entire way outside.

"Gabriel, that was scary," she whispered.

"I know, baby. Did you get triggered?"

I didn't like seeing her upset.

"Not too much," but her eyes were stark and her usually warm face was pale. Whited out. Something in my chest tightened seeing her like this.

I didn't have much time with her. This was stupid.

After she passed?

They might put her literally anywhere in the globe. Not near me.

This was the dumbest thing I could be doing—and I still felt the urge to follow through with it because something in my gut told me this woman was important to me.

The worst thing was? I could still hear the ghost of her moans.

The internal longing in me to pull her into my lap, to warm her up differently was there.

I drove us to her apartment with Liam. But some part of me didn't want to let her out alone.

I parked the car and got off on her side helping her out. Not even hesitating to pick her up in my arms.

Taking her into the apartment felt natural now.

Like I belonged here with her. In a short time I had become a part of her world.

Life in this world moved differently. Time was judged by the vulnerable moments and not the mundane day to day.

Right now, she was slowly becoming important to me.

Liam stood in the kitchen without his shirt on, a half-eaten bowl of noodles in his hand he dropped immediately seeing her in my arms.

"Isa!" His worry was palpable. "What happened to her?"

"No—"

Isobel cut me off saying something to him in Spanish.

Whatever she said to him, it carried something that made Liam's expression change instantly.

His eyes took us both in semi wet, her in my hoodie, and me shirtless, and I saw his brows furrowing with everything she said.

For a moment, something in his face cracked open.

Raw and stark concern etched into every line as he watched her.

For a nanosecond then I realized what I was looking at. It went beyond his love for her as a sister.

In my downtime, I had enough time to analyze him. And I realized that I was looking at him, while holding his entire world in my arms.

Isobel and I talked sometimes during our sessions. Sometimes.

And she told me they'd been together every single day. For what felt like forever.

They were two halves of the same coin.

He was important to her.

Liam seemed to be asking if she was all right. In that moment I noticed that Liam looked like his world was ending when she looked at him. I saw it now.

He looks devastated.

They said something to each other I didn't understand and he flushed a little red.

His Adam's apple bobbed as he nodded looking at me for a second before rushing into the apartment.

I took her into her bedroom toeing off my outside shoes. That was important to her.

I helped dry her off quietly as she shivered.

"You should go clean up in the shower," my voice was gruff. "Wash off the chlorine."

Her teeth were chattering wildly as she nodded and left.

Leaving me standing there like some idiot in her space.

All gold and white and beautifully done. Like her. It was lush. Like paradise.

And my ass in here looked out of place.

I was still in my swim trunks. Still a little damp the heat of the car having helped a little but I didn't have clothes.

I didn't have anything to change into.

On cue, Liam knocked on her door and he walked in his eyes meeting mine as he handed me a set of towels, several shirts and even a pack of briefs. A pair of sweats.

I blinked at the clean socks he set down.

He'd gotten all that? Everything was still in it's packaging.

"Everything's in your size," he muttered not looking at me as he set it down on her bed. "Her heated blanket needs to be turned on," he motioned to a digital pad on the floor he hit to a number. "And she sleeps on that side. It's almost midnight so you can stay here tonight."

But he didn't look at me.

His inky hair messier than usual like he'd ran his hands through it. Tattoos I didn't have roping his skin like art. There were two sides to Liam.

The one Isobel got.

The one the world got.

And I got the later all the time.

His jaw clenched as he looked at me with eerily dark eyes now.

"She's my sister. This is our home. You so much as hurt her or say a word against her—"

"I would never hurt her." I swallowed cutting him off and feeling out of my skin. I was ice around everyone else.

But something about Liam Santos felt important.

Unlike his sister who was warm, next to her he was all shadow and edge. His tattoos. Piercings.

"I would never do anything to her," I kept my voice down with the shower running in the background where Isobel was. "You trusted me to train her. Her physical safety. You don't trust me not to hurt her? I would never take advantage of her. Seems a bit unlike you to doubt that."

I could give it back too.

"Did you think I'd change my mind?" I asked him. He didn't say a word and just took me in. "You don't love her the way I like her. You think I'd ever take her away from you?"

I knew him. I knew exactly what he was about. It was my job to know people.

When he first came to me, he was acting out of love for her.

He knew that I was an expert, and he knew that I was good at my job. So he asked me for help. It was all for her. I had nothing to do with it.

I didn't think even he understood what was happening between me and Isobel. I sure as fuck didn't.

I was drawn to her sure. I kissed her. And I would do it again.

I was still figuring it out. I wasn't exactly trained in that.

And I figured out in training Liam was her shadow. He would make sure nothing would hurt her.

Not even me.

He didn't say a word. The shower stopped running and both of our heads turned to the door. He snapped back to me.

"Not a fucking toe out of line with her."

He walked out of the door, the snick of the door as loud as a slam.

∾

"Why do you have so many products in your bathroom?"

I lay next to Isobel an hour later having cleaned in her shower and put on a pair of clean briefs, sweats, and Liam's plain white t-shirts.

I was laying under her heated blanket—something I didn't even fucking fathom I ever would love—cuddling next to her.

The heat of the blanket draped over me was something I never imagined would be so good.

I felt like I had been missing out on a cocoon of warmth and it made everything else outside of this little bubble we had feel unimportant.

Isobel lay facing me, her eyes tired but twinkling.

"I don't take the same shower every day."

Her grin grew as she explained some days she felt like exfoliating or scrubbing and other days she wanted a clay mask.

I blinked like she was speaking Swahili. "A clay mask?"

She nodded with that twinkle in her eyes that made me smile. "Maybe I can show you?"

Her casually throwing in future plans always made my throat tight. The unfamiliar sensations crested my throat again and again with her.

"Sure." I nodded feeling too large for her enormous space and also like I was exactly by her side which was all I needed. Anything to be around her again and again.

After a busy day, after training, knowing we had class tomorrow, I should've been tired.

But instead, I laid there feeling wide awake watching her.

When she'd come out of the shower, I ducked my head, and I waited until she was good before I went in.

101

But now I knew both of us were in our pajamas, looking at each other—wide awake.

"What is your favorite color?" She whispered in the dark to me coming closer.

"I don't have one."

She frowned. "Not true. You like grey. Everything you have is grey. Your water bottle. Your truck. Your shoes."

She paid attention to me?

I never thought about it like that.

"I like grey. It's a good color."

"It's a shade, Gabriel." She looked at me with a tiny bit of disapproval and for some reason my lips stretched tipping up.

"Gray is nice. But gold is nice too," I looked around her room. "What's yours?"

Her eyes twinkled. "Gold. What kind of music do you listen to?"

I grinned wider now. "Are we on a late night date?"

"I cannot sleep."

Me either. But I felt like I couldn't sleep because I was counting the days I had left with her. I was waiting for the moment for her to get the letter that said she'd be in Japan or something.

Nowhere near me.

"Scared?"

"I don't know. I just know tomorrow we are going to be very tired."

I was going to feel it. It was probably two in the morning.

We had to be up at six.

I was going to be dead on my feet and I couldn't stop staring at her. Counting down my seconds with her.

Every agonizing one passing slowly. Thankfully.

She blinked at me waiting for her answer.

"I listen to everything," I answered. "You?"

"You listen to reggaeton or salsa music?"

"Probably not that. But everything else?"

"Opera?"

I laughed lightly. "I listen to alternative rock—maybe. But I don't listen to anything you listen to, I can tell you that."

Her laughter made me smile wider. "You want to try for me?"

"Sure." I would try anything for her. Underneath this heated blanket she could convince me of everything she wanted. With her eyes simultaneously felt…

Her smile was infectious. "Where are you from?"

"A small town in Boston. I grew up pretty shitty and poor. You?"

"Liam and I lived together in Connecticut. We went to college in Boston. But neither one of us have your accent."

"Thank fuck," I laughed easily with her. She drifted closer to me and I moved even closer until our noses brushed.

"What was your life like?" She whispered like it was a secret in her eyes. Those eyes were wide and curious. "Before this, before the military? Who are you, Gabriel?"

Gabri-el.

Nobody said my name like she did.

Nobody spoke to me like her.

There was this innocent curiosity about the way she spoke all the time.

That was the voice that hit somewhere deep inside of me.

She was intelligent, sharper than any knife, when it came to computers and training.

She's smarter than me.

And I don't think she knows it.

I think she thinks...we're equals.

And isn't that something.

But there was something about her that was also untouched, when she spoke, everything sounded more pure.

Who are you, Gabriel?

Who was I? I couldn't tell her the truth. In a few weeks?

I might never see her again. And this would be but a dream. Like a deployment.

I could never tell a woman like her that I knew almost everything about—I was who I was. What I was. What I had been.

"I'm a nobody," I whispered back, my nose brushing hers. "No parents. No home."

Her eyes were curious. "Tienes nada?" At my expression she whispered. "You have nothing?"

"I have the Agency." I whispered back feeling like a kid around her.

A kid who felt safe to exist around her.

I didn't know her well, but my entire heart knew this woman. It understood her. She could be an alien from another planet speaking multiple languages—and I'd know her.

"This is my entire life, Isobel. I only go up from here."

"And what do you want from *here?*"

I shrugged. I had never considered what I wanted. I did whatever anyone else around me wanted. "Everything."

She shook her head watching me earnestly. *"No, what do you want Gabriel?"*

What?

I paused.

I didn't know what I wanted.

Something about the way, she asked that question it hit harder than anything else. Because nobody ever asked. Nobody cared.

I was doing everything possible to rise up in the world.

I had joined the military to set myself free. To get out of a shit situation. I was in the agency because I was good at my job.

That was it. I didn't know what I wanted.

I didn't care to think about it.

"I don't know," I whispered again. "Just whatever comes my way I'm open to it." She paused watching me with those eyes. "What about you?"

Her smile was back. "I'm going to do this for a little bit and then leave."

Now I was surprised. "Leave? But you're good at what you do."

Even in the dark she ducked her head from me and I drew her closer.

"I want to own my own dance studio." Her smile was bright. "Liam wants to own a martial arts studio next to me too. He does you know, Kyokushin. It's karate but harder. My father put Liam in class when he saw Liam was very angry."

"Liam is angry. With me sometimes."

Her eyes softened on me. "It's okay. He's just protecting me."

"He's always been protecting you?"

She nodded.

"Did something happen to make him protect you more?"

Her throat worked. The delicate lines obviously stressed.

"When I was in college, I was with this guy. I meet him in computer class. He was nice. He said he liked me. And we went out on maybe a few dates."

As she said it I felt her shivering and I don't know why it felt so right to move closer other, comfort her.

"One night we went back to his place. He lives off campus and we were kissing, but I did not want to be with him that night. You understand?"

I swallowed. I did.

I did.

I fucking did. She had no idea how much I did.

"But I feel like I could not say no. He was a nice man. It was no big deal for me. Liam he was always with women so I thought it would be fine for me to be with someone too."

"Liam is a man-whore at best."

She blinked. "You know?"

"I guess. I've seen his hickies on occasion." I didn't know how the fuck he was getting laid with his schedule, but crazier things had happened.

Isobel continued. "I found out that week he told his friends on campus."

That little fucking shit. My vision went red. Blood-thirsty.

Wild. For how vulnerable she had been.

"Please tell me Liam took care of it." I didn't even notice how hard I was holding her until I gripped her tighter and she made a noise.

She nodded ducking her head. "He was almost suspended for how much he hit him, but I told the Dean, thankfully she was Latina and she moved the other guy but...after that, I did not...I was not with anyone else."

I nodded like I understood. Like in my head I wasn't dismembering him joint by joint.

"What's his name?"

She shook her head a little. "Jonathan...I don't remember I think...something like Brown? I don't remember. Liam does. He remembers everything. Much better than me."

Then I'd be talking to Liam in the morning.

"Liam was the one who said we should be in the CIA in college, you know? He said maybe we can make a bit better money and leave together."

"Together?"

She nodded earnestly. "He's my brother." She said something in Spanish and then she translated. "He's important to me. He always has been."

"I know you love him. But..." I swallowed my fear in my throat. Had to ask the question I didn't know how to ask. I had never had a girlfriend. Not really. Maybe high school, but life was a hot mess then. It didn't count. "You ever think about...being with anyone?"

"Like a boyfriend?"

I nodded.

"Si. You." And just like that she had me stumped. I blinked and at my surprised expression she smiled almost shy. "That's you, *Gabriel.*"

This woman is going to kill me.

I didn't know how to breathe. "And you're okay with that?"

She nodded with certainty. But there was a lot haunting me right now and I didn't know how to tell her.

I had told her about Kourtney earlier and she'd been upset. She'd texted it to Liam who'd cursed Kourtney out in the texts.

But right now? I was haunted by the inevitable and yet, I felt safe enough to share it with her.

"What if you graduate the program and we're miles apart?"

"I don't want anyone else. Do you?"

Not like her.

Never like her.

I had been drawn to her from the start, like gravity, like something that had been written into my fucking bones. She felt like she was made for me. A part of me.

I couldn't explain it.

It was the way her eyes twinkled, her open laughs, like something in my gut just knew I had to be around her.

"What do you want Gabriel?" She asked me again quietly.

But that was the thing. Up until her?

It didn't matter what I wanted.

I only did what I needed to do. I moved, determined—I knew exactly who I was. And it wasn't until now that I didn't.

But I knew one thing.

"You."

Her smile lit up the space between us as she drifted closer.

"What else do you want with your dance studio?" I asked her.

"I want to be someone's wife one day," she whispered back. "A normal quiet life. Just a normal man's wife. Maybe have children. Make cookies. One day."

That's it?

Can I be normal?

"A normal wife," I whispered feeling my chest clench. "A normal life."

She smiled at me with warm. "Si. A normal wife. A normal life."

Sunday mornings with pancakes.

Bickering over soccer practice.

Halloween candy in front of the house.

Candles lit before the kids went to bed.

The kids.

Fuck.

I could see it.

I could.

Me and her. A life. Normalcy.

"Cookies?"

Are you fucking retarded?

She just told you this and your profound statement is cookies?

Idiot.

Isobel being her—smiled. "Pancakes on Sunday. I would bring them too much candy and you would tell me no—"

"During Halloween—"

My heart was losing its ever loving mind.

"Si, and then sometimes after the kids go to bed I'd sit there and pretend like I didn't exist—"

"I could rub your feet from your day—"

"Or my hair—"

"I'd rub your hair—" I broke off feeling like my heart was cracking open.

She laughed lightly.

Suddenly I don't know why I doubted if everything I ever wanted was real.

Because I had never seen these things before. I always thought for a man like me—they were farther away than close.

A dream I had as a kid and nothing I could have right now.

But I could with her. Not in another lifetime.

In this lifetime.

I could have it all.

Dark hair. Caramel eyes. Soft skin. Isobel.

She was right fucking *there*.

Everything I wanted was worth reaching for in that moment.With her.

Because I wanted nothing more than to lay here forever.

107

Wrapped in a heated blanket to the smell of butterscotch and candy and possibilities.

"A normal life," I whispered back.

A normal wife.

I want to give this woman everything and it doesn't make any sense to me.

But maybe it didn't have to.

She nodded drifted so close she almost kissed me. Her smile was light.

My throat worked as I closed the distance between us sealing my lips against hers.

A normal wife.

CHAPTER 16
ISOBEL/GABRIEL

I WENT TO GO SEE HIM TODAY AWARE WE HAD BOTH BARELY SLEPT.

I didn't want to train anymore today.

I didn't care how much time we had left. I wanted to take him home and keep him there.

I wanted to tell him in a short time, I was starting to like him because of the way he felt like my family.

His hands and his eyes were like my father's and Liam's.

Some part of me recognized him like he was my own.

Slipping into his office I found him holding his head in his hands looking exhausted.

"Gabriel." I kept my voice low as I crossed the distance into his arms, my fingers going to his scalp.

For a second his eyes went wide, pale blue before they closed as the feel of me rubbing his hair.

He groaned tipping his head into my chest.

"Come home with me tonight. We can sleep together."

Another low rumble left him. "How am I supposed to say no to you?"

A light laugh left me, my fingers working on his scalp . "You don't."

It felt too easy to be with him. I wasn't expecting him to tip his beautiful head up and kiss me. Or pull me onto his lap and let me sit there while we made out.

"Home." I whispered into his lips. "*Vamos.*"

He stumbled toward the door half-asleep and when we got to the grey truck he looked ready to fall over.

"Gabriel," I grabbed his keys taking them from him and helping him into the passenger seat. I knew he was tired when he didn't even protest. I barely got him home to the apartment and in through the door.

"Liam!" I asked him for help and the two of us got Gabriel into my bed where he passed out.

❧

I WOKE UP TO THE SUN PAINTING GOLDEN STRIPES ACROSS MY SHEETS through the blinds.

I had one more week with this man wrapped around me. Tugging me closer to him like his favorite teddy-bear. Slowly, I became aware of him. The heat radiating off of him, the brush of his skin against mine, his heartbeat. And then the way his lips trailed fire across my neck.

"Gabriel," I whispered. In another second I was flattened, caged in by his massive arms, his weight over me.

His lips moved over mine.

"...nothing's going to stop me..." he was half-asleep muttering as he ran his lips down my neck.

And then he stamped his lips over mine. I gasped opening my mouth immediately, my body burned—I burned for him.

I want you, I've wanted you the moment I saw you.

I was whispering something to him, unintelligible and half asleep in a mixture of my native tongue and English that made his eyes go dark. My fingers finding my way to his wheat-colored hair that had grown longer with me. Holding him closer. Needing him deeper.

"I'm going to start recording you when you talk," he whispered, sending a rush through me at that idea. "You needed this just as badly as I did, didn't you?"

I nodded desperately.

"What did you do to me?" I panted, aware Liam was right around the corner in his room, but he wouldn't interrupt. Nothing existed in this moment but this man.

"*Me?*"

As though he was outraged at the notion. I kissed him like my life depended on it.

Like he was the only hope I had to not fall to not drown. And he was. I'd never felt this before and I felt like...I was pouring myself and my love into him. I just knew deep down in my soul this man was mine.

He was mine.

"I don't know what you do to me," I panted against his lips, my entire body felt like it was primed for a moment with Gabriel that I hadn't really had. Save for that one time and that had not been good, but with Gabriel...I felt different with him. I trusted him more. "I don't understand."

I hadn't ever felt this.

His eyes locked with mine and we breathed together. Winter blue meeting mine and something in his eyes made me stop.

"Gabriel..."

"I'm supposed to stay away from you. But...I can't. I can't—and nothing will stop me. Nothing is going to keep me from you ever."

I didn't understand why he said that.

I was right there.

"And you will not hurt me?" I whispered unable to stop it. Awareness that if he did, it might hurt a lot more than college.

"I'm going to tell you something, nod if you understand me." Winter blue held my eyes with an intensity that rocked through me, softening a little at my curiosity. "I would rather be shot by a firing squad—do you know what that is?"

I nodded feeling my throat tighten at the idea of Gabriel ever in danger. I didn't care what he had done in his past. That wasn't him now. "Painful."

"It is," he looked like he was remembering something. "I would rather hurt myself first, before I hurt you. Do you understand me? I would never take you and brag to other men about sleeping with yo —" his eyes drifted to my lips. "At least...not like *that.*"

'What do you mean?" My heart was beating rapidly, thundering inside of my ribs like a trapped bird.

He smiled then softly but slowly enough that I knew he was dangerous when pushed. "There are other ways to brag about you. Show other men I'm proud to be your man."

"How?" Even now a pale gleam passed through those eyes and

sent heat rushing to my center, but Gabriel looked at me like he wanted to eat me for breakfast. "You are a lot."

"So are you."

I blinked in surprise a soft smile rising to my lips, one he mirrored. "You did not answer my question."

"If I told you the answer, you'd run from me."

"No." I bristled. "I cannot run right now."

He looked down at my body as if to say *no, you couldn't.*

And it made me excited.

He looked upward as if for patience. "I don't think I'd ever say no to you." It had been weeks of this. Dancing around him. *I want you.*

"I would put my ring on your finger, my collar around your throat, and—" he took a breath like my heart didn't get stuck in my throat. I heard him struggling.

"Take you, keep you mine. All of you. Every part, you would never be able to hide it. And nobody else. I'd brag about you in all the right ways, and not a single man would *ever* doubt who you belonged to." He paused. "Nod if you understand me."

I did. His smile was dangerously soft.

And I realized I was a fool for thinking that Gabriel would be ice cold.

Gabriel

I NEVER HAD THIS.

Never had someone humming while making me breakfast in her kitchen she shared with her brother. But Isobel did, measuring and making chocolate chip pancakes. She insisted they be chocolate chips when she found out I hadn't had them.

I didn't know if this was normal.

The way she turned over her shoulder and asked if I wanted some juice. Coffee. More milk? More sugar?

I drank my coffee black but not today.

Today I watched her pour cream and sugar and pass me some bacon and eggs before going to make pancakes.

I watched her body in my t-shirt as she walked around the

cozier space filled with odd plants, seasoning containers, and pots and pans.

The way my heart sputtered or the way my entire body pointed to her like a compass finding it's north.

Gabriel Raphael Monroe had no previous point of reference for what...this was. None of it.

Not a relationship. Not a love. Not a heart.

I didn't know if she was...a miracle or not. She felt like it. She felt like sunlight or water filling in cracks in a drought.

Me, the kid who'd never truly been loved.

Isobel was as unfamiliar to me as I was familiar to her. She stated that part of her familiarity to me was because of me reminding her of her own family. Like I was like Liam. I was a part of her.

I hadn't known this girl for very long but every single cellular part of me was screaming for her.

Screaming at the top of my lungs. I had never known love. Never. Not once did I think love factored into the equation.

Not when CPS realized my parents were drug addicts. Not when I ran away from home at a young age.

Not when I was being violently abused.

Not when I ran away and enlisted.

I spent years building walls up so high that nobody was supposed to ever scale past them. Nobody could. Structure, rules, discipline, it was my peace within my chaos. Or so I thought.

I never expected a tiny five foot nothing girl to peek through a crack she made and pull me through my walls. That's what it felt like. In the short time we'd been together, in less than three months since I met her?

She'd reached in and pulled me out.

I wondered if she'd done the same to Liam.

She said her father had picked him up and took him home like a wild animal and Isobel had learned to live with that. She'd learned to love Liam. I knew Liam's entire file. They had no idea about mine.

Isobel's words, her kisses, her touch was turning into oxygen for me. I felt like I was releasing a breath I'd been holding and re-learning how to breathe again. As she settled into spaces I didn't even know existed.

"All done," she set the pancakes down in front of me in a stack with butter and syrup.

Passing me utensils, fluttering around me, and I felt the sunlight hit me from the thin gauzy curtains in her kitchen.

"Did you want something else? More syrup?" She hovered over me. I did want something. I didn't even feel myself reaching for her pulling her into my lap.

My lips meeting hers with a curious sensation that I never felt around women.

Women liked me. I was far from unattractive, something that made me viciously uncomfortable. Something I weaponized now in assignments where women could not longer weaponize me.

But Isobel smoothed her hands over my face and kissed me back.

Softly. Slowly. Until I was melting like butter.

"Gabriel, your food is getting cold," she whispered.

"That's okay." I kept on going until I heard a groan from behind us.

She smiled into my kisses. "You are hungry."

I was. But I didn't know for what. I just couldn't stop inhaling her into my lungs, the scent of butterscotch, something warmer, something softer invading my bones.

She was lovely.

"Mom, Dad, you have a kid in the house!" Liam's voice groaned playfully as he padded in shirtless in his pajama bottoms giving me time to peer up at his tattoos.

Even if he was teasing, I heard a playful edge to his voice. The warning under his tone. She was his sister. And while Liam wasn't a threat, I was currently making out with the most important person in his life.

I didn't feel embarrassed, but I did break off to Isobel ducking her head with a giggle. She cuddled into me as he shuffled in.

"Oh shit, you made pancakes?"

Liam had bedhead as he turned his inky hair sticking up all over the place as he rummaged around the kitchen making his coffee, adding butter to it out of all things, and then sitting down across from us.

The domestic scene felt surreal to me. I had experienced camaraderie with my team before, but I'd always held myself quiet and apart from everyone.

Now? I was in a family.

"Give it a second," she whispered. It took Liam a few sips of his coffee to wake up before his eyes previous sleepy, now widened.

"I can't believe you made chocolate-chip pancakes for him. I had to beg you for weeks."

"Yours are better than mine," she tossed back at him sitting in my lap. I hadn't even had them but Liam moaned as he took a bite.

"God, these are so good," he chugged his coffee with it.

"My father used to make these for us," she murmured. "Try some, Gabriel. I made plenty."

And so while Isobel slowly peeled herself off me, she went to get herself a plate and Liam's eyes met mine across the table. Sleepy, but aware.

I didn't say a word and neither did he as she buzzed around us. We held an entire conversation with his narrowed eyes on me.

Isobel breezed over him with butter and syrup and he schooled his expression.

He didn't like me.

Which was fine.

I meant what I said—nothing was going to stop me from having her.

CHAPTER 17
ISOBEL/GABRIEL

I WAS ALL OVER HIM.

I couldn't stop it.

Gabriel and I made out in my bedroom like we were teenagers making up for lost time.

He drove me home from now on instead of Liam coming to get me or even me taking a cab.

We made out until Liam knocked our door.

"Dinner's ready kids!"

I giggled into Gabriel's kisses as he grumbled. "He does this on purpose."

"You will like him eventually," I whispered. "He's a lot like you."

We had dinner with Liam and we practiced. Drills where Gabriel would toss me into the water now. And even if I panicked underwater, I saw him swimming to me, his eyes holding me steady, his hands pushing me up.

He would swim closer. "Breathe, I gotcha. I won't let anything happen. Breathe for me…and go."

Gabriel pressed his forehead to mine and we would submerge together. Sometimes, I would sink and rise effortlessly. Other times I panic.

"Why do I do that?" I panted as he untied me.

"You overthink," his lips brushed against mine. "Don't do that."

I frowned splashing him a little. "How?"

He didn't say anything as he kissed me over and over again. If I choked underwater, he quickly dragged me back to the surface urging me to breathe.

"How did you get so skilled at this?" I asked once, admiring his patience.

He laughed without humor. "I got thrown to the bottom and had to figure it out for myself."

I stared at him in dismayed shock, realizing someone must have traumatized him terribly in training him this way.

If he sensed my thoughts, he reassured. "I would never hurt you like that."

"I'm not thinking about me."

But someone had deeply hurt him, I could see it in the shadows lingering in his eyes. He didn't tell me anything about his life. A nobody. A son of a nobody. From nowhere. With nothing.

"I am thinking about you," I croaked in the water floating around him in a half circle. "You do not talk about yourself. Or who you are. Why?"

His eyes went dark sometimes like now. I sensed I hit a nerve as Liam would say. I swam closer to him. "Why won't you tell me? Do you think I would love you any less if you did?"

He blinked as though surprised at what I said. His lips parted, opening and closing like a fish.

"I would not love you any less Gabriel," I whispered. "Love is not conditional. My father always told me and Liam, his love is not conditional. It will never be conditional. You understand?" I whispered it over his lips. "My love for you will never be conditional." I brushed my lips over his again and again as he processed my words.

Maybe I scare him. Maybe he has not had this.

"Love…" it was a whisper from his lips. He stared at me like he was confused. Like he had never seen him. I was right about him.

He was alone.

He went home to me and Liam now.

We had taken him in.

As a child, I remembered being taught to kiss away wounds to make them better.

My father had done that for me when I was injured. For Liam even if he acted too tough for him. Papi always hugged him closer.

Where did I kiss Gabriel?

Without overthinking it, I leaned in and pressed my lips to the steadily beating pulse over his heart.

I wish for his heart to heal.

I pressed it into his skin.

"What did you say?"

"You smell like salt." I bit back tears as I rose up again.

He gently gripped my throat, and I don't know why it made me clench internally. "I know when you're lying to me." He whispered over my lips. "I know when you're going to run too."

"No," I whispered back. "You just know when I want to be kissed."

"That so?"

"Mhm."

I kissed him steadily. Until he pulled back and breathed. "Why did you...why did you say that?"

"Say what?"

"Your..." he ran his fingers over my lips. "Why did you say you—"

"That I love you?" I blinked droplets out of my eyes as we floated together in the blue lights of the pool. "I cannot love you, Gabriel?"

He blinked as though surprised.

"Why?"

"Why what?" I liked teasing him. He got all flustered. Liam and I enjoyed making Gabriel look like this. Like he was breaking a little bit to grow.

"Why do you love me?" He sounded like he was choking it out.

"You are a kind man," I whispered back into his lips. "A protector. Strong. You are open-minded. Intelligent. Funny—"

"I never make a joke—"

"Not like that," I laughed lightly. He looked adorably confused. I decided to give him a break tonight like he was giving me. "I love you because I don't need to know you forever to know who you are."

I pressed my hand over his heart.

"I know you, Gabriel Monroe. I know your heart. You are like the sun. I think you are a great man—"

He shook his head adorably. "I'm nothing—"

"You are *everything*," I held onto him my eyes watching his. "I recognize you like I recognize myself. From the day I saw you, I saw something in your eyes something in me responded to." I shrugged lightly. I didn't know how to say it in English so I told him the only way I knew how.

"*En otra vida ya te conocía.*"

In another life, I already knew you.

"*Cuando te vi, mi alma te reconoció.*"

When I saw you, my soul recognized you.

"*Cuando mi padre vio a Liam, lo reconoció en su sangre como hijo.*"

When my father saw Liam, he recognized him in his blood as his son.

"*Cuando yo vi a Liam, lo sentí mío en el alma.*"

When I saw Liam, I felt him in my soul.

Y cuando te vi a ti, sentí esa misma certeza por primera vez.

Eres mío. No necesito que pasen años para saber la profundidad de mi amor por ti. No importa donde nos lleve el destino, Gabriel.

Jamás te dejaré. Eres mío ahora. Y yo soy tuyo por completo.

I translated it to him in English.

"And when I saw you, I felt that same certainty for the first time. You are mine. I don't need years to pass to know the depth of my love for you. It doesn't matter where destiny takes us, Gabriel. I will never leave you. You are mine now. And I am yours completely."

"You're mine…" he whispered back his eyes not blinking.

"I am yours." I smiled at the look in his eyes. "But you are also mine."

He was a part of my family.

It did not matter where the world took us. I felt something for him that was so familiar? I felt like I had known him forever. When he sat next to me, when he slept in my bed, I didn't need anything else in the world to confirm it.

He was mine.

~

"You told him you loved him!" Liam shot up from the couch where he sat reading. "Isa! You don't know the guy!"

The guy in question sat quietly next to me blinking at the two of us fighting. Over him. About him.

In his white hoodie and wheat-colored hair with his wintery eyes he looked like a snow leopard lounging on my couch next to me while I broke the news to Liam that Gabriel was now my boyfriend and he would stay with us often.

Liam looked ready to kill Gabriel. Which confused me.

"I didn't know you and you slept in my bed the first night you came to me." I shot back in Spanish. "I held you all night and fed you cookies until you went to sleep. Papi brought you home when he didn't know you. Because we trusted you. And your heart! He let you sleep in the same bed as me!"

Liam turned a brilliant shade of red as he blushed. "That's *different.*"

He looked embarrassed and I realized my brother like Gabriel was also a child sometimes.

"*Why?*"

"*I was thirteen!*" Liam shot back in English. "He's twenty-four. *He's a man!*"

I knew that. I liked this man. He was mine.

"Yes, but you were a stranger." I blinked up at him and I spoke in Spanish so Gabriel wouldn't know what I was saying.

I did not want him to think anything about me and Liam ever being together.

"*I am confused. You wanted him to help me, no? He is helping—*"

"*I wanted him to help my sister,*" Liam shouted. "I didn't think he'd actually help himself to my sister." He shot Gabriel a mean look. "You, Frosty. Get out of my house. Get out."

I jumped in front of Gabriel who blinked surprised.

"*No! He belongs here with me! I don't understand why you're being like this. I thought you liked him. I already told him, if he is in my life, he's in your life. And he's mine and I'm keeping him. And there's nothing that you're gonna say for me to get rid of him.*"

I huffed out a breath, crossing my arms over my chest. "Take it back, Liam. Say you are sorry!"

He looked insulted and down at his e-reader. "Fine." He shot Gabriel a look. "I will tolerate your presence in my house. If she so much as cries once, I will break both of your fucking legs. I don't give a fuck if you were a SEAL. You're going to be a fucking cripple if you do anything to her."

Gabriel blinked a little, his eyes narrowing lazily on Liam who took his things and stormed away.

I didn't understand why Liam was losing his mind about Gabriel. I thought he wanted us to be together because he went to Gabriel and told him about me.

I turned to Gabriel. "I'm sorry, I don't understand why he is like this."

"I think I do." He murmured softly staring after Liam. "Let me go talk to him."

I tried to stop him but Gabriel insisted. I didn't want Liam to fight him.

So I sat on the couch waiting for the two men in my life to sort it out.

～

Gabriel

I WAS ALREADY REELING WITH HER LOVE.

Her love. Something I never imagined I would say.

She told me loved me all the time.

And I never said the words back barely able to formulate them but I did...I did right?

I felt something cracking in my chest every single time she said it.

Like sunlight on frost, it etched into my soul.

Her words were delicate but they slammed into me every single time. If Isobel knew every single time she told me she loved?

It sank deep in me burning me throughout?

She didn't let it on.

But she did want me and Liam to get along.

And so there I was closing the distance to his room where I knew he'd be. He hadn't settled down.

Almost like, he was always waiting to leave. It was part of why I never took her over to my place. Because my place looked exactly the same.

In my deep dive of Liam Sullivan—not Santos—I discovered a lot.

Besides abuse and neglect he endured from his parents who never even cared if he was missing or not?

Both of our biological parents were drug addicts. I didn't know if he had gone through what I did, but I recognized the signs.

So we had everything in common except one thing.

Liam had been adopted.

Isobel wasn't his sister.

She was his foundation.

I did a deep dive into Liam psyche, and I discovered she had been his glue since childhood, she was the first person to love him.

He supported her through that love. He was her protector. He was her safety net.

And in turn? My new girlfriend was his anchor.

His home.

His life.

And he saw me taking it all away. Like I was ripping her from the roots of his chest and stealing her for myself.

I knew deep down, he did not love her romantically. That's not what this was about. Liam didn't want to be abandoned or replaced.

No amount of reassurance from her could calm him down. Because losing her would be losing himself.

And the only person who could was me.

I was the monster in his life he never fucking expected her to fall for. Maybe he did know I liked her a lot. I think he thought I'd come and go in passing. He never expected her to love me.

I never expected her to love me.

Me.

The boy from nothing.

I knocked on his door.

"Go away, Isa. I don't wanna talk about this with—" he paused when he saw me from his bed. He tossed his e-reader down and he stood so fluidly I closed the door locking it fully aware of him wanting to fight.

His voice was a growl, his eyes flashing wild green and violent.

"I asked you to help her!" He snarled. "Not seduce her."

He was coming at me like a tank.

"I didn't seduce her—" I broke off to duck his swings.

Why was he always fucking fighting? I ducked with him nearly missing my jaw.

"It just happened!"

I moved as his eyes flashed with a fury I had never seen. "I trusted you to not take advantage of her—"

I moved slamming into him then taking him down to the floor with a growl. "I would never take advantage!"

His form was perfect as he rolled me over. "She trusted you—"

"I trust her!" I shouted back as he slammed his fist into my face.

A loud noise left me as I shoved him off. We traded hits, his legs were like iron. This fucking kid was a machine.

I had fought people before. Skilled fighters.

I didn't even remember what form of karate he did—I just knew he was a trained killer coming after me.

"She's my fucking sister!"

"She's my girlfriend."

We both paused choking each other out to the door banging. "Liam! Gabriel! Are you two fighting?"

Both of us looked at each other again panting.

"No!"

"No!"

We both shouted at the same time and I grunted throwing him off.

"You listen to me, motherfucker. I have no intention of taking her away from me. And I would never hurt her. I'm not trying to replace you either. I know how much you mean to her, and I'm not trying to take your place."

I was trying to find mine in their family.

He was panting as he watched me looking more like a feral wolf than man. "She's all I have."

In that moment I realized why he was lashing out.

Even deeper.

I huffed out a breath. She was all I had. "I'm not trying to tear you two apart. I swear."

"And if she get's hurt?" Liam shook his head. "If anything happens to her. You don't think I know they send you on dangerous assignments? What if she's on your team? What if she—" he broke off aware Isobel was probably on the other side of the door.

I had an eye swelling and Liam lip was split and cheek bruising.

I put my hand over my heart. "I fucking promise you, as long as I'm alive, nothing will happen to her. She's my world as much as she is yours."

She loves me. She chose me.

"We both want whats best for her. If I miss something you got her back, and if you can't hear people trying to get her—I can. Instead of me being your enemy, I can protect her in ways you can't. And there's no guarantee she'll be on my team."

Even if I hoped after all this was done?

Someone plucked both of them into my watch. I wouldn't let them down.

Liam listened to the words coming out of my mouth and very slowly he lowered his stance.

"Nothing will happen to her?"

"Nothing will ever happen to her. I'll make sure of it." I would do anything to make sure no harm ever came to Isobel.

I swore it on my life.

He held out his hand. I took it.

"Promise."

"I promise." She was my girl as much as she was. I got the feeling he loved Isobel more than I did and I wasn't a fool.

I would never come between them.

"I would never tear her away from you."

He nodded and then he tried—he really did—to flip me over his head. I caught it though as we both went down to the floor and Isobel burst in through the door screaming at us to stop.

Both of us froze awkwardly me on top of Liam holding him down.

"Isa," he whimpered. *"He's killing me."*

I snarled. *"You little shit—"*

"Nice try," Isobel stepped in hauling me off him. "I heard you fighting with Gabriel…" and then she went off on him in Spanish while I stood there looking at my girl flaming mad.

Aware something was changing in me that felt foreign but right.

Later that week, Isobel swam up undoing her ties in record time and I broke through the water watching her with a grin.

Her laughter bounced off the walls. "Amor!" She threw herself at me. "Did you see? I did it!"

"I saw, baby." I had her lips on mine in another instant. "I saw you."

When she passed her final exam on the last week?

I had already gotten the call from Koller in my office letting me know come Monday morning I was moving out of this facility back to my old one.

And I was taking three new trainee's with me.

"You should be pleased, I pulled some strings because someone else wanted Liam Santos, but I got Liam on your team along with his buddy, Jeremy Bradford."

Koller let out a breath.

"The only reason I'm putting this one on your team and not anybody else's is because I saw her file and I don't trust anyone else."

"What?" What was he talking about? Besides the fact that Liam and Jeremy were with me. *Who was he—*

Oh. Fucking. Shit.

Isobel.

"Isobel Santos is going to be the third. Figured she'd want to be near her brother and nobody else is gonna stand up for her what with the pack of idiots we got running around now. You're the only one I trust to not get her killed. Clear?"

My voice was gruff since my heart was racing in my chest. My smile tipped my lips up. I kept my voice steady.

"Copy that, sir."

"See you and your team Monday morning, Monroe."

CHAPTER 18
ISOBEL

I PASSED.

I did it.

The words exploded like fireworks as I ran through the door, my heart found it in my ribs.

After months of training, I ran into Liam's arms first. He was the first person I saw.

I laughed as he lifted me up off the floor.

"We did it!" I cried.

His laughter echoed off the walls. "We did, like always. Together."

"Together," I pulled back kissing his forehead. "Always together."

His smile was wide, his face red as Jeremy bounded over to his us his energy always excited around the two of us.

Out of everyone in the class, Jeremy was like an old man trapped in a young boy's body.

Liam liked talking to him because he thought Jeremy was intelligent. And funny.

Liam said Jeremy said the wildest shit with a straight face and my brother thought he was hilarious.

"Hey guys, I'm having a thing over the restaurant, you know? The chocolate factory looking place. Do you guys wanna come?"

I laughed as Liam put me down.

"Hey Jay, yeah we'd be down. When is it?"

Liam talked to Jeremy who we both adored like a little brother as I searched the hall.

I didn't have to for long. Gabriel was on his way over to his, a hard set of his jaw telling me this wasn't going to be good.

The moment he approached I saw Jeremy melt.

Towering over everyone, with his cut jaw, his wheat hair gleaming under the lights and winter blue eyes that seemed more intense today as they focused on me, Jeremy practically disappeared.

"Congratulation," his eyes never left mine.

Although his voice was low and controlled, I knew his secret.

I saw it in the way his fingers trembled.

He wanted to kiss me.

"I have all three of your new assignments."

And suddenly my heart began to pound rapidly. Much faster than before.

Was this—was he?

I caught Liam's eyes as he took the folder Gabriel passed him. Liam didn't even hesitate opening it up rapidly. I did the same.

Team Lead : Gabriel Monroe

Isobel Santos reassigned to Quantico under his supervision...

I SAW NOTHING ELSE. I SHUT IT WITH A GASP AND FOR A MOMENT I would've thrown myself on Gabriel who was biting his cheeks.

As I felt my body shift and move, I was aware of Liam's arms banding around me.

Tight. Protective.

Reminding me of who I was.

Who Gabriel was.

Where we were.

And how we couldn't be together on paper. He was my instructor. He was already breaking thousands of rules for me.

We never explicitly said it but we both knew.

I remembered for a second where I was as I looked at my shoes and composed myself. Breathing deeply at seeing that I was...I was with him. *Him*.

I didn't dare look at Gabriel anymore but I felt his eyes on me.

I knew what he had been doing was not...I held it back. He was two years older than me, but right now it felt like he was twenty years away from me as Liam grinned ear to ear.

"You fucking pulled strings," his sly smile aimed at Gabriel. "No fucking way they put me and her and Jay on the same team."

Gabriel shook his head at him his eyes softening a fraction. Just enough for me to know how he felt.

"This is awesome," Jeremy commented. "I'm with you guys. This couldn't be better."

As Jeremy chattered to Liam about baking us all banana bread to celebrate, Gabriel looked at me with a wry smile.

One that I wanted to kiss when we got home.

"They didn't want to separate you two. But Bradford over here has all the complimentary skills from you guys...so it fits well."

Every single word of his was carefully chosen as he blinked slowly, tipping his head to me. Even if he was composed, I bit back my laugh. I felt eyes on me from everywhere. I nodded keeping my face neutral.

Secrets. This life was new for me. And for a moment, for just a second I wondered if Gabriel felt that fissure of frustration I felt.

At not being able to throw my arms around him and kiss his smile off of his face.

I saw the way his throat worked.

"Jay is having a celebration..." I trailed off motioning to Jeremy who was making Liam grin with stories he told. "I'm pretty sure everyone is invited."

Gabriel looked over at Jeremy and I saw him fighting a laugh. I saw it. The way he shook his head. "Not my thing."

"I'm going." I kept my voice low as I realized how close we were standing.

Liam drew closer on my other side if he noticed as though making it look like it was normal. He might not agree with what I wanted—but he wasn't going to stop me.

"I'm going," I repeated. "Tonight. I was going to go home and get dressed after cleaning up...and then Liam and I probably will get there at..." I spoke to him carefully and I saw his lips twitch.

Liam shot us both a sly grin unable to help himself and I laughed it off.

"You guys, I can't wait," Jeremy's eyes blue and brighter than anything in the auditorium lit up as someone called Gabriel away. An older man and Gabriel's light smile immediately dipped.

I watched him walk over to a bunch of people who all heralded him like a god.

"Senior officials," Liam whispered. "The one who he's going to? Jim Koller? Heavy-weight in the Agency. Guy's retired military with take-no-shit attitude. He's known for being one of the best trainers in Agency history. He practically raised Monroe."

Was that…his real life?

"Koller's the one who got Monroe where he is today," Liam said as I turned to him.

Jeremy was listening to our conversation, but for some reason I knew he wouldn't say a word.

Jeremy wasn't a gossip. If anything he was Liam's good friend.

"I heard Koller's got Monroe on track to climb the ranks after this," Jeremy whispered to us. Liam looked at him surprised and Jeremy shrugged. "What? I pay attention too."

Liam's grin was one of surprise. "Keep going."

"Koller's got plans. Bigger assignments. You realize if we're on his team? It's always going to be that way for us too," Jeremy's blue eyes were warmer now. "I'm excited. I can't fucking wait."

What did that mean?

I turned to look at Gabriel nod at something the imposing man, still shorter than him said to him.

He looked at place in the world of influence. Of power.

A rising star. Gabriel was like the king of the sun. Where did I fit in? Did I?

I turned back to Liam finding him watching Gabriel as well.

His lighter green eyes met mine. "Don't worry," he whispered to me quietly. "You're going to be fine. I'm always going to be by your side."

I smiled up at my brother letting out a breath I didn't even know I was holding. And nodded. "Together."

He held out his index finger and I linked it with mine.

"Together."

∿

I GOT DRESSED THAT NIGHT READY TO GO OUT.

I didn't think Gabriel would make it to dinner.

It really wasn't his thing but a bunch of us were around the table having a good time regardless. The restaurant buzzed with good energy even if I missed him.

Liam sat between me and Jeremy and kept us both laughing at their outrageous banter.

Jeremy and Liam went back and forth.

"...I can't do that man my fiancé she left me for her personal trainer," Jeremy said a little tipsy.

Liam laughed outright. And I gaped.

"You do not look old enough to drive," I was stunned.

Jeremy grinned his entire face mottled red. "No, I'm just teasing, mi'lady...I was fucking with ya."

I laughed as Jeremy switched to an old Southern wife voice.

"Why are you like this?" I asked him teasing as the waitress who kept coming by our table bent to talk to Liam.

My brother was a flirt. A shameless one. And right now he was flirting to get with *her*.

I rolled my eyes as Jeremy looked at Liam in awe.

"He's so good with girls," Jeremy lamented. "He's been trying to help me pick up Cathy, you know the blonde girl sometimes Liam partners with?"

"That is why he talks to her?" My brother was currently watching the waitress fumble over talking to him with a knowing look in his eyes.

Combined with the tattoos and the ripped tee's and women all but threw their panties at him.

"Yeah, he told me I could borrow his cool band-tee's and skater shirts to impress her but so far I kinda feel like a clown. But I've been meaning to ask her out."

I was surprised. "I did not realize you liked Cathy. She's a nice girl."

He nodded eagerly. "And she's stationed at Quantico with us. I think I might ask her out once we get settled."

Surprised, I chatted with Jeremy about his crush a bit more.

"By the way," Jeremy whispered. "Can I ask you something?" His eyes met mine and I felt my heart sinking a little.

I really hoped he didn't ask me about Gabriel.

There was a knowing look in Jeremy's eyes as he watched me

and time felt frozen for a second before he said. "You gonna finish your cheesy bread?"

I looked down and shook my head as I passed it to him. "You can have it. I have plenty."

The seat next to me was empty and I saw Liam following the waitress to no doubt flirt with her and pay for our food.

"He's so smooth," Jeremy sighed. "I'm not. I get so fucking awkward around Cathy..."

As Jeremy talked about his crush my mind drifting. To the one person who wasn't there.

When Jeremy excused himself to go to the bathroom, I dared to peek at my phone.

Liam was no doubt all over his waitress and I sat alone for a second to gather myself.

I took my phone out. I had sent Gabriel a photo of me getting dressed earlier and hadn't checked my messages until now.

Where are you now?

My heart flipped a little.

Liam and I are going to a club after this called Havana.

We just finished eating but Liam is trying to date the waitress.

Temporarily.

I saw the bubbles.

Text me the address.

I did.

I'll be there.

That's all he said?

I felt my heart leap in my stomach as Liam and I separated from Jeremy who had to feed his cat, and we went to Havana.

Liam had come out from the back of the restaurant and I knew instantly by the lipstick he was wiping off he had gotten some. He was trying to tame his hair down.

"If you were not my brother, you would disgust me," I whispered as he shook his head. Liam had always been more...active than me in many ways.

Where I held back in safe neutral ground, Liam threw himself headfirst. Into fights, into women, into his feelings, and into everything he had ever done.

"I'm your brother and I still disgust you," he muttered.

"That's not true, I don't see why you don't find a nice girl—" I broke off at his groan.

"Isa," he looked at me with wild eyes then and messy hair. "I don't want a nice girl. I want a girl who can give me problems. Send me to jail. Something excited."

I frowned because he was lying. I knew him. As we talked the chill in the air sank into my skin as I cuddled closer to him smelling the cheap perfume of hers mixing with his own. "It doesn't have to be that way."

I wished Gabriel had a sister to pass onto Liam. Then we would all be family. Happier. Over the years Liam had changed, shifting into someone that I was worried about. He'd become more and more reckless and I thought the Agency might've helped me with more structure.

Gabriel might help him.

My brother had no discernment from anything. Throwing himself into bed with whoever walked his way.

He never stopped and thought about it and so far it was lucky nobody had surprisingly gotten pregnant.

So far.

Sometimes I thought Liam felt ashamed of where he had started in life. Ashamed to feel like a Sullivan and not a Santos.

I wished sometimes a woman would come into his life and take him by surprise. Make him see she was worth it. Someone who might help him feel like he belonged.

Make him want to stay somewhere for once. Settle down.

"We're here," he motioned to the lights of Club Havana as we walked our way down the steps leading to an underground basement of a club.

The Cuban inspired dance hall was all neon lights and palm trees when we stepped inside, Liam paying the all cash fee.

Liam wanted to take me somewhere nice tonight that I could cut loose in.

"I know how much you missed this," he shouted over the music. "So fucking grateful I took those lessons with you."

I laughed as he hauled me onto the floor.

Even if my father had barely been able to afford lessons, I did love dancing since I was a child. Liam and I sometimes babysat or mowed lawns to pay for our classes. Liam for karate and me for dancing.

When Liam first moved into my home, he didn't want to leave me alone.

"How could I forget?" I laughed as he spun me a little. "Papi never let you live it down."

He turned red under the lights. "Yeah, but I'm solid now." I laughed at his moves. Liam had gone to my classes with me sitting on the side and watching me with a little smile on his face. On the way back, I would split my cash with him, buy two watered down ice creams and come home together a mess from the sun melting it down in my hand.

"You were the only boy in the class," I teased.

"And I was damn good at it."

I giggled as I moved with him.

"You always move so light and easy," I yelled at him over the music.

"You taught me." He shot back with a grin.

Dancing was my thing.

In return, Liam taught me how to ice skate. Sort of.

I wasn't very good but he would pick me up spin me around in his arms and that was fine.

The day my father welcomed Liam into our home, I gained not just a brother, but a protector and a best friend for life.

Liam and Isa. We had our names on my door. Our drawings.

We shared a room, shared our dreams and our fears, and faced the world together.

I realized I had a protector and he was my life.

I had held onto him so tightly my entire life. But recently my heart had expanded.

"Liam," I said over the music as he tugged me back to him. "I really like Gabriel."

Liam stiffened a little as he held me closer now changing with the song.

"I don't want to lose him." I said it out loud. "I'm scared of the future and I don't know what to do about it."

Liam's usually brighter eyes were dark as he listened to me. I still remembered him in memories. Splices of life. A thirteen year old boy who held my hand tightly.

The first night he snuck into my room asking if I could sleep next to him because he was scared. Eating lunch every single day with him.

Maybe in another life I would've been his.

But not this one. This one I wanted someone else.

"I promised your father I would take care of you," he said it like he wasn't related to me then. His eyes met mine. "I promised him I would never let anything happen to you."

I nodded as I realized we had stopped moving and he held me tighter.

"I will never let anything hurt you," he was so close now. "Not even me." I frowned confused by what he was saying. "I *always* keep my word. Even if means watching you love someone like Monroe." Liam's eyes locked on mine as he let out a breath. "I'll take care of him."

My eyes widened then as my heart sputtered. "You will?"

Liam tipped his head. "I would do anything for you, shortcake. Even if it means being around him forever." At that I lightly pushed his chest.

"Gabriel is not a bad man."

"No," Liam shook his head and over the music he said. "But I don't think he knows who he is. Let alone you. I don't think he or any man will ever deserve you."

The bass pounded through the floor, and this conversation wasn't right here, but the moment he said it—I had to respond.

"I want you to be friends with him," I said. It burst from my lips. "I want you to get along with him. I think you two have a lot in common. You would like him if you did."

"What do you like about him?"

I didn't even have to think. "I like *everything* about him. Even the way he puts on his socks. The way he hangs up his towel. The way he takes his coffee. The way he looks at me. I can tell." Gabriel liked me.

"But you don't know him Isa, he's the Agency golden boy—"

"So what?" I shrugged. Even if I didn't feel confident in it.

"He chose me. He chose to help me. To break the rules. To be there when nobody else would. I choose him for what he does not what he says."

And all the things he doesn't say.

"Liam, I know you are protecting me. But I love Gabriel. I do. And I want you to try. Just try."

I stopped realizing the defeat in Liam's eyes.

"I know why you are scared of him."

I said it.

"I know he reminds you of you. Because he reminds me of you." My brother stiffened and he looked ready to let me go and bolt and so I clung to him. "I know he makes you think of yourself and you don't want that reminder. But I don't think any less of you or him."

I shook my head. "Liam, this isn't the place. I don't know why you are being like this—"

"I'm terrified." His eyes met mine. "Monroe isn't known for easy assignments. You said to me this was a desk job. It isn't a desk job anymore. It isn't us relaxing and getting weekends. Being on his team means traveling a lot, complex and dangerous jobs. If he's climbing we are automatically climbing with him—"

"But you wanted this!" I shot back not understanding why he was upset. "You wanted this life—"

"No, I wanted to take care of you and your father—"

"He's your father too—"

"No," he shook his head and for once I didn't recognize my brother. "It's not the same for me as it is for you."

I don't know why, but in that moment my eyes stung. "Yes it is. You are a part of us. *Why do you—"*

"Because one day," his eyes held mine as he grabbed my face then forcing me to look at him. "One day you are going to end up with Monroe. I fucking see it all over his face. He's not letting you go. I sure as fuck wouldn't. But I realize one day you won't be a Santos. You won't be my sister—"

"I will always be your sister—"

"You're Monroe's." He said it like it was final. "I see it, Isa. I know it. If you want me to get along with him, I will. If you want me to his best friend, I will. And if he ever does anything to hurt a single hair on your head—I'll bury him too. I don't give a fuck."

And then I realized what was happening.

The more I became Gabriel's, in Liam's eyes, the less I was his. I was moving. Shifting. Changing.

From Isobel Santos to someone who was her own person.

I didn't want the Agency. I didn't want this life.

I wanted my studio.

But now as I said it, I realized something.

Since meeting Gabriel...my wants had changed.

My needs had changed ever so slightly letting me know why Liam was afraid.

I saw it all over his eyes.

"You think I will change too?"

He shook his head with a sad look in his eyes. "Isa, you already have." His eyes flickered above my head then. And hardened even if a smirk lit his lips. Mischief lit his expression. "Didn't you say he was coming? He looks out of place here."

My mouth opened and Liam looked behind me and the wicked gleam was back.

"Shortcake, I think my plan worked a little too well."

A little thrill went through me. He grinned and winked moving onto to another woman eyeing him down, leaving me on the dance floor feeling energy crackle around me.

That was my brother.

The one who went from serious conversations to shameless flirting in a nanosecond.

But that meant— I felt a hard chest at my back.

He didn't say a word.

And even if Liam's words left my chest tight.

I couldn't move right now.

I felt *his* hand slide around my waist.

I gasped, as his lips brushed my ear, my throat, my pulse and I leaned back against him, as his hand gripped my belly possessively.

"*Gabriel.*"

CHAPTER 19
GABRIEL

I wanted to fuck her right there.

Watching her dance? I was going to kill him.

Fuck her right there to show him who she belonged to.

It didn't matter they were family. They weren't family by blood. Scientific facts and all.

He could take her from me and the worst part was—I was afraid of that. I was.

Privately, I might've been physically aware of Liam from the start. I always had been. Even if he was flirting with other girls, I knew he was living with only one.

Nothing was stopping him.

And all it would take was me fucking up.

And then I'd seen him wrapped around her holding her close, close enough to kiss her.

I could feel the thrumming tension between us, the air almost sparking with it.

Every brush of her body against mine sent shivers racing along my nerve endings. It did nothing to calm my fury.

And then she said my fucking name like *that*.

I splayed my hand on her abdomen hating that fucking red dress with no back.

It split all the way down revealing a sexy row of buttons right where I knew I could spread her open and sink deep inside of her— I pulled her back against me loving the way her lips parted.

I was *furious*.

Rage, red hot mixed with desire at seeing her dressed like this, with him, coursed through my veins brining emotions bubbling to the surface I had never felt before.

I never got jealous and now?

That ugly sensation rose like a wave, threatening my sanity, my heart was pounding, as my tongue darted out tasting her skin.

Me, who had been trained to control myself. My every fucking emotion, unraveling at the sight of my girl in the arms of another man.

I nipped her throat, loving the way her head laid back on my chest. She trusted me. She surrendered to me. She was perfect.

For me.

Not him.

"I thought you'd wait for me." The image of her moving her hips as she moved would forever be in engraved in my brain.

"I didn't—"

"You did."

My hand skated up holding her throat as I trailed my tongue around her neck, sucking her pulse into my mouth loving the noise that left her lips.

The entire dance floor was filled with people. It didn't matter that I was doing this to her.

I thought I passed a couple straight up fucking—this was…wild. And she was with *him*.

"You did, baby. Did you take him inside of you?"

She gasped and her eyes filled with such horror it broke the moment, and for a moment I knew she had never—nor did she ever dream of—taking Liam to her bed.

I had seen him grabbing another woman and moving away when he saw me coming. "*Amor*."

"He was fucking with me."

"He's my—we always dance together—" I heard her mention how they'd been dancing for years together and they trusted each other. He had been to her dance classes.

"Amor, I would never—" she shook her head as though the idea of being with anyone else was ridiculous.

But the image of her body moving left me shaking, my emotions a tumultuous blend of lust and arousal combine with the ugly sensations I didn't recognize that demanded I do something, that I gain release.

Her hands moved to my hair, brushing it back, she liked it longer—I swallowed as she did that like a balm soothing my nerves.

Something feral inside of me calming down the moment she did. I was trained to go after everything. Like an animal.

This woman humanized me beyond measure. Instead of destroying, I heeled.

Easing the beast in me demanding to take my cut of her.

I hadn't known her long at all. And she had this hold over me even now. I was aware of Koller warning me that time moved differently in our world. He'd met his wife and married her in ten months. Less than. In fucking South Korea.

They'd been married for twenty plus years. In the Agency partnerships were formed in seconds in the heat of moments where life and death was common.

I knew why Isobel trusted me. I understood the psyche behind why me holding her up between life and death would make her logically bond with me.

Scientifically—I understood it.

Emotionally? I was wrecked by it. Those eyes glittered watching me.

"I would never dance with him like with you."

How did she do that? She moved me from this...thing to human so fast.

The sound was raw out of my throat.

"How would you dance with me?"

Her eyes gleamed. "I show you?"

I didn't feel the nod, I just moved.

I felt her hands moving me, tugging me somewhere, I followed her like I was on an invisible leash she held. Maybe that's why relationships were different in this world. We lived closer to death, closer to danger, and we recognized things faster than civilians ever could.

We knew people.

It was our job.

And Isobel knew me better than she understood.

There were these booths lining the wall, in the dark Isobel tugged me against the wall.

"I never dance with Liam how I want to with you. Never."

She put my arms her waist and I was dipping my head watching her. She tugged me closer, the feel of her soothing everything even if I knew—I knew I *wanted* her.

I was moving my thigh between her legs automatically as she held my collar and her hips *moved*, her cheeks flushed, hair falling over her eyes just enough, the strands falling over one eye as she panted.

Isobel's hair was pitch black in the light gone from its usual raven blue and black making her skin look paler.

I took her lips hungrily as Isobel moved her hips in the sexiest way ever—no she didn't move with Liam like that—by contrast it was demure.

I stopped breathing, not being able to look away, and then she smiled, and arched her back bending backwards in a smooth arc.

I caught her from falling but she was nowhere close. Not around me. I'd never let her drop.

"I didn't know you danced like that."

Her smile was infectious. "I danced since I was young. I loved it. Come, I show you. And after…" her eyes were shy. "You can show me how you move."

I'd like to show you now.

My throat tightened at her words, desire coursing through my veins.

I pulled her closer, our hips moving in tandem as the music swelled around us.

The rest of the world fell away, until there was only Isobel. I captured her mouth.

Every roll of her hips against mine felt like heaven and I wanted to lift her up and sink into her, dropping her down on my aching cock over and over.

Feeling her scream and pant my name.

I didn't ever want to stop kissing her, warm, alive, so real in my arms.

I spun Isobel out, watching as her tiny dress flared around her thighs, before tugging her back into my embrace.

She laughed in delight, her cheeks flushed and her eyes bright.

Our bodies moved as one, the heat between us growing with every step, every touch.

"Where did you learn that!"

I loved seeing her surprised.

My lips stretched in an easy grin.

"I had a few ballroom dancing classes in high school," I laughed at her expression. "I swear it was that or home economics, and I used to burn water."

Her eyes went wide and I moved her, a little rusty but I was still present.

"You're good at everything you do?" She gasped as I pulled her into my arms.

"Just about," my lips moved overs hers. "I live to please."

You. Her eyes heated and I didn't let her go. I dipped her low, supporting her weight easily.

Her hair brushed the floor, exposing the elegant column of her throat.

I held her there for a moment, our faces mere inches apart, our breath mingling.

And just like that, I felt my chest crack open completely when I lifted her back up.

"Take me home, Gabriel. With you. To your home."

CHAPTER 20
ISOBEL

I HADN'T EVER BEEN TO HIS HOME.

I was trembling as he carried me to his room. He didn't put me down since I left the car. Anticipation flowed through my veins.

I'm with him. I want him.

Every nerve was set alight with raw need, I needed him since the moment I saw him.

And any moment I'd finally get to feel Gabriel, moving inside of my body was a moment I wanted to come quicker and quicker.

I was breathless as I grabbed his shirt hungrily tearing it from his skin, the moment his lips met mine.

It felt like I had known him my entire life. Time moved differently with us.

The intense training, the life-or-death modules, the emotions running high all the time.

A single stressful day for a civilian? Was every single day for us. And it reshaped my mind differently around him.

I trusted Gabriel with my life.

The moment he set me down in his room, I caught the sparse and minimal space, not surprised that unlike mine he was meticulous and organized about everything.

I was right. He was like Liam.

He didn't settle down anywhere. I knew it then. I turned to find him stalking towards me slamming the door shut as his hands roamed my body.

I don't know how our clothes fell off, I just knew I pulled back my hair as he tore at my dress, my hair fell around me some of the strands covering my nipples and Gabriel—*Why did I ever think he was cold?*

Heat thrummed through my veins, through the air, buzzing and barely contained in the room as winter blue eyes raked over me while he tore his shirt off. Wheat-hair. Golden skin. His chiseled abs. His entire body cut from marble. I knew how hard he worked.

I had seen him.

My eyes trailed down his chest, broad shouldered and lower over his dark slacks. *"Gabriel."*

"I dreamed of you—" he broke off, his eyes heating to dark pools as he took me down to the bed. "Of this. Spread out under me. Panting my name like that." His voice dropped lower. "I wanna hear you say my name like that over and over when I'm inside of you."

I clenched at his words. *"Gabriel—"*

"Just like that, baby."

His eyes raked down my body and I realized I had nothing but panties on. Every inch of him pressed to every inch of me.

My chest was heaving, nipples painfully hard seeking relief from him.

"Fuck, you're so beautiful. You're so soft," his voice caressed my skin as my heart raced.

Pounding against my ribcage as I made out with this man like my life depended on it. Hungry for him, I spread my legs wider to accommodate him feeling something else overcome my senses.

It happened every single time I was with him.

Something just felt right.

"Need you," I panted. "Take me, Gabriel."

His groan muffled in my mouth as his mouth worked down my body. His tongue tracing patterns into my skin.

The moment his mouth closed around one of my nipples, I arched my back. It was white-hot pleasure and he began playing with the other. I was aching.

I didn't care about foreplay or any of that.

Please, just get inside of me.

I cried out tangling my fingers in his hair. And he instantly stopped pulling back.

His lips were wet, his eyes eerily bright as he rose up and

twisted to grab something from his dresser. I didn't know what was going on.

"Do you want to try something with me?"

I nodded. Whatever it was, I wanted it.

"I don't fuck like this."

The confession fell from his lips like a secret, and I could barely breathe as he held up ropes and cuffs. His eyes never left mine, watching, waiting. "I need this."

I nodded, feeling like I could barely breathe. "I trust you."

He had *always* been like this. I knew that much.

Whenever I reached for him I knew.

And somehow, it made perfect sense that the man who controlled every single aspect of his life would need something like this too.

I had *never* done anything like this.

My one experience in college had stunted me unlike Liam who was with anything and everything.

My stomach fluttered, and I saw the look in his eyes.

He looked helpless, almost like he didn't know what to do with me. But he wanted to use those restraints in bed. I wasn't nervous at all.

Not around him.

"Baby, you look at me like that—" he broke off shaking his head. "*Nothing* will stop me from taking you. But I need you to be okay with it."

"Take me," I looked at the icy blue of his eyes practically glowing on his face. "Please."

"You need a safe word," his voice was gruff as he moved over me still in his slacks. "Something you can remember."

"A safe word…" I blinked confused.

He tipped his head slowly. "Something to make me stop."

I swallowed suddenly aware Gabriel was into things I couldn't even imagine. But I trusted him. Even still, it was a little scary.

"I say this word, and you stop?"

He slowly blinked and tipped his head looking like he was restraining himself from pouncing while holding onto those restraints. Raw hunger in his eyes made my heart pound even harder.

I swallowed thinking. "Snowman."

His lips tipped up just a little. He slowly moved back over me and I laid perfectly still letting him adjust, moving the restraints as he needed to.

"Keep them there, baby."

His voice was two octaves deeper wrapping soft rope around my wrists with enough slack before tying them to the headboard.

I could feel myself growing wetter with each tie until my inner thighs were shaking.

"So pretty," he whispered. "I fucking knew you'd be like this."

I panted as his hands traced down my body, his mouth working lower against this time around my nipples, sucking and biting gently.

I almost came off the bed and a dark chuckle left him as he worked lower.

I was shaking wildly now and nearly jumped out of my skin when I realized he intended to do the same to my feet. I drew back shaking now.

"Shh, I got you," his eyes pale and so light on his face glanced up. "Promise, I won't hurt."

"This is n-new."

He nodded. "I know, baby. Do you wanna leave it? Do you want me to stop?"

I swallowed as he tugged at my panties. Soaking wet and completely ruined. I just wanted him to take me.

Just take me.

My head rolled right to left and I whispered. "No." I closed my eyes as his eyes gleamed and he dipped to tie the restraints around my thighs. I was confused until he lifted one leg.

And clipped it to the headboard exposing me in a way that seemed too vulnerable. Spread open. At his mercy.

My breathing was shallow as he slowly traced over my stomach with his lips.

Dio Mio. Is this how I go?

By the time he did it to the other side I was shaking. I felt so helpless but none of the terror from before.

Instead I felt like I was his plaything. His possession. And I wanted nothing else but to belong to Gabriel.

"You look like a present," he breathed against my inner thigh, eyes flashing up to me. "Like it's my fucking birthday watching you."

"Gabriel." I didn't even know what I was asking for twisting in my restraints and a dangerously slow smile curved his lips.

He looked like a sun-warmed god who was taking a human for the first time. If it wasn't for the color in his cheeks and the way his eyes glittered—I would think he wasn't affected.

"Please." I didn't know what I was asking for. Taste me. Fuck me. Anything but this.

Both of us were panting and I felt my eyes watering at the pleasure mingling with frustration. With anxiety. I was shaking for this man and all he'd done is taste my nipples.

"Restless?" His hands went to his slacks and drew them down agonizing slow like he was taking his time.

Torturing me. Leaving me stretched thin waiting for him.

"Are you on anything?"

I shook my head. I never had a reason to.

And then he drew his pants down with a nod.

My eyes shyly trekked down his gloriously ripped figure.

Agency life kept him working out harder than most people and I knew he'd been a solider, but Gabriel was the kind of fit I had to suspend my reality for.

I always felt his strength in bed and when he held me.

Or in the pool I felt the outline of his cock against my body. But this was different.

Gabriel in the nude was not human.

His body cut and molded from marble and his cock rising between his legs, long and thick and proud. He stroked himself once as he watched me and I wanted to come right then.

"You're beautiful." *Now get inside me.*

His lips quirked up as he grabbed something—condoms—out of his dresser and climbed back on top of me.

His mouth immediately landed over mine, working his way down faster now. Until they sealed over my core.

I came off the bed then. Or I tried to.

And now I understood why the restraints were important to him. Held down like this? I could only take. Every single thing was amplified.

His tongue flicked at my clit over and over until it thrust into my pussy. Soaking wet, I all but shrieked.

"That's it," his voice was rough with need and desire. "Let me hear you. I want you to come for me just like this, baby. I wanna taste you before I fuck that little pussy."

Dio. Mio.

His words, his tongue fucking inside of me, was going to drive me to the edge.

I struggled against him, bucking my hips up. Agonized noises left me, whimpers, pleas as he sucked harder.

"Fuck, I love feeling you squeezing my tongue like that," he groaned and then he did something. "Again, baby. Let me feel you."

Reaching up, he cupped both of my breasts, toying with my nipples.

The sensations that had been winding higher and tighter in me reached a peak I hadn't experienced with a man.

Only by myself.

It was electric.

A sob left me as I struggled in my restraints, bucking my hips as pure pleasure tore through me.

I screamed a little as I gripped the restraints and it rocked through my system.

All the while Gabriel growled, the sound vibrating against my clit as he tugged my nipples.

"Amor," I whimpered as I coasted down.

I heard the sound of something tearing, the head of him pressing into me then, and I moaned unable to stop.

"I'm going to do that to you every single fucking day," he was over me then and I wanted his weight on me. But instead, he positioned himself and sank into me. Or tried to.

The sheer size of him took my breath away.

"Amor—" I broke off as he sank in a few inches and I whimpered. "*Dio.*"

His eyes were pale and low-lidded as he watched me. "Fuck, there you fucking go, baby. Take every inch of me like the good girl you are."

Gabriel was panting. The look in his eyes was one of pure unfiltered hunger as I turned vibrantly red as I peered up at him. "Say my name. Beg me to fuck that pretty little pussy."

I clenched at the words, I was shaking, this was new for me, a little scary, but the thrill only succeeded in pooling more moisture between my legs where his cock was spreading me open.

This was agonizing.

147

"Gabriel, take me, please."

In this position he was kneeling between my legs, his body jutting out proudly and intimidating, his hands running over my body, tugging my nipples, running over my pussy, and my thighs.

"I've wanted you like this since the moment I saw you, tied up, so wet you ruin my sheets—" I turned pink at that. "God, you're so irresistible, I knew you'd get all shy," his smile made me turn even more red.

"Gabriel-"

"Are you mine? Can I keep you?"

My heart stopped as he said it.

I looked at those pale eyes filled with heat, and I didn't know how to communicate with him at that moment.

I was tied up in the most provocative position I could've been in, at his mercy, and he was still asking me if….if I was his woman?

I was always his. Since the moment I saw him.

"I'm yours. I belong to you," it left my lips like a promise.

A noise left my lips as he sank in deeper. Stretching me beyond my limits. We both groaned and I whimpered finding it impossible to take him deeper.

"Shh, baby look at me." I did. He was there like a god kneeling between my legs. "My eyes." I did. I met them head on.

He gasped as he slid in the rest of the way when I watched him.

I could've came right then as I squeezed down on the thick stalk of him. "You're big."

His smile was tight. "You're mine, baby."

And he was mine. *So big. So much. It hurt just a little.*

"I can feel you right now, soaking wet, losing it," he whispered, swearing softly, rolling his hips in a hint—as he reached down and pressed down my clit, rubbing in circles that made me overheat and implode.

I had been built up so tightly, the pressure in me curled and he felt more intense as I clenched and clenched around his length.

I came apart on the heels of my previous orgasm. That's all it took.

I was shaking the ties, and I was working, helpless noises leaving my lips, throwing my head back. His name left my lips.

"Gabriel."

His voice was like dark sensual promise. "Oh fuck, just like that, come for me, baby. God, you're so sensitive."

I *was.*

When I came back down I looked at him panting, and he hadn't moved just watched me with wonder.

"Just like that?"

He whispered. "I didn't even do anything."

I turned violently pink gasping and panting for breath. I didn't think I could take anymore.

I knew I did as his lips quirked.

"Are you sensitive, baby?"

A whimper left my lips as he dipped down his lips brushing over mine but his body still apart, changing the angle now.

"Would you like to try something?" I nodded, unable to speak. His lips were in a wicked smile. "Do you remember your safe word? Good girl, I want something from you, I want you to come as much as you can when I fuck you."

A helpless noise left my lips.

His smile was dangerous.

"As much as you can. If not, I'll fuck them all out of you. One by one. Until you're limp. A mess."

Oh God, who *was* this man?

He hadn't even moved and I was clenching down on him.

"Nod if you understand me, baby."

I managed a weaker one my heart unable to take anymore.

"Gabriel...I don't think I can take anymore," my words were a croak. His smile was back.

"Let's try it out."

And then he began to *move.*

My mouth opened as he watched me delivering steady strokes over and over with precision, until I was clenching. "You're close already...*Come for me.*"

I wasn't even in control of my own body. My mouth fell open gasping for air as he drove deeper.

As I came he groaned falling over me grabbing the headboard tightly, using it as leverage to work me through the tidal wave of my orgasm.

An agonized scream left me as I came harder. "*Gabriel.*"

"Don't stop," he growled and grabbed my throat and squeezed. The pressure sent electric white hot sensations skating through me.

A silent scream came to lips as I felt every single thrust prolonging it.

"Don't you dare stop coming."

I couldn't even if I wanted to. I was so oversensitized as I sobbed and it got *too* much. I shook my head.

Too much. Too intense.

"Please no more—"

Every single stroke felt like a mini orgasm.

"Yes."

He bore down on me and I screamed as he hit that spot inside of me, and I lost it. *Dio. I'm going to die.*

The restraints intensified every single sensation ten-fold and I was writhing from every single one.

"Fuck." He closed his eyes, his hips moving in a way that more animal than man and driving himself deeper.

I *screamed.*

And yet, even as he buried in me, something was wrong. Sensitized and aware, his body only touched mine where he was inside of me. That was it.

Even through my orgasms something was missing.

Something's wrong.

This isn't.

This isn't him.

It felt...I felt him sinking deeper as he tipped his head back and groaned. Even farther.

I just wanted him close.

Something is wrong.

It's his eyes.

"You're perfect," he groaned throwing his head back and suddenly my body went cold.

He can't touch me.

He doesn't want to.

I looked at the restraints and a noise left me.

Panic. Filled. Me. Something's wrong.

The word ripped out of my soul.

"Snowman!"

CHAPTER 21
GABRIEL

IT WASN'T A CRY.

It was a *scream*.

Laced with panic and fear and I froze.

Concern for her always overrode all of my primary functions.

I stopped my hands roaming over her, holding her face. *"Baby-babybaby."*

I was all over her in a second, stopping myself from fucking her like a savage. Not moving I braced myself over her hands roaming her body. "Baby, talk to me. What happened? Too much?"

She sniffled a little and that tiny little sound broke me.

"Untie me…please…"

"Did I hurt you?" I went to pull out before I did, grabbing a knife I had in the drawer.

"Stop moving."

I froze.

I didn't move, a little stunned at her voice. I couldn't think straight. I blamed—I couldn't *form* thoughts.

"Gabriél." Nobody said my name like that. Ever. It was a prayer on her lips.

I was breathing hard. "Did I hurt you?"

"Amor." My head snapped to her eyes. If I anchored her, she anchored me. "Let me hold you." Her eyes watered.

Oh.

Shit.

Nobody holds me. *Nobody.*

"I don't...I've never—" I was struggling. "No one—" I didn't know how to say it. I was currently feeling her walls clamping down on me hungrily. Viciously.

And I couldn't think inside of her but I knew one solid thing.

No one touched me during sex. *No one.*

It was my one fucking rule.

Hence the restraints.

But her eyes. I made her cry. Because right now those soft eyes were watering tearing up at me as she sniffled.

"Baby…"

"Amor. Let me go."

I closed my eyes those words sinking somewhere deep in me.

"Isobel—" I was struggling. "I *can't.*"

Tipping my head back I was struggling with myself. Struggling with every single sensation I could've ever had around her.

How did I tell her if she touched me when we fucked I would freak out? I didn't like anyone's hands on me.

"I can't."

I was breathing harder now as I drew out of her. I couldn't. I couldn't breathe. I couldn't look at her.

Since the day I met her, I knew if she gave me those eyes I wouldn't deny her anything. Wide-eyed and soft. I couldn't stay in her.

I couldn't think like this.

Earlier tonight I wanted to possess her and I had been worried about this exact moment. Now I felt terrified she might turn me away. Tell me I was being insane. Tell me I was too much.

Not enough for her.

I drew back snapping her wrists and turned away. Ashamed. Broken. Aware something inside of me was deeply fucked up and it had to stay that way.

I was terrified of my own emotions and terrified if she saw those parts of me she would judge me.

She would be disgusted. I couldn't breathe around it.

I heard her moving. She was untying herself. I heard the little sniffles as she did. The last I expected was her to reach for me. I stiffened.

When I was inside of her, my brain functioned differently. Now,

I tolerated it from all the other times as an onslaught of memories washed over me.

The smell of cheap perfume from my memories lingered in my lungs. I couldn't see straight as I kept my back to her.

"*Gabriel,*" she whispered. I felt her hands over me, her hair tickling me. *"Gabriel, mirame. Que te pasa, amor?"*

Her lips brushed my ear as her hand coasted around wrapping around me over my heart. Resting there. She pressed her lips into my neck and my face.

Until I felt my vision blur.

"I don't...I don't do that. I don't let people hold me. Nobody touches me in bed," I couldn't speak. Barely.

Sure, women sucked me off but even then?

I didn't stay, I tied up my women, fucked them for as long as we both needed and left.

That was my life.

"I've never—I've never been with a woman and let her hold me." Lies. That had been my earlier life. But I hadn't chosen it.

I couldn't even say it. "There is no love in it for me."

Isobel stilled behind me. She was quiet for a long moment.

"Someone...someone hurt you..." her voice was barely above a whisper. But it was hoarse, like it hurt her to say the words. "Like someone hurt me? Someone did that to you?"

Yes.

"No." But even I knew it sounded like a lie. I didn't want to say it. I didn't want to tell her.

I couldn't form the words that nobody knew. Nobody on this fucking planet knew what happened to me.

Gabriel Monroe was a ghost.

And he would stay that way.

"I don't wanna talk about it." My voice came out harder than intended.

"Someone hurt you," she whispered again with more force. "That's why you don't let me touch you when you are making love to me. You do this with other women...like this?"

Yes.

"There's no love in it for me." but even as I said it I felt her drawing back. Her hand moving from my heart where it was pressing its heat into it.

I didn't know why I turned over my shoulder to find her gloriously naked and rosy cheeked, her eyes on me in the moonlight watching me softly. "But there is love here."

And just like that she did this thing to my head where she took every single fucking rational thought I had or any thought I had— and obliterated it.

"There is love here." She motioned to herself and then me looking confused and surprised. Her eyes watered and I was turning around realizing I fucked up.

Again.

"Baby, don't cry like that—"

"No," she batted my hands away. "Why do you do this to me? Why would you—"

"I'm sorry, I'm sorry—" I didn't even know why I was fucking apologizing.

I just knew I was ready to repent with those eyes looking completely broken and I had my arms around her, hauling her tight to me.

"I'm sorry, it's *all* I know."

She blinked rapidly confused at me as she pushed back a little. Both of us on our knees as I wrapped my arms around her.

"I don't want that," she whispered, her eyes meeting mine. "I want my Gabriel." *Gabri-el.*

I didn't know who he was. The version of me she saw. I didn't know him. He didn't have a soul or an identity or a name. No family. Barely any money.

All I had was her.

That's all I have.

"You want me to fuck you like this?" I motioned to us. Her arms looping around my neck.

"No, I want you to love me like this."

I blinked as though it was a foreign concept.

"I want you to—" She turned pink. "I liked earlier, but I don't always want that. I want you."

Me? Who the fuck was I? I didn't say a word.

"I don't know how to," I admitted. "I have never—"

Her eyes softened even more. "Somebody hurt you." I didn't say a word as her eyes watered even more. "Someone hurt *you.*"

"Baby, don't cry like that," but it was too late. Isobel wrapped her arms around me and held me like I was hers.

She said something over my lips as she sobbed, and I didn't

understand. I told myself I'd pick up a fucking Spanish class. Several of them. I needed to understand her.

I brushed her hair back, laying us both down, tendrils all over my pillow like spilled ink. *Fuck her hair was pretty.*

"You don't like when I touch you, on top of me?" She whispered as I wiped her eyes.

I nodded feeling the words struggle to form after being a carefully constructed lie. "I don't like being touched when I fuck. Period. Nobody...I never..." I couldn't say it.

She took a shuddering breath. We were both laying on our sides now and I was watching her taking me in.

"And now?" She motioned between us. "What about now? Like this?"

I shook my head now an unfamiliar sensation cresting in my chest along with confusion. "I've never tried that."

Her eyes were shy then but there was a quiet strength in them I recognized from all our training sessions. "Do you want to?"

I mean...fuck yeah. I had never...not like this.

Not like her.

"I think I have to change the condom," I experimentally kissed her a little. Again. And again. And again. Until my body accepted it and she was softer with me. Almost tender. Like she knew.

She knew.

She had to know.

And she wasn't turning me away.

She's working with me.

"You still want me?" My hands were shaking cupping her face. Holding her steady. "You don't...you don't care..."

"I want you," she whispered back like it was impossible to not want me. "You are mine. I am yours."

And it was that simple?

"And you..." How did I even say it?

"I love you." Her eyes held mine. "I love you. I'm not going anywhere."

This time when I slid into her after changing the condom and making out with her like my life depended on it, I groaned. This was different. New. Her arms looped around me as she kissed me steadily.

"Are you okay?" She rubbed my hair back and I closed my eyes trying to inhale butterscotch and vanilla and not anything else. Not someone else.

I nodded but I was barely hanging on. I closed my eyes again breathing hard.

"Gabriel." I opened my eyes to find honey soft ones on me. "Look at my eyes. Focus on me."

And I realized what she was doing.

"I have you," she whispered and to my surprise, she moved her hips on me rocking in a subtle motion that was enough to make my breath catch. "I won't let anything happen to you."

"You have me?"

"I have you. Always."

Her eyes met mine and I hung on as Isobel clenched out on me rocking her hips in a way that made me see stars. "Stay with me."

I would. And I felt something else in me splice into place with her. Something waking up.

This fucking woman meets me every step of the way.

"Say it," I gasped moving with her. "*Say it.*"

"I love you."

"*Good girl,*" I loved how she clenched around me as I said it, I wasn't one to give praise but to her?

I pumped back in, loving the way she stretched open for me, her eyes low lidded and hazy.

I knew she'd be like this.

"You wanted to hold me?" Those eyes met mine. "Hold on then."

I sealed my mouth over hers.

Isobel's fingers tangled in my hair and I swallowed every single sweet cry as I moved. "I've got you, baby. Let me hear those pretty sounds."

And then, I made love to a woman for the first time in my life.

CHAPTER 22
GABRIEL

"Monroe, I need you in my office."

Koller called my phone and I stepped out of the new space I was in.

An underground center with plenty of offices clustered down long hallways.

A technological maze. It was modern, sleek, and professional. But it was new for me as well to navigate.

I poked my head into the office where my five man team sat.

Only one of those current team members, were the one I raked my eyes over first. In her pencil skirt and button-up I was going to die of blue balls before I made it out alive today.

"I'm going to Koller's, Sutton, you're in charge."

Claire Sutton rose, her blonde ponytail down to her waist bobbing as I left as she turned to Jeremy who turned red-faced on her.

My eyes raking in Isobel's sexy pencil skirt clad form one last time before I did. That damn dress shirt was stretched so tight across her breasts I was losing my mind as I stepped out of the first office.

I had two.

A private room for sensitive work. And a larger space where I could sit with my team.

Along with Isobel, Liam, and Jeremy?

I had two experienced techs working alongside them so they weren't alone and fucking up.

Besides Claire Sutton, I had a Vincent Grant.

Both of them were experienced techs and comfortable. They were also completely approachable.

Claire having a keen eye for detail while Vince got the bigger picture.

The two of them were helping the newbies get acclimated while I attended meetings and briefings.

And I wasn't completely SOL. We were a part of a bigger ops group, but this one was for them.

Isobel showed up behind Liam both of them in business casual that Monday morning. She winced a tiny bit in her flat shoes.

She'd texted me in the morning telling me she was too sore to wear anything else. And I'd smirked wearing that shit eating grin to work where I kept it to myself.

Nobody needed to know. Isobel and I had vowed to keep it to ourselves and to Liam.

The latter of whom made it look indecent with his shirt slightly unbuttoned enough and tie askew like he'd rolled out of bed.

I smirked as Claire sputtered at the sight of him when he'd taken off his shirt leaving him in a white t-shirt with his tattoos on full display.

He'd gotten bigger one done over the weekend and Claire had all but drooled.

His messy hair and ear and tongue piercings back in action along with darker rimmed glasses.

Women were already chattering about him.

"Sup Sutton," he shot her way his tongue piercing clicked against his teeth and Claire all but died.

Isobel and I shared a grin as Liam winked at us playing it up.

My eyes softened on her. *You look beautiful, baby.*

That's what I wanted to say.

But Liam beat me to it. "You look hot as fuck, Sutton."

"Don't think I won't shoot you," she shot back, but I saw how red she turned. Vincent had grinned at us being married with three kids.

Isobel looked edible in that pencil skirt. And I would know.

I'd spent the entire weekend inside of her. Making love to her like a menace. Slowly she coaxed me through my fears. She didn't ask any further questions.

Just kissed me steadily and let me love her in a way that helped both of us.

Neither one of us on top of the other but trying to find what worked for both of us. And what didn't work.

When I panicked, if I panicked, she was there by my side working me through it.

And now I couldn't stop thinking about her as I walked to Koller's office.

Once there, I knocked and entered clad in my black slacks and white shirt I tidied up nice.

"You wanted to see me, sir?"

"Monroe," Koller looked up looking miserable as always. His default expression was one where he looked pissed off but he meant well. He pulled up a file in the screen behind him. "You recognize the name Marcus Hagen?"

"No, sir."

The lights in his office cast a shadow across his face, and it just made him look more tired and weathered.

"Good, means we're doing our job," Koller looked at me with grey eyes. "The higher-ups in Intel heard of whispers, but it's only been whispers. No photos. No evidence. Guy's a fucking ghost. We think Marcus Hagen is an alias for someone bigger. Someone fucking with us."

I frowned sitting down. "What do you got?"

"Trails of money and bodies and blood. Six agents dead in the last six months—"

Jesus.

"We think Hagen's got an inside man or he's familiar with our ops enough to know when to spot an operative. He's got someone sharp on his team taking us out..."

Koller continued to talk to me and I saw image after image of bodies. Dead operatives. In all of them.

"Hang on," I asked him to go back. "What the fuck is that?"

I had seen it several times.

"This is a marker," Koller handed me a piece of paper from his desk and I looked down at a copy of a black card. With gold claw marks. "Hagen's got a team. There's no fucking way this guy works alone. No way. He's everywhere and he's too precise. We think he's got a contract killer working for him. The headshots are precise. Arrowhead bullets shattering everyone's skull."

I didn't know why my stomach turned a little as I looked down at the black card with gold claw marks.

"This is a calling card?"

Koller nodded looking grim. "Every single operative who gets it? Ends up dead. Arms dealing, drugs. Every thing you can imagine, but Hagen's primary source of income is information. We think he operates through other folks like proxies. Shell companies..."

And then he hit me with the real reason I was here.

"We have a small lead," his eyes met mine. "Small enough to make it bigger. One of our operatives settled into his role so much he made a few friends who said Hagen might've been someone elite. We're talking top ten percent of the globe. He thinks Hagen's associates are related to prime families. One of them being the Nash's, the Marchand's, the Spencers..." he listed several prominent family members in the globe.

"That's insane," I muttered. "You want me to build a profile with my team of who the likely contenders are?"

Koller nodded. "Between the two Santos siblings and Bradford, I suspect they can dig."

They would. They could.

But I had one question.

"What do you want when we find him?"

"We take 'em out," Koller said. "Intel says Hagen comes into the city once or twice a year. In a couple of months he should be swinging back this way from wherever he camps out at. We think whoever he is, he comes out does his business—and leaves."

"And you want to catch Hagen in the act?"

Koller nodded. But something about the look in his eyes made my stomach turn. "How dangerous is this assignment? I can't take them with me."

I can't take Isobel on a suicide mission.

Koller was quiet then. And he nodded. "I know. Which is why I'm hoping it never comes to that."

Me too. I was too.

"You've got the best team in years, Bradford and Isobel are solid for code, Liam's got an eye for digital footprints and deception, and

Sutton and Grant are there to make sure nobody dies. You guys can find it."

But once we did?

My team was…

"Leadership wants us on this?"

Koller nodded. "Says this is a career maker."

Or a career ender if I didn't do it.

"One thing is clear, make sure only your team knows. We don't know how Hagen gets information. We just know once we start telling people? Everyone gets taken out."

He motioned to the black card copy in my hand.

"If you even remotely see this? Run. Get your things. And find me. We'll get your new identities and get you out. Hagen isn't someone you want to mess with."

My throat worked as my anxiety spiked but my face remained composed.

"Yes, sir. Anything else?"

"Yeah, I got a few cases here…"

But the entire time I was suddenly aware I was holding a ticking time bomb.

CHAPTER 23
ISOBEL

I didn't make it through his front door.

He was on me in a heartbeat.

All controlled power.

Barely leashed and caged in rage from earlier.

His hands shook and trembled tearing at my skirt, my blouse the moment I stepped into the door.

"Gabriel—"

"This fucking skirt," he growled as he tore at it. Like it personally had offended him.

The sound of ripping material made me gasp at this version of Gabriel I had never seen before.

I knew what it was.

He was jealous.

On our walk home Liam and I had been walking out when I saw a group of guys staring at us.

I thought they were looking at Gabriel who was walking next to Vincent Grant our new team mate.

Both of them cut impressive figures with Vincent's blonde softer and friendlier than Gabriels icy king.

But then they'd said something 'feisty sexy Latinas' and all three men next to me had whipped their heads at them.

Vincent had cursed them out and one look from Gabriel had sent them scattering.

Liam wrapped an arm around me tugging me to him glaring at them like he was memorizing all their faces.

But I'd seen Gabriel's eyes. The way they moved over me as Liam had.

The way his hands had trembled. Liam had seen him too and gotten out of his way as I'd all but rushed out with Liam.

I could tell the sight of Liam's hands on me was enough to send Gabriel into a rage. Even if Liam was my brother, it didn't matter— I saw the possessive fury all over Gabriel's stunned face.

I quickly looked away from him.

Liam who had dropped me off at Gabriel's place knowing I would want to see him had been concerned.

Now? I knew why.

I gasped, unable to stop Gabriel as he tore at my shirt, my bra.

I braced my hands on the wall as he ripped my stockings to pieces leaving me exposed.

Nothing was safe around this man.

"Gabriel." I couldn't even tell him to calm down because I felt the same. The desperation he felt. I needed him to know it was okay. I was his.

I heard the tear of a condom and he was groaning as he shoved into me. Tried to.

I whimpered immediately wiggling my hips. "Too much."

"I gotcha, baby. Spread your legs a little wider."

I obeyed in nothing but my bra tugged down, my breasts obscenely exposed, and my panties and stockings ripped. I could only imagine the sight I made.

It only fueled my need for him some more.

He slid in further and I moaned as my hips worked back on his length.

"That's my good girl, look at you struggling to take all of me. Did you want me all day, baby?"

Dio. I couldn't think when he spoke like that.

"I always want you."

It wasn't just out of character, when we were in bed the silent quiet strong Gabriel became my man. Now? Possessed like this with his green eyed monster? He was completely different.

Every single inch of him felt like he was claiming me.

Pushing deeper now I felt noises leave me, gasps and moans as he slid further, one hand wrapping around my throat, the other at my clit. I squealed as he rubbed circles and sank even further.

"Why are you so big?"

His chuckle was dark. "You can take me, baby. I've felt you all weekend."

I could still feel him.

Even though I was a tiny bit sore still, I ached for him.

In a way I couldn't even describe. Liam had taken one look at my disheveled self in Gabriel's shirt and smirked.

I groaned as he bottomed out and gave me every last inch of him.

My head tipping back onto his shoulder as he molded himself to my back.

My palms flattened on the wall pressing down as his fingers worked my clit. That sensation was growing tighter and tighter inside of me.

"*Gabriel.*"

"I know, baby. I can feel it. Let it come."

I whimpered as he squeezed my throat tighter and worked his hips in a slow grind as I imploded.

My orgasm rocked through me as Gabriel continued to move his hips in a way that drew out every single wave after wave.

I cried out his name as my legs shook wildly. His hand at my throat moved, wrapping around my waist to catch me from falling.

"Nobody gets to see you like this," his voice was so low I almost didn't hear it. "Not a single fucking person get's this. Not like me."

There was no reason for him to be jealous.

But he was. I hadn't ever seen this side to him. But right now it was out in full force.

"Gonna use this pussy how I need it now, baby." His voice was dark sin and velvet. "Going to make sure you never forget I was here."

I would never, but words left me as he began a pounding brutal vicious rhythm I didn't make it through.

"Such a good girl," he growled as I screamed through another orgasm. My eyes rolled back as he fucked deep. "That's it, show me how much you love it."

Dio. He was determined to kill me like this.

"Gabriel, please." I held onto him as he bent me over more and my hips angled up. In this position I was gone, seeing stars with the way he hit me so deep.

Every thrust made any coherent thought virtually impossible.

"Gonna take care of this little spot," he groaned gripping my hips harder than ever and setting a pace that felt ruthless.

I screamed at the bite of pain with every thrust.

The sensation borderline insane with how good it felt. Between pleasure and just a little too much.

"So." Thrust. "Fucking. Thrust. *"Perfect."*

My screams echoed off the walls.

I shattered around him again and again and again until I couldn't tell if I was having multiple mini-orgasms or just one big one that wouldn't stop. I turned to liquid and I felt like I was falling.

I couldn't hold still and he wrapped both of his arms around me, holding me steady for him as he bit down on my neck. My head fell back as he took from me.

I felt the moment he came with a deep groan.

It took long moments for him to calm down. His hands coming up to rub my nipples. I moaned.

"Not again," I whispered feeling him semi-hard. "You just finished."

"Again."

I clenched at the sound of that word.

"I won't be able to walk tomorrow."

"Perfect, I can carry you in." His satisfaction was possessive as he tugged at my nipples and I all but squealed.

A low laugh left me at the thought of us ever coming out with our relationship.

Especially after today when he'd lost it.

I moaned as he slid out of me and heard the tear of another condom.

I almost slid to the floor but he picked me up and carried me into the bedroom where I knew he would destroy me.

~

HOURS LATER, I WAS MUSH.

I couldn't think let alone speak.

He'd taken me two more times and now I ached. My inner

thighs ached. Every part of me shivered and trembled. Hypersensitive to him.

Gabriel was laying over me kissing every part of me he could reach. Kissing everywhere he had to. Like he was worried I wouldn't be his. Like he wanted to make sure I was still here.

Still his.

The fury had faded sometime on the third round when he'd growled that I was his girl over and over until I'd come so hard I'd almost blacked out.

"Amor," I pushed at his head too sensitized for anything else. I laced my finger into his hair bringing his lips up to kiss him. He'd cleaned us both up but right now he still had a wild look on his face. "Shhh."

I kissed him over and over.

Soothing him.

Calming him down.

"No me voy a ningún lado," I whispered. "I'm not going anywhere. Breathe for me, amor. Tell me what's wrong. Is it about your assignment? *Por qué estás tan asustado?*"

His breathing slowed. "What does that last one mean?"

"Are you scared?"

His nod was slow. But he was. "It's dangerous. I fucking hate people staring at you like that. Saying anything to you. Like you're not ten times smarter. Brighter."

I let out a breath as his breathing slowly steadied under my touch. I rubbed his back.

Gabriel spoke softly to the team.

After he had told us we had multiple cases including the one about Marcus Hagen. He'd shown us all the card to look out for.

We knew now. Sutton and Grant had been fine but Liam had cast Gabriel a look of concern.

I didn't understand it until now.

"You think once we find Hagen, we'll be sent out on the assignment?"

He nodded. "I can't let you go."

I frowned unable to sit up. "Gabriel. Let me? I am my own person."

Now he moved rising up a little, pale eyes eerily on me. "Hagen is a suicide mission. You and I both know, you and Liam and Jeremy will not be going."

166

My anger flared at those winter blue eyes. "And you will?"

His head tipped down. "I have to."

Now *I* was pissed. *"Are you insane?"* Winter blue eyes met mine a little wide. "Just because you love me like you own me, doesn't mean you do. I make my own choices. I would not let you go alone. Ever. I will come with you. Always. You don't get to decide these things for me."

I saw a flare of something in his eyes he didn't recognize in me as he looked at me.

"Isa—"

"No," I pushed at his chest my fury evident in the way I touched him. "You cannot just ship me off to where you think it is safe. I heard you. If you go out alone, Hagen has eyes everywhere. Just because you go does not mean Liam or me are safe. What if he comes after us and you going to find him in the city is a...how you say—"

"A distraction," Gabriel paled.

"Si, but if I come with you, I can protect you—"

"Isa—"

"I can take care of you!" I held onto him. "No, you are not going to stop me. Because I would not stop you! I would go with you. We can protect each other—" I broke off at his expression. "You do not think I am good enough?"

"No," he was all over me but I saw something in his eyes. "Isobel, listen to me. I saw the bodies of six operatives in six months bloody and their brains completely blown out. Whoever these guys are on Hagen's team—they're professionals and every single time I looked at those photos, I kept seeing you or Liam in every single one."

His face was pale, his eyes eerily bright now strikingly so.

I held his face in my hands as he spoke. "Isa, I saw them. I knew one of them. I trained with these people. And they're gone. Koller says every single time Hagen kills someone, he has to put the entire family into WITSEC. Do you know what that means? Koller has to make them vanish. They can't exist because Hagen doesn't stop at the operative. He takes out everyone."

His hands gripped my arm. "That combined with those fuckers hitting on you? I felt like a grenade went off in me."

I shook my head holding onto him. "Gabriel, whatever happens. Whatever happens. We will face it together even if my stomach is turning right now and I am scared—I cannot and I will not let you go alone. Ever."

My eyes met winter blues head on. "Ever. Entiendes?"

"That means understood?"

I nodded. "*Juntos*. Together. You don't go without me, not ever." He mouthed the word in Spanish back to me. I smiled softly. "You are learning?"

He ducked his head embarrassed. "I've got a shit accent."

I giggled at that. "Try with me. Tu y yo, para siempre. You and me, always. Is not just you alone ever."

Gabriel tried to mouth the words slowly. "I can teach you," I whispered. "Liam wants to bring us food. He says he thinks you need a burger."

"I need six, baby."

I laughed into his kisses. "Practice."

He sighed as he laid back on top of me even if my heart raced with the assignment we'd gotten today.

Worrying about it would do me no good.

Even if we found the information about Marcus Hagen we needed—there was no guarantee the Agency would send us or another team.

Even if I hoped it was another team.

Something dark in my mind emerged at the thought of Hagen.

Something familiar like those nightmares I had before I met Gabriel.

And I was worried deep down.

"I will tell Liam to bring six burgers."

"Nothing vegan."

"Nothing vegan, amor."

I giggled as he grumbled about vegan food Sutton was already bringing into the office again. Even if I felt the shadow in my vision now.

I felt something wrong.

I just didn't know what it was.

~

A FEW WEEKS LATER I WAS JOGGING ON A FAMILIAR TRAIL. MY MIND was spinning as I finished my run.

The hairs on the back of my neck stood up and my stomach turned with unease.

Liam and I had been working together to piece together with Jeremy who Marcus Hagen was.

Who he was connected to. He clearly had multiple alias's. But if he was a wealthier man who could he be?

We had been working over weeks now and I was sometimes with Gabriel and sometimes staying with Liam who'd been adjusting.

He still flirted shamelessly with Sutton but I knew he wouldn't sleep with her. Not when she was on our team.

He was helping Jeremy talk to Cathy his crush. And my relationship with Gabriel was blossoming more and more. The nights filled with searing pleasure and during the days off, I spent it wrapped around him.

We traded movies, music, TV shows, and I sometimes caught him studying Spanish. It was his second language now he said and he wanted to learn.

Even if he had an accent.

I giggled at it but I encouraged him to keep going.

Love with Gabriel was all-consuming.

"Teach me some phrases," he said, his eyes sparkling with curiosity one night after he'd finished inside of me.

He was a lazy lion kissing my face all over.

"I'm trying, but nothing compares to you." He paused, then added. "You speak Portuguese and Spanish?"

Why did he talk like that?

I nodded, keeping my knowledge of Latin and French to myself. I didn't like to brag, as Liam always reminded me.

"What should I teach you?" I asked, my heart fluttering as his gaze met mine with open admiration.

"Anything," he replied, his voice soft and eager. Winter blues softening with my smile. He was...changing. Something was happening to Gabriel in front of my eyes.

It was like watching him blossom like a flower. Something new in his eyes now. He laughed more. He smiled eagerly. He did things with me and Liam who slowly was warming up to him now.

A playful smile tugged at my lips. "How about I teach you some phrases?"

His grin lit up his features, boyish handsomeness radiating from every angle. "You're not going to teach me a curse word for 'I love you,' are you?"

The phrase rolled off his tongue, making my heart skip a beat.

"No," I said quickly, looking away to process the warmth spreading through my chest at his words. "Repeat after me."

I began to recite sentences slowly, allowing him to follow along and gently correcting his accent with each attempt.

He grabbed his phone. He was always recording our conversations and I knew he would replay them.

"I can listen to your voice forever. I need to remember this."

I laughed. I continued.

"Repeat after me: *Mi nombre es Gabriel.*"

He followed, his accent endearingly imperfect. *My name is Gabriel.*

I like to protect people. I smiled, appreciating his effort.

"What does that mean?" he asked, curiosity gleaming in his eyes.

I couldn't resist teasing him. "You smell funny."

He shook his head, his eyes lit up with joy, a knowing grin on his face. "I can tell when you lie." I laughed.

"I think I need kisses now," I said, leaning in. He captured my mouth for a brief, passionate moment, but I stayed focused.

I make Isobel cry when I'm sweet. I felt my heart swell as he continued. *I'm the best man in the world. I carry love in my soul.*

"What does that mean?" he asked, a playful glint in his eye.

"I am a couch potato," I replied, barely containing my laughter.

He shook his head, grinning. "How do I know you're not telling me terrible things?"

His eyes met mine, and I couldn't help but feel a rush of affection. "You won't tell me, will you?"

"One more," I said, and he sighed dramatically.

In that moment, I realized I was falling in love with this disarmed version of him.

I am an amazing man capable of incredible things.

He repeated the words.

One day I will be everything I dreamed of.

I have the biggest heart in the world.

As he spoke, he looked at me, his eyes searching mine.

"What about my heart?"

I rolled my eyes, trying to hide the depth of my emotions. "It's the size of a very small bean."

I put my fingers together, mimicking a tiny space.

He laughed easily, and then he moved closer grabbing me easily. "You're not complaining about my—"

I put my hand over his mouth loving the way his eyes gleamed. His hands moved my legs and he slid into me.

Or tried to.

I put one hand on his chest, pushing him back to sit. I could tell I surprised him, when I wrapped my legs on either side of his waist with him. "Sit back."

He did, never taking his eyes off me.

Straddling him, lifting myself up to sliding myself—"I need help."

His lips quirked as he grabbed my ass, his legs flexing under me, and shoved up. I gasped. Just like *that*.

I panted, feeling the heady energy between us, as I immediately began rocking, my arms looped around his neck, keeping our mouths locked, as I worked on him.

He was stiff in my arms—I paused, his eyes were closed and his jaw clenched. "I'm trying, don't stop, keeping going."

"Amor—"

"Just move."

"*Gabriel.*" When his eyes popped open, I didn't recognize him. Something passed through him, cold desolate.

"Is this…" I made a move to get off him. "Gabriel, is this…" I didn't need him to say it. I knew.

This is how it happened.

Gabriel never talked about it. But he was slowly breaking through to me touching him in bed over me.

Slowly. It took some discomfort for him, but he wanted me to touch him.

But I hadn't ever been on top of him like this.

I felt sick. As I went to scramble off he held me tight.

His eyes bright and pale on mine. "Talk to me. Say something. *Anything*, just talk to me. *Please.*"

And just like another part of me broke.

"*Amor*," I held his face feeling my eyes water. And I spoke my truth in the only way I knew how.

Whispering over his lips as he began to move his hips. Words fell from me. Words of love. For him. For us. Something shifting inside of me with his love.

"I want to erase her," he said. "I want to forget, replace it with you..." *I want that too.*

I understood, as I began to move with him, holding him, my eyes never leaving his eyes.

I smiled softly as I began to move, holding his face in my hands.

"Focus on me. My eyes, Amor. *I love you...*"

I told him all the ways I wanted him, and worked on him until he groaned, and I trembled with my release.

I love you, I love you. I love you.

CHAPTER 24
GABRIEL

"This is our first *unofficial* official date."

Isobel looked proud as I sat across from her in the cherry red booth. I thought she might love this diner I found driving around the area.

I laughed low. That sensation was easier with her.

Everything was easier with her.

I couldn't put my finger on her. Something about this girl got under my skin. And stayed there. And I loved it.

"Amor, this place looks good. Did you find it on your own?"

"I thought you might like it."

Her eyes twinkled as she smile, her canines sharp making her look mischievous. My girl. *Goddamn, she was pretty.*

"I love it," she smiled up at me then.

"Do you know what you want?" I asked her. Right as I did a waft of cheap perfume and hairspray came over to my side.

"Can I take your order, baby cakes?"

I turned to find a woman who look like she gotten lost on her way to a Vegas show. About thirty decades ago.

She had platinum blonde hair tease to define gravity and make up that was so bright. I could see it from the moon.

Isobel smiled up at her. "Not yet. How is your day?"

"Not as good as my tits I'll tell you that." I pressed my fist to my mouth as Isobel giggled, she did that fucking laugh. "It was so cold this morning I couldn't even feel my nipples. But the boys like it so who cares amiright? I'm telling ya babycakes, you should appreciate those tits while you got 'em..." As she spoke I saw Isobel's face flaming.

And I was suddenly wondering if I made the right choice.

And I sat there stunned as Isobel laughed. "It's so cold I don't know how anyone lives on this coast."

She did get cold often.

I had gotten her a pair of blue gloves and a matching scarf. Well, she'd picked it out. She said the color reminded her of my eyes.

Her new favorite color was the color of my eyes.

I watched as she tugged on gloves when the weather dipped below sixty.

Her fingers were always cold. Part of the reason why I'd given her my jacket and the other part in due to her nipples being diamond hard and everyone else salivating over her.

"Oh honey as soon as I find me a nice younger man to settle down with? I'm out of this shit show." Her eyes drifted over to me. "I mean you're younger but with the way you're staring at her like you want to pork her right here I'd say you're taken."

I think I swallowed wrong as I coughed Fiona continued as though I wasn't there to Isobel who laughed delighted. At least she liked it because I was turning several shades of red.

"Babycakes, I didn't know you liked them tall and frosty. So what will you two have? Chocolate chip pancakes or mushroom omelette today with a side of bacon?"

That was oddly specific. Isobel hadn't been here before but somehow the damn waitress had guessed my girls favorite foods.

"That sounds good. Can we get that number 1, with pancakes, chocolate chip, please?" Isobel said, seemingly deciding on her order.

"And you, Frosty?" Fiona asked, turning to me.

"I'll take the cinnamon roll pancakes."

Fiona looked up at me, a hint of surprise in her eyes. "Hmm, maybe I was wrong about you. Maybe underneath all that, you're just a cinnamon roll."

I shook my head. "No ma'am."

My voice was still as cold as ice. Fiona cackled, and Isobel smiled sheepishly at her as she refilled our coffee cups.

As Fiona walked away, she hummed a familiar tune.

"Is that—" I began.

"Frosty the Snowman," Isobel confirmed with a giggle. "You were right this place is good."

She laughed at my expression and I couldn't stop smiling from grinning ear to ear with her.

"So tell me, how was your meeting?" Her eyes sparkled as I talked and when she looked at me, I was the center of her world. Her entire universe. I was falling for this girl. Not slowly. Careening. And I didn't give a shit.

Her eyes met mine as I finished. "Liam and I are working on something but you have to promise me you won't tell anyone." She held out her pinky. I took it easily linking our hands together as Fiona brought out breakfast. "Liam was building it quietly, but he just made it perfect. And you will see her today. I want to take you to meet it."

"Meet who?"

Isobel leaned in her eyes wide and excited. "Liam and I built an AI. Artificial Intelligence inside of his computer. Her name is Oracle. After me. You know we have call signs?"

I did. I was Apollo. She was Oracle. Liam was Pluto.

It was fitting Isobel had picked Oracle after the Oracle of Delphi without even knowing my call-sign. When she had she'd kissed me surprised.

"Liam designed her in college, but he spent years getting her off the ground."

"Alone?" I blinked at the sheer magnitude of that.

She nodded. "He used my voice to make her talk. So she sounds like me."

I grinned ear to ear. "A replacement girlfriend."

"*Gabriel.*"

"Right, sorry," but the smile played on my lips. Isobel would get jealous too.

Once we went to the mall which I fucking hated and she was trying on a bunch of these tiny dresses which drove me insane.

A gaggle of women passing me stopped to ask me for my number.

I just pretended to not speak English until Isobel had come out in a red number that blew me away.

I had slipped out with. "Baby—" and froze when the girls frowned at me. I herded her back into the dressing rooms to her frown.

175

We'd spent the next thirty minutes with her riding my cock like her life depended on it.

Turned out a jealous Isobel was just as bad as a jealous me.

I refocused as she talked about Oracle when Fiona brought the food out.

"...Liam says he still has a few things he has to fix, but he wants us to go check it out. He's been secretly working on her for years."

"Why didn't he say anything?" I shook my head. "The Agency would love this shit."

"Gabriel, that is why he will never share it. Liam never wanted to use Oracle for spying or anything. It's a program to find missing people and track assets. One day I think Liam wants to get out of the Agency. He says he wants to start his own martial arts studio. But I think he wants to start a security company."

"Liam wants to start a security company? Like private sector?"

"Si, he has a name and *everything*. He wants to call it Titan Security. He wants to have people working for him while he sits in the shadows..." she explained Liam wanted to secretly have Oracle as their baseline and she wanted to help him with it.

"Liam wants Oracle for his use only?"

Isobel had pride in her eyes as she smiled.

"At Titan. I saw his notes. I know he thinks about it. He won't say anything though."

That was pretty impressive. I didn't know Liam Santos had goals like that.

"Titan Security has a nice ring to it."

"It does. Liam is good at this. I only help him sometimes, but we both put Oracle together and now she is almost finished. You can come see her. I know Liam wants us there. Sometimes I think he wants me to work with him. Liam says when he does, he wants everyone to be able to speak Spanish so I won't struggle."

That was sweet of him.

Fiona came by with our food as she told me about Liam and helped me practice some words in Spanish pointing at the food.

"I love pancakes for breakfast," she looked at me with a serious expression. "Is the only time I get to eat cake."

"You have a sweet tooth, baby."

"But it's good."

"I know it's good, you fucking love it."

"Yes, but it's delicious. You should have some."

"I will. We have to go see Liam after this?" I asked curious. "Did you want to stay there today instead of with me?"

Her eyes were twinkling. "I always want to stay with you Gabriel."

"Then move in with me."

Her smile fell. "*Como?*"

I shrugged not phased by it even if my heart was hammering in my ribcage.

This was a huge deal for her.

"Move in with me. You practically live there anyway."

Her eyes were wide as she watched me and Fiona refilled our cups of coffee. I watched Isobel though.

"Live with you?"

I nodded. Why did she look like that?

"And leave...Liam?"

Oh.

That was why. I didn't know what to say. If Liam was attached to her, she was equally attached to him in their own ways.

She thought about it a little looking almost heartbroken and I felt something aching in my chest at the idea of asking her to leave him.

Because this is what he had been afraid of.

Taking away a piece of his heart. Even more.

"He's going to hate me even more, isn't he?"

She shook her head, the light bouncing off the raven color turning it blue. This woman looked like a goddess compared to me.

"He does not hate you now."

Really? At my expression her eyes met mine.

"He doesn't hate you, Gabriel. He's my best friend. Maybe he can be yours."

I'd never seen it like that. Being friends with Liam instead of... whatever it was with him.

"Just consider it. Be his friend instead of his enemy. I think you'd like him a lot. He likes you."

"No way."

"*Way.*" She smiled teasing me. "Okay, I will move in with you. We can tell Liam. But you and Liam must work on getting along. When you marry me he will be your brother too, you know?"

I sputtered on my coffee then. "When?"

She nodded matter-of-fact with a sly look on her face. "Si, *when*. I don't have pancakes with just anybody, Gabriel—"

I started laughing. *This fucking woman.*

Her eyes were warm on mine and for another second—everything stopped existing but her. Everything. Bright eyes. Dark hair. That mischievous smile.

She always looked like she was causing mischief. And I'd protect her through it.

I felt another sensation blossom in me.

A normal wife. A normal life.

"When." I hid my smile in my coffee mug as we both laughed low. "Is there a code in the pancakes for how I should propose?"

She laughed harder. "No. As long as you don't make it a show."

"I was thinking about blasting it in the sky—"

"No, Gabriel."

I laughed. Gabri-el. Nobody made my name sound like they were happy to say it. Everyone gave me orders. People came to me for a job. I was responsible. Dependable. Good at what I did.

She was the only one who wanted me to be me.

Just me.

Gabriel.

Nothing else.

A normal wife.

For me?

The question didn't seem impossible anymore. With Isobel, everything felt possible.

Like I had…a life.

An identity.

Memories.

I was a *somebody*.

Nobody made me sound like I was just there. To be.

Maybe I had started out as the son of a nobody.

But I wouldn't be the husband of one.

I'd be hers.

And that alone was enough for me to know what I felt.

∾

FIONA HAD LAID OUT THE CHECK ON THE TABLE AT SOME POINT AND I saw Isobel grab it.

"Uh-uh," I shook my head. "I said I'd marry you, that means I pay all the bills."

She turned a bright red. "No, Gabriel, not this one. It's just one time." For some reason was turning a flaming shade of red. "It's not a big deal."

"Yes, it is." I wasn't about to have her pay for any of it. Not when I made more money than her. "Baby, give me the check."

"I cannot." She hid it in her pocket.

And I felt myself rising to the challenge.

"I will take you in the fucking truck," I whispered low for her ears only. "And you will not come. Not now. Not at home. Not for a week."

She gasped holding her hand to her chest at my smug smile.

"Okay, but—" she broke off holding her hands out in a staying motion. "But you cannot be angry."

Why would I be angry?

I looked at the check Isobel whipped out of her pocket. Satisfaction turned to curiosity at the zero balance.

"Why is it zero? When did you pay it?"

Her lip biting told me a completely different story.

"Isobel."

"Don't be upset." She held out her hands again. "It was a long time ago..."

And then I sat there my jaw progressively dropping as Isobel started explaining.

"You've been here before?" I gaped at her. "That's why Fiona knew your order. You and Liam—" I broke off as she rushed to explain.

"One day, she was crying, so Liam asked her why. He always flirts with all the women. You know?"

"I do know."

"So Liam asked Fiona and she said her ex-boyfriend stole her dog."

Oh. Motherfucker. I *knew* where this was going.

As she explained my jaw was on the floor. I was sweeping pieces of it as I whispered in complete horror what she was saying as she rapidly explained half in English, half Spanish, and one hundred percent terrified of me. As she should be in that moment.

When she finished I didn't know if I wanted to spank her ass raw or fuck her right there for that shit.

I pinched the bridge of my nose. "You and Liam broke into someone's house on the second week of training—"

"We did not break in. I distracted him, Liam snuck in—"

"Through an open window. On the second floor." I blew out a breath. "To steal back a Weiner dog—"

"Gretchen," Isobel bit her lip nervously. "Her name is Gretchen. From *Mean Girls*, you know the movie? Stop trying to make fetch happen?"

"Stop what?" I blinked confused. "Baby, I'm trying to process how to get your ass in the car and not tear into you right now."

Isobel turned a violent red which would no doubt be the same shade as her ass tonight.

Forget a week.

She'd be lucky if she came at all. I was going to light her up.

"Do you have any idea how dangerous that was?"

"It was fine," she insisted not realizing how much fucking trouble that little squirming was getting her into. "Liam ran in, grabbed Gretchen, I distracted him—"

"How?"

I didn't like the way she said it. I knew her tells. I knew when my girl was lying. She squirmed some more. Biting her lip.

I stopped breathing.

"How. Did. You. Distract. Him?" My voice was deadly soft.

Because my girl was close to being eaten up right now.

Her throat worked and she hung her head. "It was only the second week of training! Remember you were the enemy!"

If I wasn't harder than steel right now, I would've laughed.

But nothing was getting her out of this.

I didn't say a word as I watched her ears turn red a sure fire sign she was going to destroy my sanity as she mumbled.

"I...dressed up in a costume with feathers."

What?

My brain was executing a system malfunction as I listened to my girlfriend rattle off an explanation that defied logic.

"It had a wig! It was blonde! I swear nobody knew me. So I go and I steal this costume. I dress up. I distract him. I did a dance." She did a weird wiggle I covered my mouth not to laugh at. "And then Liam takes the dog. I ran. And now...we eat for free."

This woman is insane and I love her.

I fucking love her.

180

She motioned to the check.

"I did nothing wrong, Gabriel. I saved a dog."

I was sitting there covering my mouth because I didn't know whether or not to laugh or bend her over right now and spank her.

I had been trained to torture, infiltrate, assassinate, and steal.

Nothing had prepared me in my training for a singular Isobel Santos.

Not a single fucking thing.

It took every single ounce of my blood to compose myself.

"You and Liam conducted a black-ops raid on a civilian's the second week of training. And now you two eat for free at this diner that you acted surprised when I brought you to."

No wonder she loved it so much.

This woman was going to be chaos and I'd love every bit of her.

At my expression she paled.

"Gabriel, you cannot tell anyone. Please. I did not even think you would ever come here and I did not see Fiona on shift."

"That's even worse! If I didn't catch you red-handed you would've gotten away."

"I am not a criminal, Gabriel."

"No, you're a rebel."

"What?"

"Someone who breaks the rules in a non-traditional way."

Someone who made me love that she made me question every single thing I knew in life about right and wrong. Someone who made me grateful for taking a chance on her out of everyone.

"Si," she nodded seriously. "If the rules are stupid, why would I follow them?"

I gaped as a wild noise escaped me.

Something in me broke loose.

Snapping into pieces.

And I realized I was laughing. Failing to hold it back as I couldn't stop. Once it started I realized how ridiculous it was.

Her eyes went wide. "Forget it. Now you are scaring me."

I couldn't stop laughing. The more I laughed covering my mouth or trying to hold back Isobel looked uneasy. I couldn't stop it.

She kept this from me for weeks.

Months. We'd been together for fucking months.

Since the second week of training. Her and Liam had been

181

fucking sneaking around. Running fucking ops on dogs and civilians while I was yelling at her to hydrate.

"Gabriel. You are very scary right now."

I don't know why that made me laugh even harder.

My grin was in place when I said. "Get your things, baby. Get in the car."

She shook her head. "No, you don't look very nice right now."

"You don't say?"

She squirmed again. "But you are angry."

"Are you kidding me right now? I'm not angry. I'm so fucking *pissed*," I leaned back. "You stole the dog, back?"

A shy grin lit her face then. She was so fucking proud.

Sweet brave girl.

"He's not cute, but Fiona loves him. And it was all smooth."

And then she did that little thing again.

Oh. Baby. I fucking knew when she was lying.

Did she just squirm? I looked at her eyes. "I know when you're lying. What happened?"

Isobel shivered at my tone and something dark unfurled in my veins then, the ice settling into the cracks with her name on it.

"*No.*"

"Baby, you should never become a spy. *What did he do?*"

Her big brown eyes widened. "You can't kill him, *Gabriel.*"

Watch me.

I already knew Fiona's name and her stupid dog's. I could find her ex-boyfriend tonight. Have him strung up in—"No, come back."

I blinked, returning to her eyes, looking almost sorry she'd told me the story. I wasn't sorry. It had been a good laugh until I realized something happened to her.

"*What happened?*" I hoped I sounded better than I felt.

"Nothing—"

I was going to kill him.

"Did he touch you?" And I know the way she didn't meet my eyes and shook her head. I knew every micro-expression. I knew her inside and out.

"No, it's fine."

"He *did.*" I took a deep breath, struggling to process that she'd put herself in danger because of her heart.

Even with Liam there, he was robbing a fucking dog for an old lady, and yet—all I felt was ice in my veins.

"Oh no, please—"

"Do you have any idea how reckless that was?"

Her eyes flared at my tone. "Yes, but I would've done it to help Fiona. She's sweet old lady—"

"She sent you into a situation where God knows what could've happened to you."

I was going to strangle Fiona behind the diner, and then go after her boyfriend, shoot him in the head—*no, that's too kind.*

No, I needed space.

Plastic wrap.

Knives.

A chainsaw. A hacksaw.

"I put myself in that situation. I came here one morning, and she looked so sad. I asked Liam for his help. I came up with a plan. It was my fault. If you're going to be angry with anyone, be angry with me."

"I'm not angry with Isobel, I'm downright livid. Now get your things."

This woman is going to destroy me.

CHAPTER 25
ISOBEL

"Gabriel...we can talk about this."

"Not another word." His voice was dangerously low.

I texted Liam letting him know we would be there the next day.

It was afternoon when we made it home.

Gabriel was silent on the drive home.

I was a little afraid. Just enough. More excited because so far the things he had done to me?

I knew he would never hurt me.

But I was a little nervous.

And I got out the car quickly walking into the house tearing off my coat leaving me in my date night dress under.

He was on me a second later his mouth moving over mine.

"You went and came up with this plan?" Winter blue eyes met mine.

"Yes." I stood my ground, refusing to be intimidated by his intensity, even if my stomach knew—I was in danger. I was.

"And then you went and distracted him so Liam could sneak in—"

"Yes!"

"And you were doing whatever the fuck it was that show girls do—"

"Yes." I met winter blue head on.

"And that's when he touched you?"

"*Yes!* What do you want me to say, Gabriel? He groped me and touched my ass, so I threatened to shoot him!"

I huffed out a breath and walked away from him. I was so...I didn't know what I felt. My skin prickled. My body clenched waiting for him to do something to me. Anything at all.

And then I froze, my hand on the bedroom doorknob, ready to rip off my clothes in a fit of rage.

And then I realized what I had done.

Oh. He is scary.

I had just admitted what happened.

He had played me, maneuvered me into a corner until I had no choice but to confess.

Before I could even react, I felt his strong arms like iron wrapping around my waist. I squealed lifted up into his arms.

My stomach dropped as my world tilted and he had me over his shoulder.

"Gabriel!"

"Not another fucking word out of you."

My stomach turned as the blood rushed to my head and I caught the way the sun faded a little as he dropped me onto his bed.

Our bed.

Now completely at his mercy, bathed in minimal sunlight streaming in from our curtains, Gabriel yanked his sweater off.

The white sheets felt like silk this morning but now I felt every nerve ending agonized watching him, his golden skin in the sunlight.

Pushing up on my elbows I was ready to argue.

Ready to say anything until he grabbed one ankle and dragged me down the bed.

I squealed.

He looked like an angry avenging angel ready to take me—the mortal woman he'd found on Earth.

His icy pale eyes blazing on his face. His hands moved gripping my legs first. I didn't even see the restraints at the end of the bed.

"I'm going to teach you another lesson today," his voice was gruff as he leaned over me and my head tipped back as his fingers worked at my panties, nearly tearing at them.

"You always ruin my panties."

His smirk was devilish. "I'm going to ruin a lot more than that."

And then without looking away, I didn't know how he knew his head dipped and he took my lips as I felt something cinch around my ankles.

I looked down and realized Gabriel had left ties on the edge of the bed. Tucked away but there.

Nobody ever visited us and if Liam did, he wouldn't exactly find the bedroom the place to visit.

Gabriel clamped them around my ankle right now and I felt him pressing me back, his tongue thrusting into me and I moaned around him.

"You still taste like candy," he whispered, gruff and husky over my lips as he took me down to the bed, his hands moving to undo my dress.

I panted as he trailed his lips down my body now that I couldn't move properly.

Dragging the fabric lower until it exposed my bra, Gabriel moved his mouth over my skin.

I was shaking already as he drew something out from his dresser.

He was going to drive me crazy.

I whimpered as he grabbed his belt.

Laying there helpless, I felt Gabriel move to straddle my face.

I gasped as he rubbed his cock on my lips, long and thick and hard I moaned around the tip.

"Suck."

I obeyed. Hungrily. Taking him deeper, my lips stretched wide to accommodate his size. His length.

He barely fit halfway into my mouth and I struggled.

"There you go," he kneeled in front of me as I felt his hand move. One hand gripping my hair and holding me down and he sank deeper. "Relax your throat, baby. Relax...there you go."

I gagged and gasped breathing through my nose. And he stayed there twisting his torso a bit to tug my nipple clamps.

The dual sensation made me see stars, and I felt him sinking even deeper.

I moaned and he drew out letting me gasp for air.

As he tugged my clamps, Gabriel began fucking my mouth. Over and over. Sinking deeper. Until it became easier.

"I knew you'd be like this," his voice was sin wrapped in rough octaves over my skin. "So fucking pretty taking my cock so deep. Deeper, baby, be a good girl and take it deeper."

186

I obeyed whimpering helpless on him.

My hands gripped the sheets at my side as he fucked my throat coming down and pumping his hips into it. I moaned not realizing how much I'd love him like this.

The dual sensations warred in my body each one making me hungrier for him. More and more.

I gasped when he pulled out crooning. "I wanna see how long you can hold back for me, baby."

What? I felt light-headed as he drew out completely and slid off me coming to lay down next to me.

The belt was still in his hands and he didn't move.

"What's your safe word?"

I could barely think, my mind filled with mist and smoke rising like tendrils all around me, I licked my lips. "Snowman."

It was the only warning I had as he brought the belt down over my pussy. I gasped at the contact.

"*Gabriel.*"

I squealed trying to close my legs now but I couldn't.

"Does it hurt?"

My eyes watered as I watched him and nodded. "A little."

"Do you like it?"

I nodded again feeling shy even if I was all trussed up for him. He did it again. And again.

It was light enough but I saw his jaw clench as he did it again and again, the heat of the leather snapping against my sensitized flesh making me gasp and writhe.

"*Gabriel.*"

"I'm only getting started." It was a promise as he rose up and the sensations began snapping harder. Each downward slap of leather became harder and harder until I was crying out.

"That's my girl. Scream for me. Beg for me to fuck that little pussy. I bet it's sore isn't it?"

"Yes," I shrieked. I couldn't stop twisting but I was completely helpless. Arms bound to my sides every movement shaking my nipple clamps.

Gabriel whipped my pussy with the edge of his belt. Harder and harder until pain and pleasure blurred together.

Each strike was reminding me of this man. Determined to leave his mark on my body, on my soul, driving me wild.

Noises left me, helpless and pleading.

I was crying harder now.

"Keep your legs open," his voice was gravel. "Wide." The belt came down again and my inner thighs shook wildly.

"Gabriel..." I moaned. "Please...Please...I need your eyes..." I needed to come. So bad. "I need—I need you—"

I heard the clink of it drop from his hands.

If I thought Gabriel was done—I was wrong. He licked his way down my body, ripping off his condom to eat my pussy out again.

Tongue fucking me relentlessly in that sensitive area until I cried. I could feel another orgasm brewing.

Whenever it built too long, he would slow down his strokes lapping at me lazily. I squealed as it built and dropped so many times I felt like I was going crazy.

"Please—" I cried.

"Were you close?"

I nodded desperately, and the smile that spread across his face made my stomach flip.

Understanding dawned—*this* was how he planned to torture me.

"Good." He settled back between my trembling thighs. "Let's try this again."

I gasped as he sucked my sensitive clit between his lips.

He paused just long enough to add. "You are not allowed to come." His smile held no mercy. "If you do? I'll finish what I started with my belt. And you won't walk."

Dio mío.

It was endless and when he began tugging at the clamps? I was screaming to get away. It was *torture*.

He ate at me, tugging and sucking and licking until I wanted to orgasm like nothing else.

"Gabriel!" My cries took on a hoarse note. I was losing my voice.

Dimly I heard the tearing of foil in the background as my head lolled in delirious pleasure.

Every shake of the clamps was designed to drive me insane.

He was going to tear into me at this rate.

I felt him moving and I saw wheat-colored hair and pale, so pale, eyes moving over me.

The moment he speared into me, the blood flow to my pussy after his belt was so intense, I could come right there.

The sheer size of him so thick and overwhelming I felt stretched beyond my limits.

Always.

"That's my girl, you can take it. Spread those legs wider... wider...good girl."

He filled me even deeper. I was soaking wet and primed for him. On the edge of an orgasm that I felt like would kill me.

The combination of his body on me, his weight pressing me down, cock stretching me so wide and painfully hard inside of me, and those winter blues? Was deadly. I was dying. This was too much

"Hold. It."

It was a struggle as his eyes locked onto mine and I breathed out desperately trying. But like this? It was impossible.

Every single tiny movement sent a shockwave through me and I bit back a scream.

"Yesyesyesyes." I cried out. A helpless noise left me then mixed with a scream. *"Gabriel! I can't—"*

He drew out of me and for a panicked second I thought he was going to pull out and I wanted to scream again until he slammed back in.

My orgasm hit me with the force of a tsunami. His eyes locked onto mine, his arms bracketed my head as he thrust in and groaned.

"Fuck, there you go, baby. Come all over my cock."

I was. I couldn't stop myself anymore a ragged noise leaving me as I locked eyes with him feeling wave after wave take me over, my eyelids dropping lower as he held me tighter.

Pounding so deep I felt it like one enormous orgasm.

Each wave more intense than the last.

All the while, my eyes low-lidded watched the winter blues locked on them—both of us caught between each other. Vulnerability in them as he watched me breaking.

He was moving in me like an animal. Rougher than he'd ever been. And it was exactly what I needed.

"Gonna destroy this little pussy, and you're going to love it."

"Yes."

A wicked glint lit his eyes up. "There you fucking go, keep going, baby. Let me feel you coming."

I didn't even scream anymore. I felt like I couldn't breathe as he groaned over me. My breath came in small pants as he groaned over me.

"Such a good girl," he panted over my lips. "Give me those eyes."

I didn't look away memorizing those winter blues as he filled me with his heat searing and hot. I could do nothing but take.

Liquid heat rushing through me.

His arms wrapped tighter around me as his head buried in the crook of my neck groaning praises and filthy things as I shook.

I closed my eyes feeling him pulse and swell, shuddering.

Agreed.

I couldn't even speak as we both shook wildly.

I can't believe I ever thought he was made of ice.

CHAPTER 26
GABRIEL

I wasn't saying I *dreamt* of sexually tormenting Isobel.

I thought about it twenty-four seven.

Not just in my dreams.

I spent the day in bed with her, testing her limits, tormenting her, until finally taking her ass with a fervor she echoed.

By the end, she was wrung dry, I was panting over her like a wild animal—and I was certain this woman was perfect for me.

When I woke up that morning she was still passed out and Liam texted me.

> You guys coming today?
>
> I need to make dinner if you do

> Yeah. We'll be there.

> Is she okay? She sounded out of it.

I couldn't exactly tell him I fucked her until she blacked out, could I?

> Still asleep. Had a long night.

> Gross.

I grinned as my heart flipped at the text of Liam calling me his brother.

I glanced over her bruised body. Red and purple against the golden color of her skin. My work. My claim on her.

Everywhere. Including between her legs which was redder than anywhere else.

But Isobel met me every step of the way. Urging for more.

Her light meeting my darkness begging me for it—letting me loose with her. I usually kept parts of me chained.

I never had come undone for a woman like this.

But now I was exploring my darker aspects with her.

She loved me between every round even after I did in fact go back and whip that pussy up.

She loved it, begging me for it harder. And harder.

Until it was so red she was sobbing while I fucked her.

Until the light in her eyes looked like worship.

Until her surrender felt heavenly.

Until animal noises left her as she came over and over rubbed raw from me.

Say it.

I love you, I love you, I love you.

She was gasping the words under me as I fucked her harder than I would've dared but she was so sensitive after being whipped —it was magnified for her and for me.

Both of our sensations heightened allowed me to take her with violence that felt nothing like that. It felt like…love.

Because…there was none of the animalistic need to hurt. No. I just wanted to love her, but I knew we both needed… more.

We looked like we'd mauled each other.

Even as we held on and Isobel kept whispering she loved me weakly.

What was the last name of the guy you tried to kill in college?

> The guy who hurt her.

> Jonathan what?

There was a pause.

> Wallace. I broke his arm.

> Isa pulled me off him.

> She told you?

Good man.
Of course she told me.
What didn't she tell me?
I texted Liam on my way to the kitchen for coffee as I tugged on my shirt and sweats. Clean boxers. I'd clean up our bedroom and the sheets later.

It was a wreck in there.

> She did. So he's still alive.

> I'm guessing by your texts that's a 'he's alive for now' instead of a 'did I let him live'

I didn't respond.
I did however get a text two minutes later with an address.
An address.
I smirked.

> He lives here.

> I don't even wanna know how you know.

> I got dossier's bitch

> Files. Maps. Info.

> I'm a broker baby

> Don't ask me why his internet service is shit and why his sprinklers go off every so often when he's wearing his nice clothes.

> Fucker

I bit back a laugh glancing down at my phone.
Nerds. Leave it to them to find the best revenge.
Liam was still fucking with that guy. *Shit.*
Great minds thought alike. Liam texted me again.

> His wife's cheating on him with his best friend and
> he has no idea.

> I don't even think his kid is his.

> > Send me everything you got on him.

> Ohhhhhh.

> Dun dun dunnnnnnnn

> If you kill him, I wanna watch.

> Please, let me watch.

> It turns me on you know?

I almost snorted out my water.

> > You're worse than me.

> Bitch, I am you

> > That's disgusting

I felt almost chipper making my coffee the way Isobel and Liam took theirs. With butter. Whole milk.

I was absorbing things about her. I knew every single fucking thing about this woman. I paid attention.

Absorbing how she whispered affection to me bringing me back to my life.

I sat down at my computer knocking out some work before I went to check on Isobel.

She didn't even stir. I smiled going over to her, her skin cooler to the touch and thankfully, she was snuggled into my side now.

"Baby," I whispered crawling into the space with her now fully clothed. "It's late, come on."

She grumbled.

"I made coffee." She stirred. Barely. I grinned. "Liam's here. In the room."

She shot up covering herself swearing up a storm in Spanish as I chuckled cuddling her to me then.

She shot me a dirty look. "Gabriel, that is not funny!"

I chuckled. It was pretty funny. "Come here, baby."

Isobel all but harrumphed disappearing into the covers again. *She always wants to stay in bed.*

I ducked under them with her laughing lightly.

"We have to go see him today."

"I know," she croaked. "But I cannot walk."

I bit back my laughter finding her curling into a ball.

"I'll carry you."

She laughed as I wrapped myself around her. I never took myself for a man who played under my sheets. "Besides, the bed is filthy."

She groaned. "I know, I slept in it."

We both burst into laughter as I tried to kiss her and she kept wiggling until I pinned her down. Laughter left us as pressed kisses everywhere.

"Come on, baby, I made breakfast."

"Hmm, pancakes?"

"Maybe," I kissed her again. I wasn't capable of doing anything and I could burn water. But I could try.

Isobel smiled up at me. Soft warm eyes that filled me with heat.

"You are dressed."

"Mhm."

She groaned. "Fine, I will get up. But you have to carry me everywhere."

"Deal." I chuckled. "But you gotta kiss me every single time."

"I can do that." Her laughter blended with mine as she pulled me down on her.

~

BEFORE WE WENT TO SEE LIAM, I DROPPED US BY THE GROCERY store.

Liam had said he wanted to make dinner but Isobel told him not to.

"He likes those fancy sandwiches," she muttered walking slower next to me.

195

"I told you to sit in the car," I laughed low at her frown. "You just said you were sore."

"I have to get this, Gabriel." *Gabri-el.* "We need seasoning."

Her accent coasted over me as she spoke to the deli counter and told them exactly how to make the sandwiches.

"Do not put the onions, but that garlic sauce you have..."

I grinned behind her at how precise she wanted in. The lady at deli-counter blinked at her taking notes with an earnest expression.

"You're a woman on a mission, baby." I grinned ear to ear.

"Come Gabriel," she tossed me a look over her shoulder. "Let's go get the chocolate cake cups he likes before they run out."

I grinned ear to ear. "Stay here, I'll go grab 'em."

She frowned. "With the whip cream?"

"Yes, baby. With the whip cream. I got it."

I kissed her steadily before walking down the long grocery aisles to the bakery section in the back.

I shook my head with a stupid grin on my face at fucking shopping for cake out of all things.

Before Isobel I would get what I needed and just what I needed. Healthy things. Never diverging. Now?

She got what she craved. What she wanted.

I just went along with it because it was fun. An experience, she would say.

She liked going out. I liked staying in.

She liked trying new things. I liked to play it safe.

She liked keeping me on my toes. I liked keeping her grounded.

She was wilder than me, but I was adept at handling a handful.

In all fairness, we balanced each other reasonably enough.

I found the cups she wanted for Liam grabbing a few of them into the basket I had gotten for him.

Isobel felt bad about ditching him the last few days and she said Liam always was convinced with snacks and food.

"Monroe."

I stilled a little at the sound of my voice.

I turned to my horror and saw Richard Young out of all people standing there.

Still short. Still angsty.

"You back in Quantico? Heard you got my sister kicked out of the fucking trainee camp."

Jesus. Fucking. *Shit.*

196

Isobel was here.

It wouldn't take a genius to put it together. Me. Her. This.

I tucked the basket at my side with all the things my girl loved.

Had he seen her?

I took in his mixed race features, his eyes narrowed on me like he could scare me. Like I hadn't faced down worse with less to lose.

In the past I had done dangerous assignments. Handled every single threat with lethal assessments.

Now? Young was nothing.

"Your sister threatened and sexually harassed a female trainee."

My girlfriend.

Your sister tried to hurt my girlfriend.

You know, the one I'm falling in love with.

I looked around feeling the anxiety crawl on my skin at the thought of Isobel daring to come back here to see us.

"Do you really wanna do this shit here or take it outside?"

No. He couldn't know.

I felt my face blank out the moment I saw him pasting on a bored expression. Anxiety underneath my skin felt like fire ants at the thought of Isobel near him.

His face heated. "She's a kid—"

"I'm not doing this with you—" I broke off. "The fucking frozen cake aisle is not the one you start shit in. Or did the Air Force not teach you any better?"

Of course, it fucking didn't. Bunch of prep school pussies.

Young had made to being a staff sergeant which was another word for leadership's bitch.

And now he thought every single civilian he came across needed his shit rank to be pulled. I glanced down. Yup. Combat boots on at the grocery store with his jeans and he'd been out for a few years?

Fucking goblin. His entire family was full of 'em.

"I need to get going." I met his eyes and I saw his banked rage. "For your fucking sake, watch your fucking mouth. Clearly you and your fucking family failed that."

I shook my head disgusted out of all things.

He was still here so I couldn't just walk back to Isobel. I texted her what happened.

She was typing.

So I called her. "Baby, not now. Go."

"I don't like this."

"I don't care, I take care of you." Even if my stomach twisted as I gripped the fucking basket. "I fucking hate this."

She was quiet. "Me too."

We hadn't told anyone.

We were keeping our entire relationship a fucking secret because if anyone found out about me and her? That was a wrap for my career and she'd be crucified.

Koller could only protect us so much.

They might move her out of my sight. I couldn't protect her anymore or Liam. And then came the fucking nine thousand questions they'd have.

My stomach burned with acid rolling in it. "Baby—"

"Amor—"

I stopped.

And she knew it too.

"Go to the car. You have my keys right? Wait there for me. I'll take care of it."

When I got to the deli counter, the woman there was waiting for me, Isobel's shopping cart still there with a few things she'd found for Liam in it.

I bumped into Young one more time at check out and I took my sweet ass time.

When I got to Isobel, she frowned looking a little lost in the car.

In the backseat. Where people couldn't see her.

She looked so small in her coat as she smiled up at me with those eyes, her canines out. Mischievous. Dark eyes sparkling wide at me.

Fuck, my girl is adorable.

"That was close, Gabriel."

Gabri-el.

My chest cracked open.

"Come here, baby." I got in with her and she hugged me tighter crawling into my lap a little.

"I hate this."

"I hate this."

We stayed holding each other for long moments.

I didn't want to let her go.

"This means that *maldita* Kourtney is here too."

I nodded already working on it. I could ask Vincent. "I'll find out tomorrow morning where."

Isobel pulled back nervously. "He left before you in his car. It's okay for us to go now."

I hated it. I hated keeping my girl a secret.

I hated the lies that came up when I saw her at work and wanted to kiss her.

I hated every single fucking bit of it. Hated keeping her a secret. Hated us being like this. Hated having to feel like I was hiding her.

"I'm proud of you," I whispered feeling the ache in my chest intensify. "I always have been."

Her smile was soft and understanding. "Gabriel, just because we are keeping secrets does not mean I think any less of you. It does not matter who knows and who does not. I would never want to be the reason you do not make in the Agency."

"I don't give a shit about making it if it's without you," it spilled from my lips as I held her to me. "None of this means anything without you."

She'd agreed to move in with me.

She was becoming a part of my life.

A part of my soul.

Isobel was etching herself into my skin so deep, I couldn't fathom going anywhere and losing her in the process.

Her palm pressed over my heart, the heat warming me from the inside out. "Breathe, amor. It's okay."

She was mine.

Her eyes met mine. "Maybe when you move up and when I leave you can say something then. It will be more natural. Like we started dating. Nobody has to know then."

That was true.

But how long was that? How long? I wanted to marry this girl.

"You still want to have your own dance studio," I breathed. I sometimes forgot despite all that she was, she didn't want anything fancy. She didn't want too much.

I wanted to climb the ranks up the Agency to sit at the top.

But Isobel? She wanted to own that studio. Create art and be around music.

Isobel wanted me to come home for dinner to her and our future kids. I knew that.

Somehow watching her dream, made me want it too. I wanted every bit of the picture she painted in the future.

She nodded with that smile of hers, canines out. "A normal life."

"A normal wife." I whispered kissing her softly this time. "How's your body?"

"Sore," she whispered back. I turned my head to the patter of rain drops pelting down on the truck. "Let's go. Liam is hungry and the hungrier he gets the angrier."

I chuckled. "Can't have that. Love you, baby."

"Love you, amor."

Liam opened the door with a knowing smirk in his eyes at my arm wrapped around Isobel. I held up sandwiches.

"Don't even fucking think about it."

"I wasn't going to," he grinned. He winked at Isobel. "I was going to." She slapped his arm slowly walking forward trying to maintain composure.

I bit back my laughter as I blocked her from his view. Luckily Liam was excited about the sandwiches and Oracle.

"You wanted to show us Oracle," I said out loud helping Isobel hang up her clothes and she whimpered a little into my kisses.

"*Yeah yeah*, as soon as you two stop canoodling like teenagers, I wanna show you my baby too."

Isobel smacked my chest. "Come on, he's proud of his project. And so am I."

I grinned watching her trying to walk normally.

"I'm coming, baby. Don't run off without me."

"I cannot walk," she hissed. "This is your fault."

Guilty. But I wouldn't have changed it for the world.

CHAPTER 27
ISOBEL

"So she's this incredible free-thinking AI, and Isa and I spent years putting emotions into it, so when she gives you answers—"

"She has no constraints," Gabriel whispered staring at Oracle in amazement.

The program was colorful on Liam's screen.

He motioned to his phone. "Look, I have her imbedded into my phone, and into Isa's. I can put her on yours. She responds to your call sign." He paused holding up his phone. "Oracle, this is Pluto."

And then my voice came on.

"Good evening, sir. What can I do for you today?"

I giggled at Gabriel's jaw dropping.

Liam grinned at us. "Show me the current coordinates of Isobel Santos."

And then on screen, Oracle began pulling data from everywhere she could until it showed the dot of me sitting at my apartment with Liam and Gabriel.

Gabriel's jaw dropped. "Do you have any idea what this is?" He looked stunned. "This is…great."

"It get's better," Liam looked delighted. "Oracle, show me every single mechanic in a ten mile radius."

She did.

"Narrow it down to ones with only good reviews."

She dropped the hundreds down to five.

"And narrow it down based off how long they've been in business."

She left it at one.

Gabriel blinked his pale eyes widening. "You can have a conversation with her."

"Sure, I mean you have the real version of it," Liam motioned to me. "I just stole her voice and had Isa do a few commands but for the most part she runs off anything you tell her. She ingests the information and she spits it back out like a normal person only more advanced. And she's attuned to you as a person. She's genius. Well...I am. But it's fantastic."

Gabriel looked impressed as I sat there eating my sandwich and chips. "This is what you wanted to take with you when you start Titan?"

Liam's smile dipped and his eyes met mine. I shot him an apologetic look. I explained carefully. "I talked to Gabriel, he think's its a good idea."

"I think it's a great idea," Gabriel admitted openly. "It's insanely clever. Long term planning outside of this life is great to have. I want to stay in, but if you don't? This is the way forward. I can't believe it when she told me you kept it to yourself."

He was a lot more open with us now and I felt pride warm my chest as he spoke. I felt myself smiling as he reassured Liam.

"I have a friend Reed. He works for another three-letter but he was debating working in the private sector. This is a great project and Reed's tech savvy, he would eat this up if you ever trust him enough. Isobel explained why you didn't want to tell anyone and I won't share it with anyone, but this would be insane for the Agency to use."

Liam's jaw went tight and I saw him closing in a little at the sound of that. "That's exactly why I don't want them to know about it."

Gabriel nodded and I knew he understood. "You think the Agency would misuse it."

"They misuse everything." Liam shook his head. "Half of the items we use are outdated and old. For all the technological advances we can't seem to advance because they insist on archaic methods of everything."

Gabriel nodded. Not taking offense because he felt the same sometimes. "I won't tell anyone. This program is helpful either way.

When you start Titan, you can do so much with inputting information into it."

Liam's eyes watched Gabriel with a knowing look. "If you feed Oracle enough information, she is trained to be free-thinking."

Which meant...

"She can do half of the job for you," Liam smirked and I knew that twinkle in his eyes. "And if she picks up your personality? She can do it with you in mind, with your thoughts like...if Isa controls her Oracle, it begins taking aspects of her personality. The problem with AI, is that it doesn't have that. It has no soul—"

"You gave it life," Gabriel whispered.

"No," Liam correct. "We are giving it life. The program swallows everything you give it. Eventually, it just runs on its own."

In my entire life knowing Liam I had always known how smart he was.

From the day I brought him home. I knew him.

And right now? He was sharing his personal life with Gabriel. A breakthrough for him.

"All of it. And all you have to do is ensure she stays within her bounds and doesn't randomly control missiles into foreign countries. Not that she would—"

Gabriel paled as he realized how powerful Oracle was. *"That's what you want to build?"*

"Not right now, but one day I wanna grow," Liam sat with Gabriel and showed him how it worked. "I wanna do something good with my life. Have power. Use it for good."

I already knew but I didn't know Gabriel was not a tech savvy as Liam.

Liam operated on a different level.

He was so smart Papi began sharing everything with him about our finances and at a young age Liam began to help him more.

Most people saw my brother as a little wild with his piercings and his tattoos. His ripped clothing.

Most people never saw him the way I did.

The boy who took care of me, who taught himself programming languages.

This mind who created artificial intelligence at the age of eighteen in college with me. Nobody knew how smart he was.

I knew. Liam functioned like an entire IT department. If Gabriel fired everyone today—Liam would do every single job and then some.

I watched Liam build Oracle with me piece by piece.

But I saw Gabriel's reaction when he realized what I already knew. Liam was a genius.

He could change the world if he wanted to.

But Liam wanted to start Titan Security.

I knew this.

He didn't even talk about the martial arts studio anymore.

Almost like he wanted the dream because it was my dream—not his dream.

Gabriel sat with Liam for a while asking him questions about Oracle and the two of them side by side were a picture.

I snapped a photo on my phone of them. They were getting along more now.

And we were turning into a family.

I walked out into the kitchen, the sound of Liam explaining things to Gabriel fading behind me.

I was searching around the fridge for a drink when I heard footsteps.

I had opened it when Liam walked into the kitchen heading for me.

"You good, shortcake?" His hands were in my hair pushing it back out of my face. "I haven't seen you in forever." His arms wrapped around me tighter.

"I'm good." I had to tell him about moving out. "I wanted to say something." I pulled back. "I was so excited about Oracle I completely forgot to tell you."

His eyes were bright on me, as he held me. "Anything."

I slowly said. "You know, Gabriel and I are getting more serious. And I was thinking I should move in with him..." I said it and I saw Liam's brows rise. His eyes widening as he gripped me tighter.

His chest rose and fell for a second as he searched my face.

"I love him and I think with all the time I spend with him, it's easier."

I felt guilt twisting my gut.

For a long second, Liam didn't say anything. He just held me to him. He cleared his throat. "That's what you want."

I nodded slowly. "I do." I hoped my face wasn't flaming. Moving in with Gabriel was a big deal.

204

It was the first time I had willingly separated myself from Liam not counting college.

And even then I would've wanted to share a space with him.

He nodded blinking back his emotions. "Okay. I'll help. Whenever you want. Whatever you want."

I blinked up at him surprised. "Really?"

His smile was soft on me. And my heart began pounding in my ribcage. "Yeah, whatever you want."

He brushed my hair back, lips pressing into my forehead as I heard footsteps.

Gabriel was usually quiet, silently moving through the apartment, but I knew now he was making noise so we both knew he was here.

Liam didn't turn but I looked around Liam to see him. Winter blue eyes on us.

Not jealous.

He knew.

"I'm moving in with you!" I felt my smile stretch my lips and Gabriel's echoed mine. Liam held me a little tighter as I laughed.

~

AFTER I MOVED IN WITH GABRIEL, WE ADJUSTED TO US LIVING together. To doing everything together now.

He felt more like home than anyone else I had known.

Our love felt different me.

Somehow I knew Gabriel as much as I knew myself.

Gabriel woke up before his alarm clock, groaning a little about it. It always made me laugh when he cuddled me in the mornings.

How he took his coffee now. How he liked to workout. The way he rubbed his neck when stressed.

Which side of the bed he wanted, how he did his laundry.

The way he grabbed his second cup of coffee and me asking for snuggles.

In turn, he learned things about me.

Besides the s'mores and heating pad on my period?

He learned everything he could about me, picking up on where I lost my hairbrush, where I put my makeup, how I liked my clothes hung up—and everything in between.

He began keeping butterscotch candies on him. Everywhere. In the car. At home. On his desk.

It was tiny things.

But it fit.

We were complimentary. More than me and Liam. Gabriel adjusted to me. All of me.

Living with a man like this had always been normal for me.

But now? It was different.

Now this man wanted to know why I had fifty bath products. He wanted to get in with me. He played with me in the mornings when we had time off.

He drove me to work with him and because we got there early we walked in together. I made breakfast for us. Until one morning when Jeremy said. "Shit, you and Monroe are eating omelettes and now I want one."

I almost choked on my bite until Liam who caught it said. "I want some too." I didn't protest as he took my breakfast with an easy grin. But my heart was racing.

Sutton glanced over at Liam. "Only you eat like a bear stealing Isobel's food."

"Do you want some Sutton?" Liam clicked his tongue piercing at her. She promptly turned red and ducked as everyone else laughed.

"Are you—" I motioned with my head to her.

He shook his head. "Nah, too clean cut for me. Think she's got a man. Civilian. Firefighter." He looked impressed. "Solid guy."

I didn't even want to know how he knew. "Stop eating like that," I batted his hands away. "You act like since I've been gone, you don't eat normal food anymore."

"It's not the same without you," he said slowly. Like it made him uncomfortable to say it out loud. "Who am I supposed to tease now?"

His smile was light as he said it, but my heart broke a little.

I realized with work and a relationship I saw Liam less, which hurt me sometimes.

"Come over for dinner," I whispered. "Come over."

"I'm not staying if you two start making out—"

I clapped my hand over his mouth and his eyes twinkled as he dropped it. "Fine," he bit into the omelette like a civilized person. "I'll come over for dinner."

"And I will bring you breakfast more."

I brushed his hair back, the inky locks growing out longer now. He sighed as he tipped his head back.

"Tell me you love me, please. I think I'm dying."

I chuckled. "I love you, stupid. Come here."

He did come closer and rubbed his hair as he ate like we were kids.

I realized in my time I spent with my new life...I hadn't paid much attention to my old one.

And so Liam made it his business to come over to see us for dinner.

I began decorating Gabriel's home. As my home too. Our home.

Gabriel was sneaking in Spanish lessons thinking I wouldn't know. But I saw the app on his phone.

Or when he practiced with Oracle.

Liam had put it on Gabriel's phone as well.

This morning as he wolfed down the extra breakfast I made, my brother glanced at me on a break outside. I walked to Liam's car while Gabriel went to a meeting.

"I made a copy of something for you." Liam passed me a USB drive. "This is a beta-copy of Oracle. If anything happens to ones on our phone or my computer, since it's stored locally, this copy unlocks it again." He passed it to me.

"What's the password?"

"For you," he grinned. "Apollo."

After Gabriel. Oracle was named after the Oracle of Delphi. But Liam had used my voice to program her to be her in a way. It fit.

"Just tell her you're Isobel Santos. She'll unlock herself since she is you. I just input everything about you into Oracle, so she always makes choices like you do. But that's the only copy in existence." He grinned at me. "See, I still always have a piece of you no matter what."

I was the voice of the Oracle...

"And if I don't enter the password?" I frowned over it. "Does she just exist without the improvements? Not mine?"

"Exactly. If you don't know the password which why would anyone else know that? You don't unlock Oracle." Liam smiled over at me. "I miss you."

I felt my heart ache as I pocketed the drive. "I wish I could marry you *and* Gabriel."

207

At that Liam laughed looking embarrassed for once. "You probably could. We're not *technically* related."

I shuddered. Gross. Liam was as close as a brother got. And Liam laughed even harder.

"Why are you so stupid?"

"Why are you so easy to tease?"

I grumbled as he got out of his car motioning for me to jump on him. "Come on, I'll give you a piggyback ride into the office."

"I'm not twelve." But I couldn't resist leaping on him laughing. "This is my *favorite*."

"I know," he grinned carrying me in. "As long as you don't yank my ear—Ow, Isa—"

"You got another piercing recently?"

"Yeah, and you don't wanna know where."

"Carajo!"

He laughed louder.

CHAPTER 28

GABRIEL

WE HAD A LEAD ON HAGEN.

Something.

He was coming to New York in a few months.

"Intel says he swings by around this time," Koller pointed at his calender. "This is the three month window. We have a contact in Havana who gather's Intelligence and says Hagen plans on swinging by there. If your team is up for it, when we get more information, we can get further than whispers and body counts."

I felt my stomach fill with what felt like acid. That was fast.

Even Oracle couldn't get a read on who it was. Even with Liam feeding it all the data in the world.

Not only was getting Intel on Hagen rare. The level of dangerous this assignment would be even in New York—was insanity. The pressure for my team to actually preform and be put out there, and the implications for every one?

Insanity. Urgent insanity.

"What do you want from my team?"

"I'll send out a second unit with you guys, but you're taking this one," Koller looked at me. "You can do this. If you bring him back, or even someone on his team—it'll be the one for you."

The one that got me another wrung on the ladder.

The one that took me from a nobody to a somebody?

But wasn't I already Isobel's somebody?

Did I need to be anyone else's?

The thought popped up into my head and I knew something was wrong with me when I stepped out of Koller's office more shaken up than anything else.

Because now I had to tell the team. And they took about as well as they could. Isobel composed herself and Liam frowned. He inched closer to her until he was all but shielding her from everyone. Even me.

I tried not to let that bother me and failed.

"Santos, both of you guys dig up anything you got on that area of Midtown. And the hotels around it. We think Hagen's going to be staying at the Primrose. Matches with him celebrity profile..."

Claire and Vincent were experienced and they were worried.

Vincent came up to me. "Are they making you take all of us?"

I shook my head. "One of you guys will stay back. Koller's going to send in a secondary team to shadow us. Hopefully."

Hopefully, they weren't mauled out and killed by whatever Hagen had on his team.

I sat there in my office and failed to remain composed. As soon as Vincent left my hands were shaking. I was shaking.

I couldn't take my girl out with me. But she wasn't supposed to be my girl. I couldn't do this.

I didn't know how to.

We were supposed to catch bad guys together.

But right now? My stomach soured at imagining her soft face. Those eyes. Completely obliterated.

A knock came at my door and she stepped in then like a vision of raven and soft caramel.

The scent of butterscotch came off her and I got that privately, I was aware the office had noticed the candy.

But Sutton only stole some off my desk and Vincent had one on his desk.

Now the entire office smelled like her.

She shut the door and locked it as I stood from my desk.

I didn't even think I was all over her in a second aware of everything wrong we were doing.

"Baby—"

"Amor," she held my face in her hands. "It's okay. I'm okay. Nothing's going to happen."

I held her for long long long moments. Longer than I should've. Longer than it was safe.

"Amor."

I looked down at her. "I don't know what I want." I admitted it. Her eyes widened on me as I said. My hands found their way into her hair, threading into it and staying there. "I don't know what I want anymore.

Every single moment that I had build myself up to be, none of it mattered anymore. All of it was crumbling like a sandcastle. Because without her none of it mattered anymore.

"I thought I knew," I whispered. "I thought I knew. And then you look at me. You take me home. And I don't—" I shook my head closing my eyes. I couldn't form the words.

She made me ask questions on whether power and control were worth it.

My entire life I had always thought that the ability to prove who I was made me—me.

Not the kid I used to be. Not the homeless runt.

Not useless. Not a soldier.

"You make me feel like something I want, is something different than what it was." I swallowed opening my eyes. "Does that make sense?"

Her eyes were confused on me. But she nodded.

Her fingertips reached up brushing my eyebrows, smoothing over my lips. "I want to take you home."

"You are my home." I nuzzled my nose against hers. "I don't understand you. How you do this to me. I have never had to be anything for you but me."

"You are enough, Gabriel," her words soothed every single ache in my soul. "It's going to be okay. You are going to get everything you want in this world. I know it. It may not be how you imagine. Sometimes my father says life throws you unexpected things, but you will get there." She held my face. "It's been too long, I must go. I will see you at home. And then I will snuggle you and kiss you everywhere."

She pressed her lips to me over and over again until I smiled. Her canines peeked out and I tickled her a little.

"Love you, baby."

"Te amo, mucho. Amor."

"I've been practicing too," I whispered. Her eyes shimmered with pride.

"Yeah?" She smiled up at me. "You want to take me home and show me?"

I groaned as she kissed me until someone knocked on the door. We flew apart and I found Liam waiting outside.

He held up a sandwich at his sister. "Lunch?"

She left her arm linked in his and he shot me a look that was more of a warning. He didn't want her getting into trouble either over me.

I blew out a breath wondering when the taste of butterscotch had become normal for me, and when I had started measuring success differently.

But even still, becoming somebody in the Agency. Being powerful. Having the world at my fingertips?

It was...everything I ever wanted.

I could feel Isobel's weight against my body.

Her kisses against my skin.

I was at war with myself and I didn't know which side was winning.

~

As a distraction Liam took us both ice skating.

Isobel mentioned he wanted to play hockey growing up. He wanted to do everything.

I think I skated once as a teenager and landed on my face.

But Liam was *active*. I got that he was trying outrun his own demons which I knew all too well about.

"I wanted to play hockey," he puffed out into the colder winter air. "Isobel's dad put me into martial arts to get my anger out and when I was awful, he would bring me out to the lake and make me do circles to run it off."

He grinned down at Isobel, his green eyes sparkling a little as he helped her with her skates. Tying them several times. "Easy, shortcake. You always did have the chubbiest fingers—"

Isobel swore at him and he chuckled. He moved onto me. "You did a decent job too." He adjusted them to make sure they were right on both of us and helped us up.

"Liam is good at everything," Isobel rolled her eyes.

"Kyokushin?" I asked him as I took a few strides not immediately falling on my ass.

212

He tipped his head looking over fucking joyed to be on the ice. He did a few test laps leaving me and Isobel holding onto each other. "You'd love it, Monroe. That's how I always kick your ass."

I blew out a breath as Isobel almost went down. And then I definitely went down.

Her laughter mingled with mine as she kissed me. Liam swung back to us helping us both up, teaching us how to stand without his help. He grinned wider looking happier than I had ever seen him.

"He likes the activity," I murmured to her as we both panted.

She nodded, her cheeks rosier, her canines out and eyes twinkling. She looked fucking adorable. "He needs it. Otherwise he goes crazy."

I watched Liam skating around us. I couldn't ice skate but Isobel and Liam had all the patience in the world teasing me and helping me.

He was active and muscled in ways I wasn't.

Leaner and meaner as Isobel said.

And he carted Isobel around on his back all the time standing next to her like a sentinel ready to take out everything around her.

He still kicked my ass from time to time, but I always had more weight than he did.

Working out with him cut me down to just lean muscle, more muscle than I had before without it showing up in bulk.

Isobel had noticed. Tracing my body with her tongue and leaving me a wreck under her.

I settled.

I watched as Isobel went down and slid, Liam *swooped* in like a torpedo coming for her. His legs moved too quickly for me to keep up.

He's scary good.

That's why he never put on bulk, because he was *faster* like this.

He moved backwards around her easily like a hawk, always watching and never letting her stray, never moving far, always around her orbit.

"Come on, shortcake. I gotcha." He had his arms around her every so often lifting her up. "I gotcha, sweetheart. Come here."

While I stood back I watched Liam practically lift her up and she screamed a little at his laughter. I grinned ear to ear as he moved her around the rink. "Easy," he put his arms around her head protecting her as she held on.

"Monroe, you're next!"

I grinned wider. "Touch me and die, motherfucker."

Both siblings laughed into the rink echoing loudly. They skated over to me as he grinned holding his hand out. Both of them reached for me.

"Come, Gabriel." Her eyes twinkled.

"Yeah, what she said." And I followed them. I fell a few times and I saw Isobel caught on fairly faster than me.

"We have you," she held onto me as much as possible. Liam skated by me and helped. And I had a fucking blast.

Isobel's words rang true in my ear.

Papi says love is not conditional.

My love for you will never be conditional.

My love for you will never ever be conditional, Gabriel.

"Shortcake, you're like Bambi..." She scowled at his laughter when she fell once more. I went to go help her and Liam skated up.

"I got her, here."

There was nothing he could do to make them stop loving him. For a moment I realized what I was doing. I was taking *her* from him. In more ways than one. His love wasn't romantic. It went beyond that.

If Isobel asked for something it was hers.

The first time she saw me she looked at me and he had known.

And he made it happen for her.

She was his entire life. His *everything*.

But now, she was also mine.

"Come on, hold onto me, shortcake."

Liam moved around her, grabbing her by the arm and lifting her his eyes fierce and focused as he used his body, the traction of his skates to haul her up, into his arms as he laughed at her expression. "Monroe, one of these days you gotta get good at ice skating so you can do this too."

He crossed the entire length fast, his eyes focused. Sharp. Now, the way he leaned back told me he was a fucking pro. And then *faster* until he was crossing the length of the pond with her on him.

Liam grinned in apparent joy brushing her back as he skated with her on him. I watched and my heart filled with something else watching them.

Family. That's what these two were.

Liam would always take care of her. If anything happened to me on the assignment with Hagen—he was her rock. Her shield.

Isobel brought him home.

And he stayed with her.

He made himself her other half.

And I was coming in between. Deep down I knew he had set me up with her.

I could see it in the way he looked at me sometimes. *Like he saw something in me.* He approved.

And I didn't want to disappoint him.

His everything was my *everything*.

I was family.

THE FIRST DAY LIAM TOOK ME TO KYOKUSHIN.

He wiped the floor with my ass.

His laughter rang in my ear as Isobel winced in the background.

"Get up, Monroe. Don't be a punk bitch," he grinned all canines out. For people that weren't related, they had the same fucking smile. Only his came with tattoos, piercings, and a wicked grin. And he did it again and again. I grinned. *This was awesome.*

Liam and I sparred all the time. Despite being leaner, he had the grace and charisma of a fighter. I swore.

I had fought people. And then I fought Liam and got my ass handed to me. Isobel had to walk out after realizing the two of us weren't giving up.

I wasn't quitting. And he didn't want me to.

"You've got potential," he smirked. "But you don't have motivation."

I frowned. "What the fuck is that supposed to mean?"

He held up his hands ready to go again. "It means, when you fight, you have to fight like something is on the line for you. You fight like a man who doesn't care if he lives or dies."

"How the fuck do you know that?"

"Because I fight," he motioned to himself. "Like I have to go home. Like I have something to go home to. Someone."

He motioned to Isobel's form on her e-reader now. Sutton and Jeremy had a book club where ironically Jeremy read romance novels.

He'd introduced them to Isobel and Sutton. The former of whom began making a list of things she wanted to try with me from her books.

If she felt us staring she looked up, eyes shimmering a little on me. Her entire focus was on me. I felt my lips split into a smile. *Hey, baby.*

Her lips tipped up and she waved a little. Adorable.

Her eyes went wide at what she saw next.

Liam moved then like lightening, and I barely caught his leg as he swung at me. His green eyes held a predator's focus to them, deadly with intent.

"*Focus.* You don't fight like a man who cares to win. You fight like a man who doesn't care if he does," his eyes were light and shrewd on me. "You fight like a man who doesn't care *if* he goes home. You need to shift your mindset." He aimed another kick at me and this time, I blocked it moving out of his way. "Better. She sees something in you worth saving. You need to live in a way where you honor that. *Entiendes?*"

In Spanish Liam told me I needed to be better.

It caught me off guard.

"Entiendes." I could taste the word on my tongue.

His grin was feral and wide as he tore into me. Nobody fought like that. Nobody human.

I groaned taking every hit and giving it back on my own.

Liam and I began going to workout together. And he was turning into my best friend, a brother, a family. Our workout days became a ritual, Isobel relieved to have some time to herself as Liam and I connected.

Liam and I talked about everything, realizing we had more in common.

"No fucking way you listen to this band," he motioned to the White Strokes. "Teague Lawson is a legend."

I grinned. "I met Teague Lawson."

"You did not!" Liam was all eyes and excitement as we got on over the same band we followed. "How, motherfucker?"

He was a lot like me. I began picking up his mannerisms and he picked up mine until Isobel had groaned at how alike we were. He wore his heart on his sleeves and I kept mine somewhere deeper in me.

I was just quieter than he was.

But it was clear we both agreed on one thing—her. She was the epicenter of our lives. Our family. Connected through one woman who kept it together.

And in some ways we weren't alike.

One evening, we'd both been so tired we crashed in her old bedroom where Liam had left it untouched.

In the morning, I'd woken up, rolled Isobel over onto her stomach, with a pillow under it, and slid deep into her with the intent of making love to my girlfriend.

We both groaned at the position and I was kissing her when the door burst open. She screamed. I swore.

I covered her as he swore covering his eyes and closing the door. In his briefs I swung my head to him.

"It's okay, baby." It was not okay. I was losing my shit. "What the fuck do you want Liam?"

"Jesus, things I did not need to see number ten thousand. Can you two help me?"

I pulled out aware I was so fucking close to killing him as I tucked her under me. He had his back to me and I blinked at his tattoos running down his arms.

"What the fuck happened that you had to come in here for?" I swore.

"Is it safe to turn around, Mom and Dad?"

"Every single time he says that, I know something bad has happened," Isobel whispered ferociously. I agreed.

"I heard that," Liam shot back. "Walls are thin as fuck, remember?" He didn't let us finish as he whimpered. "Look, last night I brought this girl home, okay?"

"When?" I asked. "You came home with us."

"I couldn't sleep—" he started. "So she comes in. And she spent the night."

"I knew I heard something," Isobel whispered. "This little *pendejo* was busy."

I snickered at her misery as she pawed my chest turning around in my arms. I was already missing her heat. I was just as frustrated as her.

"Now she won't leave you guys."

Both of us burst into laughter.

I buried my face into her hair as she laughed outright both of us shaking as Liam turned around red-faced. "Isa. Please. Do something. I think she's in the kitchen touching your things."

Even with me still laughing that got Isobel up and moving. "Turn around, I have to put clothes on."

He did and I helped her put on a shirt I borrowed from Liam. So technically it was his. She motioned to him red-faced. "Let's go."

I laughed harder as he whispered. "Please scare her."

It took her maybe thirty seconds of Isobel screaming like she caught her man cheating for the girl to leave.

Liam thanked her, promised us both breakfast, Isobel shut the door and ran over to me.

We laughed so hard I caught a stitch in my side she rubbed out.

"Amor, I am never staying here again."

I laughed harder. "It's all fine if we do, I bet he misses you too."

She pouted as I kissed her our laughter mingling as she rolled on top of me. "Now where were we?"

CHAPTER 29
ISOBEL

"You're on your period?"

Gabriel snuggled me tighter to him.

He was very sweet.

I hadn't been with Gabriel in a few days, I had put it off as not feeling good, and he'd been worried.

I just lied and told him I was on my period and he'd been this sweet all week.

Bringing me flowers, my favorite snacks, wrapping me in a heated blanket until I was asleep in his arms.

I never ever thought he was made of ice anymore.

I felt bad lying to him but today—I finally felt better.

"I have to tell you something," I looked at the condoms. "You don't need those anymore. I was not sick. Or on my period. But I got on birth control. I was just seeing how my body reacted to it."

Pale eyes met mine as he blinked, his head tipping a little to the side confused. I smiled and nodded feeling shy.

A soft smile drifted on his lips making him look adorable.

"You didn't have to."

"No, I wanted to, especially since…"

Since sometimes we almost forgot them. Both of us too absorbed in each other.

I didn't mind it, I just wanted to feel him, but also not worry about having kids right now, there were times we didn't have condoms or ran out and—I shook my head.

"I did not want to worry about it."

"*That's why* you made me wait." He looked at me with relief. "I thought something was wrong."

At the look on his face I instantly apologized. "I was just trying to take it and get used to it."

"As happy as that makes me, *tell* me those things, baby." I nodded, feeling an unfamiliar sensation crest in my chest. "I was—" he closed his eyes puffing out air. I kissed him. I reached for him. "I was worried about you all week."

And then he laid me down and made love to me. The first time he was in me without anything he was intense.

"I love you like this," I gasped into his mouth, loving the way he grinned.

The first thrust inside of me, I cried out, head tossing back, his answering groan one of nothing but pure pleasure.

I whimpered his name as he invaded deeper and deeper until I felt the slight twinge of pain.

He let me adjust until I urged him to move and then the white-hot pleasure at Gabriel losing it over me was nothing I was prepared for. Sometimes he was sweet.

Sometimes he was not.

Whenever I'd give him an attitude or he felt jealous of something, he tied me up, and did things to me that left me a pile of mush.

It was so intense I'd cry afterwards and Gabriel explained it to me as a drop in endorphins and he was there holding me, wrapping me into the blankets, and cuddling me.

He liked when I cooked, but I liked that he did everything else.

The laundry in the mornings before he went to work, putting away when he was home while I ran around living with him most of the time.

I added my touches to his apartment, little things I liked and I liked the way it surprised him.

And in a way he made my dreams come true. I liked doing my job, but I loved coming home to my partner.

Just Gabriel. *Su amor vive en mi alma.*

His love lived inside of my soul.

My father always said he loved Mama no matter where they were in the world.

Without her he said he felt incomplete, like a shadow missing the light. He said they could not exist without the other and he did for me. For Liam.

I felt like Gabriel had sank into the shadows in my head and soothed him and only he could.

More than anyone else, I felt like the darkness in my brain was something only Gabriel could help. Heal. Soothe.

I was in the bath one Saturday afternoon, the bubbly water scented and hot before soaking on my scrubbing day.

A little smile played on his lips as he brushed his teeth. Domestic life with Gabriel felt different.

"What kind…is today?" He gestured to my bath products. Since moving in with Gabriel I had to explain why I needed fifty of them.

"Today's just a body scrub day." He didn't look like he'd like that. He looked adorably lost as he finished brushing his teeth. "Have you taken a bath today?" I asked. He shook his head rinsing.

"Come here," I held out my hand. "I'll show you."

His eyes heated as he took off his clothes and sank into the bath with me. I smiled. "No, Gabriel, that's not why I got you here."

And then Gabriel Monroe sat in the bath with narrowed eyes looking like an angry cat and wet hair, as I introduced sugar scrubs. I laughed lightly and then a lot as he sputtered.

"Relax Gabriel…it's nice, no?"

He closed his eyes with a sigh as I scrubbed. "We should do this more often." Laughter bubbled in my throat as I helped clean him up. His eyes lit up.

"We can do whatever you want." He needed more self care, he worked so hard, and I wanted to give him some peace sometimes. And I moved onto my body.

"Let me," He mimicked what I had done for him, and I learned Gabriel was someone who liked to absorb everything, he didn't want to just learn *everything*, he wanted to master it.

I live to please.

As I sank with my back to his chest I exhaled. "I want to make you feel good too."

When we finally rinsed off, he marveled at how soft I was. I knew where he was going with this when we got back to his bed.

"*Gabriel…*"

I felt his smile as he kissed me. "We definitely should do this more often."

"I COULD STARE AT YOU FOREVER." I FELT MY CHEEKS HEAT AND MY body grow warm.

He smiled winter blue eyes bright and warm despite being so pale they shone on his tanned face. "You are so pretty."

I melted.

This man is so sweet.

How could I ever think he was cold?

I smiled, unable to tease him with that sweet smile of his. That was the smile that got me every time. *This is the smile I fell for.*

"Prettier than anyone else?"

He slowly oh so slowly closed his eyes and tipped his head.

All his little expressions gave him away. All of them.

I couldn't believe I'd *missed* them. Since day one.

This *entire* time.

"You are beautiful, Gabriel." *Inside and out. It's an honor to love you.*

He opened his eyes and once again hitting me with the full force of pale ice. "That so?"

"Mhm," I nodded, looping my arms around his neck. "You will love me again, *Amor*?" I smiled up at him. "As much as I want?"

His Adam's apple bobbed as he nodded. "As much as you need." Before I could process that he dipped his head to my lips. "I can't get enough of you."

Nobody loves like him.

In the last weekend alone I was sore. I ached.

And cried as he took me. Over and over. I whispered over his lips. *"El amor vive en tu alma."*

Something was changing the more he made love to me.

"What does that mean?"

Love lives in your soul. "I like you."

"I know when you lie, I can feel it in your body."

"No," I panted. "You know when I want to be kissed."

I wanted it forever. When I was finally too sore, I dared to ask him.

"Why do you like me...like that?"

He replied with his eyes closed on the bed, looking more at peace than I'd ever seen him. "Why do I like being a Dom or why I like fucking you?"

"Both." His eyes opened. A soft smile played on his lips at my expression.

"That's not an answer." His low rumble of a chuckle sank into me as I frowned.

"No?" He was dangerous when he was playful. "Tell me what that sentence means in Spanish and I'll give you an honest answer."

I batted his hands away. "No, me duele."

I *hurt*. His eyes went dark as he tongue darted out between his lips. He knew what that meant. I said it enough to him.

"*Where?*" *Oh no. I knew that look.*

"*Gabriel.*" *I'm serious.*

"So am I."

He moved over me and I felt my heart lose it as my legs fell open to him and he dipped his head kissing my inner thighs.

"It's like I'm fuck drunk off you."

He dipped his head lower and as he licked, there was no intent —nothing wild or crazy, just—I panted.

I lost track of my thoughts and time.

My fingers tangled in wheat hair and tugged.

My eyes unseeing as he tasted and licked and tongued and when he did finally slid his tongue into me I shook around him in the gentlest wave crashing over me.

I laid there boneless as he lapped.

"Tell me," his voice was gruff. "I can keep you here like this."

Dio. "I can't think—"

"Try harder." I screamed a little as he sucked my clit into his mouth.

"I like watching you break. Over and over." He whispered. "I like control over you, your body, forcing orgasms out of you for me. You have your safe word and you know I'll stop whenever you tell me. And if you don't use it I won't stop."

Gabriel was devious like this.

He lapped at my body like he owned it. Like he had all the time in the world. My skin against his contrasted and the sight of it was something else.

"I like that you use your safe word outside of sex too. It's like you have me around your finger and all you do is say Snowman and I yield. Not that I mind—" he licked again leaving me a mess.

"I need *more* control. I need *everything*. Need to rise. I just want it with you now. I love you helpless, not thinking for once, letting

223

me control it all, love how it calms me down," he continued on me like he wasn't tearing me apart from the inside out. "Calms me down and….drives me crazy."

He looked up at me, his lips wet, eyes bright and face utterly the most beautiful man I'd ever met. "Does that scare you?"

He protected me, defended me, got on my nerves, drove me crazy, and let me lead, took my ideas, let me be free, and he was asking me if him wanting to make me come, *scared me?*

I didn't answer him.

I reached down and pulled him to me kissing him, reaching between his legs, between mine. Letting him slide against me.

"You're sore."

"Don't move." I *rarely* got to command him. "*No te muevas.*"

Rarely. I rolled him until he was sitting up and I straddled him.

It would ache a little, a lot, it would hurt, and it did. But as I slid him in me I sighed.

I wrapped my legs around his waist and he moved adjusting me until his arms were around me.

"You're sore." I knew he caught my wince.

"I want to feel you." And then I told him in Spanish everything I wanted to say.

Everything. "Wait, I know that look—" he reached for his phone. "I'll be damned if I don't know what you say."

A light laugh left me. It wouldn't matter.

He didn't understand Spanish. He was trying to learn and it took time between our jobs for him to learn.

I smiled into his kisses. "*El amor vive en tu alma. Estás lleno de amor. Te amo…*"

I said love lives in your soul. You are so full of love. I love you.

I know you don't understand me.

I love you, I love you like the moon follows and loves the sun, just like that amor. I will always be yours. I take no one else but you. When I first saw you I thought you were the most beautiful man I had ever seen. And now every single day I love you—

I had to stop because my eyes were watering as I kissed him over and over.

Thank you for defending my honor, my best friend, my intelligence, my strength, my future, and my culture. I would never be afraid of the man who pretends he has a heart made of ice and burns like fire for those around him. I vow to always love you, in equal measures as you love me.

I don't think it's possible to love anyone the way you love. I never saw you coming. Liam, wanted me to do this, for my future. But now my future has changed. It's changed completely with you.

My future is with you. Our children. Our love. I would stand by you through everything, Gabriel. I don't know how to exist without you.

"I—" he was struggling. "I got some of that. You're my future too."

I was so proud of him. "You are learning fast."

"I still have my accent," he whispered with soft eyes. "But I'm trying."

I smiled at the thought of ever being like him, as good as him.

"One day, Gabriel, you will have everything you want." I whispered in English. *"The world will be yours."*

I pray to everything out there your heart heals, you heal, and one day maybe I could be yours.

"What does that mean?"

I vow to love you. I vow to give you the all consuming love you are. You are everything good in this world, Gabriel. I pray you rise in this world.

You will have everything one day.

Nobody will ever take anything away from you.

"Say it."

I took his lips in mine. In English. "I am yours."

He kissed me with equal fervor pulsing in me.

I tugged his hair back, nipping his jaw. *"Make love to me, Gabriel."*

If Gabriel could feel my desperation he returned it.

His phone lay forgotten.

And I kissed him with everything I had.

For some reasons the shadows he was calming in me were stirring, moving around him like they could protect him from what was coming.

I felt a storm on the horizon.

I felt something in my bones. In Mexico my mother would say she could always feel when something bad was coming for us.

She held onto Evie the entire time she did.

Gabriel will make it. He has to.

You will rise.

You will heal.

You don't need to be great Gabriel Raphael Monroe.

You already are.

CHAPTER 30
GABRIEL

It was a few weeks before we went after Hagen that Liam came to my office.

Something was wrong. I knew it the moment he looked at me.

"Hey," he looked lost, the shadows in his eyes deeper, the way his hands shook. "I need to—" he broke off shutting the door. "We need to talk."

All the spark of mischief he and Isobel had was gone. I felt my stomach turn and anxiety creep into me.

"What the fuck happened?"

I got onto my haunches as he sat down meeting him eye to eye. I wasn't his boss now. I was his brother. Her man. His family.

"Her father was in an accident." I knew who *she* was. Panic skated down my spine.

"She doesn't know yet. The hospital called me for some reason. I was listed as his emergency contact." Wild green eyes met mine panicked and desperate. "I need to go see him. But I can't without her knowing."

"You want me to…" He couldn't be asking me to distract her.

"We're going after Hagen soon," Liam's eyes met mine. He shook his head. "She can't go to him. She has to stay here with Sutton and Vince and Jay. I can go. I'll take care of it." Something was wrong.

"What happened to him?"

"Head injury, he got into a car accident." Liam looked more shaken up than I'd ever seen him. And I saw the tremor in his body.

"You can't go alone."

"I have to."

I shook my head in disbelief. "I can take care of her, but I have to tell her. She's gonna wanna go."

"We *can't* both go. If she goes?" He looked at me. "She's gonna completely fucking shatter. I can go. I'll handle it."

Lying to Isobel was not something I did. Not well.

She knew instantly something was up with Liam and me. She frowned at both of us. Both of us trying to protect her for different reasons.

That night at home she asked me what was wrong over and over. She knew something was up.

"Gabriel," she whispered to me in bed. "Liam would only leave for a few reasons. I know one of them." Her eyes watered. *"Dimelo, amor."*

"I can't, baby. I can't." I brushed back her raven hair growing even longer with me. "I was thinking about the house you wanted to show me. You said you guys lived in Connecticut for a bit? Liam went to go look at it. I think he's scoping it out for you." But she knew I was lying. Her eyes watered. "Show me, baby."

She wiped her eyes as she brought her phone out. It was a decent enough distraction.

"This is Heron Manor," she pointed it out. It was a massive structure. A couple of million dollars.

A pretty penny for real-estate.

Her hands trembled at the photos and I held her tightly as she told me about her dream house.

"It was owned by some rich family," she whispered. "But now, it's empty..." she said she drove by it as a kid and imagined living there.

Liam had said he'd get it for her one day when he made money.

It looked like a fucking castle and I saw why she loved it.

"It's called a Georgian style mansion?" I looked at the description choosing to distract her over tell her the truth. I had never lied to Isobel. I was pretty pissed off with Liam for putting me in this position. "It's in Greenwich?"

She nodded. "It's good for children."

Her voice softened as she said it and something blossomed in my chest at the image of someone smaller than us.

227

Someone who looked like her. Someone with her eyes and that mischievous smile glancing at me from coloring books.

Maybe dance classes.

Her voice dropped to something even more vulnerable.

"Liam said he liked the sunroom. I always thought after we fixed up Oracle, I could find Evie and Mama. I would bring my family back together." Warm eyes met mine. "One day."

"I can help." I don't know why every moment with her felt different. Recently everything felt different. "I can help with that. I can help you find your sister." Evie Santos.

How hard could it be to find her?

Somehow while our lives went on, Evie was put on the back burner but now? As her boss, I might be able to say I was doing Isobel and Liam a favor by finding their long lost sister.

Her smile softened on me as she watched me, but I saw the way her eyes turned red, watery. "Liam is with our father isn't he? I know you, I know when you lie to me."

I didn't say a word. I knew when she lied to me too.

"Something happened to my father." I had her in my arms as she sobbed. "You won't tell me because it is bad."

I held her tighter.

"Did I ever tell you why I fell in love with you?" I whispered into her hair. She shook her head. The words came from somewhere deep inside of me. Somewhere she unlocked.

"It started with your sass," I smiled into her hair inhaling butterscotch and warmth. "You're fiery and beautiful, absolutely breathtaking. And then I got to know you and I realized despite your trauma and pain—you have never let it define you. Not once. You give me everything so openly, so freely, so much of it—I don't know what to do with it. I just know I want it. All the time."

I took a shuddering breath.

"I wanted your challenge. Matching me step for step. You never back down."

If I was ice, she was fire. Melting every bit of my resolve until all that was left was a man at his base. I was drowning in her. I didn't want to come up for any other thing. Any other reason.

"And then I think I started falling you harder when you told me your love for me would never be conditional. Not even once. And you prove it all the time. You make me believe I can heal. I can be great. Even when I feel like I don't deserve it. And it makes me want

228

to be worthy of you. You're my compass. You're my faith. You're my everything. And I would do anything to protect that."

She pulled back, her eyes watering as she took me in.

I took a breath as I held her face in my hands.

"I have never…ever…once known this. But then I meet you and I feel like I've known my entire life. You don't wanna fix me or change me, you don't expect anything from me."

She shook her head. "I want to be by your side. I want to walk with you—"

"I know, baby." Independence within interdependence.

She was my whole fucking world.

"And you stay."

"I will." She held onto me tighter then with worry. "I will stay."

I dipped my head. "And that's exactly why I have to keep you safe."

A WEEK LATER LIAM DID COME BACK. AND I SAW IT ALL OVER HIS face.

Isobel didn't make a sound as he showed up at our door haunted, eyes dark, and his entire expression blank.

His eyes met mine and I knew.

But so did she. Her jaw dropped open as she stared at him.

"You…you kept him from me?" She whispered horrified. "This is why?"

In another second she on him tearing at his shirt like she was sinking asking him questions.

I translated it roughly in my head.

How could you?

What happened? Why did you keep it from me?

You're supposed to be my brother!

Liam looked numb as she gripped his shirt for the answers he didn't give her.

I knew why he didn't say a word. I fucking *knew* him.

We were in a critical state and Liam knew if both of them were out—we'd be in a shit situation. I got it.

But I saw the devastation in her face. I saw how Liam didn't meet her eyes. I saw him fighting his emotions in a way that tugged at my heart.

Instead he held her elbows like he wanted to hold her and held back. I was the one peeling her off him and she whirled on me. "You kept this from me! You hid this!"

There was nothing but fire in her eyes now and I had one hundred percent of that anger directed at me.

Liam's lower lip wobbled as an animal noise left her. "He didn't want me to tell you."

She turned to him with a stunned expression, her eyes wide, hands shaking. "What?"

Liam nodded. His eyes usually bright green and vibrant shuttered now. Turning into a duller hunter shade.

And it stayed that way.

"He asked me not to..." and he explained to her, her father hadn't wanted her to stop her life.

And if Isobel could ever look like someone had shot her—that was how she looked right now.

"He asked me to see him. Because you would've dropped your world to stop for him."

As Liam said it I saw something else in his eyes when he looked at her.

I couldn't pinpoint what it was but the regret was all over his expression.

She covered her mouth and I watched her crumble sinking back into the island, and I couldn't see her face but I saw the way Liam watched her.

The way his face crumbled as he swiped at his eyes.

I blinked back my emotion at both of them.

I had never seen them like this. Isobel didn't say a word. And somehow that was worse. The silence cut deeper into me. I was the quiet one.

Those two were louder than life when together.

This was my first time seeing them breaking. And I fucking hated it.

She left the room. Leaving him standing there, staring at her like someone had carved out a piece of him. Sheer agony written in his eyes. One thing about Liam I had always respected—he always wore his emotions on his face.

Right now? Liam looked devastated.

He didn't stick around and I didn't know what to do.

There was nothing in my system that knew what to do for

230

them.

My brother and girlfriend were at odds.

At work everything changed between them.

Isobel was devastated, not saying a word to him.

Sutton picked up on it immediately and she shot worried glances at Liam who stopped teasing her with his tongue ring.

Her and Vince traded looks about the siblings all the time.

Liam didn't talk to anyone. He just stopped being...Liam. Every single day he just sat and worked and passed his info to Jeremy who gave it to me instead.

Vincent began bringing them food from his wife who knew, and even Jeremy was baking more often for them.

"I thought you guys might like some banana bread, it's my Nana's recipe."

Fucking Jeremy didn't belong in the CIA.

I didn't know who let him in, but the kid was too sweet.

But it was the worst at home.

She was my other half and she shut me out. Like I had shut her out. The silence between us bothered me more than anything I could've even fathomed.

She didn't say a word to me.

One night I came home with flowers recognizing while pathetic, I didn't know what to do.

I didn't have a playbook for angry upset girlfriend I lied to keep her out of seeing her father at his lowest.

I knew why he'd asked for Liam.

Liam could stomach seeing him like that. He wasn't blood even if he loved the man.

I had no doubt if Isobel had seen him?

She would've quit the CIA, gone home to him and buried herself with him.

Isobel loved her father.

He was something she had been looking forward to.

Not only did I keep it from her, Liam buried him and she would never see him again. I found her in bed, curled away from me, and something in my chest twisted.

"Baby." I cleared my throat setting the flowers aside and crawling in with her on the bed. "You awake?"

With the heated blanket on she was cozy but I knew she was

numbed out. Like a ghost in my house. Her features shuttered. Even her eyes had changed.

Every instinct in my body screamed to fix this. My accent was horrible, but I couldn't get through to her otherwise.

I curled around her, pulling her closer to me, her body into my chest. My lips brushed over her temple. "Lo siento…"

I felt her stiffen a little as I said the words like I surprised her.

"Yo…uh…" I was searching the mental dictionary in my head. "Cuidar…tu?" I had a hard time putting it together. I was trying to tell her I wanted to take care of her.

But I knew I fucked up. Liam too.

Sometimes those decisions hit the hardest.

I pressed my face into her hair feeling her move against me a little. "Yo quiero…mmm….necesito? Eres mia. I can say that. No me dejas? Degas? I can't tell. I'm trying. Para ti. For you. Uhh…por favor, mirame…." I butchered it.

All of it. But I was struggling.

This whole learning Spanish while trying to hunt down a potential criminal was hard.

I took some steadying breaths.

For a long moment she didn't say anything.

And then she said. "Dejes," her voice was a croak. "It's *no me dejes.*"

I didn't know what else to do. It was the first thing she said to me in days. I just mimicked her accent. "No me dejes."

Don't leave me.

"Your accent is terrible," she whispered.

I let out a light laugh feeling something crack open in my chest.

"But you are trying."

"I am, baby. I'm trying." My voice was a quiet shudder. My fingers trembled running through her hair as she sniffled.

Isobel whispered. "*Estoy enojada contigo.*"

Ummm….what did that one mean again?

"Estoy enamorado too." I tried. That sounded the same. Was she telling me she loved me?

A light laugh left her. "It means I'm angry with you stupid."

"That too."

Her shoulders shook lightly and I felt my lips tip up. Fuck, I missed her like this.

I dipped lower until my eyes met hers. Soft and wet and so

pissed off at me. I cupped her face with one hand, thumbing her tear tracks.

"I'm sorry, baby. I didn't know how bad it was until Liam showed up. I just knew he'd been in accident. I'm sorry I didn't tell you. Liam asked me—"

"But I am with you, no?" Her lower lip wobbled. "I am yours. Your everything? You did not give me a choice. To know. To pick. To choose." Her eyes watered again making me realize why she was angry.

Liam and I never gave her a choice.

We were so hell bent on protecting her?

I forgot she deserved every right to break and make it.

"I'm selfish," I admitted, the truth was burning in my throat. "I didn't want to lose you. I thought if I gave you what I thought you needed. You'd leave me too. You'd go home and you'd abandon me."

There. That was the truth. My darkest fear was that the moment Isobel did break—she couldn't put herself together for me.

That I wasn't enough.

I had never been enough. Not for anyone.

"I didn't tell you, because I thought he was going to be fine. I thought Liam was going to see him and he was alive. And you wouldn't have to care for him during his time when you'd already been stressed out. And then I was terrified if you did, you would leave me, you would leave Quantico, you would leave my life—"

"I would never leave you."

"But I don't know that—" I broke off at that feeling because everyone left. Everything was obliterated in my life except for her. "I don't know if you will or if one day you wake up and you decide this isn't what you wanted anymore—when Liam told me—"

"I would never—"

"When Liam told me, I knew if I told you, you'd leave too. Was it fair? Fuck no. Liam and I didn't think it was the last time you'd see him. He didn't even know until he got there. And that's when shit hit the fan for both of us—"

"But you kept it from me—"

"I did. And I will spend the rest of my life feeling that guilt. But you are the one good thing I have in this world. I didn't want to ever risk that. Liam thought he would be fine."

Her face crumbled. "He was my world."

"I know, baby." I tucked her into my chest again as she cried.

"I'm angry with you. I don't like you right now."

"I know, baby."

And the worst feeling was? I was such a fucking bastard. I was. Because I knew deep down, William Santos did the same fucking thing asking Liam to not let Isobel see him like this.

Which was cruel letting Liam shoulder that all alone. All three of us had tried to protect her. Out of love. Not out of malice.

And all three of us had fucked up.

~

LIAM WASN'T OKAY.

I went over to the immaculate apartment now like it was an empty home. Liam had packed up some items into boxes neat against the wall.

But his room?

I walked in and I saw the bin with liquor bottles.

He was drunk out of his mind when his eyes met mine. On a weekday.

"What happened?" I sat across from him aware, I could smell the alcohol on him and he was staring at his wall. I had Isobel's keys and I let myself in.

But I knew I couldn't leave him alone.

"He had head trauma," Liam voice was a whisper. "A brain injury from the car crash. She didn't need to see him like that. She's got a softer heart than I do."

He shook his head taking a sip from the cup he had. I felt the darkness coming off him in waves. My stomach twisted at the sight of him.

"He figured if she came she'd be devastated. She'd give it all up to be with him. And she would. He didn't want that."

I had experienced loss. With my team-mates. With others. I'd lost a lot.

But I never felt that same loss as these two did. I understand the same way.

Until the two of them? I'd never loved anything enough.

Liam's gaze was fixed on the wall, his eyes distant as he spoke, "I promised her father I'd take care of her."

I nodded, my heart heavy with the weight of Liam's words. His eyes held a faraway look to them.

234

"That's not what I promised him," Liam continued, his voice low and thick with emotion. "I promised Isobel's father, I would marry her."

And just like that—my heart shattered.

I felt it plummet to my stomach, a cold dread seeping into my bones. The fire ants trailed a path on my skin. Staying there.

Liam's confession hung in the air between us, the gravity of his words settling like a physical weight.

I couldn't breathe, couldn't think.

The idea of Liam marrying Isobel, the woman I loved more than myself, was like a knife twisting in my gut.

"He made me promise I would give her the dance studio she wanted, a life to make her happy, babies, the house, everything."

I swallowed suddenly aware of the reality of what he was saying.

"He told me he knew I loved Isobel. He knew all those years I did. He said if I loved her, if I loved him, I would marry her."

Because he hadn't known about me. Isobel wanted to take me to see him once we came back from the assignment with Hagen. Now she'd never get the chance.

Liam shook his head not looking at me once as he drank now straight from the bottle.

"I don't want Isobel, I *need* her. She's my sister, my best friend, at times she's my mother," Liam laughed softly, the sound tinged with a bittersweet ache. "She's my everything, and then I watched her fall for you, and I knew—*I fucking knew*—it would never be me."

And all of a sudden, I became aware of something else.

Something that horrified me. *I had always seen him as her brother. Always. Because of her.*

Not because of him.

The hairs on the back of my neck stood up and the energy in the room shifted. I felt it instantly.

And if Liam felt it, his eyes darted over lazily to me.

"Never me." He shook his head. "It was never me."

"You're not her brother," I couldn't even say it.

"*Not even close,*" he whispered with so much darkness in his eyes I didn't know who I as looking at.

It was borderline eerie for me to look at him and see a new glint. The darkness in the room was swallowing me whole.

"But I am to *her.*"

"*You* loved her," I whispered my eyes and voice betraying my shock. But I had known all along hadn't I? I had suspected it because of how he looked at her. "Did you realize it now after me? Or did you know for years?"

And I didn't just take her away.

I had her from the moment she met me.

"I don't understand, why would you give her to me?"

If he loved her.

Because no fucking way he would wait years.

"Because I see the way she looked at you." His eyes held mine and I saw something akin to a hint of contempt, darkness, bitterness, reality all in those depths. "She never looked at me like that."

I was aware he was clutching the bottle now.

"I see her. I have always seen her, and I thought I could be her brother. I thought I could be who she needed me to be. And then I watched her fall in love with you." He tipped his head back drinking more. And then he said it. "I promised *him* I *would* to his face. And I would die by my word."

Liam stood abruptly and moved to his dresser where I fucking knew he had his gun and I didn't know what to do.

Maybe it was the alcohol.

Maybe it the pitch black in his expression.

Maybe it was his confession that he was in love with my girlfriend.

I didn't know why I knew something was coming out of there.

I moved reaching for him. I didn't bring my gun but Liam knew —and he held his hands up. His back was turned to me still.

"Relax Monroe. If I kill you, she'll never forgive me."

The way that he said it I realized something then. Liam would kill me. He would.

Because his priorities weren't that he wouldn't, it was that if he did, she wouldn't love him anymore.

It was always about her.

He reached into his dresser slowly and pulled out a black box. He tossed it my way and I caught it deftly.

"That is her mother's. Adrianna. He gave it to me. He didn't want to split up their family. But he said he did so that nobody would hurt his girls again. He was afraid if the cartels told their Stateside counterparts they would go after Evie. Or Isobel. So he left and hid and split his family apart. He still loved Adrianna and

Evie. Isobel's middle name is her mom's." His voice cracked. "Everything he did was for them. He still loves them."

With trembling fingers, I took the box, my heart racing as I opened it. Inside, nestled on a bed of velvet, was a simple gold band.

I knew how much it would mean to Isobel, the sentimental value it held.

Liam's voice was raw and breaking.

I didn't think it would hurt.

"I'm giving you this, because I want you to know I fucking hate you for making me break my promises. You have always made it hard for me to hate you. But this time—I do. I hate you. I hate William. I hate everyone. But *her*."

He loves her.

All this time.

The first time I had seen Liam, I saw something in his eyes that made me assume he was with her.

The way he touched her, his hand on her waist—that moment felt like eons ago.

Now I knew, I wasn't imagining it. I had always known. Always wondered.

Isobel had never seen it because she had never seen him like that.

The boy who snuck into her life and shared her room and become this man.

Of course he fell for her. And William fucking *knew.*

"I can't keep my promise to the man who saved my life." Liam's voice shook as he looked down at his hands his back to me still. "I'm changing my name back to Sullivan. Not just for the Hagen assignment, but losing William made me realize I was *never* a Santos." Liam didn't even look at me. "I'm so fucking pissed at him for what the fuck he did."

I was angry with William Santos.

In his efforts to protect his family—he'd done this.

I was angry he split his family apart, angry he shouldered Liam with his death, angry he cut his daughter out at the end, angry for making Liam make a promise without knowing what she would want.

I didn't understand if my heart was breaking with him or for him or for Isobel who had no fucking idea the lengths he could go to for her.

"Everything you did—" I began.

"Has *always* been for her." He finished. "It will *always* be her."

But the ring. I looked down at the box. "You're giving me your blessing."

Liam tipped his head deliberately and he finally turned to face me.

His eyes wet and red. "I want you to marry her. You have my blessing. Don't fuck it up. *If you do, if you hurt her ever—*"

The words ripped out of me. "*I would never hurt her—*"

"*I will put a bullet in your brain,*" Liam said, his eyes wet and unapologetic.

"I promised. *You* are the reason I am breaking that promise. *If anything happens to her, I will kill you.* If anything happens to *you?*"

His eyes were hunter green now after William's death they had never gone back to being light.

"*I will keep my promise.*"

CHAPTER 31
ISOBEL

"DID YOU READ THE NEW BOOK? ABOUT THE GUY WHO STALKS HIS girl and then breaks into her house to seduce her?"

"I did," I whispered back to Claire. "I did not like it, it was a little creepy—"

"Yeah, tell me about it. She wasn't even phased. She's like 'oh no I'm so horny whatever shall I do'?"

I giggled as Jeremy caught our convo.

Ever since I started working at the office, I learned Claire liked extremely filthy books. And so did Jeremy. Out of all people I did not see this coming.

Jeremy read all sorts of romance novels. Historical. Contemporary. Thrillers. And supernatural dragon shifter romance novels where the men transformed into...well dragons. I did not know such romance novels existed but here we were.

In the modern day.

Reading about dragons making love to unsuspecting innocent women and bringing them cows...

It took me a little to get around to it as my brain tried to rationalize the dragons, and when I told Gabriel he looked ready to have a heart attack.

Dragons? Jeremy? Jesus fucking Christ, I knew that kid was weird.

Amor, look—

No, Isa I'm traumatized.

Amor—

Fine, just one....

"Sutton, I gave that to you a week ago," Jeremy pitched in. "And I found some super dark stalker novels where he fucks her with—"

"Jeremy!" Claire threw a textbook at him. "Not at work."

"It's okay, Sutton, I won't tell anyone you're a closeted whore."

"Dio! Jeremy!" It was my turn. And he cackled. His little round body tipped over in his cheap plastic chair as he giggled.

Jeremy was the one who recommended the romance novels to us out of all people. He had a stack of them he read for "research purposes."

For a sweet faced round boy who baked us chocolate chip cookies—he read some of the nastiest things I could imagine.

Ever since I started working with Jeremy, he seemed to come out of his shell. Slowly.

"I'm not the one who spends their day knitting," Claire shot back.

"I make cats sweaters at the animal shelter I volunteer at," he shrugged adorably turning red in the face. I pinched his chubby cheeks making him giggle.

Que bendito. How cute.

"You are a strange little boy," I agreed. "Dragon shifter pornography and now you are eating pickles?"

"Isa, I'm basically a pregnant woman in a man's body. If I didn't have a dick, I'd ask questions."

Claire and I burst into giggles at that.

"All right, all right," Jeremy laughed with us turning even redder. "That's enough of your shenanigans."

I laughed harder as Claire wiped her eyes.

Every so often I was sure Jeremy was an old man. He would throw a really big word into a sentence that made no sense. Like *flabbergasted, bamboozled,* and *jolly good. Or fiddlesticks.*

Into the middle of some random sentence.

I was *flabbergasted* by Jeremy.

"It helped me seduce Cathy, you know? I just think dragon shifter romances have their own appeal. At least I'm into werewolf sex."

"Dragon sex and werewolf sex are different?" Claire remarked dryly.

"Duh, they have different cocks, Sutton. I'm gobsmacked you don't know that—"

I burst into tears with how hard I was laughing. And Claire shot me a look. "If he says fiddlesticks I'm gonna kill him—"

"Ladies, fiddlesticks is a great word—"

"I do not know what this means—" I started.

"It means what it means, Isa. Language is an art. You wound't understand. Peasants."

"Contemporary art or modern art, King Jeremy?" Claire shot back.

Jeremy thought about it as he said. "Look, Liam told me I had to be cool, but I didn't know how so I just started reading romance novels. And definitely classical art. I couldn't imagine the word *skedaddle* in contemporary art."

"Ske—daddle—" I practiced.

"Isobel, don't sound like this douchecanoe over here. Jeremy, stop speaking English and start speaking in Spanish. Maybe we'll understand you more."

"Fiddlesticks."

Claire through a textbook at him as I laughed so hard my side ached. This was life in the CIA.

Sometimes you almost died.

Other days, your coworkers were strange people who spent hours talking and hanging out.

"How is Cathy?" I asked Jeremy. "And do not tell me anything about dragon penises."

"Or werewolf cock—" Claire grumbled. "I draw the line after stalker romances."

"Sutton, you literally read a trilogy about a vampire demon lord—"

"Jeremy—" Claire eyed him down. "Tell us about Cathy before I cause a *kerfuffle* with you."

Now she was speaking his language.

Jeremy was dating Cathy. Finally.

His crush was his girlfriend and life had moved on for us. We were all...progressing. Life moved really fast in the CIA than civilian life and I couldn't imagine what I would be without Gabriel.

"I don't know why I ever thought you were a sweet man," I whispered to him. "Now I know you're completely *sucio*."

"I don't know what that means, but sure sounds like you wanna have a kerfuffle with me."

"I will kerfuffle you," Claire growled.

Claire quietly hid her smile as Gabriel walked in looking angrier than usual.

He went over to Vincent and Liam who were tracking a few updates for him.

Jeremy looked at me quickly. He raised his brows to ask me if I was good.

And this is why I liked Jeremy. People like Jeremy were assets to the intelligence community because he looked like a cupcake and had the brain of a killer.

He knew about me and Gabriel. I knew he knew.

Even though Jeremy did not say anything I knew he *suspected* I had something with Gabriel.

He never judged.

He never asked.

He checked on me with his eyes, his entire demeanor shifting from chubby pickle lover and romance novel reader to something else.

It was so subtle but I caught it now.

I felt like if he wanted to—he could kill someone for his romance novels. Everyone had a motivation.

I just shrugged a little at him.

He dipped his head closer. "Are you upset with him or is he upset with you?"

I always knew Jeremy knew.

I didn't say anything.

I shook my head not wanting to out me or Gabriel. Jeremy looked around and then dipped his head back again.

"Whatever he did, I think he's stressed right now, I don't think his head is in the right place. At all. I'm a little worried myself. I looked into Hagen. And I have some ideas about who it might be. I haven't pitched it to Gabriel yet. I wanted to run it by you and Sutton since you two think differently than Vince and Liam."

I nodded as he opened up his computer and I looked at his suspects. "You think Hagen is one of these men?"

His suspects were all wealthy billionaires.

Phillipe Dupont.

Charles Devereaux.

Gerard Marchand.

Malcolm Nash.

A few others but those stood out at the top.

"Who are these people?" I didn't know any of these names. I didn't even know Jeremy had narrowed a list down.

Jeremy explained he narrowed the listing down by people who he knew owned property across all the locations Hagen had been to.

These were the only people who matched his description. Somewhat.

"Hagen is either Caucasian or mixed race. People say they can't tell. He has black hair but white skin some have said. But he's *connected*. The guys a fucking ghost." Jeremy explained quietly. "I haven't said anything because I'm afraid the Marchand's are royalty or at least they're connected to enough royal families for me to know not to fuck with them. But who else would it be?"

I shook my head. "Who is Malcolm Nash? He is the only one without a clear picture."

Jeremy smiled. "Ah, that man is what got me thinking it might be a Nash. The more private the man, the more I knew something is worth seeking out."

Jeremy began showing me his notes about Malcolm Nash.

Charles Devereaux.

"He has a son, Lucas," I muttered. "His daughter Lucy. No, it can't be him. He does not look bright." Lucas Devereaux was a boy. A year younger than Gabriel, but Gabriel looked like he had been alive for three thousand years.

Lucas looked inexperienced as a civilian.

Jeremy snickered as we went through the people. "We can bookmark Lucas Devereaux because he's a NAVY SEAL."

We were so absorbed we didn't hear Gabriel coming over to us.

"A word, Bradford." Jeremy stood up and almost saluted Gabriel until he remembered where he was. And I bit back a laugh looking down at the file of Malcolm Nash.

Something about him rubbed me the wrong way. I couldn't put my finger on it.

But so did Gerard Marchand. I didn't know why.

Both of them had a daughter. Gemma Marchand seemed too sweet looking and thin. A model. Not her.

But Malcolm Nash had a daughter. Without a photo.

Talia Nash.

What were the odds...what did she do?

Before I could keep digging, I felt someone to my side and I thought it was Gabriel.

It wasn't. I turned to look into my brother's eyes.

"You got a sec?"

I felt my chest ache as I looked at him. His eyes had changed.

Becoming dark and shadowed like they had been when he'd been younger.

Claire sat up in her seat. "I can manage the desk," she added to me. Motioning for me to go with Liam.

He held out his hand to me.

I didn't even hesitate to take it.

~

"I'M SORRY," HE WHISPERED.

I didn't even know what to say I was so angry with him. So angry in so many ways. Angry with my father. Angry with Liam.

A little angry with Gabriel caught between everyone.

I folded my hands in my lap. "This is not the best time."

"No," his voice was gruff. I knew he had been crying. I could see it on his face. I always knew when Liam cried.

"You should not have kept that from me. It doesn't matter what Papi wanted." It shouldn't have mattered.

"But it does," Liam said honestly. "It does. Because he knows you just like he knows me."

Something about how he said that made me look at him.

What did he mean?

"I'm sorry," Liam's voice was raw with pain. "I thought he would be okay."

"What happened?" I realized in me hating him. Being angry with him. I didn't know.

Liam looked away. "He thought he was fine after the accident. I saw him in the hospital. We talked." His voice was a whisper. "We talked for a long time. He said he was fine. He was stubborn about it." I nodded I knew he could be. "We went home. He said he had a headache and he wanted to go to sleep. The doctor's said he was fine, but he should come back if he felt off."

I was shaking wiping my eyes.

"I went to go shower thinking he just wanted to rest," Liam wiped his eyes.

His voice broke. I realized Liam was there to watch him die and not in a way he wanted. Liam thought he failed my father. I saw how much he kept from me. From *everyone*.

"The doctors said it was an epidural hematoma. The short version is...his brain was bleeding. I woke up...he was cold...I called an ambulance."

He shook wildly then and I reached for him without even thinking as he broke. "I'm sorry." My entire being crumbled as I held him.

He hadn't said it. He kept it to himself. This *entire* time.

"I'm not angry with you," I sobbed. I held him tighter than I ever had. "I'm not."

"I didn't think about the CT scan," he whispered over and over. "I left him. I went to go shower..."

"But you couldn't stop it—" I broke off seeing his expression. "Not your fault."

He nodded like he understood me but he didn't hear me.

I held onto him so hard then I felt like I would break his spine. It was awkward over the console of the car. But I wasn't letting him go.

"I'm sorry."

But the words weren't adequate at all.

The shadows in my mind closed around me like they could protect Liam from himself.

Even if I knew—I had no idea what Liam was going through or how to get through to him.

∼

I TOLD GABRIEL ABOUT IT.

At home. He looked out of it too. Nervous almost.

Definitely distracted.

He was acting stranger than he usually did and most of the time it was endearing. He never fumbled with things but today he did.

But now with Liam out of it, Jeremy trying to find Hagen's identity, and Gabriel acting nervous?

It was getting on my nerves.

"Gabriel," I watched him almost drop something in the bedroom. "What is wrong?"

He turned to me then and I saw him holding something in his

fist. "I was going to wait. I wanted to do it right. Not here. Not like this. Not so soon."

"What?" I was confused. I had spent most of my time breaking down and now I was a little more than emotional. "What is it?"

He turned and I saw a chain dangling from his hand.

He walked up to me looking more nervous than I'd ever seen him. "Sit, please." He looked like he was deep in thought. "Sorry, uhh...lo siento. *Siéntate*, por favor."

I did. If he was trying to speak Spanish it was serious.

He took his phone out. "I wrote this down and translated it so let me say it to you."

And then he got on his knees in front of me that object in his fist like a child holding onto his toy.

"Amor," he started looking at his phone and then me. Poor baby hadn't even started and he was struggling. "El primer moment que te vi," he began. *From the moment I saw you.* "Estaba...ummm...captivado por ti."

I felt my lips curve into a smile. "Captivated."

"Yes. I mean, si."

My smile grew as he stumbled. "Tus ojos, tu pelo," he was searching for the word. "I can't pronounce the word for beauty."

"Belleza."

"Right," he looked embarrassed now and unsure of himself.

The light on his wheat colored hair and his eyes so pale and bright as he looked down and back at me. *"Era como me miraste con luz y sol en los ojos."*

Light and sun in my eyes. That's how I looked at him.

"Yo trataba de ser...scary? Serio? Y tu...you smiled. Me..."

"I teased you," I helped him gently. "Bromeaste. I teased you."

He nodded. "Si, me bromaste." I covered my mouth to not laugh. *Still wrong. But he's trying.* "En es moment, estaba...I was obsessed. Contigo."

I know, amor.

He took a deep breath. Gabriel stumbled over his words and I gently corrected him as I listened.

I never thought I was become your instructor. I never thought your brother asked me to take care of you.

I never thought you'd become my love.

And suddenly I realized what he was saying. I stopped correcting him as I realized what was happening.

In that moment I knew. He was on his knees and I sat up my eyes widening as he swallowed, his Adam's apple bobbing as he continued.

"En el tiempo que te conozco, sé que eres mi corazón. Tu amor es mi alma. Vive dentro de mi."

In the time I have known you. I know that you are my heart. Your love is in my soul.

It lives within me. You have taught me to be human. How to love. How to live. How to be a better man. As your boyfriend.

My heart was pounding in my ribs. "Gabriel—"

He continued switching to English. "I cannot imagine a life without you. A love without yours. Nor do I want to."

And then in perfect Spanish he said. "Isobel Adrianna Santos. *quieres casarte conmigo?"*

I blinked rapidly my heart racing as he took out the object in his hand. It was a necklace. Intricate designs on it. Heart-shaped. He held out something. A geometric shape.

And stuck it inside of it at the top. I frowned as it came undone into a clover. A four leaf clover.

"It unlocks it."

"This is the key, it's geometric. It's your name on the inside." He held the key up and I saw it. His smile was genuine and he blinked rapidly. "It's an antique. I figured you'd like it. I got it thinking I would put our photos. But when Liam gave me your mom's ring...I found another use for it."

My heart stopped beating as he took out a gold ring from his pocket. His voice was raw. "I had the jeweler carve it out. Liam gave me your mom's ring. Your father had it. And now it's yours. If you want it."

He held it up and his eyes met mine.

"Will you marry me?"

It wasn't even a question. "Yes." My lips met his instantly and I saw his little smile as I kissed him. "Gabriel. Yes. A thousand times."

His little grin was one I knew. He had been nervous. My hands shook but the ring fit perfectly on my left ring finger.

He showed me how to close the necklace and open it. "If you don't want to wear it...anywhere. It fits inside here." He took off the ring and showed me but I wasn't even listening.

I just wanted to kiss him over and over again.

He continued though. "I know what we talked about at work. I know. But I wanted to wear something for you too. This half is mine."

He showed me how the key necklace fit around his neck, low enough under his shirt.

And the heart did the same around mine.

It settled like a heavy weight and I read the engraving on the outside. "Monroe..."

"It's your name as much as mine, if you'll take it," he whispered "That half is yours. And your ring fits inside."

"But the only way to get it is with you," I murmured. The other half of me.

He tipped his head slowly, when he opened his eyes they were burning pale fire. Blonde hair. Tanned skin.

Beautiful.

I think I found him...the man from my dream who was swimming closer and closer...he's...Gabriel.

"Exactly."

I wiped my eyes over and over as I kissed him.

CHAPTER 32
GABRIEL

WE GOT MARRIED.

It was a small courthouse affair.

I wore a white dress shirt and slacks.

I should've fucking known my girl would've defied all mention of tradition when she stepped in with a slinkier red dress.

Liam walked her down the aisle. He'd put on his brotherly mask that I saw through now and his eyes had shimmered watching her. She'd talked to me about his guilt.

I never told her Liam loved her the way I did.

It would gut her twice. Even now I kept secrets.

But I wouldn't let either one of them down. Not Liam for his choices. Not Isobel—as my wife.

"Red," I whispered as I caught the glint of necklace between her breasts. She looked radiant. I wasn't expecting it. But I fucking loved it. Even the embroidered veil with the floral touches from her culture.

"It's good luck in some cultures," she whispered back at the alter. "Good fortune. Where is your grey?" I adjusted my cufflinks she got me to show her.

Her smile was wide and her eyes shimmered.

When we recited our vows.

Amor, I will love you in this lifetime. In every lifetime. I feel like I have waited for you...

Isa, I promise to love you forever. I promise to take care of you, your

249

heart, our kids in the future, and everything in between. You will never struggle with me...

I see you.

I see you.

I waited forever for a love like yours.

I will never compromise my values for you.

I will always be your shield.

I will always care for your soul.

I promise.

I promise.

We both got emotional. Liam was there with a box of tissues we laughed at.

But he was using them too.

I couldn't even imagine how he felt. Or why he tortured himself. Maybe he felt like he never truly deserved her.

I knew I didn't deserve her. But I didn't let that stop me. Nothing had ever stopped me from her.

I knew he wouldn't have let me marry her if he didn't truly know—I was her number one.

Her boyfriend.

And then I was her husband.

She looked ready to explode. I laughed around her kisses.

Liam's voice made us turn to him outside the courthouse. He held up his phone. "I didn't even get a good photo of you two!"

I grinned as she scoffed. *"But I was crying—"*

"You look beautiful," he said with an easier smile and warmth in his eyes. It was always there for her. But now it shifted into something else. Something like acceptance.

Liam knew she'd never love him like me. I didn't know how it made me feel.

"Now come on. Let me take a single photo of the two of you. It's your damn wedding day. Monroe, look at you—shit. I can't call you just Monroe anymore, can I?"

Isobel smiled ear to ear and her canines flashed. "That's Mrs. Monroe to you."

I grinned down at her as she burst out laughing at Liam rolling his eyes as he took the photo. Both of us wore our necklace.

I asked him for it later.

And he sent me all the photos he'd taken of us over the months.

Out of all of them, that one was my favorite.

"I cannot believe you're married," he put his arm around her shoulder as I glanced down at our photos.

"Si, now it's your turn," she teased. "We have to find you a nice girl, right Gabriel?"

"Yes, baby."

Liam snorted. "You're not even married five fucking minutes and she's got you wrapped around her finger!"

Isobel cursed at him playfully while I grinned. "She had me wrapped around her finger before she was my wife—"

"Si," Isobel cut in with her laughter. "He is just my husband now."

Goddamn. I looked down at her. "I'm sorry it took me so long, baby."

"It's okay," she kissed me and we just started making out while Liam groaned pelting us with flowers he'd gotten as our makeshift flower girl.

"Fuck my life! Mom! Dad! I'm right here!"

She laughed into my kisses.

And for one fucking second—I had everything I could've ever wanted in the world.

∾

Isobel

I HAD NOT BEEN FEELING GOOD.

Maybe that's why I had been emotional. Until I went to the clinic.

I looked down at the ultrasound in my hand.

Lucky for me, he didn't read the same books I did, and I didn't think he'd look.

Birth control could fail sometimes apparently.

Which explained why I had been emotional.

I had lots of questions for the doctor.

How many weeks was I? Was it a boy or girl?

We were less than two weeks out from going to New York.

This was not the time to be pregnant.

I didn't know how to say the words. I just stared at the doctor and then the stick in front of me that said I was pregnant.

Pregnant.

I was having a *baby*.

I didn't feel ready to be a mother. Not right now. But I also did not want to get rid of…no. Not that. I wanted to have babies with Gabriel. Plenty of them.

But I saw the look in his eyes.

This was…the most dangerous mission we could've gone on. But it wasn't true. Gabriel thought this was.

I knew this was one of many.

One of plenty.

I was in the CIA. Not college. Everything was harder. Any mission could be my last. I understood that the day I was on his team. All my quiet was gone.

My little life? My little dream. My little studio. Somewhere in the life of Agency, in being Gabriel's? I lost it all. But I didn't mind.

"I'm having a baby." I whispered to myself as I looked for ways to tell Gabriel. I could order him a shirt.

I browsed the Internet for the right one.

He thought this assignment was really scary, but to me, after doing research, I realize that this was just my new life. I wasn't afraid. I had a good team.

The assignment was the least of my concerns as I found a shirt to announce I was pregnant.

A baby shirt.

I could customize it and put 'Monroe' on the back of it.

I was eleven weeks along.

I think with the death of my father, Liam and me being upset with each other, and thinking birth control was safe? I hadn't ever imagined I might be having a baby.

I needed to tell Gabriel. If I told him before the assignment though? He would pull me off it. If I told him after? He might be angry that I kept it from him.

I decided to risk the later on. I'd rather be punished than be the reason he did not make it home.

That night he came back from the grocery store. "Honey! I'm home!"

My life felt like a sitcom as Liam would say.

"Is Liam coming for dinner?" He asked.

"No," I shook my head tucking the ultrasound into my e-reader. As I walked to the entryway of the apartment where Gabriel brought in groceries his phone rang.

"Shit," he swore. "It's Koller." He rolled his eyes picking the phone up. "Sir."

I helped quietly put the groceries away feeling my stomach turn. I needed to tell him.

But when Gabriel got off the phone his eyes were dark.

"Koller says they're moving up the Hagen assignment. He's going to be in New York sooner. Intel says next week." My stomach bottomed out.

"We are leaving next week?"

Gabriel tipped his head. "I need to go talk to him tonight. Now."

I nodded understanding.

As Gabriel ran off, I realized he didn't have dinner. I called Liam to tell him to come over.

When he did he saw my worry all over my face.

I was in his arms the moment he was there.

Gabriel wouldn't mind. Liam always took care of us.

"Don't worry, Isa." Liam held me tight to him. "I won't let anything to you or him."

I put my hand over my stomach. Or her. *Maybe.*

CHAPTER 33
GABRIEL

"You want Kourtney Young to switch places with Claire Sutton because her fucking congressman shit show of a father meddled in Agency politics?"

I repeated back what Koller just said to me. At ten at night. I had left dinner with my wife. For this bullshit?

"Are you fucking insane?" I lost my cool.

Nobody was in the office right now.

I didn't give a shit about losing it.

I just got married and nobody fucking knew.

And now? Koller was threatening my assignment with my wife and my brother-in-law with the one thing that would take it from dangerous to deadly?

"You thought Kourtney fucking Young was a liability the moment I knew about her. Her brother is a piece of shit—"

"I'm sorry, Monroe."

"And now you tell me Marcus Hagen is a dangerous op. And somehow a brand new congressman in office knows about this? Knows about me? And he wants his fucking daughter on my fucking team!" I was livid.

Livid.

"HAVE YOU LOST YOUR FUCKING MIND!"

This was how he shattered everything for me.

Koller's last minute meeting with me for the New York assignment was garbage. Complete fucking ass.

I was beyond livid standing there in my civilian clothes. Isobel's necklace burning into my skin with my secrets.

"You're insane," I whispered. I felt the rage boiling in my blood. *You're fucking insane. I cannot believe you right now.*

He shook his head looking regretful. "Her father is powerful."

"You're. Fucking. Out. Of. Your. Fucking. Mind."

And power hungry.

I never thought I would wake up and hate Koller.

"I never thought I wake up and hate you." I growled. The low but savage sensation rising. Now that Isobel was my wife?

Something wilder had spurned inside of me.

Something that hated the Agency.

Hated the identity I wore to uphold.

Because that person?

Gabriel Monroe the operative? Couldn't have her. Only the civilian side of me could. Isobel and I hadn't told a fucking soul. Just Liam.

But after I got married? Every single thing that happened to her was my business. It was like a feral primitive part of me reared up when she got a fucking paper cut.

I was livid.

And right now? Right now, I was going to kill Koller.

He wasn't shit to me anymore.

Not him. Not my friend. Not my mentor.

"You are going to sell out my fucking team for a promotion!" I was ripping into him now. "I fucking hate you! Fuck you!"

Koller looked at me uncomfortably like he knew the position he was in and I didn't care.

"Leadership wants me to drop Sutton. *Claire fucking Sutton.* The one fucking technician who can fight. And you want me to take Kourtney fucking Young on the most dangerous assignment of the Santos siblings and Bradford's life? She's fucking insane!"

Koller looked at me grim faced.

I knew the difference in the military and in ops. I knew the difference with operational reality and political theater.

And Koller was a fucking *puppet.*

"You taught me that weakness is not teachable! You taught me good enough gets people killed! Kourtney fucking Young will get my team killed!"

"But her father somehow found out about the assignment—"

I was done with Koller.

I was fucking done.

"How! YOU DON'T THINK THAT'S A FUCKING PROB-LEM!" I shouted now. "Nobody was supposed to fucking know! Why is a congressman somehow finding out! This op is compromised now!"

And Koller wanted us to go. Absolutely not.

No fucking way.

"WHAT THE FUCK HAPPENED TO TRUST? You let politics influence our family?"

Koller held up his hands. "I don't know. But Congressman Young said this is great on his daughter's resume—"

A wild noise left me. "Are you fucking crazy! A resume! This is life or death and you have people fucking worried about plating their paperwork? Thats about as shit as the Air Force making you hug orphans every fucking Christmas so news outlets think you're humane! That's my team out there! Not Congressman's fucking resume!"

I was beyond livid. I had passed the point of no return.

I had always been aware that institutional corruption was real. I had always been aware of it. It had never once impacted me like today.

"I refuse." I looked at Koller. "I fucking *refuse* to take Kourtney Young on any assignment. She has sexually harassed females in the unit. *Not just Santos.* She's a fucking problem. *And you know it.* And you allowing her to stay in the Agency because of her fucking father is part of why—"

I broke off.

This was why Liam never gave the Agency anything.

Not Oracle.

Not his heart.

Liam knew.

The only enemy was the enemy within.

I ran a hand through my hair. "*No.*"

Everything I had built, everything had protected, my entire family, was now crumbling because some garbage congressman wanted to polish his daughter's résumé at the cost of innocent lives of other people.

Fuck politics.

Fuck the Agency.

Fuck the system.

This is why Liam and Isobel break the rules.

This is why they hate it here.

This is why they entered knowing it was temporary.

I *knew* this was a documented issue.

I knew this happened all the time.

But it never happened to me.

And I never realized how absolutely fucking agonizing the sensation was ripping through me right now.

At understanding that my family's death in the future would be padding for a congressman to boast about it.

Koller's entire expression was downright dark and grim.

"Monroe. If you don't do it. They wanna replace you with someone who will." My heart dropped.

It completely shattered as a wild smile lit my lips. I could tell Koller saw my wild eyes then.

"Of course they fucking would," I whispered. "Of course they would replace me to appease politicians who will never lose their loved ones."

Of course.

I closed my eyes as Koller said. "So it's you taking in your team. Or is someone less qualified taking them into this mission. Either way, congressman wants his daughter on the table."

I stood unable to sit there for any longer.

My blood was boiling right now. My blood turned to fucking acid. There was no choice.

I either went into a war and led my team, my wife, into danger, knowing full well there was an unstable element on that team.

Or I abandoned them when they needed me the most to somebody who wouldn't protect them like I would.

Somebody who would probably cater to every single thing leadership wanted.

Even if it meant watching Isobel or Liam die.

Someone who didn't know Isobel needed cover.

Or that Liam wore glasses and he couldn't shoot as well as Isobel could.

"Fuck you." I growled. "Fuck you. Fuck this place."

My wife. The woman who made me human. My entire soul.

My brother. The man who trusted me with his heart.

They were both under me.

I knew better.

I gasped clutching my heart. Fuck.

Fuck.

Fuck.

Fuck.

Fuck.

Fuck.

"I'll take the fucking job. And the cuban operative," I bit out. "Selena Tavares."

"One of Finch guys got her—you remember him."

"Yeah, he's a scumbag." So Selena Tavares was in a shit situation with Agency shit heads. "Like everyone else around me."

"Monroe," Koller sounded regretful. "I know you're upset. But it's a quick gig. You'll be in and out. We have Intel, Hagen is supposed to stay at the Primrose Hotel in Midtown. You guys will stay two blocks away. We have everything set. I can talk to the Young family and make sure she's on her best behavior—"

I scoffed. Fucking pussies.

"And the secondary team?" I didn't even look at Koller. I was disgusted with everyone.

"Leadership says you shouldn't need it."

I whirled on him.

He held his hands up. "They think they have enough on him to know he's operating solo. I don't know why he's coming alone, but it's just him."

"You're insane," my eyes were wild. "You're a fucking puppet. A sell-out."

I walked the fuck out aware Koller was a fucking muppet.

I was done.

In that moment I knew, I would get my wife and brother-in-law through this assignment.

I knew.

Because it was my last.

A normal wife. A normal life.

I promised her in my vows—a normal wife. A normal life.

"Fuck!" I shouted into the night sky. *"FUCK!"*

I WENT HOME AND FOUND LIAM ON OUR COUCH, ISOBEL NEXT TO HIM curled up into his side. Both of them turned to me.

The moment they saw my face, they both stood.

I wasn't even shocked to find him in my house. I trusted him ironically not to sleep with my fucking wife.

As I told them woodenly what Koller said both of them erupted. Isobel was cursing in Spanish and Liam's jaw looked unhinged.

"They can't do that!" Liam shouted. "Koller's fucking insane! Sutton for Young? What the fuck! I fucking told you man. I fucking told you. Fuck this place. They don't give a fuck about their people."

He swore looking at me with wild dark eyes now. After William's death they never changed back.

"Gabriel." He never called me by my first name. "Don't do it."

Isobel and I both looked at him.

"Don't do it." He shook his head. "I did research on Hagen. I picked up briefings where they dissected him. He's good at what he does. I think he's got a team. We can't do this. We can't go in there without backup."

"What do you want to do?" I looked at him with wild eyes myself. "You want me to quit? Koller said they would replace me if I did—"

"I want us to quit!" Liam shouted. "Leave! Leave tonight. Quit. Leave Quantico!"

"I can't!" I shouted back. "I can't leave! I can't leave you two!"

"You wouldn't!" Liam's dark eyes now hunter green were in my face. "We go with you! The end!"

"What?" I whispered it. "You want to walk with me?"

Liam looked at me like I was insane for even saying it. "I have Oracle. We can set up Titan. We can get it all together. Isobel and me—" he motioned to her. And her jaw dropped. "We can do it. We can all leave. Let's go. It's next week."

"You're insane too," I whispered feeling like every which way I turned I was losing my mind. "I can't walk away from all of this. This is my life."

Liam took a step back stunned with me. "Kourtney Young for Claire Sutton. And you are still wondering if this is your life?" He tapped his head with two fingers. "You're the only one that's insane here, G."

"Stop it!" Isobel got between us. "Both of you!"

She was shaking, I swear her hands were trembling harder than mine.

"We can talk about this," she was trembling as both of us looked down at her. "We don't need to fight about this. It isn't as simple as walking away or staying. You both know it. Both of you sit down. Just because Young is on the team doesn't mean we all die." She looked at me. "You need to breathe. Get some air. Breathe. You are still a leader and you are in charge. Even if she does something stupid—the only person who will die is her. Jeremy and I would never let anything happen. And you—" she turned to Liam. "Stop screaming at him. He does not know everything and this is his entire life, you are asking him to leave all that he knows for the unknown, that decision isn't made in a day."

She was breathing harder and I reached for her hand feeling the way it shook. She looked paler. "Baby, sit down."

Liam let out a breath I didn't realize he was holding.

"That's true," he said looking at her. His eyes met mine. "I'm not trying to freak you out. I know it's a big choice. If you can handle Young on your team—we can do this. I'll be there. Jeremy is solid. A baker. But solid."

Isobel nodded as the three of us sat down and she was in my arms. She was freezing. I needed to get her blanket.

"It's one assignment," I said out loud. "I don't want Young anywhere near us."

"But maybe with her father watching it'll make her..." Isobel started. "More...better?"

Liam and I shared a look. But Isobel wasn't wrong. Making a choice on my own to leave? Wouldn't just be career suicide.

It would mean that for the rest of my life?

I would watch my back in my own way.

I would be known as the guy who walked the fuck out of this. Nobody would look at me seriously or Liam.

I looked at Liam. "If we do this successfully, you can start Titan without a fucking argument from the world. Everyone would know you. You did it. If we leave now—we get nothing."

And that was the truth.

I saw Liam's jaw set. Hard. "You're saying we either enter a suicide mission or we dip out now and get shit."

I nodded. "If you leave now? It means fuck all if your reputation is blacked out by the Agency. Does that make sense? Nobody will work with Titan Security with cowards."

"So Koller put you in check." Liam muttered looking down at Isobel who looked a little more than defeated. She looked...out of it.

She nodded then slowly. "Gabriel is telling the truth." She looked at her brother. "Even Oracle cannot stop the Agency from bad mouthing you or Gabriel. The two of you cannot walk away. And even if I did, we would always be known for this. People talk. That will never stop."

Liam looked beyond upset. Frustration etched into every line of his face. "Fuck this."

"Agreed." She whispered. "This world is small. Walking away from critical assignments is bad."

"It's career suicide." Of course my girl would get it. "It's a security risk, it shows nobody can trust us, we abandon our duty, we abandon our team. The Agency could flag our clearances and now we got shit to work with. And now we have unofficial black marks that follow us if we choose not to do it." I shook my head in frustration. Koller put me in check.

Koller put my wife in check.

Koller put my brother-in-law in check.

And I was in charge of both of them.

I didn't even realize I was clutching Isobel tighter until she turned to me. "Amor."

"Sorry, baby."

But I was now aware of the fucking shit show of a position I was in. The intelligence community was small. The network itself is still powerful. Reputation would make her break a career. And word-of-mouth would close every single door in the private sector completely for us.

"In order for you to start Titan," I whispered to Liam who looked uneasy still. "You need reputation. Professionalism. Credibility. Not this. You can't run. They're counting on it. If you do? It'll destroy your entire life."

"So I'm fucked if I go on this assignment and fucked if I don't."

"Exactly." I eyed him down.

"Both of you stop." Her voice was calmer than ours. "None of us know what will happen on this assignment. None of us. For all we know? In a few days? We will go. Everything will work out. We'll come back and be good. It'll be okay. We go. We watch each others backs. Gabriel will be fine. Liam you can go start Titan Security. And I will…" her eyes looked at her lap. "I'll be here too. All of us."

Her eyes met mine. "It'll be okay, amor. We'll be okay."

I didn't know how to tell Isobel, I didn't believe her for once.

CHAPTER 34
ISOBEL

I WAS HAVING A GIRL.

No.

We were having a girl.

Gabriel made a soft comment one morning before we left.

Tangled in the sheets, I got the feeling he didn't want to leave. He always did this.

He woke up before his alarm, turned it off, and laid there with me with his eyes closed.

I smiled into his cheek as he grumbled about the morning.

"You look different," he murmured kissing me. "Everything okay? Your skin's glowing more than usual."

I smiled up at his pale eyes. He looked more tired than usual. "New lotion."

"Hm, you do smell different. In a good way, baby..." he drifted off as he held me tighter. "You feel soft."

I laughed low, holding onto him. "Yeah?"

"Hmmm." Gabriel would be an amazing father. I could see him doing this with our daughter. Our daughter.

The shirt came in. I hid it in the closet. I could just show him after. I got the feeling we would be okay.

Maybe some things in life did not happen the way we wanted them to happen.

But they were okay.

"You are going to be amazing," I whispered. "We're going to make it."

"When I'm done with this shit, I'm gonna give you the fucking world," he muttered into my hair. Neither one of us wanted to leave.

I felt his words hit me somewhere deeper. Softer this time. "You already have, Gabriel. You don't have to prove anything to me."

He pulled back, the pale blue of his eyes watching me carefully. "I thought about what Liam said. Sometimes when you say all the right things to me, it makes me want nothing more than to be with you. To leave it all behind. Move into the Heron Manor with you, Liam, Evie, your Mom."

My eyes watered as he spoke. I thought it was the hormones but I realized Gabriel made me emotional all the time now. Especially because he had no idea what he already gave me.

I didn't know how to say it. I knew him and Liam—if they knew? They would stop me from going.

I was an asset.

I could help them. If anything happened to them and they died because of me? I would never forgive myself.

And after what Gabriel told me about the Intelligence community? I did not want to be known as a woman who got pregnant to get out of an assignment.

Or abandoning my team.

"A dream." I whispered.

He tipped his head slowly. "A dream. But a real one. We can give Liam and Evie the sunroom—"

"We can have babies." I blinked up at him feeling my emotions burst in waves over and over in me.

Gabriel, we're having a baby. She's so tiny.

I got you a shirt with her name on it.

His eyes softened, winter blue now something else to me. Now his eyes were the only things that helped me focus.

"Is that what you want?"

Yes. "Yes."

I promise to give you the world.

Together? Together.

~

264

New York was a lot of noise.

I had been here before once with Liam in the past. But it was a lot of noise now. Constant sirens, lights, and something happening in every direction. It made sense why Marcus Hagen was here.

He could blend into anyone. Anywhere.

We were in Midtown staying at a hotel two blocks down from the Primrose.

So far, everything was good. Gabriel ran command. His eyes watched me when he thought I didn't know, those pale blues worried about me.

Liam was on edge but he was always on edge. His darker eyes now taking in everything differently.

Jeremy was browsing bakeries for pastries he was sending to Cathy. "Cathy likes these," he muttered obsessed with his new girl-friend. "I think things are pretty serious between us and I might bring her home to my nana after this assignment."

"Oh yeah?" I teased him. "Are you going to propose to your Cathy?"

He blushed turning an adorable shade of red that made me laugh. "Maybe. I don't know it's a leap." He looked around making sure the coast was clear. "You and Monroe...you guys good? You seem better?"

This was the first time he had ever asked me about Gabriel in a long time. Out right.

"Sorry," his clear blue eyes met mine, his blonde hair slightly messy. "It's just nobody's here and it's our first time off base. I thought I'd ask."

I smiled looking around feeling my hands on my stomach gently. "We are good." All of us were good. She was healthy. He was holding on. We would make it out of this. "I am invited to your wedding, hm?"

I got to laugh at Jeremy turning red.

Sutton and Vincent kept in touch with us.

And Kourtney Young was there.

She existed. Like a splinter under your skin or a tumor. She knew she wasn't welcome. Sutton had made it clear before we left she hated the ground Kourtney walked on.

Nobody wanted to work with her so she annoyed Jeremy the most but Jeremy was too polite to tell her to fuck off.

And so far she had been fine.

So far. But my morning sickness might have been acting up lately because I did not feel good around her.

Until I had to put on my mic. Gabriel got me these beautiful blue gloves and a matching scarf I had on in the winter.

They were brighter than his eyes but I loved it.

Blue was becoming my new favorite color. I bought his shirt in that color.

I was shivering in the cold as I walked back to the hotel, one hand on my stomach. Gabriel was in another quick meeting, probably trying to manage leadership checking in on him every single minute. They were micro-managing us.

Gabriel knew it.

I was walking into the hotel when Sutton called me.

"Hola."

"Hola, Isa," Claire spoke Spanish but not too often with me but she understood it enough. "How's everything going?"

"Good…" I filled her in as much as I could since we had been given new phones and these were more secure than our personal ones. "You?"

"I'm going insane, Isa." She sounded like she was pacing. "Vince and I are trying to gather some information. Listen, I was going to tell Monroe, but I saw Jeremy's notes on potentials and I was going to do some digging. I noticed a few of these folks are in the area…." She told me some more information she had and if it checked out with what I knew.

At the same time, I was alone in the hallway waiting for the elevator.

When it dinged, I went to get on when Kourtney looked up from her phone and walked out. I didn't even think twice to say anything to her. Until she shoulder checked me.

"Watch where you're going," she snapped. "Jeez Santos you can't even be bothered to not harass me outside of work."

"What? Hang on Claire," I didn't mute the call. "You pushed me. Just like you stole my towel and tried to attack me—"

"Bitch please, get a hold of yourself," Kourtney said at the same time I heard Claire talking on the phone. "Nobody is more obsessed with you than you—"

"What?"

I was so confused. I didn't understand why Kourtney Young

hated me. I didn't know who she was. I didn't understand her. I only knew she was more confident the more she got away with.

My father taught me about people like her.

The kind that had life handed to them so now they felt like the world owed them something.

People who never knew hard work.

They only knew how to be little *pendeja's*.

"My father says once I'm done with this bullshit assignment if you try anything, he'll have your ass deported right back to where you fucking came from. He already knows you're a fucking problem. So watch your fucking mouth."

I was livid now.

"Watch your fucking mouth you little *puta, I can't believe you're a real fucking person. And if you think you and your stupid father can scare me? You better fucking believe when those immigration agents come to deport my ass I'm taking your mixed race bitch self with me.*"

"I heard your Dad might be white, but your Mama is Filipina and Black right? So you know all about not *belonging*. It's crazy to me for a woman of color, you hate everyone else just like you. You think you're the only brown girl to have ever existed? You're insane if you think trying to take out girls like you will ever make anyone else like you more. And if you ever call me an immigrant ever again, I will show your stupid skinny ass what my immigrant hands can do."

I huffed out a breath. "My father worked his immigrant ass off to provide for me. I would never let a crazy woman like you insult me."

I had the satisfaction of seeing her speechless for a bit.

I had grown up. I gave her the finger and the elevator shut on her face. *"This stupid bitch."*

"Holy...fucking shit...."

And then I remembered Claire Sutton on the phone.

"Are you—" she was sputtering. "Isobel. Did she just—"

"Claire—"

"No, listen to me. Listen to me. I have been in the Agency for five years. I have never seen that shit in real life. I have never seen that level of —" she broke off.

"It's fine—" I began.

"It's not fine!" Claire was not the kind of woman who got angry.

Maybe she teased Liam. But she didn't get angry. "*Oh my God! Isobel! You have to tell Monroe.*"

"And say what?" I puffed out a breath. "The congressman's daughter insulted me for the fifth time? I don't know who she's sleeping with to get here, but whoever it is? They are working overtime to make sure she is here. I cannot say anything."

"Isobel—" Claire sounded so fed up. "*Isobel. I cannot stand by that.*"

"True," I kept my voice calm. "Neither can I but if I am deported to Mexico. At this point? I want to go. It is warm there and it is cold here."

Claire let out a laugh that sounded forced. "Vincent heard that. You have no idea how angry we both are. I am so angry that stupid bitch got on the assignment and now I'm even more angry she said that to you."

"It's okay," I got to my floor. I was at the top of the floor above everyone for some reason. "I'll be okay. It's one stupid girl. Like we said. Anyways, let me go now. I need to get some sleep."

"Goodnight, Isa. Tell us if she tries to kill you in your sleep or something. Vincent and I are ready to go to the fucking Director at this rate."

I laughed it off.

"My father always told me the worst discrimination comes from other minorities who think they have to prove they are different." I laughed low as I walked into my hotel room. "Kourtney does not scare me anymore. I already have my life together."

I was married.

I was pregnant.

I had my whole world downstairs on the seventh floor working away.

"Isobel, what Kourtney said to you is not okay," Claire whispered. "It's not."

"It doesn't matter if it's not okay," I shrugged it off even if it did. "It's not true and after this assignment, I don't care what she says she's going back to her…whatever office she works in."

Before Claire hung up she said. "We shall see about that."

CHAPTER 35
GABRIEL

I GOT THE CALL I LEAST EXPECTED.

It was the Deputy of Operation.

"Ma'am."

"Gabriel," Cindy Roberts was a fucking legend.

She was in the Agency when they still thought women were home-makers.

Cindy was a former colonel and the only other woman in the Agency who scared the shit out of everyone around her.

She was the kind of woman who made operatives straighten their spine a little bit more because they could hear her and her drill sergeant voice screaming at us.

She was also Koller's boss.

"Is everything all right?"

"No," she began her voice low but I heard the rage in it. "I'm calling because there's been a change of plans. Claire Sutton was actually a mentee of mine. And I forgot about her. I forgot she was on your team. And I didn't know that she was taken off an operation that she was supposed to be on. Even though I'm supposed to know everything. As you can imagine, that might've pissed me off."

Oh shit. It sounded like it more than pissed her off.

I didn't know what to say.

If Cindy was pissed? Koller's ass was about to get chewed the fuck up.

"Claire also had some information for me about a Kourtney Young."

I swallowed.

And then Cindy Roberts told me about how Kourtney had attacked Isobel in the elevator of the hotel. Again.

And how Vincent had backed up everything Claire had said and without me knowing?

Claire at Quantico called Cindy late at night in her home to tell Cindy fucking Roberts that Kourtney Young was a liability.

Go Claire.

I always knew women in my career field always got away with a little bit more when it came to certain things.

Because it wasn't like they played on the same level as men.

What Claire effectively did was make an enemy out of Koller, but an ally with Cindy Roberts.

Which meant Claire was using her cards too.

But I was also aware my wife had been assaulted verbally. Again.

"What?"

"Don't worry," Cindy sounded annoyed more than angry. "I worked it out with the ADD." The associate deputy. "He's getting Kourtney off. I don't care who sucked her father's dick enough to get her on the op. Fucking can't stand these Washington folks meddling like it's a goddamn school project. Let me just put all my fucking kids on assassinating the next prime minister of a country why don't I? We can all grade them from far away." I heard her sarcasm but I didn't feel it at all.

I felt my heart racing in my chest as she went on and I barely heard her.

I only heard. "Kourtney Young is off the op. What a shitshow. I fucking hate when Koller does this shit without me..."

I didn't know that my boss had stepped on the wrong toes. And this woman was now reminding me of why she survived decades.

"Idiots." Cindy muttered. "I'm getting Young off. I am trying to get a hold of Tavares in Havana. Sending her your way to Quantico first. She doesn't speak a lick of English but the girls got spirit. I'll give her that..."

As Cindy talked I wanted to run to find Isobel but I forced myself to focus feeling free and trapped at the same time. My wife had kept this from me? Why?

"Thank you ma'am."

"Anytime. If Young acts up, call me. This is my number and I don't intend on sleeping tonight. I need to make sure Congressman Young understands his fucking place."

I felt my own eyes widen at her tone as she hung up. I needed to go find my wife and ask her why she kept things from me.

ASAP.

My phone dinged from Liam. I looked down.

> I just met this girl at Teaser's. It's a burlesque club. On paper. Except...I don't think it's a club, bro.
>
> Her name's Melina Mendoza.
>
> I think somethings wrong here with the club. We can look into it after the op.

I frowned. I didn't need this right now.

> What do you mean somethings wrong?

> I think she's trafficked. I think she's a victim of trafficking.

What?

"You gotta be fucking kidding me." I whispered looking at Liam's texts. "He's out of his mind right now."

> Get out. Do you hear me? Get the fuck out of the club right now.

> G, she's young. She's got this mark on her.

And then Liam sent me a fucking photo of a young woman's wrist.

> She says she was brought here by the O'Hara family. Look, it's called Teaser's.
>
> She says some guy named Cormac owns the club. Just look into it when you get a chance. She's a nice girl.
>
> Cormac O'Hara. His son's name is Aidan.

My headache was blossoming in full force. First Kourtney, then Cindy Roberts. Now this? Liam was losing his mind.

> If I promise you to look into Melina Mendoza. Will you leave Teasers and come to the hotel? I need to talk to you.

> Yeah, I will. But we'll come back for Melina once the op is done. We have to.

> Fine. I will personally go back for Melina Mendoza. Now get the fuck out and come here.

My brother-in-law was going to end up in trouble.
I texted Vincent and Claire.

> Thank you guys for standing up for Santos. When you get a chance I need you to look into Cormac O'Hara. New York City. Club: Teasers.

Vincent answered with a thumbs up. Claire left an angry face with a knife next to it that said.

> Fuck Kourtney Young.

I snorted going to look for my wife.
The night was never going to end.

CHAPTER 36
ISOBEL

I COULDN'T SLEEP IN MY ROOM. MY THOUGHTS WERE SPIRALING.

I wasn't supposed to technically leave the hotel.

But I needed to get some air.

I didn't recognize the person I was anymore.

The girl who had begun dating Gabriel was gone. Now I was someone's *wife*. I hadn't really gotten over my father and now with my pregnancy? It felt worse.

Liam had kept a polite distance from me but the stress of the job had brought us closer.

All I craved was peace. Calm. Normalcy. Sunshine.

Isobel, my entire career is riding on this.

I'm going to make it.

I'm going to give you the world.

I wanted to tell him I was pregnant.

I already had the world.

And just like that, the hormones got the best of me. I wiped my eyes, my body shaking harder as I shook my head.

I couldn't say the words.

Liam would tell Gabriel. He would be angry. Both of them.

He would leave this mission. I couldn't abandon Gabriel.

Ever.

He was so alone. Sometimes when I looked at him I saw that sweet boy who was abandoned by everyone and not my husband. I saw that earnest look in his eyes when he asked me if I liked his slightly burnt pancakes.

I did. And then I imagined the softness in his eyes wiped out with the arctic chill he had months months months ago.

I didn't want that.

I couldn't leave him.

I already have the world.

I have you and her, and Liam.

I don't want anything else. I want to go home.

Once, I wanted to be a normal wife.

A normal life.

Now? I didn't know.

I walked back to my hotel room after walking around the block.

In the distance I saw the Primrose Hotel from my window. The strikingly beautiful tall structure looked imposing but not menacing. Actually, the Primrose was beautifully feminine and pink.

Nothing like what I imagined a man would stay in. Especially not a big tough guy like Marcus Hagen. Unless…it wasn't a man.

The primrose is feminine. It has roses trailing down the side...

I felt my brain working further as I watched the Primrose pink lights. Flashing. Feminine lights. Flowers.

Feminine. Soft. Like a girl…

I sat back in my bed looking out as a thought occurred to me then. My hand on my belly rubbing slowly.

"This entire time, I thought Marcus Hagen was a man…" I ran to my notes talking to myself and maybe my daughter.

What if the Agency was wrong?

What if…Marcus Hagen wasn't a man?

What if…she was a woman?

That would change *everything*.

CHAPTER 37
GABRIEL

Isobel wasn't in her room.

Liam was on his way back from the club Teaser's.

I went to see if Isobel was hanging out with Jeremy. It was the only other option.

I reached his door and knocked, my knuckles rapping against the wood with a sense of impatience.

No answer. I knocked again, harder this time. Still nothing.

"Bradford, I need you to open the fucking door," I sighed, reaching into my pocket for my key card. "If Isa and you are in there I swear to God—Jeremy fucking Bradford if you're in there jacking off to dragon porn, I swear to God—"

I was so done with this kid. Jeremy had always been a rotund little ball of happy go-lucky energy that was getting on my nerves now.

I slid the card into the lock, the little light blinking green as the mechanism clicked.

"Bradford! I'm coming in! You better be wearing pants!"

I pushed the door open, and that's when I saw it.

Blood. Crimson and viscous, it pooled on the floor.

My heart. Shattered.

So much blood.

"Jer? Jeremy!" I rushed forward, my heart leaping into my throat.

He was there, lying motionless on the ground.

"Jeremy. Jeremy. Jeremy. Jeremy. Nonononononono. Jer! Bradford, I swear to fucking—"

I dropped to my knees beside him, my hands shaking as I reached out to turn him over.

The moment I touched him, I knew.

He was dead. Shot. Several times.

Holy.

Shit.

His body was cold, the life already drained from him. How long had he been lying here? How did this happen?

"Jeremy…"

Jeremy Bradford was…gone?

My mind raced, trying to make sense of the scene before me. And then, like a punch to the gut, it hit me.

Compromised. We've been *compromised*.

I need help.

I fucked up.

I'm done. I'm done. I'm done for.

My wife...shit shit shit.

Ice-cold fear gripped my heart as a single thought consumed me.

Isobel. Find her. Find her now. Her and Liam.

I stumbled to my feet, my legs feeling like lead as I fought against the rising panic.

I had to get to her, had to make sure she was safe. I couldn't lose her, not like this, not now.

I ran from the room, leaving Bradford's lifeless body behind calling for help.

The hallway blurred as I sprinted, my breath coming in sharp gasps.

I didn't know where she was, but I had to find her. I had to protect her.

Please, God, let her be okay. Let me find her in time.

The hotel seemed to stretch on forever, each second feeling like an eternity.

I burst into the stairwell, taking the steps two at a time, my heart hammering against my ribs.

Isobel, where are you? Please, please be safe.

I reached her floor, my hand slamming against the door as I pushed through.

Isobel.

The hallway was empty, the silence deafening.

I raced to her room, my trembling fingers fumbling with the key card.

Please be here. Please be okay.

I opened the door, my eyes frantically scanning the room. It was empty. No sign of her. No sign of a struggle.

I sank to the floor, my back against the wall, my chest heaving as I tried to catch my breath.

She wasn't here. Where was she?

What had happened?

I pulled out my phone, my fingers already dialing her number.

"Baby, where are you?" My voice broke. "Please pick up. I think… something happened. Babybabybabybaby, *just call me back."*

I ended the call, my hand clenching around the phone.

I had to move, had to act. Every second counted.

Hold on, Isobel. I'm coming for you.

I won't let anything happen to you.

I promise to be your shield. I promise to take care of you.

Please. Don't let me fail.

I would tear this city apart if I had to.

Because I couldn't lose her.

Not now, not ever.

I felt like I had waited three thousand fucking years for this woman. She was mine. She had been mine since the day I knew what love was.

I just needed to find her.

Now.

CHAPTER 38
ISOBEL

I WAS SO FOCUSED ON READING INTO MARCUS HAGEN BEING A woman, I didn't realize I couldn't find my phone.

I must've lost it outside on my walk.

I ran downstairs to get it at some point leaving my notes on the bed.

It would be quick.

Pregnancy brain was real.

It was freezing in Midtown.

The sea on either side making it frigid.

Gabriel. I just want to go home.

The bitter cold bit into my skin as I walked down the street, my hands numb and stiff.

I cursed myself for not wearing the blue gloves Gabriel had given me.

"Excuse me," I mumbled, nearly colliding with a woman who seemed to appear out of nowhere.

The brightest green eyes I had ever seen landed on me.

Jade green. Intelligent. Tip-tilted like a cat's. Frightening.

This woman was a little scary beautiful.

Her smile was wide as she landed on me.

"*Well*, hello there," her accent was subtle and she looked...a little scary. "What a night to find you."

What?

Her striking eyes flickered over me, assessing, and I automatically apologized in Spanish, the words falling from my lips out of habit.

"Lo siento, I was looking for my phone."

Her black hair shimmered a little as her smile dipped.

"Have you seen a phone anywhere?" I asked, though I knew it was a futile effort. "It's got a red case?"

She had just arrived, and the chances of her stumbling upon a lost phone were slim to none.

As expected, she shook her head, but her gaze remained fixed on me, intense and unwavering.

She reached into her pocket, and for a moment, I thought she might actually produce a phone.

But then, a voice cut through the frigid air like a knife, shattering the illusion of a simple interaction.

"You stupid bitch!"

I whirled around to the sound of the one person I never expected.

"Kourtney?"

Only...it couldn't be Kourtney. Not...

"Why are you covered in blood?"

It was Kourtney. But enraged like I had never seen her before.

And then I saw it, clutched in her trembling hand. A gun.

Oh my God.

My breath caught in my throat, my body frozen in place as if the cold had seeped into my very bones.

The chill that ran down my spine had nothing to do with the temperature and everything to do with the unhinged woman before me.

"You took him from me! I had a crush on him first. Everyone, everyone wants to be you. You stupid bitch."

Kourtney waved the gun at me, her words dripping with venom and barely contained hysteria. "You did this to me! Roberts called my father! I'm off the fucking op because of you!"

The woman behind me breathed. "Jesus fucking Christ."

"Don't move," I whispered to her. She was a civilian. Innocent.

"Don't worry," she whispered back. "I intend to."

What? I couldn't turn around to see her.

"I might not be my father," she whispered. "But I'll be damned if I don't see the truth."

I didn't understand her. It was like...she spoke in code.

"You did this to me!" Kourtney had lost her mind. That much was clear. Ranting about Gabriel this and Gabriel that.

And a horrifying thought occurred to me. "Did you kill him?"

Was that blood—a sickening sensation crashed over me. She blamed me for everything, her words becoming more and more unhinged with each passing second.

"Who the fuck are you? He was mine! And now I have to go back and face my fucking father and tell him I failed an op because a stupid Mexican slut can't get her life together?"

The realization hit me like a ton of bricks. She was mentally ill, her grasp on reality tenuous at best.

"*What did you do to him?*" I demanded, my hand drifting instinctively to my stomach, a protective gesture that I couldn't quite control. "WHAT DID YOU DO TO HIM!"

"*Shut up! Just shut the fuck up!*" She stepped closer, the gun now pointed directly at me, her finger twitching on the trigger.

And then it hit me, the reality of the situation slamming into me with the force of a speeding train. The blood. *Oh God, no.*

"*Did you kill Gabriel?*" The thought made my stomach turn, rage and fear rising inside of me.

I was going to kill her.

She laughed again, the sound grating against my nerves. "You don't get to say his name you fucking bitch."

I hated this bitch.

I hate this bitch.

"This is Reaper One," the one behind me muttered. "I thought the New York job was easier."

My eyes widened. The woman behind me was not a civilian.

"But this bitch is getting on my nerves."

She was an operative. I heard the static on her.

"You took my life from me." Kourtney shouted at me pointing the gun at me on the streets of the city. The street where civilians had scattered.

"Reaper One. Lights out." A man's voice sounded in the static.

The woman behind me was speaking. "If you shoot her, spook. I will bathe the city in your blood."

"Fuck you, Isobel!" Kourtney's face already dark and hideous twisted into something nastier.

"Reaper One. Requesting Clearance."

"Copy that, Reaper One. Target sighted. Cleared hot."

Dio.

The woman behind me was an operative. Enemy.

She wasn't a friend.

Cleared hot…meant…attack. She was coming—

"I'm taking it." The woman behind me was the one I was listening to. Because she wasn't a normal operative. My heart dropped into my stomach.

"Go to hell, Isobel." Kourtney shouted and then she fired her gun.

The gunshot rang out, shattering the cold air. I froze.

The woman behind me growled and aimed her gun.

At Kourtney.

"I'm already there, bitch." Green eyes. She isn't human. What is this lady?

One after the other. I saw Kourtney go down.

And so did I.

CHAPTER 39
GABRIEL

THE STENCH OF BLOOD ASSAULTED MY SENSES AS I BURST INTO LIAM'S room, the metallic scent so thick it coated my tongue and made my eyes water.

My heart pounded against my ribs, a frantic drumbeat that echoed the chaos around me.

"*Liam!*" I shouted. I ran to him. My *brother.* "*Liam, what happened? Shit shit shit, stay with me. Stay with me.*"

He was moaning on the floor, his legs twisted at an unnatural angle, the sight so grotesque it made my stomach heave, bile burning the back of my throat.

"*Liam.*"

I had seen dead bodies before, the gore and violence a familiar companion in my line of work.

But this...this was different.

This was personal.

He's my family.

He is my brother.

"Gabriel." Liam's anguished cry pierced the air, his face a mask of agony as he writhed on the blood-soaked carpet.

"*Kourtney...*My leg, I can't feel it. She was here." His words were jumbled and he was reaching for his broken phone, shattered screen, glass cutting into his hands. "*Isa.*"

His words came in broken gasps, each syllable laced with unimaginable pain.

He's your brother.

I dropped to my knees beside him, the warm, sticky blood seeping into my pants, staining my skin.

"Liam. I gotta find her. Let me call for help."

Even as I spoke, my hands were already fumbling for my phone, my fingers slick with sweat and blood. I dialed for help.

I couldn't tear my gaze away from the ever-widening pool of crimson beneath Liam, the metallic tang of it filling my nostrils, making my head spin.

It was too much, too fucking much.

But I had to focus. I had to push past the horror and the fear. *Isobel.*

Where was Isobel?

"I need an ambulance!" I barked into the phone, my voice shaking with barely contained panic. "I've got an agent down!"

I rattled off the address, the words spilling from my lips in a frenzied rush. *"Yes, Midtown! Near the Primrose Hotel! Hurry!"*

Liam shook his head, his skin ashen and slick with sweat.

With a herculean effort, he reached up and grasped the collar of my suit, yanking me down, a guttural groan of pain escaping his lips as he did.

"I can't feel my legs...Find her. I'm scared. Kourtney—find her. Find her!"

His words cut off abruptly as another wave of agony crashed over him, his body convulsing beneath my hands.

"Dad. I'm sorry. It hurts so fucking bad right now—"

An animal noise left Liam as I held him feeling the fear claw up my throat. Kourtney killed her own teammates.

Kourtney was a psychopathic loose cannon.

This was my fault.

I let her on my team.

I did this to my family.

"I can't leave you—You're my brother!"

"She's your wife!" Liam roared, his voice cracking with the effort. *"Find her! I promised...Dad...I'm sorry, I promised. I swear—I didn't mean it..."* Liam was delirious.

Tears streamed down his face, mingling with the sweat and grime. "I fucking promised—Fuck! I promised!"

Her father.

"She's my girl too. She's my—I promised him. I promised him."

283

Liam was crying so hard my vision blurred as he rubbed his chest his teeth gritted in pain.

I couldn't breathe. Couldn't see.

I was usually composed and right now—I was losing my ever loving mind.

Trying to push down my emotions but my family was bleeding out in front of me.

I stumbled to my feet, my legs barely supporting my weight as I bolted from the room.

Where is she?

Powerless.

Helpless.

Weak.

In that moment, I was a kid again, lost and frightened, the hallways of the piece of shit Midtown hotel blurring before my eyes as I ran.

Why was this place so fucking awful? Isobel! Where are you?

My hands shook, my breath coming in ragged gasps. Was it Sullivan shaking or was it me? I couldn't tell anymore.

All I could think about was Isobel.

She wasn't in her room. Where was she? Panic clawed at my chest, squeezing the air from my lungs, making it hard to breathe.

I had to find her. I had to find my girl.

The thought consumed me, driving me forward even as my mind reeled from the horror I had just witnessed.

I had to get to Isobel.

The fear was a living thing inside me, twisting my gut, making my heart race.

I couldn't lose her. Not now. Not ever.

I stumbled out of the room, my feet carrying me forward even as my mind screamed at me.

Please, let her be okay. Let me find her in time.

The hallways stretched out before me, an endless maze of doors and carpeted floors, the sounds of my own ragged breathing and pounding footsteps filling my ears.

"Fuck! I hate this!"

I ran blindly, my heart leading me forward, my soul crying out for her.

Isobel, where are you?

CHAPTER 40
ISOBEL

PAIN. BLINDING, SEARING PAIN.

It consumed me, engulfed me, as if my very soul was being ripped apart.

"Move, move, move!" A woman shouted.

"I'm fucking trying!" A man yelled back. "You're the one who brought a bloody CIA agent into this fucking car."

I swear to fucking God, Duke, if you don't get your ass moving—"

"I'm moving as fast as I can!"

A pair of green eyes entered my vision. "Isobel? Isobel Santos? Focus on my voice. I got you. I promise I got you—"

I promise. I gotcha. I won't let anything happen to you.

"Gabriel."

"No, my name's Talia." She shook her head. Her hand at her earpiece. "This is Reaper One. Do you copy? Shut it down. Shut all of Midtown down."

All I knew was the agony that coursed through my body, centering on my chest. My lungs. I was coughing up blood. I could see it.

"Shit shit shit," Talia held my face her eyes stark and bright. *"Don't you fucking die on me. I didn't save you to let you fall."*

What?

I tried to focus on it, to cling to the words like a lifeline, but the darkness was pulling me under, dragging me into its inky depths.

Each touch sent fresh waves of pain crashing over me, threatening to drown me in a sea of suffering.

Someone was shouting, their voice laced with urgency and fear. *Gunshot wound.*

My chest was on fire, the agony consuming me from the inside out. I was dying.

I wanted to cry, to rage against the unfairness of it all. I wasn't ready. I had so much left to do, so much left to say.

"She's not going to fucking make it...shit shit, stay with me, you're not going to go!"

The darkness was closing in now, the edges of my vision blurring, the world around me fading into a muted grey.

I was freezing cold.

Gabriel. Where are you?

"She's bleeding too fast-

"...in the shoulder...chest—" I couldn't *breathe. "...lungs, help her or I will fucking kill you!"*

That woman was angry.

My body felt heavy, my limbs numb and unresponsive.

The pain in my chest was a dull, throbbing ache.

Only overshadowed by the desperate thoughts. Frantic thoughts that raced through my mind. Frantic. Desperate.

One word shot out through the madness.

GABRIEL.

No. Gabriel. I love you. I'm so sorry I—I messed up.

She's so tiny, Gabriel. I love her so much.

I messed up.

I messed up.

I messed up.

I messed up.

I never told him.

Talia. Tell Gabriel. Tell him.

Find Liam.

Liam—Liam is looking for me.

I was losing it.

Tears streamed down my face, hot against my icy skin. I wanted to scream, to beg, to plead with whatever higher power might be listening.

To the universe.

Please, take me back, I don't want to go.

I will do anything. I will give you anything.

Please if anyone out there is listening—bring me back to him. Bring me back.

Bring me. BACK.

Gabriel.

I just wanted my family.

I wanted my family.

One day I'll come back and my family...

I was shaking uncontrollably, my teeth chattering as violent shivers wracked my body.

The cold was a living thing, wrapping around me like a shroud, sapping the last of my strength.

My head pounded, the pain so intense that I could barely think straight.

"She's going to crash!"

I was in Hell, my body betraying me as I fought against the tide sweeping over me.

I'm not going down without a fight.

I will do anything to go back to him.

He's my soul. He's my entire life. I can't leave him.

I clung to the memories, to the love that had sustained me.

Gabriel's face swam before my eyes, his eyes over me, his gentle smile, the way he looked at me like I was the only thing that mattered in the world.

Gabriel, I love you. I love you. I love you.

"Shit, stay with me, stay with me, stay with me, stay with me—" She kept screaming it. *"No! Doc Perla I swear to fucking God if you don't help her—"*

The last thing in my head I heard—was his voice.

"Juntos, you and me. Amor. Si?"

"Yeah, baby. We'll always be together."

"Miss Nash. Talia, she's not going to make it. She's dying."

"Yes she fucking is—Wake up, Isobel. I'll be damned if I let you die."

"You and me, baby. Always."

"Will you marry me?"

Yes.

The last thing I saw was his eyes. Winter. Pale blue. In my eyes. Smiling. Practicing Spanish. Telling me he loved me. Laughing.

His eyes. Icy.
Pale. Blue.
I love you too.
I was gone.

CHAPTER 41
GABRIEL

"Isobel!"

I roared, my voice echoing through the empty streets.

The icy wind whipped around me, stinging my face and numbing my fingers. My heart tightened with a panic I had never felt before.

"Isobel!"

My phone rang, the sound jarring in the eerie stillness.

I answered without thinking, my voice raw and desperate.

Vincent Grant was shaking. I could hear it.

"Where is she? Where is my girl?"

The voice on the other end was apologetic, frustrated, just some analyst, "We have her pinging near the hotel. I can't get a read on it, I'm trying boss. I'm trying right now."

I frowned, my mind racing. "What? What do you mean the footage is wiped?"

"Sir, it's like it never existed in the first place. I see her in the frame and then she's wiped—"

"It's Hagen."

"I think so, I'm trying sir—"

"Try harder! It's not good enough! Isobel is gone! Liam said he was shot—"

We were burned. Someone was coming for us. *And Isobel got caught in it.*

I forced myself to think, to focus, even as the cold threatened to overwhelm me. "There's a hospital nearby, she could be there."

"Sending you the address now," I heard Sutton's voice shaking with panic as they both worked overtime.

I looked down, my stomach turning at the sight of blood on the sidewalk, stark against the white snow.

Kourtney was dead.

Someone shot her.

But all I could think about was Isobel.

Where are you? Amor. Where did you go?

I don't remember how I got to the clinic, my feet numb and my face raw from the biting wind.

Please, please, be alive.

I could feel her, sense her nearby.

She's my soul.

I feel her.

"Let me in," I growled, pulling out my gun with stiff, frozen fingers. They held up their hands and let me pass.

"I need to know if there are gunshot wound victims—female, twenty two, dark hair, five four," I demanded, my voice hoarse from the cold.

Beautiful eyes. Isobel. Where are you? Come on, Amor.

She lies on her ID card.

She's five-four maybe. She's so small. She's tiny compared to me and I know she's hurting.

I know she's hurt.

"Where are you?" I gasped, my eyes scanning the clinic desperately. And then I stilled, my heart stopping in my chest.

Bloody clothes in the trash, gauze, the unmistakable signs of *something.*

I pulled my gun back, my hands shaking from more than just the cold.

"She was here." I whirled on the scared faces, my eyes wild. *"Where is she?"*

They took her.

They tried to kill my wife.

"Sir," one of them uttered, their voice trembling, "The people who came here threatened—"

I read her name tag. *Perla.*

"Where the fuck is she?" I snarled, my patience snapping like an icicle. Ice was casing over me. Something was happening to me.

"Ww-we d-don't know where they took h-her."

"Who is they? Who took her?"

I cocked my gun back, the sound deafening in the tense silence. Every second that went by was another second *without her.*

Perla held out a shaking hand.

"Sir....they left this." She was shaking so hard she almost dropped it and I blanked out.

Black.

Gold claw marks.

Hagen takes out everything.

Hagen took my wife.

Hagen took.

My.

Wife.

Rage burned through my bloodstream.

She's cold. I'm freezing.

Something is happening to me.

Amor.

Something is happening to me.

Something was happening to my heart.

In that moment something in me snapped.

I'm going to kill everyone in this room.

"WHERE IS MY FUCKING WIFE?"

PART TWO | 煉獄 | RENGOKU
PURGATORY | A REALM OF HUNGRY GHOSTS

CHAPTER 42
ISOBEL
CAPE VERDE

I FELT SOFT.

Quiet.

Something…in my vision I saw white.

The world swam into focus as I opened my eyes, a haze of blue and white that slowly resolved into a sky above me.

It was like water color paint in my eyes.

I was…I was somewhere. Not in the car with Liam.

Did I fall asleep?

I stirred, a soft noise escaping my lips as a violent headache pounded behind my eyes.

"Talia…" an English voice said, the sound muffled as if I were underwater. "Your case study is awake." The English voice was sardonic.

"*Samara*, she has a name." A pair of green eyes swam into my vision. Her dark hair framing her elegant features. "Isobel, you're awake. Good to see you. It's only been two weeks and you're doing much better."

"For a dead woman," came the dry haughty response. I felt like I was…underwater and asleep at the same time. "Two weeks is an eternity in hell."

What?

"What…what happened?" I asked, my voice hoarse and raspy.

Graduation, a man with green eyes.

Liam...

The headache intensified, throbbing in time with my heartbeat.

My dad, he was waiting for me.

I needed to go to see my family.

"What's the agency doing sending children to catch big fish?" The woman with the green eyes. *Talia.* She watched me carefully. "You're not the usual roundup of clowns they send after me."

After her? *Agency?*

She was speaking in tongues.

"What agency?" I managed, confusion swirling through me.

My body ached all over. I felt dry and uncomfortable. Every part of me felt...wrong.

Something was wrong.

Talia frowned at me.

And the woman across from me, with the English voice, dark eyes and even darker hair sat up suddenly.

Both of them looked at each other.

Then me.

Then each other.

Like a cartoon movie.

"*....who are you?*" The woman with dark eyes widened. "Who are you and where do you work?"

The words formed like I was underwater.

"Isobel Santos. I just graduated. Is that...where I work? What agency do you work for? Liam went to get gas..." He was going to pay for snacks...I saw him leaving.

And that was it.

That's all I had in my brain. Liam's grin as he walked away from me.

Talia blinked several times staring at me like a three headed alien.

"You know what? Perla said after she woke up there might be some damage. But I didn't guess this, Samara get her something to drink. She looks pale."

The woman named Samara stood and I realized they were both wearing the same outfits. Uniforms almost. Black.

Talia's had gold markings on one shoulder like armor.

Her eyes met mine a little concerned.

Who was Perla? What was happening?

"Where am I?" Talia looked more approachable than the other woman. Samara. "What is this?"

I was in a hospital gown. Somewhere near water.

"Liam was driving...he stopped at a gas station..."

Talia's eyes met mine then with a softer approach. "Where do you go to...what do you do?"

"I go to college. I just graduated school, I work on computers... What am I doing here? Liam and I..."

We were going somewhere, but the memory was hazy, indistinct. "I woke up in a gas station. I had a nightmare. Liam...where is he?"

"Liam Sullivan," Samara said out loud.

She handed me a bottle of water and I slowly sat up only to feel a twinge in my left shoulder. I looked down.

His name was Santos...

"Why am I..." I had bandages across my chest.

"You were shot," Samara's eyes despite being cold, her voice softened as well. She sat back to her perch across the room from me as Talia sat by me.

"Samara." Talia's voice was firm. Whatever she conveyed in that tone Samara's expression blanked out. But me?

I felt nothing but panic. Until Talia said. "Isobel, do you know what Lazarus syndrome is?"

I shook my head. "Why am I...why am I here? Why do I have bandages? Why am I in a hospital? What is this—"

"Lazarus Syndrome is when a patient clinically dies."

I stopped talking as Talia met me head on. She was maybe my height, maybe shorter. Her body leaner and more toned than my own. Her eyes sharp, almost cruel in how pretty she was.

"You died."

I blinked. I was in...whatever this was because—

"I'm dead right now?"

Samara laughed low. And Talia's face broke out into a wide smile, her canines flashing and the green in her eyes looking delighted.

"No. But you did die. Back in..." she was watching her words. "You were shot. I saved you. Well...Samara and Duke helped. This is Cape Verde. It's an island I have property on. I flew you out here thinking you'd be safer. Turns out I was right." Her eyes softened on me. "Do you remember anything but Liam and the gas station?"

Both her and Samara watched me.

I shook my head.

"Are you my family?" I asked, the words feeling foreign on my tongue. "Why am I here? I don't remember you two."

We were going to Quantico...to...join the CIA...Liam convinced me to join it. Liam wanted us to have a better life...

I felt the memories slowly infiltrating my brain. But we had never made it there. I didn't remember making it there.

"We were on a trip," I whispered. "He went to get gas."

I didn't know these women.

Where was Liam?

Talia sat back her expression changing as she watched me.

"Samara give us a second. Bring her some clothes." And Samara moved like a doll, elegant and graceful as she left doing exactly as asked and Talia's entire face softened the moment the doors shut. "You don't remember anything?"

Was I supposed to?

I felt hollow. Empty. Aching in ways I didn't understand.

"What do you mean I was shot?"

Was I in the CIA?

Jade green eyes met mine. "You know I'd forget the world too if I could. Duke wiped the clinic and the entire city so you're all good. You have no idea what I'm saying, do you?"

I didn't.

I didn't know who she was.

"I was there," her voice was a whisper. "I saw you die. Saw you... lose your world in front of me. Don't worry." Her eyes were wide like a child's now. "I killed the bitch who killed you. Eye for an eye. But Isobel, Liam was shot by her. His name was Sullivan. If you hadn't told me—I wouldn't have known. Your team is gone. I don't know a gentle way to tell you about this. So I'm going to rip the bandaid off given your trauma."

What? My team? Liam was shot? By the woman who tried to kill me?

Liam...

"He was driving."

Did we get into an accident? How did we die?

I felt the panic rising and Talia's hand was on my face holding it as the headache made my vision swim.

"Don't freak out," her eyes were eerie. A little frightening.

"You're safe. I'm sorry for your loss. I did what I could. Took you to a clinic. To Germany. Now here. I did the best I could. If my father found out he would have my head." Her smile was wide again like that was funny. "If you ask me, loss isn't real if you can't remember it."

What? What was this woman? What was she saying? Who was she?

Liam was dead? My heart was pounding. I didn't even know how to form words.

"My father—Liam—"

"They're both gone."

I felt like I was going to implode a little at how calmly she spoke to me holding me.

The physical contact making me aware of my position in bed helpless and her predatory gaze on mine.

My memory of Liam was fuzzy. Our memories like film blacking out. Everything else? Was empty. The panic was in my throat again as the room spun.

"Who are you?"

Her smile was back. "My name is Talia Morningsr. But since you don't remember me—my name is also Marcus Hagen." She looked delighted as she said it. "Do you recognize that name?"

I shook my head.

Her eyes gentled then. Something about Talia was a little spooky. *Liam was gone...*

How?

"Don't worry Isobel, I won't ever fail you. I promise I'm not as big of a cunt as the world makes me out to be. Maybe Samara. She's definitely capable of eating you alive. But I won't hurt you." She looked at me then softening completely, her smile dropping. "I am you. I know exactly how you feel. And since I know everything about the game—I'm going to do you a solid." She let me go and sat back as though waiting for me to ask.

"What...is...what are you going to do?"

"I'm going to give you a new life." She smiled softly. She motioned around to the room, to her uniform and she passed me a black card with gold claw marks.

"I think you'll do great things here. I'm not a complete fool. And believe it or not, my father might be a demon, but he did teach me a few things. And one of them—is to keep my mouth shut."

I took the card gingerly aware of how pale I looked.

She smiled at my expression wider again, those jade green eyes sparkling with her excitement.

"Welcome to Talon, Isobel."

CHAPTER 43
GABRIEL

I DIDN'T LEAVE MIDTOWN.

I stayed there. Searching for her all night.

Vincent on the phone with me listening to me unravel while Sutton had been crying. Running around.

Cindy Roberts raising hell for the operation on my behalf.

But it was too late.

I quit. I was done.

Just like that.

Vincent wasn't done.

Vincent had a fucked up sense of loyalty in him.

With the entire team murdered—Vincent who had been sent home began helping me pick up the pieces virtually from his home.

I was covered in Liam's blood that night. Somewhere I lost the key to the necklace. I didn't know where it went.

And my wife was nowhere to be found.

Hagen took my wife.

Perla ended up telling me what she knew her hands shaking. She was a resident. A woman brought Isobel in. Dark hair. Green eyes. Same build as my wife.

A *woman* brought my wife bleeding.

Marcus Hagen was a girl?

Perla had tried to stabilize her but ultimately needed a trauma surgeon. Because Isobel had been shot.

Several times.

But the woman who brought her in was trying to save her life.

Who? Who the fuck would do that?

Where was my wife now?

Was she dead or alive?

I sat at the hotel aware I needed to give briefings and reports which Cindy and Sutton stepped in for.

Liam's words were that Kourtney shot him.

The security footage that Sutton had found had shown that once Kourtney had found out. She had been with Jeremy.

He had been the first.

Her snapping came from her being absolutely fucking batshit. She went after Liam when he'd come back from Teasers.

And Isobel had been the last one. Except Isobel is where the camera footage went dark.

And then all of Midtown went dark.

My wife was gone.

I had a mission I was on. I couldn't leave my wife behind. I didn't know where she was that week.

I just knew I descended into a level of madness I didn't even know was possible.

Now two weeks later, Liam was in the hospital. He had been flown back to Quantico with Sutton at his side.

She stayed with him taking a leave of absence.

Liam. My fucking brother.

Who could no longer walk properly and needed a wheelchair.

Jeremy Bradford was dead. His girlfriend Cathy had been a wreck and Sutton juggled Liam and Cathy on her own.

The ironic part?

Koller was found with a bullet in his brain this week.

The black card with gold claw marks somehow reaching him. His family was dead.

And every single person on the team was declared dead.

All of our names changed.

I was now Raphael Santos.

In the hotel room my mind was a mess. I found Isobel's gloves at the hospital. I found pieces of my wife everywhere. Her hair brush. Her suitcase unpacked and untouched in her room. I held onto her things like if I held tighter—I could save her.

Vincent and I worked together.

I was officially a free agent.

"Sir," Vincent was on the phone. "I got information about Cormac O'Hara you had asked for. Liam was at club Teaser's and he said he met Melina Mendoza. I hacked into the club feed. It's a human trafficking ring. She's just another victim. I think that club is owned by the mob though. The O'Hara crime syndicate. They span New York and Chicago...he's got three sons..."

I processed what Vincent was saying.

"Aidan O'Hara is the oldest..."

I swallowed feeling numbed out. Liam couldn't walk.

Liam. The karate black belt and ice-skater.

The one who lived for activity.

Melina was the last thing he asked me for.

"I also got a call from a man named Reed Whittaker. He says he heard through several people on the grapevine something happened in New York. He heard you were involved. He says he wants to make sure you were good."

"He doesn't need to know anything. Don't say anything yet."

"Yes, sir."

I wasn't his boss anymore. But Vincent and Claire had been the two people who stepped in. When I went to go kill everything for my family.

Reed was the one I had been friends with in high school. A long time ago. We kept in touch every so often.

Every so often.

He was the one who would've liked to be in Titan with Liam. I hadn't even gotten the chance to tell him.

"I'm digging into Evie Santos, Selena Tavares, and the Heron Manor. All cameras at Teaser's are out for you. The entire block is dead. You're all good when you're ready."

I head out into the evening.

"Good shit." My voice was numb. "I'll go look into it."

I had nothing else to do but retrace Liam's steps.

I did go to Teaser's with my ball cap on. And I felt numbed out at the women around me. Clearly younger than normal and I searched out the bar.

Melina Mendoza.

I asked the bartender for her name in the seedy joint. The woman who was brought to me looked frail. Barely five feet tall. Track marks on her arms. Black hair, wide eyes like she afraid of me. She was pretty.

302

When I went to the back with her I honestly thought she thought I was going to sleep with her.

Instead when she approached me shaking. I held up my phone with a photo of me and Liam. I zoomed in on his face. Her eyes lit up wide and a smile broke out on her expression.

"Liam!" She said. "Donde esta?" *Where was he?*

"Do you speak English?"

"A little." I handed her my phone typing it into translate it.

This is my brother Liam. Do you know him?

I showed it to her in Spanish. Never in my life did I hate not having learned it properly until that moment. Never in my life did I hate myself more.

She nodded eagerly her eyes going wide at the photo.

I kept typing hating myself as the minute grew.

He was here to see you?

She shook her head. She motioned for my phone.

He said he was here...to...forget himself. But he found me.

I read her notes. *Forget himself?* I frowned down at it.

But I had more pressing concerns.

I typed. *Liam told me you needed my help. Do you need my help?*

I passed Melina my phone again and her eyes went wide. She shook her head looking concerned.

"I'm not a trap," I said in English. And then I typed frustrated with myself.

I can get you out. Get you to Liam. Make you safe. I can do this. You trusted Liam. You can trust me. Liam said you are under Cormac O'Hara. Is that the man who did this to you?

I pointed to the shamrock brand on her wrist. Human cattle.

But Liam...Liam saw something in her.

She was shaking as she took the phone from me her eyes haunted. Her nod was quick.

"Where is he?" I asked her in English before typing it in and translating it. My hands didn't shake anymore. The layer of ice covering my heart was getting harder. But I stayed focused on this girl. Liam would've wanted me to look into her, and I also knew what I needed to know about his time here.

She told me.

I looked at her dark eyes looking at mine with hope in them.

"Tu nombre?"

"Gabriel." I held out my hand. "Nice to meet you."

She dipped her head in an embarrassed smile. I hadn't looked at her body long enough to know the flimsy outfit she wore was barely a shirt with plenty of rips and tears. She had bruises on her arm.

It had been two weeks since Liam had been shot.

What did she go through?

"I'm going to get you out of here. For Liam. And then I'm going to look at the security footage to trace his steps."

She frowned. And pointed beneath us. "Basement."

I smirked. "Cormac's downstairs. Can you take me there?"

I typed it in. She nodded.

And so I left Melina at the top of the steps, and went to see Cormac. I didn't really have anything to say. I already knew he was scum based off the shit show the place was.

Cormac O'Hara was the head of the Irish mob.

And he was about to be a dead man.

CHAPTER 44
GABRIEL

I walked into the basement of the place and I heard the sound of something being hit. A person. I passed by a group of men surrounding a few girls.

I held up my hands. "Sorry, I'm a little lost."

I pasted on a grin that felt foreign but I was trained. Still. "You guys know where the bathroom is?"

One of them swore at me and shoved me into the deeper part of the hallway and took his gun out. Perfect. I felt my grin slip the moment I was out of sight and had him disarmed in another second.

"Where's Cormac?" His eyes widened as I didn't hesitate. I aimed it right at his skull. I peered at the gun. "Silencer. Nice shit." I grinned wider. "Where is he?"

His throat bobbed as he pointed to a closed door where I heard the sound of a man groaning. In pain. Cormac was beating on someone. Fun.

I kept my eyes on the man. "Thanks."

And then I shot him.

I made my way into the room, shooting the locked door open, and bursting into the room to find Cormac O'Hara kicking a young man in the stomach on the floor.

"Piece of shit you are, Aidan!"

His son. That was his son.

I didn't hesitate. I didn't need to. Every single thing I knew about Cormac so far let me know this was beyond talking. I didn't even hesitate, I shot him in the face.

A groan came from the man on the floor as he raised his bloodied face up to mine. Amber eyes locked on me.

"Who—who the fuck are you?"

I scoffed. "I'm the motherfucker who just met you the next King. You Aidan O'Hara?"

He nodded slowly rising up, his hands up as he watched me like a wild animal.

"I want one of your girls for good. She's done here. Melina Mendoza." I pointed the gun at him. "And I want a cut of this." I motioned to the room. "Whatever the fuck it is."

He spit out blood looking at me with rage in those amber eyes, his dark hair a mess. "What makes you think I'm going to give it to you?"

He was bleeding and holding his side.

Even when he wasn't in a position to be questioning my authority since I held the gun he was proud. Bloody. But proud. His jaw when not bloody would be regal.

As he spoke I heard movement behind me. Someone else approached. One of the guys from earlier who had found his friend's body.

I didn't even hesitate as I shut the door.

"I'm going to offer you a fucking deal Aidan O'Hara. I can give you props. You're gonna give me a way forward. Starting with your security tapes." I heard pounding on the door as Aidan looked past me. He couldn't be older than me.

"And you think after you shot my father I would ever—"

"I shot your abuser. I know enough. I know you've been working with the Feds. I know they haven't done shit for you. Not surprising. Did he find out you were a snake?" I ignored the pounding behind me. "Or was he trying to kill you because he thought you were taking over?"

Amber eyes widened on me like he was shocked. He wasn't a small guy either. So him taking a beating from his father came from loyalty. Loyalty was good.

"You could work with me. Or I can shoot you right here and make for an impressive power vacuum even the Fed's won't be able to stop."

His Adam's apple bobbed.

As he looked down at his father. Dead.

Gone.

I aimed my gun at him. "Well?"

He swallowed looking exhausted for the first time. "How much do you want?"

I grinned. "I want a *permanent* cut. A partnership. And your security tapes. I want Melina. This club shut down effective immediately. I have a guy Vincent he can help you—"

"*What the fuck are you—Agency? Fed?*"

"*I'm a fucking nobody.*" The son of a nobody. Who belonged to no one right now. But her. I blinked my emotion back. Not now.

Not in front of him.

"But I'll be damned if I turn down opportunity anymore."

I fucked up.

I got my family killed.

I fucked up.

My wife is missing.

My brother can't walk.

I fucked up.

Aidan noted looking at me like he'd seen the devil in real life. "Deal."

"Deal." I dropped my gun. "If you renege on it, I know where you live. And I know you've got two brother's you protect. I won't kill you. I'll kill them starting with the one with the freaky eyes."

His jaw clenched as he looked at me and I dropped Vincent's number. And then I took Melina with me.

I stepped out of the club giving her my hoodie and she quickly put it on.

Vincent would give her a new identity. A new name.

I typed it into the translator. "What name do you want?" I asked her as she read what I typed.

Her eyes met mine. Wide. Dark. She was so young.

"Liam…" she whispered.

"Liam isn't here right now, Melina. I need you to pick a name or Vincent will get you one."

She swallowed nervously. She didn't understand what I was saying. I hated every second I couldn't talk to her.

"When I'm better, you can help me with my Spanish. Where are you from," I said it as I typed it showing her the text.

"Mexico," she blinked up at me. And in that moment as I looked down at her it took everything in me not to cry. My eyes welled a little watching her. "Liam?"

Her eyes watered watching me. "Liam?"

She was like a baby bird. I swore a little moving automatically taking her in my arms without thinking. "¿cómo te llamas?"

What is your name?

She wiped her eyes typing into my phone.

Why do you want me to pick a name?

My hands shook as I typed. "Because this is the first choice you're going to get in your new life. Something tells me you haven't been given many choices." I typed it. I showed it to her wiping my eyes and I motioned to the brand on her wrist. "Choice. You know what that is?"

She nodded and I saw her think about it.

She grabbed my phone and typed into it again. Her fingers shook even harder.

Liam gave me a nickname.

I smiled a little. "What is it?"

She typed again. *Lara. He called me Lara after my middle name Melina Larissa Mendoza.*

"You wanna be called Lara?" She nodded. "Good shit." Vincent was going to make sure someone from New York could take Lara to a safe house temporarily. Somewhere to cool off. Shower. Heal. After I dug into Aidan O'Hara I would have him answer for what the fuck his father was doing.

Vincent had said the sons weren't involved in anything their father did. Victims. Not vultures.

I'd make do with that. I waited until the female operative Vincent sent came. In the meantime, Lara stared at a photo of Liam on my phone with a smile on her face.

He's a saint. She said it to me in Spanish. *Un Santo.*

He was. He was a Santos.

Now I didn't know how he was doing.

I knew Sutton told me Liam had been in and out of surgeries. Multiple ones after Kourtney hadn't killed him.

She'd gone for his legs. Liam. The one who was fast, active—the ice skater. The karate black belt.

I could feel from here how wrecked he was.

I couldn't even look at my brother right now.

When Melina—*Lara*—left with the female operative I got a chance to breathe.

Vincent texted me.

> O'Hara got in touch.

> Selena Tavares was never brought out from Havana. What do you want to do about her?

I didn't know. But I couldn't leave her in Havana. I knew some of the guys she was with.

There was a reason why they were there.

Selena was the one who didn't make it to New York.

The one who was alive. But not in a good place.

Havana wasn't ideal.

> Can you get her to Quantico?

> Yeah. I need to work on it.

> Did you want the keys and address for Heron Manor?

> I want you to pull the money from the O'Hara's. Take Heron Manor.

> Aidan won't give a shit.

> Not after that.

> And then I want the address for Evie Santos.

> She's in California?

> Yes, sir.

> Reed Whittaker said he can fly out to meet you in a few days.

> Send him to Heron Manor. I need to get there first.

> Yes, sir. Flight tickets for Evie sent to your phone now.

> You might need to rush. Her mom's in and out of the hospital.

I stared down at my phone to find a photo of a young girl. Fifteen.

And the moment I saw her eyes—I saw my wife.

"Oh, she's a baby." I blinked back my emotions as I realized Vincent had sent me her mother's file.

Adrianna Santos works for a smaller motel line owned by the Devereaux family...they've reported issues there with a few of the staff...

I blew out a breath passing by a tattoo parlor on the way to my rental car reading Vincent's messages about Evie Santos.

Adrianna Santos had cancer.

I needed to figure out my house.

Get Reed out here.

Get Evie out of California and bury her dying mother. I was burying my wife's entire family at this rate.

My head was spinning. But I felt like in that moment if I stopped, and if I stayed still, I would break into a million fucking pieces.

I would shatter.

And I couldn't afford that right now.

I had failed my family. I failed my wife.

I let her down. And it was burning in my blood to do something. Anything. But sit still.

An hour later I had my wife's named tattooed on my left pec. If not the necklace? It was permanent now.

On my heart. Isobel didn't know I kept everything she had.

Her name. On me. Until I died. I left to get Evie. For my wife. For the promises I broke.

For the way I failed her.

I let her down.

I fucking hated myself.

Hated the Agency.

Hated my world.

With all my pretenses and rules obliterated? I felt myself sliding so further into a grey area I knew there was no coming back out.

And I realized something in that moment—I would cross whatever line, whatever bridge, whatever rule I had to—to get where I needed to go.

To find my wife.

And suddenly, without any rules, the possibilities of where I could go were limitless.

By the end of the month?

The sun was going down and I hadn't moved all day since I'd come back to our apartment.

My hand on the space next to me she sat. I lost...

I lost the key that night.

My key.

I didn't know where it was.

It must've dropped it. I may never find it.

Or *her*.

My eyes drifted around our home. Her home. How she'd settled. Into my heart.

I did see Liam briefly. He was in his hospital bed staring at his lap like a ghost. He looked thinner, weaker, fragile.

Sutton by his bedside, eyes rimmed red as she held onto his hands. Liam didn't look like himself. He looked like a specter.

She wiped her eyes and the moment I stepped in, he had taken one look at me. One.

I saw a dead man in his eyes.

He *knew*. He looked away his hand moving over his heart as he closed his eyes, his fist gripped his gown tightly.

Sutton's face broke again.

In that moment—I lost him.

I broke every promise I made to him. I broke every promise to her. I told my family—I'd protect them.

I'd take care of them.

And I failed both of them.

CHAPTER 45
GABRIEL

It was before I had to go see Evie, after I got Heron Manor secured. Vincent went to Heron Manor while I packed up my home.

Her things.

Her scarf, trinkets, flashes of red all over my white rooms.

Her bath products.

I didn't realize it would eat me alive being in my own house.

I was suffocating touching it. I couldn't go near her clothes, her wedding dress, her shoes—without snapping.

Isobel's e-reader was by our bedside. Suddenly, seeing her and Jeremy and Sutton trying to hide their romance novels for me at work, felt like eons ago.

I reached for it and opened it, almost falling before I caught it. It was several black and white and grainy photos.

I frowned down at them.

Now? I felt like I was searching for clues about my wife now. Everything she had I held onto.

I didn't even wanna throw out her trash.

On the back Isobel's handwriting had some things written into it.

Alma Gabrielle Monroe.

Alma...

And for a second I stopped breathing. My hands shook.

"Due..." I muttered, staring at the two dates scribbled.

The first date, from what I could tell, was the day the image was taken. And then...another date.

I did the math.

Seven months from there...my thoughts spiraled.

Amor, I ran too hard, I forgot....

I'm just tired, I haven't been able to rest while building Oracle.

What if you could make it in other ways?

Like what?

Like a family. Life. Her.

I'm going to make it, baby. I'm going to give you the world.

I already have the world, Gabriel.

Isa said she has a stomach bug or something. She hasn't been feeling well. She's been sick and she went to the doctor.

Your cheeks and hips look fuller. You're glowing.

My chest was on fire.

I couldn't see straight.

Love lives inside your soul.

No, it lived in her.

It lived in her. She was my entire soul.

I'm going to give you the world.

You already have.

I don't need the world, just you.

My love for you will never be conditional.

It will never be conditional, Gabriel.

She didn't tell me.

She didn't tell me because she knew.

She didn't want to ruin the assignment.

Didn't want me distracted. I know my wife.

I know why she did it.

But that didn't mean—it didn't hurt.

And my heart, encased in ice.

Completely.

Shattered.

CHAPTER 46
ISOBEL

I caught a glimpse of myself in the mirror in the last three months I had been at the Talon Compound.

It was a private security company on paper, owned by Talia Nash.

Talia who was becoming my shadow. I recognized her. But I rarely looked at myself in the mirror anymore.

I didn't recognize the woman staring back.

She was a stranger, her eyes haunted and confused.

Black voids.

Black hair.

Nothing but darkness and shadows.

Dark circles rimmed my eyes, and my cheeks were hollow, the bones too prominent. I didn't recognize her. There was no...light in me.

I looked like a woman without a soul.

Someone missing. My hair cut to my elbows now.

My gaze drifted to my shoulder, and I winced as a dull ache throbbed beneath the skin.

My chest felt even worse, a constant, nagging pain that seemed to emanate from my very soul. What had happened to me?

I kept seeing the pale blue eyes in my vision sometimes. Every so often they floated over and the scent of something unfamiliar to me.

I reached for the pile of clothes the hospital had given me. Talia saved all my things and Samara who was a little spooky had done me justice by not throwing anything out.

As I looked through them I searched for clues for who...what happened to me.

And I found the necklace.

Monroe.

In my room at the Talon compound where Talia sometimes stayed, the necklace was heavy in my palm. I lifted it to my ear.

Something was inside of it. It clinked gently.

Talia let me stay here, I had medical care and Samara dropped by every so often with food.

I wasn't a prisoner. Not really. I got to roam around and explore the Talon compound. There were *people* here. Men and women.

Lean, fit, some looking like Liam. A fighter.

My grief over my family had transformed into something different. I held onto my necklace for weeks as I recovered.

Talia had explained my medical condition about being shot in the collarbone right over my heart.

I had pain in my left shoulder and on the left side of my body in general. I needed an emergency surgery. I had died on the operating table. I had needed a blood transfusion.

I had muscle weakness from being in bed for so long. I had limited mobility in my left arm and shoulder.

I had scars that needed healing.

And I felt like a mess. I had difficulty breathing, memory loss due to oxygen deprivation during clinical death.

I functioned slower.

And Talia kept me safe in my bedroom where Samara often came and took me out. Samara, I took it, was like her assistant. One of many.

Today I was alone.

I looked down at the necklace again, turning it over and over in my fingers. Monroe. The name meant nothing to me.

This is important, this is what is missing.

As I slipped the necklace over my head, the metal cool against my skin, my eyes were drawn to the puckered, angry scars near my left shoulder, the skin between my breasts distorted stretching out over my left breast.

The pendant settled against my chest, right over my heart, and for a moment, I felt a flicker of something familiar, something that almost felt like home.

Every single time I put it on I felt different.

But it was fleeting, gone as quickly as it had come.

There was an ache in my stomach that felt like I was getting my period.

As I stood at the window, my gaze was drawn to the endless expanse of the ocean before me.

I closed my eyes, trying to remember, trying to piece together the fragments of my past. But all I could see were flashes of icy blue eyes, piercing and intense.

The eyes haunted me, their gaze searing into my soul...I felt a shiver run down my spine, a sense of unease that I couldn't quite shake.

I turned away from the window, my hand instinctively reaching for the necklace that hung around my neck.

The pendant was warm against my skin, a tangible reminder of the life I didn't...remember?

We have the world.

Who are you?

What are you?

Are you real? Are you out there?

Come find me.

I spoke it into the wind whipping through my hair. The sun on the horizon beating down on me.

"I have the world..."

CHAPTER 47
ISOBEL

"It's going to take you another nine to twelve months to heal," Talia murmured.

She sat with me in my tower at Talon. Talia was a kind of beautiful you had to suspend all reality to take in. Dark hair. Jade green eyes that glittered. Predatory.

Talia was dangerous.

I could feel it in her energy. Like her soul was split in half.

I felt off…

After I came back from the dead, I had been off.

Talia looked a little strange in feminine clothing.

Every so often she showed up in all black like a killer and then threw me off in a sundress and her laughter with Samara. Samara Arterton was her shadow.

She followed Talia like a wraith and didn't leave her side.

The island itself was hot. And I loved it here now even if I felt a tug in my soul from another direction. Somewhere far from me but there. Blue eyes. Blonde hair. He was…right there on the tip of my tongue but I couldn't figure it out.

Talia's eyes now a brighter green met mine. "How are you?"

"Better."

"Sleeping better?"

"No, the nightmares are there." I had them all the time. Ones where I was being swallowed by shadows and sometimes a grim Reaper appeared curiously over me.

He didn't move. He just stood there confused as to why I was still walking the Earth.

It was spooky.

I told Talia about my visions and what was happening.

"Sometimes that's common," she whispered. "In parts of Asia they believe when the body dies, the vessel is empty for a few moments, and the thread between you and death is so thin, that veil is like paper."

"You think I'm…"

I felt like half of my soul was missing.

She shook her head. "Like half of you is gone, taken over by shadows?"

That's exactly what it felt like. Pale blue eyes in my vision.

Blonde hair.

I have the world.

Alma…Monroe…

I felt different. I felt things.

"After brain injuries, people aren't usually the same again. And then you died. I wouldn't think you're freaking out, it's normal for you to be sensitized now."

Talia explained it to me and I listened. We talked for hours like this. I realized when I got to know her she just looked really scary.

Talia was really funny.

She just said like offhand things with a serious face. Samara didn't any sense of humor and her personality was made from ice, but she was still a polite girl.

Nobody else was really around me which was nice.

"Why are you doing this for me?"

Even I knew this was strange. I wasn't a prisoner.

I could leave, but she offered me medical care and she was taking care of me. And I didn't have anything else left.

She told me that my family was gone. And the scars on my body weren't lies.

I had no reason to doubt her. I wore my necklace around my neck and the wind blew on my gown.

I looked out of place among all the soldiers but they just assumed I worked here too.

Her eyes took on a faraway look. It had been four months since I met her. Four month here just…existing.

I felt…weird. Because I couldn't remember anything, there was nowhere I had to be. Liam was…gone. A fact of which tore through me since Liam felt like my heart.

I knew I was missing my life and my story, but I couldn't exactly run around and do anything. I got tired easily. I needed physical therapy. I was weaker than anyone on the compound.

"You've never met my father," Talia whispered her voice low even though the door was closed. "I don't want you to meet him. I'd like to keep this between you and me and a select few people. Natasha is trust worthy, but even still…"

"Why not?"

I didn't know Malcolm Nash. I didn't think I wanted to ever meet him.

"My father isn't the best person in the world. In fact, sometimes I think he might be the worst. You're what, twenty-three?"

I just had my birthday.

She smiled softly looking much younger and warmer.

"I was eighteen. I had a medical emergency. And my father had to come out to get me in school. The only problem was…my boyfriend was there also. And my father did not know I had one. I knew better than to tell him with how protective he was."

Talia paused her eyes getting a faraway look to them.

"I was with Drew when it happened. And next thing I know I'm waking up in the hospital after having surgery. My father found out at the hospital and he kicked my boyfriend out." Her eyes met mine. "I never saw Drew again."

The wind whipped around us. Me, in a gown, her in a sundress. Like two normal women. Except one was an assassin and one was a ghost.

Talia leaned back again the window, her smile playing on her lips bittersweet.

"At the time, at *eighteen* I thought I knew what I wanted. I thought everything was the end of the world. But it never was the end. It was always a beginning."

I blew out a breath as she spoke.

"Every loss led to greater heights. Every bit of suffering led to greater things. I lost so much. I lost my health, I lost Drew, and I lost any semblance of normal in my life. Drew's brother's were like my family too. And in one swoop, I had every single thing taken away from me."

"I'm sorry."

"Me too."

"What happened to Drew?"

She shrugged. "I wasn't allowed to talk to him. Father said he would kill him and his little brother Teo. I had known them since I was eleven. Drew wasn't my love. He was my soul." Talia looked at me lazily the predatory look in her eyes back. "Do you know the worst part of being alive? It's remembering every single second of what happened that day. Of the last twenty something years of my life. And knowing, I will always live in my memories."

And one day all of it came crashing to an end. She didn't tell me what happened and why she ended up in the hospital.

"When I saw you die, I saw myself," she shook her black hair out of her face. "I saw...me at eighteen. I'm twenty-five now. I haven't seen my past in seven years. And then one day, I'm watching you die like I was watching myself and for some reason I couldn't let that happen."

Her eyes met mine with a glint in them not only did I not recognize, it scared me again. There was steel in them.

"I saw you die. You were all alone. It was freezing outside. You were..." Talia looked almost lost as she watched me. "I just saw myself. And I could never let that happen. I could never watch you go."

Behind the green there was something I recognized in her eyes I saw in my own face now.

Determination.

Resolve.

Courage.

"I know you're going through it right now. This was the hardest moment of my life. I promise you everything gets better from this point on. You don't have a past anymore. You don't have an identity anymore. You belong to no one. For the first time in your life, there is no man to define you. When I was eighteen, I thought that it was the end of my life. It was my father who told me the end is just the beginning. I might have hated my father once. But now? I see he was right."

Her eyes met me head on. Brighter now.

"You are no longer Isobel Santos. She died a long time. She died that night. I had everything taken away from you just like you. And whether you know it or not, you're just like me. Except the Universe was on your side."

I was confused now. "Why?"

Her smile was humorless. "Because you forgot your past. I can never forget mine. There isn't a world I can exist in where my past is my future. Even if I wanted it, a long time ago? It no longer exists for me now. But it exists for you. I think the Universe gave you a *second* chance. And maybe the Grim Reaper is confused as to why you exist because you're meant for greater things. Who knows?" She laughed. "Maybe you can take over Talon after me."

There was something in her eyes I searched for.

She loved him.

Talia loved Drew.

Did I love you? Are you out there?

Are you real?

Where are you?

Come find me.

Come.

Find.

Me.

I felt that reverberate through my system. Pale blue eyes. Blonde-hair. I could feel...something in the mist. But I couldn't see him.

Her smile was back soft and bitter.

"We can *never* go backwards, Isobel. Even if we try. Sometimes the past is there to stay there. From now on, you get to choose every single piece of who you are. Including, your name."

I thought about it.

I want to call her Alma. She's a piece of me...and...

Who?

Alma. Gabrielle. Monroe.

The name on my necklace.

The name's floated up to me.

Was that...who was she?

Was she...a part of me?

Are you out there?

Are you real?

Will you find me?

Come find me.

"Alma." I whispered it. "I want to be called Alma Monroe."

Come find me.

CHAPTER 48
GABRIEL

SIX MONTHS.

That's how long it took to get my shit together.

Less. I was now adjusting to Heron Manor. The house, my wife dreamed of. Sometimes I find myself searching for her and every single room. I imagined her wandering through the halls.

I swore she was haunting me. She existed in every room. Every dark corner. She was there. For me.

Today I swore I felt her when I woke up.

I was training Aidan's younger brother Killian, a twenty-year old with hetereo-chromia and anger issues that rivaled Liam's.

He was a force of nature and I knew in his eyes how much fury he had. I had seen his father laying into Aidan. I could only imagine the havoc Cormac wrecked onto his sons. All three of them reminded me of Liam in different ways.

But maybe I was just looking for my family and everybody that I found.

"Your form is shit!" I dodged a hit from Killian. Inky black hair. Piercing mismatches eyes—one aqua, one amber—glared at me.

"Stop dancing around me."

"Stop being a punk bitch." I laughed it off.

Killian threw another punch at me. Now I knew why Liam told me I fought like a man who had nothing to live for.

I saw that in Killian's eyes. At twenty—he was struggling.

"You fight like someone who's got nothing to live for," I echoed

Liam's words finding strength in my brother. The one I didn't have anymore. "You can do better!"

I side stepped him when he came at me with raw power. I used his momentum against him just like Liam had done to me so many times. Gillian went over my head in one smooth motion. He landed on the mat with a groan.

"Fuck." He swore.

"Shift your mindset when you come at me." I growled. Now I understood Liam. To his core. Killian leapt back up ready to go. "Aidan wants you better. More in control. You've got power. But all of it flaring out like that? You're going to get people *killed*."

I would know.

With the defiance in his eyes, I saw something else too. I saw someone who didn't have any parents, someone who was alone, someone with the same desperate need to prove himself. He didn't understand why his brother pawn him off to me.

But I saw in him, what Liam saw in me—the same promise.

I could teach Killian.

"Again." I motioned for him to come at me.

This time when he did, he was more focused. He parted every hit I gave him.

"Again."

He did. He moved with more grace. Killian was an inch shorter than Liam at six-three but the two of them had similar body types. Leaner, faster, made for fighting. He could do it.

"Again."

WHEN I WENT TO SEE LIAM AT THE HOSPITAL BEFORE I DID, HE didn't say a word to me.

He didn't even look at me and Sutton looked weary eyed at me. She didn't have to say anything.

I saw Liam's emotion written all over his face for me.

I didn't have family anymore.

So I left.

The last six months of my life had been insanity.

I had worked out a deal with Aidan. In exchange I trained his two brother's and him to be better. Smarter.

Carving a path of blood through the ranks of the O'Hara syndicate and forming an alliance Reed wouldn't be happy with it. Vincent for some fucking reason helped Aidan, discreetly—I thought it was guilt. For everyone. Across the board.

I had gotten Evie first. She'd been at the hospital trying not to cry over Adrianna Santos in bed. Dead.

I held her tight to me on the plane ride to Connecticut.

Heron Manor was a space I was getting accustomed to. Isobel's...dream.

Evie cuddled into me whenever she got a chance.

Reed came after her almost scaring her. He'd gotten more tattoos and while he kind of reminded me of Liam, sometimes, Reed was less emotional. He kept himself in check.

At six-four, tatted up one arm, and stormy eyes, he terrified Evie a little until she realized he didn't bite. Dark chocolate hair, piercing eyes, he was Liam's height and sometimes I swore—I saw my brother in Reed.

Selena came after Evie. Selena Tavares was definitely a reminder of the ways the Agency failed women. A feisty brunette with sharp green eyes that looked alien on her face Selena got on with Evie well.

Vincent got her to Quantico. I pulled her out of Havana.

I took her to work with me since praise from Cindy Roberts didn't come easy.

Selena had potential.

I met her in Quantico and that had been a fucking revelation. She reminded me of my wife in some ways.

And that was the thing about missing Isobel—I saw her in everyone. Everything. Just like I saw Liam.

I found myself searching for my family in everybody.

Creating copies of them in everyone.

But I never found them.

Evie had deeper hair than her sister and lighter eyes.

But they both had the same little smile. Evie curled into my arms while I sat with Reed at the counter some mornings.

She was affectionate like her sister too.

Something I took as Adrianna raising them.

"I looked over all the files you gave me, including Oracle. She's half-finished..." Reed told me the USB I had gotten out of Isobel's things, only had a shell of a version of Oracle.

I didn't even want him to play the audio.

I couldn't listen to her voice through Oracle like we were at work. It would break pieces of me and I couldn't afford to break. After I tucked the ultrasound away somewhere safer, I never broke again.

Reed had no idea he was staring at Liam's work. Liam's mind in front of him.

"You want to build up this security company with this? The blueprints in this are thorough and clean." I knew that.

Liam was a genius. He had put everything on a drive. I took that drive from my wife. I took everything from her and unpacked that side of the house. I couldn't afford to stay still.

I was building Titan Security now.

"Nathan says he can reach out to his contacts across the globe and see what he can do..." Reed was saying Nathan Wyatt, the final addition to our team that he had picked, had connections as well. We were pulling together everything that we had and all of our connections to start forming this company.

Without my heart. Everything that they had dreamed of building, everything that they had joined the agency for, Liam's brilliance, Isobel's faith, and just me.

Every single day I woke up—I felt their loss.

No Liam. No Isobel. *No...Alma.*

I couldn't think about my daughter without snapping in half.

Nothing.

Amor, what are you doing?

Giving you what I never could.

A normal life. A normal wife.

I moved like I *never* had before. I couldn't stop. There was something burning in me to keep Liam's vision intact. It was a security company that protected people, collected information, lived with profit, and I knew in my mind, it would make them proud.

Reed had no fucking clue about any of it.

I had no intention of telling anyone who I was.

She took my soul with her.

But something was *burning* inside of me. I had to move. I had to do something. She was gone. I didn't know where to start.

I got my entire family killed.

For an operation that had been a set-up. A trap.

A lie.

Gabriel Monroe was a fuck up. He didn't belong here. I ruined Liam's life. Sometimes I heard her ghost in the hall.

Amor, *what are you doing?*

Keeping my promises.

Lo siento, amor. I failed you.

I hadn't given her the world.

She in turn had taken mine.

All of me. To wherever she was.

And nothing was going to bring me back but her.

And she was gone.

I never stopped.

I barely slept.

I was a machine.

Reed worked endlessly to stand up Titan. Turns out when Reed wanted something nothing would stop him. A vision we both shared. He had gotten fucked over a couple of times and he'd been through enough for himself to know after working in the government he would never do it again.

And me?

I wouldn't ever let anyone down. Ever. I could never.

Good enough got people killed.

Weakness could never be trained.

I existed upstairs on my floor.

Haunted by her. By my mistakes. By me…I was the worst.

I got my wife killed. I broke every promise I made.

Every vow. Every single bit of me.

I kept all her stuff from the apartment in a room. Everything besides her photos. One room strictly for me to hunt for her. Wherever she was. I did my fucking best.

But it wasn't enough.

My life had changed in the last few months.

I didn't know who I was anymore. Ice invaded my body.

I didn't want to know him. Gabriel Monroe was a ghost.

He didn't exist without her.

I just wanted her.

"Yeah," Reed watched me. "Evie's in her room, did you want me to take her to therapy?"

"Get her a good tutor, therapist, and some more plants. Get her whatever she wants, she won't use my card, so you'll have to."

And then I brought up why I was there.

"Can you translate audio from a video?"

My Spanish was excelling with Lara helping me. She and Killian were oddly enough getting along. But I didn't trust Lara with this stuff.

Not with her. It took me six fucking months to listen to her voice again.

"I'll show you how to do it."

And that's why I liked Reed. Adaptable.

Always had been and flexible and determined.

He kept up with me.

And he showed me. I handed him a flash drive. Make sure Evie gets this when she's ready it can be hers. He nodded.

I went to my room, locked the door and made sure I told Reed to not let Evie anywhere near me until I said so. Nobody came near me.

I played all my audio of her.

And my heart sank to my stomach as my throat tightened.

My vision blurred. I kept going.

I replayed the auDio over and over again, each time feeling like a knife twisting in my chest. I memorized every word, every inflection of her voice. I memorized it.

She was my heart, my very fiber of being, and I couldn't bear the thought of living without her.

And I would never fail my family again. Any of them.

I had told Reed he better start brushing up on his Spanish. Selena and Evie spoke it around the house and Nathan had learned it. That was a requirement.

There would be another me.

Another fuck up.

Another ghost.

I had that photo in the frame tucked behind that night. My night with my wife. The ultrasound. Of the baby. Of my soul. It was only time I could hear her. Feel her.

Where is my fucking wife?

Nobody loves like you.

I leaned back on the bed replaying my worst nightmare over and over again until it sank into my bones until she sank into me. My soul. My heart. She was haunting me.

She was everywhere.

The truth was undeniable.

Gabriel.

I opened my eyes and I swore I saw her.

Listen to yourself.

"Why?" It led me to her. And I lost her.

What does your heart tell you?

I felt her. I felt, her fingers across my chest, her lips on mine. I could feel her.

I can feel her. I sat up.

I can still feel her. "I can still feel you."

My brain processing the facts. The photo in my hand. No body. No Isobel.

Why?

Why could I still feel her? Would Marcus Hagen whoever she was? Kill Isobel?

Gabriel, what does your heart tell you?

Gabri-el.

My girl wasn't gone. She's still alive.

I can feel her.

She was my soul.

So...where was she?

Where are you? And in that moment I knew...I knew why I was burning alive with her.

"I'm going to find you."

If it's the last thing I do, I will find you.

CHAPTER 49
ISOBEL

A YEAR PASSED IN TALON.

And then another.

There were women and men at the compound all milling about and overtime I made relationships with them.

I was changing into something else I didn't recognize. Without my past? Talia was right.

I woke up every single day free to become whoever I wanted to be.

Whoever.

The old rules of society no longer existed for me.

Talia fit me into their technical unit to work and watch what they do.

"You can choose what you want to do, but I thought you might want to do something with your hands," Talia motioned to the computer. "This was your thing."

Coding, software development, gathering intelligence felt familiar to me. I found out through Talia, Talon was beyond what I thought it was. It wasn't shadows and contract kills.

It was a way for me to be someone new.

To be reborn as Talia believed. Talia was part Japanese and she called Cape Verde the realm of hungry ghosts.

"My father wanted a way to protect his assets," she explained motioning to the screens and her friend Duke, an older gentleman with darker skin and dark short hair helped me get settled.

His eyes were wary around me but he wasn't rude.

Just reserved.

In his company memories floated to the surface of my brain. Late nights in school. Liam's laughter. Him teasing me. Sometimes I did break down.

Grief was strange when you didn't remember it.

Talia didn't tell me how I died. She said she wanted to spare me. Or Liam. Or my father.

Sparing me from that agony. She said she took care of it.

I had cut my hair to my shoulders to breathe better and heal. My head and heart healed.

But Talia was always letting me know that once I died once...

She really didn't ever want to experience that again.

Over the years I knew her?

I genuinely liked Talia.

Underneath the harder disposition was a softer woman who picked up people like rescue animals. Like me. Like Bexley Carter who was a young Dutch South African girl Talia had adopted.

So I began teaching Bexley about coding and software development.

I thought it might be a decent way for us to pass time. I began to develop Oracle, Liam's project he had started with me in college with Bexley.

Together we worked on it building it up from scratch. I remembered what he had done.

I had been a part of it.

We couldn't do much else.

Time on the island flow differently. It was a lot slower. Every single day blended into the next. And I actually really liked it.

The local markets had fresh fruit and vendors that sold in a mixture of languages.

Something about this place felt familiar to me. I remember a distant past where my father and I lived together with my mother and a girl I assumed was my sister.

Maybe.

I had a life before this once. Now? My past felt like a strange blur.

I stayed in Cape Verde for that time. Sometimes I went to other island, but my life had completely changed. I met people in Talia's life.

At fifteen Natasha Nash wasn't technically Talia's sister. But Talia protected her all the same.

With platinum blonde hair, blue eyes, she was my height—with a fragile build.

"Did you come here from your father?" I asked her one afternoon. Sometimes she came and went from the island.

"No, I don't stay with him. He's not...I'm not...Malcolm's daughter." She shook her head looking adorably young on the boat we were on but I was surprised. I always thought she was. "Not really. He just took me in because he felt sorry for me. My mom... she's...complicated. I have classes with a tutor..."

She looked a little off. Sometimes she tried to sound tough but I could tell her legs bothered her. Her right ankle in particular where there was a large scar and tissue that was rock hard like my shoulder.

Both of us had issues in different places.

I couldn't shoot a gun properly and my scar tissue ached. Natasha had a limp because of hers.

She looked at me. "Do you like being...you? Talia says you have no memories. I think that's nice."

"Was it?" I asked her.

She nodded, her pretty features delicate and her brow furrowed. "I remember everything. Too much. Sometimes I wish I didn't. I know Malcolm doesn't like me. He tolerates me because Talia fought for me." She fought for everyone it seemed. But herself.

I didn't know what to say.

Sometimes when I was around Natasha, I felt echoes of somebody from my past. A younger woman with that look in her eyes. But it drifted as quickly as it came.

"Everyone thinks I'm crippled, so for some reason they think it makes me dumb," Natasha zipped around on her scooter all the time on the compound. "But I'm not dumb!"

I laughed at her having a blast on her electric scooters. We kept them on the compound for her.

"I'm sure he still loves you," I kept my voice low. "After all, I was wondering, who all the scooters were for."

She laughed low. "Talia got me those. She thought walking everywhere was tough. I do love the electric scooters." My laughter mingled with hers.

I realized my forgotten memories around these people who

endured loss was enviable. Everyone is here because they wish they could forget their past. I was the only dead woman walking.

Over the last few years I had adjusted to a new life here. A new world.

Whenever I played around with Natasha on the compound, on the beach, her laughter reminded me of someone else's.

A long time ago. Memories of my mother in my visions. A little girl in her arms.

But the beach, the insular island—It healed me from the inside out. I couldn't remember anything but Talia wasn't wrong.

Even after grieving the loss of my family, if I couldn't remember what was out there, there was no point in me, holding onto it.

I heard people whispering about me on the compound.

The dead woman.

That was me.

In two years I never met Malcolm Nash. Talia kept me out of his way. Out of everyone's way.

From what I knew—he wasn't exactly a nice man.

I couldn't do anything too physical. I tried to run and that was about it. Talia tried to train me physically but it was a lot harder for me to learn.

My scar tissue twisted a little at my chest so I sat with Natasha in the sun sometimes. The two of us like broken birds in our world.

"He loves Talia because he loved her mother. Tatiana. She passed away and he took Talia in like his whole heart. He doesn't love anything in the world the way he loves Talia. He would kill for her." Natasha looked faraway as she said it.

"Talia and I met after few years ago. We didn't grow up together. But when she met me she said she knew I was her family. Regardless of what her father said. She convinced him to give me their last name. And in turn, I swore I would do right by her."

I listened to Natasha tell me about their lives and how Talia just came across as harsh, but she meant well.

She was Malcolm Nash's daughter after all.

A wealthy corporate businessman who didn't have anyone in his life that mattered. I had seen some photos of him from Natasha but nothing out in public. He was under-the-radar she said.

But Talon used to be his.

He gave it to Talia when he took her out of school and had her control the company instead.

I didn't know if Natasha knew about Andrei. I didn't want to say it.

Talia had said her father wouldn't stand anything against her. It was why she had never married. She would never.

Nobody would ever be good enough for Malcolm' Nash's daughter.

But I knew in Talia's heart it was always for another.

It had always been Andrei DuPont.

I had seen photos of him. Handsome in a way that seemed unreal. Electric blue eyes rimmed with black around the pupils.

He had a baby brother, Teo, and Talia had a photo of the three of them and a blonde man in the background who had looked away when they'd taken the photo.

She never talked about it and I saw how much it hurt her and I never passed.

Natasha didn't have many friends and she kept to herself.

I started healing fully my third year in Talon. And Talia began training me under her wing.

And it was in my fourth year I saw Talia shift.

She had been on an assignment in Europe. Handling business for her father.

When she came back she looked different. Her eyes alight with something new.

A few months later she brought a young angry boy to the Talon compound who looked beyond livid.

He was taller than everyone, inky hair messy on his head and the brightest blue eyes I'd ever seen.

I knew those eyes. I stopped her one day privately when I saw him.

"This is Andrei's brother, Teo."

She shook her head, black wisps floating around her face. "This is Thierry, he's the youngest—"

"You have seen Andrei?" My eyes went wide. "Your father—"

She held onto my hand pulling me into one of the darker hallways. "Isobel."

I knew it was serious when she called me by my name.

Nobody on the compound knew my real name except Samara and Talia.

"You can *never* tell anyone that he's a DuPont. His name is not DuPont. It's Mattison. Thierry Mattison. I did see Andrei, but nobody knows." Her eyes pleaded with me looking so human and so much warmer than I'd ever seen them. "I saw him by accident."

Her cheeks were flushed as she told me the assignment in Europe she'd bumped into him after almost a decade.

And he hadn't let her go.

He'd asked her to be a part of his life.

And now Talia was sneaking around with him.

Thierry was at the Talon compound which for some reason Malcolm Nash entrusted to his daughter and I realized Talia had spent so many years being sneaky?

Nobody had any reason to question her.

THIERRY WAS ONE ANGRY YOUNG MAN.

I met him time to time sparring with the Kincaid brothers who liked him enough to take him under their wing.

His anger was familiar to me.

Isa, Liam can go with you to dance practice.

My heart clenched tighter.

So I started leaving food out for him. Like a stray wild animal who would come into the room with me.

"You didn't have to feed me," he snapped, a little messy and adorable despite being so enormous. He was maybe six-four but lean muscles and tattoos. He was a little Liam.

My brother wouldn't snap at me though. Not like that. Liam had never done that. He'd softened when I was kind to him.

There were moments that I missed him. And then there were moments that I thought about different pair of eyes. Pale blue. He always appeared in my vision. He was in my dreams like smoke.

"No, but I did not feed you—" I broke off pointing at the sandwich he was eating. "That was mine. You assumed it was yours."

He gaped almost spitting it out. "I'm sorry, Alma."

I laughed outright. "You are easy to tease." He turned a violent shade of red when he realized I was messing with him.

"You don't gotta do that," he started.

"What was that in your hand?" I asked him.

I saw him holding *something.* Pink.

I never told anyone about my necklace. I didn't wear it. Not always. I tucked it away safe and sound in my drawer.

334

Thierry's frown deepened. "None of your business." But he looked so adorably angry all the time. But I thought I heard mutter about *mon couer.*

"Okay, but I put poison in the sandwich. Surprise."

I laughed harder as he spit it out now growling.

Overtime, though, I noticed that he quietly respect me, and when he saw Talia and me together, he began sitting with us.

He began spending more time with us.

I didn't tell him he reminded me of Liam until one night we had all gone down to Johannesburg to visit someone Talia knew.

Thierry and I had been there with her at her side. I had seen him playing with his little object. It was a woman's hairpin. A butterfly. Pink. Pretty. Feminine.

Did he have a girlfriend too?

I didn't ask. He wanted to keep it to himself just like my necklace.

Over the years, I learned that Talia always took extensive security measures. We existed so deep in the shadows.

Talon had this network that allowed for complete and total control of technological services wherever we went. It was tri-fold. Security. Technology. Contract kills.

It was sophisticated and large.

By the time people saw their security cameras, malfunctioning, the footage going missing, satellite images that would blur a crucial moments—it was too late.

We were already here. We just bent the technological grid to our will.

Talia believed that the less people knew about you, the longer you survived. Which is a policy she applied to everything in life.

There was not a single photo of her in any database and not one trace of her existence in the digital world unless she *wanted* to appear.

Combined with me designing Oracle slowly, little by little I made Talon's security impenetrable. I used Liam's framework to design it. Liam's brilliance into Talon.

If you went around the world and ask, nobody had heard of them, but everybody knew about the cards.

Black. Gold claw marks.

Thierry was in the security aspect of Talon.

He killed people.

And he was good at it.

Talia said he was one of the best.

I knew Talia wasn't a good person by definition, but she had saved my life and created a way for me to exist in my new life.

Even if I didn't have my past, I had a present, a future—something greater than I had in the past.

I integrated Oracle into Talon.

Until one night.

Bexley came to me.

"I made a mistake," she whispered, blue eyes wide. "I noticed a tiny crack in Oracle, I fixed her up but not before something got out. You know how you were down in Johannesburg and you guys took the ferry from Senegal?"

She showed me a photo of me, darker and blurry not quite clear, but one thing was clear.

I had forgotten to tuck my necklace into my shirt.

"This photo. This is one of the few photos that was captured. It's not a big deal right? Someone from the States was monitoring the network. I don't know who. It vanished as soon as it caught it, like they were searching for images and your necklace was one that fit. They had parameters. Specific ones."

"Maybe someone looking for a necklace?" But even as I said it a chill ran down my spine.

"That's weird," she frowned. "it's also not possible. Nobody should even know we exist. Whoever it was, they knew exactly what they were looking for. They knew exactly where to look."

"You think it was focused on the necklace?"

Bexley nodded. "I didn't even know you had one. You always keep it tucked in. It's weird. I can make a list and roundup anyone who is in Senegal or South Africa right now. I can see if there's any overlap. Maybe some errant thief or con-artist is also in the area? Why else would someone be looking for jewelry?"

Like a jewel thief? I didn't know.

I should've mentioned this to Talia.

It was a breach in our system. But something stopped me.

Something that stopped me from telling her about my necklace.

I still didn't know who Monroe was. If it was me.

My alias Alma Monroe. I picked it for whoever it was. She didn't ask questions.

Or if it was...the man with the pale blue eyes who appeared in my dreams sometimes. Faceless. Body-less.

Just his eyes. It was a man. I knew it.

I just didn't know who he was.

CHAPTER 50
GABRIEL

THE CARTOON MOVING PLAYING ON THE TELEVISION WAS ALMOST over. Evie's choice.

A romantic musical she'd picked. Something about princesses and frogs and true love.

I didn't even see it.

I just felt her curled into my side like a tiny cat, at five feet one she was so small, her dark cherry colored her spilling out over my arm and chest as she played with my hoodie strings. She might've been sixteen on paper, but to me?

She was my baby.

Even Reed admitted I treated her like my daughter.

She was the only one I chilled out for.

"Did you like it?" She yawned burrowing into my side making me laugh. I cuddled her closer.

"Shortcake, you always wanna crawl into my skin."

"I do," she murmured sleepily. "You're so warm."

I laughed easily with her.

"Well?"

Right she asked me a question. "It was great." I had no clue what the movie was about. I just kept seeing my wife in my vision and holding Evie imagining Isobel walking in and seeing us. Seeing her growing up in my arms.

Amor. Did I make you proud?

"You didn't even look."

"I did look, she kissed him. He turned into a frog."

She giggled. "That's not what happened."

"No?" I chuckled. "What happened?"

"Gabriel…do you think we can have pizza?"

I smiled into her hair. "You're half asleep on me, shortcake. You wanna eat now too?"

She nodded, bumping my chin a little making my chest ache as I pulled a heating blanket over her.

She yawned a little. "With mushrooms…"

"With mushrooms," I rubbed her hair pressing kisses into it. She didn't smell like Isobel, but every so often I got her candies on her desk and flowers every week she loved. Inhaling it always comforted me.

"Gabriel," she whispered. "Do you think you can rub my hair like that more?"

I did. "Yeah."

Slowly, she fell asleep in my arms like she always did. I stayed there holding onto her. Since Adrianna died, Evie lived in my arms. Seeking comfort and affection from me whenever she could.

I would never let anything in this world hurt her. *Nothing.*

"Love you."

"Love you too, sweetheart."

My daughter would've been six. Not a day went by where I wasn't aware.

Just having Evie near me broke through the ice in my chest whenever she threw her arms around me like I was the only reason she was here.

The guilt ate me alive.

I should've found her sooner.

Should've done this for Isobel sooner.

Amor, she's so tiny. She's five one and she thinks she's six feet tall.

Evie would run up to me as the only burst of sunshine in my life and hug me.

She knew a little bit about me.

She knew I led the op that got her sister killed. I had to be honest with her even just a little. I adopted her.

Evie knew enough.

Evie didn't know I thought Isobel was alive. Or…worse. Captive. Tortured to death. Held against her will before eventually succumbing to something.

339

Some nights I woke up screaming. I had nightmares about that night over and over for the last few years.

And I become unrecognizable even to myself. I wasn't the best person to be around, but I didn't want to be.

I wanted my wife. I wanted my daughter.

I wanted my home.

And I knew it would never be mine.

~

I STAYED UPSTAIRS OR IN THE BASEMENT WHILE REED RAN THE company.

I regretted every single choice I made even if deep down? I knew I had been fucked over in the worst way? Losing my wife had made me irreparable.

I worked with Aidan who polished up nice now after a few years of consistent money. Consistent success.

And distancing himself from his father's crimes. Aidan hadn't understood the extent of how awful Cormac was.

As an apology, Aidan and I gave Lara the club Teasers.

He and Killian and I had this idea with Lara to give her something to sustain since she didn't want to go back to her family.

His brother Killian took over different aspects of Titan for me. Including taking care of Lara who oddly enough—they both got along with. But Lara?

I knew she was Liam's girl. Always.

She taught me Spanish sometimes and rapidly learned how to speak English mimicking an American accent so well—I forgot she didn't know how to speak properly. And fast.

Survival meant everything to Lara. She adapted quickly. I was surprised, but she was one of the girls that have been there for the shortest time. So she retained her humanity.

For the most part? Any mess I needed cleaned up Killian got done.

I vanished.

Raphael Santos was my new identity.

Gabriel Monroe was a dead man. Inside and out. I was completely ice.

I had Reed take it and turn Raphael Santos into a respectable professor at Astor University. And he erased all mentions of me.

If I was hunting a ghost I would become a ghost.

I searched for her. I built up Titan from the shadows. I leverage my Intel contacts to get us jobs, doing everything possible to honor Liam's dream.

Liam himself? Never heard him from again. He vanished too.

Sutton had filled me in that she had left the Agency and spent a year or two with Liam until he'd turned to drinking instead.

"I'm sorry," she'd cried. "I tried. But he can't do anything he used to do and he left the Agency. He's done."

"I can't find him either," I told her. "It looks like he went back to Connecticut where he grew up with her and his father's home."

Sutton was privately devastated. I wasn't aware if she loved him or if she was clinging onto his remnants. But he didn't want it.

In turn, over the years, Reed became a good friend. A brother. He was solid and stable. A rock among everyone and the peaceful middle ground. When Selena needed training, when Nate fucked up over and over, and when Evie needed help.

He came a best friend.

Reed had an innate need for privacy and so did I. I never brought up my past. He never asked.

Selena became my shadow in some ways, working international jobs for me and secretly?

I wanted to know who Marcus Hagen was.

Who *she* was. Why was she even in existence. And where she had vanished to with my fucking wife.

But every time I thought I got close I never got close enough.

Over the years Killian out of all people formed a network of informants who fed us intelligence.

Over time, I began to piece together Isobel's notes from that night.

A singular one. One that had haunted me.

Talia Nash.

What did the Nash family have to do with my wife?

Why would they even care?

Malcolm Nash couldn't be the one the Agency had been looking for.

What were the fucking odds?

∼

341

THE COMPANY RESPONSIBLE FOR EVIE'S MOM'S DEATH WAS MERCURY Group.

Their CEO at that time was Charles Devereaux.

His son Lucas was put into power by Aidan and Reed.

I got rid of Charles. Motherfucker he was.

Aidan kept an eye on Lucas.

Reed kept an eye on Lucas's younger sister Lucy.

A fucking *thief.*

And it was Lucy Devereaux's mishaps around the globe for Reed that led me to the one thing I never fucking suspected.

Over the years I asked Aidan who had contacts for missing women.

He hadn't found her.

But Reed?

Reed had given me one piece closer to the puzzle. It was on his desk when he was monitoring where Lucy was in South Africa.

I just happen to see a bunch of surveillance shots. I only cared about one in particular. It was blurry. A port photo. She was getting off a boat with another darker haired man. That was the only shot it caught.

But I caught something else.

Over the years, I had given Evie the opportunity to fix the Oracle. I didn't know how to do it.

I just knew how to use it.

But I wasn't Liam.

The USB drive that I got was a form of Oracle that wasn't finished. Liam had the finished version.

So Evie kept feeding her data and I ended up using her to put out the image of the necklace, to constantly search for it in case it turned up anywhere.

I input the functions I needed and input the variables hoping to find her. It sent me a photo of a woman. Dark hair. Blurry. And the fucking necklace.

I didn't know why no matter how much I tried to un-blur it, it didn't give me a clear enough shot. Port cameras were notoriously shitty.

Even when I tried to change the quality of the frame? No dice. It was like they knew exactly how to stay visible and past checks, and then they would disappear. The woman in the shot was moving brokenly a little.

In the next shot she was gone.

There was no doubt in my mind it was Marcus Hagen. Or Talia Nash. *Whichever.*

In Senegal. Her necklace. *My* necklace.

I had no fucking clue where the key was.

I never did find it again.

But the necklace?

I was going to fucking make it mine.

Because it was the first fucking clue I got in six years.

Everyone saw me spiraling and I didn't give a damn anymore. I saw Reed casting worried glances at me.

I didn't care.

I only cared about one thing.

And that was her.

Just her.

CHAPTER 51
ISOBEL

"I'M PREGNANT."

Talia sat on my bed across from me her face pale. Her usual grace was cracked at the edges. I stayed perfectly still. Sometimes I scared people around here. I didn't move very much.

My face gaunt and darker than before.

In all the time that I had known her, I had never seen her like this. The old me would've been shocked.

The new me was now calculating security risks, potential weaknesses, and how to figure out what Talia would do with a baby that did not belong on this island.

"You have not told anyone?" Even if I had changed? My accent had not. It softened enough but not to the point where I could forget—I used to be Mexican. Brazilian. Now?

I was nothing. It was interesting being erased.

Nothing mattered but the next day.

"I just found out. My father doesn't know. He can never find out."

"Andrei knows?"

She shook her head looking even more sick. "I saw him two weeks ago, but the baby—he's four months along."

I had noticed her being off lately, the subtle changes in her behavior, but I hadn't connected the dots. Maybe because I'd spent so many years here learning not to look too closely at anything, including myself.

I wanted to give her warmth I did not have.

I was vanishing.

My body didn't feel like mine. I hadn't...lived. I was stuck in a strange purgatory in Cape Verde.

I liked it, but I felt like I was existing in a bubble. A reverse snow-globe.

Talia handled crisis really well. She was a natural. Efficient and she moved without hesitation. That's how she saved my life.

The only time I saw wavering in her eyes?

Was when it came to two people.

Her father.

And Andrei DuPont.

"I was so stressed out. I never even got a chance to focus on my pregnancy. I just found out this week. My father wants to come here and see me."

She motioned to her stomach.

"But I'm already showing. I need to got to Andrei. He'll fix this. He always does. He would be so upset if I didn't tell him, but you're the first to know."

Over the last six and a half years Talia and I had become closer.

She wasn't family, and I wasn't hers, but I couldn't explain why we were connected. Bound by something. Our shared secrets.

Her need to protect me.

For a really long time when I was around her, I almost wondered if what happened to me, scared her.

Sometimes when she looked at me for a long time, I realized she might be protecting me from something.

Because why else would somebody tried to kill me and Liam. I had years to think about why Talia saved my life.

She had given me life.

I knew why. I had known her for years.

And now she was...having a baby.

"You want to leave Talon?"

There. I said it. I asked the dreaded question. And that's all it took for her elegant features to crumble.

"I never wanted this," she shook her head. "He made me do it or Andrei would die." I let out a breath listening to her reality.

"This is *why* you lie to everyone and keep secrets."

I had always known that she was the kind of person who kept secrets from everybody. To protect.

Talia compartmentalized every single aspect of her life.

She put every single person in careful tiny little boxes and those boxes never touched anything.

Which was why I had been undisturbed by Malcolm.

The sheer genius she operated in was insanity.

Both us had descended into a different aspect of our heads where disassociating was safer than feeling. Where pain that usually needed to be felt was gone.

But I also knew that the way her father trusted her? He would only do so if she earned that trust.

Through whatever means necessary.

Nobody knew who I was. Nobody knew about Thierry. Not really. She kept everything so hidden and now I understood why she was so good at hiding things from people.

She was operating off protecting the one man she loved the most.

"What will you do?"

Regardless of what decision she made, she had given me a different life over the last few years.

Not only had I become technologically savvy, I physically got stronger.

I started running faster. I started training with Samara to fight better. I became better. Under them, I became somebody else.

And I feel like I was stepping into a new version of myself that I never imagined myself being.

Sometimes I felt like I was a machine, pretending to be human.

That hollow ache inside of me never really went away. Sometimes I wondered if anyone out there knew about me. Or if I had really been alone.

Talia looked broken. "If I run, my father will find me."

And he would kill Andrei. No loose ends.

Over the years, I didn't interact with him so much as observed him from far away.

I knew he would shoot somebody without any hesitation if they disrespected Talia.

"And if you stay, you cannot have another man's son here."

She was caught between two impossible things. And one of those had to give.

"You need to hide," I whispered. "I heard of the things your father has done to people. He is not a nice man or a good man. You need to choose what you want."

The entire time I had been here I feel like I was a spectator in my life, watching it through frosted glass.

"Take Thierry. Go to Andrei. He's in New York?"

"I don't want our son to grow up like me." Her voice was breaking. "Isobel, he is so tiny. I lost...I lost so much in the past. I can't lose my baby again."

I didn't know what happened to her and Andrei all those years ago. But I knew she was thirty-one. She was a grown woman. She could make choices.

"You need to take care of yourself," I didn't have all the answers but I knew one thing.

In cases like this? Something had to give.

"If anything happens," those jade green eyes locked on mine. "Will you take over?"

I gaped now. Me? Be the head of Talon?

Over the years, I've grown into the organization.

What started as developing Oracle turned into making decisions. Restructuring Intelligence. Talia stood in front of me while I helped her.

I was her ghost. Her shadow.

"Of Talon? Of this? What do you mean? I cannot. I'm not a fighter. Not like Samara—"

"Samara doesn't think like you do." She gripped my arm. "Samara isn't you. And you have more heart than anyone else. You don't have many casualties, no collateral damage. You protect everybody. This project was my father's. I promised I wouldn't kill innocents. You upheld it. You have to take care of this. This is my legacy too."

I didn't know what to tell her. She wasn't wrong.

Talia had filled me into Talon's operations.

And I shifted her approach a bit more.

I didn't know how I knew. I just knew whenever I was thinking —I saw winter blue. I did. He was encouraging me to tell Talia this.

Intelligence over violence. Mind games over malice.

We solved problems—with precision. Strategy. Not force.

I could drive out anything if I messed with it long enough.

But I don't know who I am. As good as I was for Talon?

I didn't know myself. What did I even do?

I dipped my head to Talia out of respect for her. But I didn't want to be the next Talia Nash. The next Marcus Hagen.

That was the alias the head of Talon took.

Talia had been that identity. I didn't know why that name gave me chills.

I didn't want to be anything but me. Or...find him. Whoever he was.

That night I had a dream—about him.

He always came in my dreams. Sometimes I was underwater and I saw his eyes.

Clear. On me. Just his eyes. I swore I heard his laughter.

Amor. Talia asked me to be...her.

He never spoke. The man with the pale blue eyes. Winter morning. Pale blue gloves. He was laughing tonight at me.

Amor?

Only this his face was blurry but more clear.

Amor?

That was my voice. Why did I call him that?

Who was he?

For years the faceless man haunted me in my dreams. I felt like he was a part of my past.

I knew because in my dreams he called me his love. I felt like a ghost trying to be human. But when I saw him, I swam to him. I woke up screaming.

"Amor!"

Who are you?

I'm a nobody.

The son of a nobody.

I was a ghost surrounded by more of them.

I would always wake up before I saw his face and tonight was no different. I felt off. I always felt off. I didn't recognize myself in the mirror anymore. My eyes sunken in more.

Scarier.

Darker.

I took out his necklace from my drawer and held it close to me. Putting it around my neck like I could take life from it.

Since Bexley said someone was looking for the necklace and so it had popped up, I heard nothing else.

For a wild crazy moment I wondered...if anyone out there knew me. If someone was looking for me.

348

If I mattered.

And the other times I accepted who I was becoming in Talon. Rising through to leading them to accepting Oracle as a part of their operations right under Talia. Samara listened to me now.

Bexley became an assistant to me.

Even Thierry respected me.

I was becoming a fixture.

It was strange having so many identities. I used to be Isobel Santos.

Now I was Alma Monroe.

But everyone thought I was related to Talia and they called me Alma Nash.

I never bothered to correct anyone.

What did a name matter anymore?

I didn't know who I was. Or who he was.

And then like I feared.

Malcolm did find out the following week.

I didn't know what happened. I just knew just like watching a building explode right in front of you, when everything bad happened. It always happens so fast. I barely remembered any of it properly. I remembered it in flashes.

Natasha came running to my room. Covered in blood. Not hers. Malcolm's. Hysterical.

"I shot him," her hands were shaking frantic, her eyes rimmed with red from crying. "Help me. I didn't know what to do."

I found Talia sitting next to his body, shaking wildly as she stared at it. I needed to get them out of here.

The first thing I did was wake up Thierry.

The next? I got Talia out of Cape Verde. Samara and I buried his body.

"What now?" She looked at me as her hair blew out in the wind. In our pajamas we both looked ridiculous. "Natasha takes Nash Group and becomes the youngest billionaire in the world. And you become the head of Talon?"

And then the impossible happened.

I did become the Head of Talon. With Samara at my side?

One week I was a shadow.

And the next week, I was leading an empire.

Talon was much bigger than I knew.

349

It was international. Months blurred. I became someone else. Samara stood by me the entire way.

And naturally, when things got hectic and busy?

That's when I shut down.

I was tired.

I was exhausted.

I couldn't do this.

I didn't know how Talia did. I needed help and I didn't know how to ask. I felt like I needed more hands.

I needed someone by my side.

And those same eyes would flash in my vision.

CHAPTER 52
GABRIEL

"What's your name?"

Garrett was six-six. Two-seventy-five. Shaved head and a little mean looking.

I already knew his fucking name. He was one of two new hires from Reed. The other was a bright eyed, bushy-tailed all American Quarterback—Kellan Watts. He was currently all over Selena who didn't complain about him.

Not even once.

Courtesy of Reed who wanted to expand Titan. He had always tried for years to bring a new people.

But every time I caught a whiff of anything related to what I knew would get us killed they were out.

Reed thought I was being difficult. I thought I was saving people lives. We agreed to disagree.

But I knew the guy in front of me.

I knew him inside and out.

I knew he didn't have a father. I knew he sent every single nickel and dime he made to his sick mother to take care of her. I knew he had a little sister who he was putting through college.

I knew his blood type and how he woke up in the morning.

Garrett Christopher Fuller. Twenty-five going on fifty at this rate.

"Garrett, sir."

"Get int," I motioned to his button down. I tore off my hoodie leaving me in my t-shirt and got into the ring.

Reed had a custom boxing ring down here for us in a different section.

"You want to fight me?" He blinked. I smirked.

Over the years I took up Kyokushin.

Everything I did I lived, and I breathed to honor my family. To atone for my mistakes.

I never let Evie down. I never would.

Later on, I motioned to Evie who was fluttering around the kitchen now making me tofu. I choked it down for her but I also needed a steak. If she was my kid—she was half Isobel's because she ate vegan food like my wife did sometimes.

I met Garrett's green eyes. Lighter than Liam's.

"She is the most important thing in this house. You will do whatever makes her happy."

He tipped his head obediently.

"Yes, sir."

Not bad.

～

REED WAS GETTING TOO CURIOUS FOR HIS OWN GOOD. BUT I DIDN'T exactly do a job of avoiding him.

In my pocket, I had one singular black card with gold claw marks. Killian had found some of them scattered throughout the city over the summer.

They're back in town.

At some point, I had told Reed about the necklace.

I told him it was in Senegal. Reed being who he was volunteered to go with me on an effective suicide mission.

He wouldn't know about the island. Malcolm Nash had a property on Cape Verde.

Which meant...maybe...just maybe...that is where my mystery started. I had long suspected Nash. For years.

The Nash family had one singular daughter.

Talia Nash. On paper.

I knew Natasha Nash was rumored to not be his daughter. But one he took on after an affair with a woman named Camilla. So Talia...if she was the one?

Talia had taken Isobel.

But why?

Why leave the entire team? *Why take my wife?*

I thought about her every single day for the last seven years.

Now, I had finally caught a break, and I wanted to go and get the necklace. I wanted to go and figure it out myself. Why did they come back? Did that mean Talia Nash was in the city? Did that mean I went after Nash Group?

They were powerful, but I was discreet. I had zero concrete evidence. All I had—was a hunch.

"You ever going to tell me why you need to find your necklace so bad?" Reed asked me after we sparred one day.

No.

"You ever going to tell me why you keep *almost* killing people and destroying their company for touching your new girl?" Reed had a girlfriend. Alisha Malhotra.

"It's almost convincing, you know, you walking around trying to blend in with the *normies*. Like you're just like everyone else."

"I'm not doing this." Reed walked away from me giving me the finger.

"Who did you hire to replace you?" I called out.

For some reason he was being secretive as fuck. Because I knew there were three hires—Reed wouldn't tell me the third one.

Like I was going to kill him or something.

"Some guy named Liam Sullivan!"

And just like that—I stopped breathing.

Just stopped moving and the world tilted on its axis for me.

I was left gaping after Reed—who had no fucking clue.

No.

Fucking.

Clue.

He hired my brother-in-law.

The one who hated me for killing the one woman he loved the most. Reed didn't even know I had been married. I never wore a ring. Never had in the Agency. I lost the one piece of me that was my ring the night I lost her.

How apt. I lost my entire world in one fucking night.

All because of a call I made.

Sometimes in the last seven years? I wondered what would have happened if the three of us had walked out that night?

Jeremy would still be dead. And so would the rest of the team. There was no winning.

Not for me.

Not for her.

And Liam? I heard his voice loud and clear.

I promised her father. I broke that promise for you.

Do not let me down.

I had. I let him down.

My heart dropped into my stomach.

"FUCK!"

IT DIDN'T JUST DERAIL MY PLANS.

It was completely earth-shattering.

Liam who never spoke to me in seven years. Had taken Reed's call. Liam had joined Titan. *My* brother.

With my new brother.

Liam had a seat with Reed at Titan Midtown. Right next to the hotel I had been at with him. And Isobel.

The building next-door had been empty at the top. That was the one the masochist in me bought.

Reed and I turned it into the Midtown office where the servers and It equipment would go.

It was my every day nightmare to be right next to the location that destroyed my life.

But he was there. I saw his name. I saw his set up. It was the exact same one at Quantico.

My brother was alive.

And he was now working for the same company he had built and designed from the ground up.

I took all of his plans and gave them to Reed to improve. Reed had amplified every idea Liam had and used his own credibility along with Nathan Wyatt's for them to grow the company.

All of us had teamed up to make Liam's project—the best.

Titan Security had started as his.

But I wonder if he knew I had done it all in his name.

For him.

Atonement was a bitch.

And Liam was now under my umbrella.

I just didn't know what to say to him.

"Liam is here," I could hear Lara smiling while tinkering. She called me. "He came to see me today." Her accent was there when she spoke to me. "You brought him back?"

Throughout the years, she had asked me about him. I told her the truth.

"Reed brought him back," I told her gruffly. "He won't speak to me."

"Maybe I can convince him." Lara didn't know what happened to me. There were still some things I didn't tell her. She didn't know I was married to Isobel. She didn't know that Liam was in love with her.

"No," I felt my voice turn gruff. "No. Just...thank him for saving you. If he hadn't found you, I wouldn't have been able to get you out."

And now he was somehow moving around the city seeing Lara.

I was still happy for him.

I was still going to find my wife.

I was going to bring my family back together. One day. Some day. Somehow.

Unless I found her body. And she wasn't alive.

Then I didn't know where I would go.

I didn't wanna stay here anymore. Not a shell of a man without a future.

I didn't want kids with anyone else. Didn't want to ever feel that ever again.

If I didn't find Isobel—at the end of the road?

I saw no point in putting one foot in front of the other.

CHAPTER 53
ISOBEL

AND THEN LIKE I FEARED.

Malcolm did find out the following week.

I didn't know what happened.

I just knew just like watching a building explode right in front of you, when everything bad happened.

It always happens so fast.

I barely remembered any of it properly. I remembered it in flashes. Just like that.

Natasha came running to my room. Covered in blood. Not hers. Malcolm's. Hysterical.

"I shot him. He was going to kill her, I knew it. I knew it. I knew it. I knew it. I knew it." Natasha's hands were shaking frantic, her eyes rimmed with red from crying. *"Help me. I don't know what to do."*

She had turned twenty. She didn't know what she was doing.

Neither did I.

I found Talia sitting next to his body, shaking wildly as she stared at the floor covered in blood. I needed to get them out of here.

The first thing I did was wake up Thierry. He helped me get Talia out of Cape Verde after Natasha got her cleaned up.

Samara and I buried Malcolm's body.

I didn't understand it. I just did it mechanically like a robot.

I moved like I didn't have any thoughts or emotions.

"What now?" Samara's sharp dark eyes looked at me as her hair blew out in the wind. Even now her jaw was set.

In our pajamas we both looked ridiculous but her braid blew out again with the night wind.

"Natasha takes Nash Group. And you become the head of Talon?"

"I promise Talia."

And I didn't want it.

I wasn't...a leader. A long time ago I recalled dreams of a dance studio. Liam sitting in the corner watching me eating his cookies with a little smile on his face.

When I turned to look at the pitch black ocean waves and the moon above me—I wondered what happened to that girl.

In the moonlight my hands were covered in blood.

Malcolm Nash was dead.

But so was I. And so was that girl with the dream of the dance studio. Liam. My father. The man with the winter eyes.

I turned back to Samara. "We need to figure this out."

Because once people found out? Chaos would ensue.

And then the impossible happened.

I *did* become the Head of Talon. With Samara at my side?

That's when I shut down. I remember stripping off my uniform at the hotel. It was almost mechanical for me at this point.

Samara and I were together at a hotel. The Nash family used the chain that belonged to the Primrose here.

When I was in the shower I knew I heard the maid.

But I disassociated so often now I didn't pay it any mind.

I was seeing the winter blue eyes in my vision. I only saw him when I was in the water.

Amor.

Some days he was quiet.

He appeared out of the mist. Quietly. Dangerously. When I got out the shower the maid was gone. My bed still messy so maybe she only took the trash and left?

I had left my clothes on the bed.

As I moved my black clothing off the bed, my fingers automatically search for the one thing that always kept me tethered to reality.

The one weight that would always calm me down. It was an anchor in my world, and it was my one secret that nobody knew.

Talia, who was gone, wouldn't care, but everybody else who didn't know who I was might.

My necklace.

I couldn't find it.

I searched everywhere. But I knew I tossed it onto the bed, I heard the noise. I couldn't find it.

Instant panic clawed up my throat.

It was building slowly like a wave, and the longer I looked for it, the longer I waited to hear the distinctive metal clink against my ear, I lost it.

I was throwing my pillows, I was stripping the bed, I was dropping to my knees.

And then all of my calm, completely shattered.

Housekeeping. Had they taken it?

The man who haunted my dreams. He was connected to that necklace. I knew it.

Without it, I felt like I was losing the final part of myself that made me a human being. I was losing my mind.

I called the hotel and they informed me that no housekeeper had gone to my room in a day.

Finally, the panic that had started turned to a block of ice. Someone had been in my room.

Someone had taken the only piece of my old life for some reason. Someone was watching me.

But why?

~

"I FOUND YOUR THIEF," BEXLEY LOOKED OVER AT ME. "NAME'S LUCY Devereaux. Daughter of Charles Devereaux, brother's Lucas he own a real estate group. Family's loaded. Old money. Why would she steal from you?"

I didn't know. For the first time in seven years, I felt something other than numb. I felt pure unadulterated rage flowing through my bloodstream.

"Where is she going next?"

"New York."

Then we were going to New York. I didn't know why a chill ran on my spine. I had never left the island.

"I'll figure out your passport situation," Bexley said. "But I'm coming with you."

"What?"

After seven years I was leaving Cape Verde.

Leaving the Talon compound.

"I'm coming with you," Bexley repeated. "You can't go alone."

Samara stood slowly. "I'm going to."

Wherever I went, she followed like my new shadow. "But this is my problem."

"No, it's ours. I don't care what it is," Bexley shook her head. "She stole from you. If it were Talia? She'd be dead right now."

"But we cannot kill her, you two are the only two who know about this necklace except for Talia." I filled them both in because right now? I had no choice. "Whoever wanted, this is tied to a life that I don't have. We're not going to New York for the necklace. We are going for answers. This is a longer game. Are you too ready for that?"

"Duh," Bexley grinned looking all of twelve.

Samara tipped her head.

Because nobody knew about the missing piece of me. Lucy had taken the last thread, connecting me to the only thing I had left.

Him.

Monroe.

And for that? I would paint New York red with her blood.

CHAPTER 54
ISOBEL

BRUNCH AT THE PRIMROSE WAS A BIG DEAL ACCORDING TO BEXLEY who loved it here.

She had spent three days eating pancakes while me and Samara watched her with alarm in our eyes.

I was filled with increasing concern.

When I was on the island, I never realized what an odd pair all of us were. Now, I realized it.

"You guys," she motioned to the chocolate chip ones she was folding into origami before shoving into her mouth. "So good. *I love America. And butter.*"

"I'm going to scope out the Devereaux properties today. Maybe leave Lucas some presents." She motioned to the black card in her hand with gold claw marks.

"Don't kill him," I muttered under my breath watching someone eye us with wary concern in their eyes for Bexley's pancake eating habits. "I want zero casualties...Bexley, chew your food. Do not eat like that."

"Mmmm trying," Bexley ate like a wolf.

"You want Lucy Devereaux's head on a platter."

"Yes, and with less syrup than this one's using...Bexley...don't growl at people. He's just staff cleaning up."

She made a low noise as she went back to her food.

Lucy's father worked with Malcolm before died.

When Bexley used Oracle to call Charles Devereaux?

He'd handed his kids over on a platter. I didn't know if Lucas was the reason why Lucy had taken my necklace.

I didn't know any of them.

"You there, chubby. Can you shut down his building for me?" Samara sardonically looked over at Bexley chowing down on pancakes like her life depended on it. "Eat slower, they'll think we don't feed you."

Bexley swallowed another pancake folding it into fourths. I frowned. She did eat like we didn't feed her. Around us, celebrities and model sat around discreetly. Most of them not eating anything.

Safe to say, Bexley was alarming. She was one sugar rush away from hacking into a company and blowing it up from the inside out for fun. And Samara looked annoyed at everyone. Now more than usual.

Now among the normal people of society?

The two of them were odd. Bexley who ate like a rapid wolf. Samara, anti-social and cold sporting a frown with her black on black.

"Yeah," Bexley drank her coffee which she didn't need. "I already hacked into his building. He's boring. He's got meetings on meetings and that's it. No life. No way he's our culprit."

I was the only one who seemed remotely normal even if I knew I looked frightening.

People were always freaked out by me.

"And the hotel," I murmured. I fingered my new platinum blonde hair to blend in like I was Natasha. That's who I was pretending to be. The real Natasha was in New York. She was making it by doing desk work and attending virtual meetings.

Lucky for her, Talia had groomed her to take over Nash Group. It didn't surprise me Talia wanted nothing to do with it.

Talia never wanted anything but Andrei.

"I trained Oracle to blank us out," Bexley said carefully. "No more mishaps."

"Keep it that way." I stood. "Charge it all to my account. Do not eat all the pancakes in America—"

"They can't stop me."

Samara snorted again over her espresso.

Sometimes I missed the island and other times I rolled my eyes at their antics.

I walked outside to the street to get some air. New York City in autumn wasn't where I wanted to be though.

The cold bit through my jacket, making my scars ache in ways they never did in Cape Verde.

I was on a mission.

But the moment I showed up? Bexley had discovered caffeine and sugar. And Samara had been irritable.

I didn't get it.

Something was happening to my team.

And I still had to find a thief.

~

THIERRY AND TALIA WERE HERE IN THE CITY. TALIA WAS STAYING somewhere with Andrei. I had to go see Thierry at some point. See how he was doing.

How old was her baby now?

Alma.

I stopped moving a little retreating to the side of the road staring at a hotel above me.

I tried not to think about how that knowledge made something in my chest ache—a phantom pain for something I couldn't quite remember losing.

I kept seeing the blue eyes in my sight. I didn't know why it mattered but it did.

It did to me.

He felt closer to me than ever before.

Monroe?

Without my necklace I felt empty.

Those winter-blue eyes haunted me more frequently here. Like the city itself was trying to tell me something.

Without my necklace, I felt untethered.

And because I was hunting for something that belonged to me didn't mean that I could just neglect everybody else on my team.

Officially on paper Talon wasn't what others thought it was.

We weren't just some private security firm that nobody had ever heard of doing the wealthy's dirty work.

Officially, we handled art security. Protection details.

Corporate in intelligence.

But only for the people who could afford it.

Over the years I had more money than I could even dream of. On paper, they were pretty legitimate.

Except for the side that wasn't.

Talon was exceptionally sophisticated and exceptionally quiet.

We were disciplined, we didn't kill innocence, not with Talia in charge.

I had left Renata in charge of the side in Cape Verde.

Solid girl. She understood exactly what we needed, and she understood Talia's vision, taking in that framework and evolving into something better.

It wasn't until Talia left, but I realize that she had always seen potential and broken things, and people at the world always forgot about.

Bexley had been one of those girls—and now she was one of my best analysts at nineteen.

Talia did not believe in tradition.

She didn't believe in anything other than nurturing people and where they were the strongest.

She believed that if you help people to unrealistic standards for themselves, they would never accomplish anything in life.

"Why would I teach someone who is good at driving to shoot? Nurture people's strengths not their weaknesses."

Samara had come from nothing to become my right hand.

We solved problems that couldn't be handled. And not through violence alone.

Taking a vacation was not the way forward.

Being in New York felt wrong to me.

In Midtown especially.

Everything about the city made my body hurt.

My scars were twisting and aching.

The shadows in my mind had become a part of me. And I didn't know what to do about it anymore.

CHAPTER 55
GABRIEL

REED DIDN'T TALK TO ME FOR DAYS.

Not until the dead body of a potential suspect turned up at Alisha's charity and we had to work together again.

Even then his words to me were clipped.

In seven years—I hadn't pissed him off this much ever.

Which told me how angry he was with me.

Something about Alisha was getting under my skin. Maybe because after seven years I finally had some semblance of a normal interaction. I told myself it was that.

I feel like the more I distanced myself over the last few years from everybody, things were slipping past my control. My world had cracks.

I had a sneaking suspicion that Evie was sneaking out of the house to go see someone.

I felt like I was slipping.

In more ways than one.

Because Alisha was a living embodiment of watching Reed falling in love like I had seven years ago. And if anything happened to her—Reed would become me.

I knew it.

While Lara told me about how Liam was doing?

I focused in on Reed and Alisha's stalker.

The same day a dead body turned up at Alisha's charity? I found out Reed was still keeping secrets from her.

Alisha had no fucking clue I had been the one to figure out there was a serial killer after her.

I had put the pieces together with what Reed had.

He was too emotionally invested, but I wasn't.

I realized that there was a pattern here. Selena had as well, when she'd come to see in Midtown with Kellan Watts in tow. He had it bad for Selena.

But it was Kellan who had explained to me that Alisha might not know anything.

Reed was trying to protect her by keeping secrets from her.

I knew secrets got people killed.

So I told Alisha. I ripped the bandaid off.

Now?

Reed was back to being pissed off. He may have tried to choke me out. Twice.

Which led me back to Titan Midtown brooding and generally not in a good mood that week.

I was never in a good mood now a days.

Not with knowing the black cards were showing up around town. Not with knowing I couldn't get my fucking necklace in Senegal. What if it moved?

All of it had been placed on the back-burner. Because now I had priorities.

Garrett was here in Midtown doing some work on Liam's computer. Liam was never here. I wasn't surprised.

Lara said he did physical therapy and worked from home. But he had made a move on her.

She didn't have to say anything. I knew from all the fucking texts she sent me like I needed an update on him.

Privately, I hoarded them. He still drank, but less. Way less. Lara said it was manageable. For the most part.

Lara loved Liam. She always had.

I didn't know too much about their conversation other than he had gone there. He had met her.

He had picked up on her being a victim after what happened to Isobel. I had a moment to myself to breathe.

Garrett had taken one look at my neck covered with Reed's handprints from choking me out and looked away.

And then my mood went to downright shit when the devil himself called me.

I answered with a sigh. This motherfucker.

"I'm surprised you have this number." I would be deleting tonight.

"You know?" What? I swear Lucas fucking Devereaux was an idiot. "I'm surprised it took you this long, but really? Shoot first. Ask questions later? That's your style?"

"What the fuck—"

"It was always about Isobel, wasn't it?"

I lost my shit the moment he said my wife's name.

Lost it. I stood so fast I didn't even see straight. I just heard her name. And I reacted.

I didn't say a word. Why the fuck did he say her name? His father had been dismissed as a suspect for being Marcus Hagen. I knew now, my hunch was Talia Nash.

But there was nothing on her. Nothing. That only confirmed it for me.

"What did you just say?"

I was going to tear into that son of a bitch limb from limb.

"Did my family do something?" Fuck, this idiot had no idea. "That's why you hate me?"

No, I hated him because his family killed one half of mine. Adrianna Santos. I was atoning for fucking up for both her daughters. I was her son-in-law. I couldn't help her until it was too late.

I buried her husband.

And then her.

And now this motherfucker had the audacity to demand answers from me?

I saw red in my vision. Garrett in the corner stood.

Oh. I was going to kill him.

I hung up the phone and didn't even look. "Let's go, G. We have a field trip."

CHAPTER 56
GABRIEL

LUCAS'S OFFICE WAS MAYBE A SOLID FIFTEEN MINUTES AWAY FROM Titan Midtown.

Garrett went with me because if there was anyone I wanted nine thousand feet away from Evie—it was Lucas fucking Devereaux.

I closed the distance so fast seeing his six-two, maybe three frame leaner than mine standing there watching me.

I didn't give a shit about Lucas Devereaux or his fucked up family. Kourtney Young had taught me apples did not fall far. The entire Young family was garbage.

People learned from their parents.

And while Aidan and I got intelligence to make sure Lucas never fucked up?

To make sure nobody ever died under his watch?

I still despised the Devereaux's.

I moved in on him. All fists and no fear. I fucking hated the look in his eyes, true blue and too much fucking stupidity for one person. And then I imagined Evie anywhere near him. I ripped into him.

For Evie. For Isobel. For him saying my wife's name and thinking that he could when I absolutely fucking despised him.

"What did you do to her?"

"I didn't—KIA. That's all I know." He was choking and I didn't give a shit.

"What do you know?" I shoved my arm into his windpipe. "I will tear your tiny empire apart for answers—"

"That's all I fucking know!" He gasped, shoving at him. "Someone's trying to kill me!"

Was he serious right now?

"You *threatened me with my wife because someone's trying to kill you?"*

"Look, I'm sorry! Someone's trying to kill me." He scrambled back when I let him go. But I was fuming at my wife's name coming from him. Right now though, Lucas Devereaux didn't look like he knew anything.

"I thought it was you—I thought you hated me because of—"

"Don't you fucking say her name!"

I was fucking pissed now as I whipped out my gun.

"I don't believe you." I aimed it at him aware the back of my neck prickled with awareness from Garrett in the room. I didn't care if he listened. He never spoke. I trusted him to not say a word.

"You're going to tell me any information you have on *my wife*. Or I will do to you *everything you did to her*. G, search his desk. *You, start talking.*"

And then he began telling me about how someone had tried to shoot him tonight in his parking garage.

"My father called me and said something about Lucy having *something* in New York. She took something of his—He said she worked for *someone* named Marcus Hagen."

I froze. Just. Like. That.

I fucking knew it.

I fucking.

Knew.

It.

The cards. The bodies. The headshots.

Talia fucking Nash was in town.

"Lucy took something that your father said belonged *previously* to Marcus Hagen?"

Charles Devereaux, Lucas's father, had called to tell him Lucy had something that belonged to Marcus.

No.

But I fucking knew one fucking person it did belong to.

Me.

It belonged to me.

It was mine. I barely heard Lucas. Because he just said his sister was working with Reed.

And in that moment I became aware of a few things.

The first?

My best friend had gone behind my back and sent Lucas's fucking sister into Senegal to get Isobel's necklace.

The second?

Lucy Devereaux gave my necklace to Reed. Who had it in his possession. Oh fuck. I was going to kill Reed and steal Alisha from him. The end.

"My father said—He said he wanted Lucy to give it to him. But then, why would she give it to Reed?" He paused. "Do you know who Marcus Hagen is?"

Did I know who she was? I had a fucking guess.

"She met with Reed..."

Because Reed hired that sneaky psychopathic thief to get it.

Of course he did.

And of course she got it.

"*Son of a bitch.*"

Lucas kept going.

"Lucy works with finding artifacts. I don't know what she was doing or why she ended up in Reed's car—"

Jesus. No fucking way Reed was fucking Lucy.

Not the way he acted with Alisha.

"And someone shot at me. I've had my driver watch over Lucy because my father said she might give it to me, but she never saw me. Is Reed involved with her *and* Alisha?"

No. This fucking moron. This is what happens when you're friends with Matteo DuPont.

Lucas's close friend, Matteo, was the CEO of his own luxury brand and wrapped around more women than he needed to be.

"I just *might* shoot you at this rate," I resisted the urge to kill him.

"Boss," Garrett, who I completely forgot about, materialized to my right. He passed me—the fucking card. Black. Gold claws. Marcus fucking Hagen.

"Why do *you* have this?" My eyes narrowed on Lucas. "*Who* gave this to you?"

"I don't know. I keep finding them on my desk. I throw it out and every single day it keeps reappearing."

Hm. He didn't know who Hagen was. He didn't have a toe in any of this? Aidan watched him but only so much he could do from Chicago.

If Lucas saw my skepticism he continued with. "I'm telling you *the truth*. I was pissed that you wanted me dead. But I can't imagine you feeling thrilled if people tried to kill you."

No.

I'd be fucking honored. It would be such a fucking favor at this point.

"I don't give a *shit* who tries to kill you. You're going to forget *her* name and that you have that number. I don't care to know how you got it. I'll find out before the night is over. Next time you want to know who tried to murder you—speak to the entitled pricks in your family. We both know I would've, at the *minimum*, picked you up and thrown your ass into Gitmo for fun…"

I swept over his office disgusted I was even wasting my time here when I couldn't stop thinking about the defeat on Alisha's face. Evie waiting for me at home. And my wife—my fucking wife.

I snapped back to reality.

"You will *never speak my wife's name again.* Not from the likes of you."

I left him standing there with his mouth fucking open.

Garrett didn't say a word. I gave him the card. "If you see any more of these I want you to report them to Killian O'Hara."

"Yes, sir."

CHAPTER 57
GABRIEL

I was going to rip into Reed. I was. But he was with Alisha at K2, ignoring my calls.

Which pissed me off. I reviewed the footage at Titan Midtown and saw Lucy fucking Devereaux sneaking over to meet Reed.

He had the fucking necklace.

He had to have had it.

But why would Talia scramble for it back? Or was it Talia?

Some part of me had privately entertained that maybe in some alternate dimension, my wife was still alive.

But then I had to entertain the question of what kind of mental state she would have to be in.

Would she be pissed off at me?

Would she remember me?

Crazier things that happened.

Or was she like Liam, and did she hate me?

Did Liam ever suspect that she was alive? Or was he told the version of the story where everybody was dead except for me and him?

I didn't know.

Was grateful that Reed had sent in a Criminal Barbie to get my necklace? I was.

I met him a year younger than me in high school—I didn't know much about him at the time but quickly we were solid. I taught Reed how to fight years ago.

In all the years he'd grown? Reed had one thing about him that didn't change—his need for privacy and his need to help me.

I had taken on Reed with me to build Titan because that man hadn't changed.

He'd just grown up into a man with unshakable loyalty. Unshakable resolve. No matter what happened or how hard things got—Reed's spine was made of steel.

Maybe thats why he was so pissed off with me for being around Alisha.

Because he had been doing everything to be there for me.

While I had been...I didn't even know what was going on with me right now. Why I felt so sick.

This obsession with my past—when my past was right here in New York—was going to kill me.

Now, sitting in Heron manor, I had no fucking clue what to do with myself. I needed to call Reed.

I didn't care what he was doing with Alisha—this was a priority. I called him early that morning.

I didn't waste any time with niceties.

"You fucking have my necklace." I growled. "You went behind my back with a Devereaux for the fucking necklace."

"You kissed my girlfriend." I fucking knew he was still angry about that. "If Alisha hadn't told me why you did it, and even then – I fucking hate you."

Did she?

Did she tell him about Isobel? She didn't know anything.

"You don't trust me at all." Reed growled. "I hired Lucy to find your treasure in Senegal. I've been feeding you information from her fucking lips for the past three years. I gave you all the ammo you needed against the Devereaux's. And you have the gall to ask me why I kept it from you? Kept secrets from Alisha? Listen to yourself. I don't even know why you want the necklace—"

"Did she have it?" I didn't care about anything. I cared that somehow Lucy had gotten an impossible piece of jewelry.

"What?"

"Did she have it?"

"You knew I met with Lucy, *but not if I had the necklace?"*

I mean, I suspected.

"I only knew because Lucas called me." I didn't tell Reed I tried to shoot Lucas.

"Does he know? Did you kill him?" But Reed knew me well.

I sighed. "No. Someone's trying to kill him, and he talked."

I gave Reed a cliff notes version.

Not the one where I'd beaten Lucas up. Probably best left unsaid.

I was confused about why someone would ever target Lucas, while at the same time…the card had shown up. And his sister had it. I was confused.

Why would they target…Lucas?

"And he thinks it's you?"

Reed's voice put me back into reality. "Do you have it?"

"Yes." I held my breath. "Do you have the key?"

What? He knew about the key? How did he—of course he fucking figured out it doesn't fucking open.

"I don't have it."

"What? Where the fuck is the key?" Reed sounded annoyed more than anything else.

I was annoyed. My wife's necklace was now in Reed's possession! *"You thought I had the key the entire time?"*

"I fucking thought you were the key!"

We both swore. If I didn't trust Reed with my life?

I would swear he was fucking with me.

"Gabriel, from now on, when you go on your fucking fantasy quests and you've got your questions, please, do it after nine am."

"When can I have the necklace?" I barely heard anything Reed and I said my eyes envisioning it in my hands.

Her necklace. Where had it been? Where was my girl?

Reed who had no fucking clue who she was—groaned.

"Goodbye. I have a woman in bed, and as I remember correctly, you do not."

"No, I'm just your work wife according to her," I muttered.

"I will give it to you. But you're going to tell me who the woman was and who Isobel is." Reed finished.

I had no intention of telling him.

"Fine," I agreed having no intent on it. "Do you know why Evie is avoiding me? She's seeing someone, I know it."

"She's got a brother who dismembers people in his basement. Let the kid try to live a normal life."

"Absolutely not." She was my baby girl. Nothing was going to take her from me.

"I'm leaving." Reed hung up the phone and left.

Leaving me to sit there reeling.

Reeling.

He had the necklace.

My necklace.

I knew.

Was she alive?

Was it hers?

Was she here in New York looking for it?

But if she was, then she had to know me right?

It didn't make any sense.

None of this made any fucking sense.

I was deep in thought for hours. I didn't eat or move or do anything.

Because now I was wondering, what the fuck was going on.

By the afternoon, a knock came at my door.

Evie, my sweet girl, poked her head in, her dark auburn locks a little wild today and her eyes rimmed red. She'd been crying.

"Evie? Is everything alright?"

"I want to talk to you about something." She wrung her hands together. She only did that when she was nervous. "I want you to know I've spent quite some time thinking about it. I did a lot of research, and I have a plan."

I was around my desk immediately.

"It's okay. Whatever it is." It was always okay. "Tell me." Why was she crying? What was going on?

She was crying even harder now.

I had her in my arms a second later. "Shortcake—"

"I'm moving out."

Evie's words hit me like a baseball bat to the chest.

I thought losing Isobel hurt. But right now? Something similar ripped through my chest at Evie saying those words. To me.

To me. After years of snuggling her, feeling her on my heart, her light in my life—

"What happened? Did I do something? Did you feel uncomfortable—"

"No, you are the best!"

"Then why?" I couldn't even breathe around my emotions. I could barely speak. "I knew something had happened to you. *Did he hurt you?*"

I was going to find the man who made her cry.

I was going to kill him.

Slowly.

Did she want to leave me because of something he said?

Death was kind.

Evie's soft eyes watered.

"Gabriel, I'm twenty-three. I want to live on my own. I feel like a kid encroaching on your territory. I don't want you to have to hide your life from me. And you should be able to live freely. I cannot play house like this. I really want my own place. I have for some time. I'd like my own space."

"You have your own space—"

"You know what I mean. I love you so much. I need to set some boundaries with you. I would like to have my own place. I would like to have my own life outside of work. And I think that independence starts with creating my own space. Look at Alisha. Even Avani has a place for herself."

I didn't want to look at anyone but her.

She was my world.

She was my family.

Isobel wanted us to live here.

"I want to grow up," she whispered.

"You can grow here. You're safe here." She was my entire fucking world.

But Evie's jaw was set. "Safe doesn't mean that I'm okay. I'm telling you, and I'm giving you the courtesy of letting you know I am moving out."

I didn't even know how to tell her the way she took an ice cream scooper to my insides ripping it out of me.

My love for Isobel is what helped me find her.

Throughout the years, she'd snuck into my arms, snuggled up to me, ran to me with hugs, and I felt like Evie was my daughter.

Our daughter.

I got to play this fucked up pretend game.

And now...I felt like I was losing it.

I couldn't stop her.

And then she hit me with. "I know if Isobel were here, that's what she would want."

Oh. I narrowed my eyes.

She had no fucking clue how much that one hurt. How it ripped through my entire bloodstream. *No.*

That isn't what she would've wanted.

I knew my wife.

I knew her heart.

I knew this went against what she wanted.

But I couldn't keep Evie chained to her sunroom.

"That was a dirty move. She wanted you to be here." I spoke woodenly. If I said too much I'd explode.

"I love you, I love her, even though I didn't know her well. I respect both of you, but you guys need to respect that I need to grow up," she countered softly. "I need you to understand where I'm coming from."

I did. But I didn't. She didn't remember Isobel.

Didn't know her. Didn't understand that the sound of Isobel's laughter and mine together were the one things that kept me sane.

Didn't know that I listened to Isobel's voice all the time.

Evie didn't know Oracle, her pet project belonged to Isobel. She didn't know the impact of it.

She had no idea. About. Anything.

I knew she had met Liam. Reed had assigned the two of them and the irony of Liam having met her? Didn't escape me. He might've figured it out. Maybe he put two and two together. With Evie. With Lara. With Titan.

Did he know I had worked my ass off to repent?

I spent seven years atoning for my sins.

Evie's soft voice and crying made me focus on her.

"Isobel lived—she lived her life. She met you. I know you were the best thing that ever happened to her—you're the best thing that ever happened to me. Maybe I want a life for *myself*...I want to be better than where I am now—"

"There's *nothing* wrong with you—"

"*Yes, there is!*"

I blinked back. Did I fail her too?

I heard her. I did. She wanted to be more than me. More than Evie Monroe.

"I love you so much, but you have to let me *grow*...You saved my life. It just means I want to live, too. Everyone else does. I need space to just be. I'll still come back and work here all the time or from my new apartment. I'd like to replant myself somewhere that's mine. I'm not gone, and I'm not far. I'm right there...I already found a place."

Did she?

I would vet it.

But it ached.

Amor, did I fail you? She wants to grow up. Is this normal? Am I supposed to feel like there's a part of me ripping out?

Evie told me the neighborhood. And then she asked me.

"Do you want to come look at it with me and help me move in… maybe vet the place and look for security issues?"

I did.

But I needed to get my fucking necklace first.

Reed passed it to me at Titan Midtown, Liam's desk was empty as usual, and Reed didn't even look at me too focused on his work.

I snatched that shit so fast leaving without saying a word.

I was surprised he didn't ask about Isobel.

But I also thought maybe his mind was on Alisha. I didn't give a shit. The moment I was alone with it, I shook it gently. Listening.

The distinctive clink sent a shiver running down my spine. I blew out a breath I had been holding for seven fucking years staring down at my name on it.

I have you.

But where are you?

Did this mean…Isobel was gone and Talia get kept it?

Because if she knew? She would've taken it out, right? So who was hunting for Lucas? Why would Lucas ever have this necklace? How was he connected?

I needed to dig. But I also had ninety other pressing things.

Within a few days I had a copy of it made. I couldn't trust anyone anymore right now.

I put the real one around my neck.

In the meantime, I went to Evie's new apartment.

It was a decent place. Even if it was one Devereaux's older properties. He didn't pay much mind to it. Not like the skyscrapers he owned.

That day she told me she was seeing Alisha who was staying at the Primrose. I blinked.

Alisha was staying at the Primrose. Absolutely not. The Nash family stayed there.

But even more unsettling?

Why the fuck was Alisha there in the first place?

I called Reed who brokenly told me Alisha had ran from him. They'd broken up. They'd gotten into a fight.

And Alisha was with Kellan at the fucking Primrose. Absolutely not.

Evie told me what time she was going.

I would just go before then.

I blew out a breath into the sky the moment I slid into one of my shitbox cars I drove to hide my identity.

"FUCK!"

CHAPTER 58
ISOBEL

"You need to sit."

Bexley looked uncharacteristically serious. Her usual playful demeanor was gone. Even if her outfit was pajamas.

She motioned me to the bed where Samara had been sitting up ramrod straight. Even her clothes seemed darker today.

"I have news about Lucy Devereaux. Samara and I went digging and we found some stuff." Bexley paused unsure. "Samara also fired a shot to scare him."

I blinked over at Samara who shrugged lightly. "He was annoying. He's got emo vibes."

"And you do not?" I motioned to her outfit. "You look like a college art student."

She smirked and turned a little pink as I said it for some reason.

"That's the point. Now, moving on from me...Lucy Devereaux works for a company," Samara cut to the chase her voice clipped and tense. "Titan Security. He's the CEO. And he's also her boss. Or we think he is. Show her."

She motioned a hand to Bexley and she pulled up surveillance footage. I felt a strange pressure in my chest.

I already knew that Lucy was a jewel thief.

But I also knew that she had gotten away with a lot more than she should've.

We looked at all of the places she had been over the last few years, and Samara was the one who realized that she might have somebody working over her.

Someone protecting her.

"I can't get footage into the towers because of Reed's network. But I did see this—" she pulled up a photo of a car entering the tower. "This license plate belongs to the Devereaux family."

She showed me a navy Maserati with a dark-haired driver. "This is Reed Whittaker. She met with him. This guy."

She showed me a photo of Reed. He was handsome, dark chocolate hair, striking pale stormy eyes. I stopped breathing.

I stared at the image of him, wondering if I should feel something. My heart was sputtering. There was something about him that I felt like I should know.

My hands trembled and I tucked them into the pocket of my coat. I was freezing in the city.

Bexley went on oblivious to my spiraling.

"She met him. And she's dating his brother. We think. When we showed up to the city, people were already whispering so I checked recently and Adam Whittaker isn't with her anymore. On paper. It doesn't hurt to scope him out and clear him off the list."

She motioned to Samara who tipped her head.

"But Lucy Devereaux met with Reed Whittaker," Samara's hard dark eyes met mine. "We suspect, she works with him. We've found several identities but none of them matter. She's connected to his family."

"You don't think it's Lucas?"

"It doesn't hurt to keep an eye on Lucas in case he's in league with Reed," Samara said. "I've already dropped by his office. Several times. But he's working with someone. He knows we're onto him. I feel it."

Bexley nodded, her space buns on tight today letting me know she was at work and had been for a while.

My chest clenched at the two of them trying to find out what happened to my necklace.

"You said you don't want to kill anyone, I won't," Bexley shrugged. "But I've been poking at Whittaker's network. I'm just digging a tiny bit. He won't even know I'm there."

I frowned at the idea of Bexley digging. "I need to go see Lucas Devereaux myself."

Samara shifted as I turned to her. "It's not that I don't trust you. I just need to interact with him." I knew people.

I would know him.

Lucas Devereaux's secretaries had one singular day they would both be out.

Sort of.

I simply slid myself into the cracks. Bexley had done the paperwork, I put on my business casual best.

And I knocked on his door.

Lucas Devereaux was sitting at his desk and for a moment I paused. He looked so familiar to me, but his eyes were a clear shade of blue. Brighter like the sea. Like Cape Verde.

Which I missed.

His golden hair under the sunlight made him look inhuman.

I knew he was tall, broad shouldered and in his navy striped suit, he looked handsome. That gleaming hair lifted when I walked in and I was met with his eyes.

"Mr. Devereaux, I have a question."

"Are you new?" That was his first question. I knew he had PTSD, and memory issues which Bexley found in his medical records. Documented veteran. He had seen horrible things. Done even worse.

I slipped on a smile at his adorable blinking.

"Do I know you from somewhere?"

"I'm just covering for Jenny this morning. I work for Mr. O'Brian." At least on paper I did.

"Where's Ella?" Hm. He didn't read his email Bexley sent him.

"She had a doctor's appointment this morning and her nephew to pick up, so I'm just covering until two o'clock." I practiced. Because Ella did have doctor's appointment's that ran late. And she didn't have to pick up her nephew.

But Bexley pulled enough strings to delay Ella long enough to get me what I needed.

My in.

"I hope it's alright, I have everything you asked for today, your meetings organized, and your father called earlier when you stepped out. I told him I would pass you the message. I also have a list of questions, including your special requests. Would it be all right if I went ahead?" He blinked again a little smile on his face.

"Where are you from?" And then he seemed to realize what he asked. "I'm sorry, your accent is beautiful."

He is adorable. He kind of reminds me of Bexley. She does not think before she speaks.

I laughed low at him. *He is not a criminal either. Even with his military background.* "Brazil."

He made a motion for me to go on and I did. He had emailed his secretaries a few requests. Odd ones.

"I contacted the store, and they just had a few questions about your request, so I wanted to go over it with you." I wrote them into my notepad. "You said several small cacti, a few ferns, a five-foot fiddle leaf fig." I was struggling with his requests. "And...a tree..." I looked up to find him smiling softer at me like he...like he found me funny. I felt a wave of embarrassment flow through me. Even after all these years my English was— "*Sorry,* my English is not the best, but—"

"*Your English is great.*" He looked almost proud of me as he waved a hand. "I would never shame you for your accent. It's wonderful."

Oh.

Something in my chest expanded as he said the words.

I knew his sister stole my necklace. I knew he was a suspect. I knew we were watching him and trying to take him out as the most likely candidate since she was his family, since his father was Malcolm's accomplice. I knew all this. And while Samara would keep an eye out on him?

I didn't know what I saw in his eyes that made me turn a little red.

His smile widened a little on me like he knew my thoughts.

"How big should the tree be?" That is what I said.

"Eight feet sounds good. This way, there's room to grow."

"Right away, sir. Eight feet. Got it." I paused glancing at him looking like he was holding back his laughter on me for some reason. "One more thing."

"Yes?"

There was one request in there. He wanted his assets moved to a woman named Eva. Eva *Monroe.*

One that Bexley and I looked into. I didn't recognize her name. I didn't know her. Because on Titan's system she was Eva Whittaker.

Bexley and I assumed it was the same woman.

Which brought Titan Security to the forefront again. She was no doubt related to Reed. She was also seeing Lucas. Which brought her and Lucas into the web.

"I will make the arrangements to move all assets to her name, as you requested. And your will has been updated. I just need your signature. Could you spell her last name again?"

I put my head down to write it.

"Eva Monroe."

My head snapped up again. Why did he call her that? Was she the same woman?

I thought it was that.

Was she...was she who I was...no.

Over the years I searched for many Monroe's. Many of them. Privately.

Not a single one was connected to me.

Until now. Was she the original owner of my necklace? He was updating his will to give everything to her. Every single thing he owned. Billions of dollars of assets to one woman.

He loved her. *All* of this was for her.

"By the way, you said you work downstairs for O'Brien."

I pasted on a smile.

"I am new. O'Brien's on a warpath with the Walters and Jennings teams today, and I'm trying to avoid him. Guilty as charged," I quipped. "Monroe, I got it. I'll be moving everything today. Will there be anything else?"

"Smart move. He should calm down by the time you get back. No, just make sure Evie—Eva's name is on everything I own. The trust and everything else—"

"Of course." I looked over Lucas Devereaux. Who was Eva Monroe? Was she the same? Why did everyone have so many names?

Then again—I had several.

"I'll email you the confirmation of everything once it's done. Mr. Devereaux, do you love her?" At his expression I explained. "I was just wondering if you'd like me to add that to the card with the seven-foot tree since you're sending your girlfriend, a jungle?"

"Eight feet," he murmured looking away. Like he was embarassed. "Yes, to both of those questions."

I had to get out of there before I embarrassed myself. Awkwardly.

I felt out of place.

Titan had a lot of information we didn't have access to. Because Reed's network was fortified. Eva Whittaker was listed as a contact on the Titan website.

According to Bexley, Eva Monroe...wasn't...real.

So I put down Eva Whittaker on Lucas's forms. All of them.

Why did he call her Monroe? Was that her name before?

It didn't make any sense.

In my head as I stood outside his office, I made a motion to the cameras and I knew Bexley would wipe them again.

She sent his IT department scattering in all different directions losing their mind.

But this meant...Lucas wasn't innocent. He knew things. He had connections. He was dating the Whittaker family. Just like his sister was too.

I texted Samara in code that Talia had taught me years ago.

Call Sign.

Message.

End Goal.

Raven. SKWITCH. DLT.

Samara sent me a thumbs up. Years ago, I didn't remember who I was. But recently, I've become a lot colder. My heart felt like ice.

This wasn't just about the necklace.

Now that I knew who he was, who his family was, I saw it as a direct threat to me.

He was connected to the same people who probably took my necklace. Which meant he was guilty. Until he wasn't.

I was still the head of Talon. And I didn't care who Lucas Devereaux or his Eva were. I didn't want to.

Raven was Samara's codename.

She would continue to shadow him.

And if Lucy came his way?

He was mine too.

384

CHAPTER 59

GABRIEL

IN THE NEXT FEW DAYS, I HELPED EVIE MOVE INTO HER NEW apartment. I sat there on her couch while she slept on me, Isobel's voice in my ear.

I listened to her audio almost every day for seven years like an addict.

Amor. Did I do a good job? Are you listening to me?

She's in her own home. Are you proud?

Did I do right by you?

Did I work hard enough to protect you?

Did I love you enough before I lost you?

And am I ever getting you back?

And much like anything wrong in the universe—all of the bad things came at once.

I was reliving an entirely new brand of hell.

Because it wasn't just Alisha.

No. Because I was picking up a pattern that when devastating things happened in my life, they happened altogether. All at once.

Selena was attacked. Alisha *and* her baby sister Avani were attacked.

And that was the worst feeling in the world.

I was bolting out of Titan Midtown where I would sit there haunted by my nightmares.

Because losing Alisha wasn't a part of the equation.

I was experiencing a different brand of hell.

385

One where I watched Kellan Watts who was in love with Selena, almost lose his world.

One where I saw Reed lose his mind over Alisha blacked out.

One where I had to bring paperwork to Avani to let her know if she lost her sister, Reed would be her family.

One where I was reliving my hell.

Over and over and over again. Watching my team fall to pieces.

And I wondered for a moment how the fuck I was supposed to hold on.

It took Alisha a few days to come to, Selena was injured deeply and it would take her time to heal.

I dealt with Watts's unstable ass by kicking him out of the hospital and booting him to Killian and Shane Alves—a Titan recruit Reed had already onboarded.

And if it wasn't enough? At some point Reed's half brother Adam had entered his life again.

Things did not happen for us easily. Or smoothly.

It was when I finally got a chance to go home to the manor, after days and days to just breathe did I get a text from Alisha.

CHAPTER 60
GABRIEL

"How did you know?"

That was the first thing Lucas said to me when he walked into his apartment that night holding her favorite flowers. Of course.

He's her boyfriend.

I felt fury like no other rage through me. Did he know? Did he know he was the reason she lost her mother?

No. He probably didn't give a shit.

I uncorked the fucking whiskey again.

I had seen her favorite drinks on his shelf.

Her favorite snacks. Her sweater on his couch. Evie, my fucking kid, was dating Lucas? The son of the man who murdered her mom.

Absolutely not.

If there was one thing in the world that would gut her? It was that.

I didn't really enjoy breaking into his apartment. I didn't want to be here. I didn't like the little fucker.

I brought out the whiskey and poured two fingers, taking the shot so I wouldn't lose my mind.

At six-two maybe three, he could've been related to me. Blonde-hair. Blue eyes. But he looked like the aristocrat he was.

Polished. Too shiny.

"Pets for Vets? Her apartment building? She's got a tracker on her keychain. It's the Lilly."

I helped Evie move out.

That day had been devastating for me. Because Isobel had wanted the family under one roof. It was my wife dream. But I was coming to realize Evie was her own person and she had wants and dreams too.

He undid his suit, tossing his jacket on the floor along with the bouquet of white lilies he got Evie.

This was the man she'd been seeing. And I had a feeling she had no idea who he was.

"How about I offer you something better?"

I took a sip. "What's that?"

"I help you find your wife's killer."

Oh. Hell. No. I watched him like a hawk. Lucas. Like his old man. Was smart. Sharp. Despite his obvious PTSD, he could still figure things out.

"*That's* how you knew about her."

"I can help you." His eyes met mine. No. He couldn't help me. He couldn't help himself. I helped him. And he had no idea.

"*What makes you think I'd want your help.*"

"You don't, but it's been seven years, and you need all the help you can get. You haven't been able to find the motherfucker who did it. I would do anything for Evie. Let me do the same for her sister. I'm not your enemy. I don't give a shit what my father did. I'm not him. The only way you'll keep me from her is killing me."

Then so be it.

"Until then, I'll take you. I know why you protect her. She's the last thing that belongs to Isobel, isn't she? You don't want to let her go because you'd let Isobel down. I'm not going to hurt her. I love Evie."

I didn't give a shit if he promised Evie the moon.

He was scum. His family was scum.

Like Young. I had to spend the last few years going after that family. It was in the back of my mind because Killian handled it.

If I got involved, I would just blow up all of their houses and torture them at a black site. I let Killian do it. As much as I relished revenge, slow revenge was nicer.

"You need to stay away from her." It came out of my lips. He needed to get him and his fucked up family out of my life.

Out of my daughter's life.

"You're not going to be enough for her. Ever. Trust me on this.

You're going to hurt her. And when you do? It's going to break her."

"What the fuck is your problem?"

I was ready for a fucking fight. I was.

I was her man.

"The only way to keep you away is to kill you. Bad enough you and...*with Evie,* but now you bring my wife into this?"

"You're insane. You know that?"

I threw the first hit. He ducked. But he wasn't fast like me. I was trained. Spent the last seven years, turning myself into this. Nobody was going to beat me.

"After you're dead, I'm going to dismantle your entire empire, just like years ago." Rage filled me as I said it.

He was on the floor. As I walked towards him, I saw his eyes focus on my chest. And then he frowned and lunged at me.

I wasn't expecting Lucas Devereaux to be strong after sitting behind a desk. *"Get down!"*

And then I heard the shot. Glass cracking. Lucas groaned. Both of us scrambling for cover. I felt my shock through my system. Lucas had thought someone was trying to kill him.

I knew that much. Now I was certain someone was.

"You took the hit for me?" After I tried to kill him? *"Stay down."*

Another shot took out the glass on the island, and the glass outside the window shattered.

"What the fuck is happening?"

I looked at Lucas who was clutching his arm. "Gabriel—*Gabriel*—let her—let her bring me back."

I was shrugging off my jacket, a second later, pressing down on him calling Reed for help.

I tersely explained it to Reed who was rushing out of his apartment, K2.

He was sending his half-brother Adam, a doctor who worked with Perla, after I hired her.

I recommended Perla discreetly to Reed.

And in turn she kept all my secrets.

After all, she had seen the woman who brought in Isobel.

There was no photos of Talia Nash on the Internet for me to show Perla.

Otherwise, I would've found her a long time ago.

Now two entire nights later, after that incident, I was now

arguing with my Evie—of course she would fall in love with a man she wasn't supposed to—now pleading with me to help him.

"It's not safe." Evie's soft eyes were wet watching me. "We need to take him to the manor until we figure out who's behind this."

She had no fucking clue Lucas's father had been responsible for her mother's death. I explained it to Reed on the ride over here after Lucas had been shot. He looked grim faced.

Years ago, when he had helped me, he did it with the blind eye. He didn't ask any questions.

Reed was the kind of man who went with it.

Always.

If I asked him for the moon he would just do it.

When it came to talking about himself and his life? He was shit at it. But he listened and I knew he had processed it all.

"He's got the money to take care of himself."

"Why do you hate him so much?" I had never heard Evie snap until that moment. Her usually warm eyes flashing fire at his bedside. Like he was something she needed to protect. "He hasn't done anything to us. *He almost died!*"

Before I could lose it—Reed kicked me out.

If I didn't leave I'd have to explain my madness to Alisha.

I won't abandon you, Gabriel. Trust me.

Please?

Talia Nash was back in the city. She had shot at Lucas. Most likely. I didn't think he even knew.

Because that gold card with the claw marks was spotted in the city. Killian had found them. Everyone was alert.

I know when you're lying.

No, you just know when I want to be kissed.

CHAPTER 61
ISOBEL

"You shot Lucas Devereaux?"

"No!"

Samara's voice was tense on the phone as she called me and Bexley.

My heart began pounding at the idea of Lucas Devereaux dying without giving me answers. Or worse?

The Titans starting a war against me in a way that impacted my entire unit. If they even knew where to look.

I couldn't risk.

I listened to Samara stumbling over her words.

"I didn't mean to—I saw the blonde guy moving at him. Someone was in his apartment. I can't tell who it is." Her dark eyes were full of remorse. "I didn't mean to—but I think I hit him. They took him to Titan hospital. Thierry—he was aware. Did you know he was aware?"

Bexley shot me a guilty look and I understood it. I spoke to Thierry after coming to the city.

"His brother's are friends with Lucas. Talia's husband Andrei, he's Lucas's friend. He was worried," I barely heard myself. I needed to go check on this.

I needed to make sure we didn't do anything stupid. I let Bexley know hanging up the phone with Samara.

"I'm already on it." Bexley was on her computer. "I have surveillance of Adam and Eva Whittaker with him."

"Got it. Send me the address." I grabbed my coat ready to leave and Bexley stood abruptly. "Hang on. You wanna go sneak into the hospital? Reed Whittaker's properties?"

I did.

"No, that's suicide, I can't cover you!"

"I know," I held her shoulders. "Which is why you must stay here and figure it out. I need to go and make sure nobody is dead. Prepare for contingency. This was not supposed to happen."

"No, Alma—"

Sometimes I forgot. She didn't know me.

Not my name.

Not my identity.

It wasn't stupid.

It was my entire world.

~

LUCAS WAS OKAY.

He was in his hospital room, and I had gotten the uniform of a nurse with my fake badge. The amount of work Bexley could do in a day was insanity. But I needed it all. I was moving fast.

Within twenty-four hours I made it to the Titan hospital with my hair platinum blonde and pulled back. I didn't even look like myself.

I felt the back of my neck prickle standing there in front of Lucas's door to find two men talking to him. He was wiping his eyes emotional. I recognized Reed Whittaker in an instant.

Stormy eyes. Muscles. White t-shirt slightly covered in specks of blood. He was enormous in person.

His demeanor shadowed by his exhaustion. I took him in discreetly, the medical mask on my face, and my clipboard in hand.

Reed. Whittaker. His eyes are not the right ones...but is he...my one? Is he...who is he?

A movement to my left made me shift. I caught Adam Whittaker looking up at me.

One look at him and every single of us had dismissed him. That was not a dangerous man.

He might've been dating Lucy—but not anymore.

And he was about as threatening as Bexley eating pancakes.

Adam Whittaker had a sweet face. A sweeter smile.

392

Messy blonde hair, softer warm eyes looked up at me.

He was the spitting image of his older brother who sat in there with Lucas but somehow his coloring tempered him into something more approachable.

And then he smiled and I felt my lips tip up.

He was not a criminal.

Not even close.

As I turned back, the back of my neck prickled.

I turned to see a blonde man walking away with a girl in his arms she looked too excited as she tugged him down the hall. He was tall. Blonde. In a gray suit. Didn't Samara say she had shot at someone who had been with Lucas in a gray suit?

Was it him?

My phone pinged from Bexley.

> I can't get into his network. It's fortified and someone's blocking me.

> They know.

> XTXT. Bluejay.

I left the hospital instead of following the man in the gray suit.

Bexley was telling me to exit out. Not to draw suspicion. The longer I stayed there, the longer they might put it together.

I needed to stay on Lucas and now Reed. They were together.

This was opportunity to gather intelligence.

> I need a hotel near his home in Greenwich.

> Get me as close as possible. Gonna try and scope it out tonight.

Reed Whittaker had two homes.

K2.

And the manor in Greenwich. A manor in Greenwich. I had the address. I would have to go and check it out while they were all here.

I had Bexley give me the address and I dropped by Nash Group tower to get weapons and whatever else I needed. I was going to break into that manor while they were all here.

I stopped a little at the name of his home on my phone now.

393

Heron Manor?

A memory slipped into my head. One of my father driving. Liam next to me.

Watcha looking at, shortcake?

I want that house one day. I pointed to Heron Manor. My house. My home. Reed Whittaker lived in...my dream?

Who was he?

> Who are the people with him? Did you see them on camera at all?

Only when one of them was coming in.

Let me do some digging.

When I got to the hotel in Greenwich, Bexley called me.

"Irish mafia," Bexley said. "You said there were two? One of them is Killian O'Hara. Guy's basically *covered* in blood. He's dating a nurse inside of the hospital. Nisha Graham. But the older one is the one you gotta watch out for. Aidan, you said the guy with Reed was big? That might be him. Might. Rumor is he killed his father to get to where he is today. They have a younger brother. He's connected to Matteo DuPont. Who is connected to Lucas."

"*Dio Mio.*"

"I know, it's like Titan Security is connected into a web. The epicenter of Titan is Reed. And his fucking network is impossible. It's like he's got another version of Oracle or something because this guy's good."

I blinked. A shiver ran down my arm at the memories I had of Liam. Working on something. A security company maybe.

I didn't know. Most of my memories were fuzzy. But I felt something for that.

"I'll follow them."

"You want to take out Reed?"

"No, I want information." In my world—that's all power was.

"Got it. I'll keep doing a mind map of the Titan's and their connections. They're all linked in this chain."

They were stronger as a unit. Fortified.

The Titan web was expansive. One always led to the other.

But I knew, how to drive people insane, how to make them know our presence.

"I want you to trip a few things in their network tonight. Scare them enough."

"Gotcha." She giggled. "They have a hacker too. I can see him. He can see me. I think he knows we exist because he keeps sending me jack-in-the-box's that appear with messages."

I frowned. "Are they playing with us."

"I think so. But I can fuck with them right back."

"Good."

I had to go stalk Reed Whittaker and his family now.

THE MOMENT I SAW THE MANOR IT WAS LATE AT NIGHT.

People were there.

They had come back from the hospital? *Mierda.*

I was watching them. Bexley had given me the go-ahead and somehow she'd gotten me this far on the grounds. Into the forrest surrounding the manor.

I was in Reed Whittaker's yard staring at the behemoth that was Heron Manor.

I grew up in Connecticut. This was...a few hours away from where Liam and I lived...with my father. Liam...he was gone. But this...this structure was here. Reed Whittaker had my home? And my necklace?

This didn't make any sense to me.

The full moon was out tonight and I stared up at it. The last time I saw the moon—I buried Malcolm Nash in the sand. Now? The blonde in my hair contrasted against my all black.

I had strapped knives down to me.

I wasn't a bad fighter.

Not terrible. But I couldn't shoot. Not with my scar tissue. The kickback hurt sometimes more than anything else.

And I just stood there. I couldn't move. Thankfully with my face covered nobody could see me.

Or so I thought. I dipped a tiny bit into the trees when I saw two lean figures, like fighters tearing through the lawn at me.

At me.

Dio!

I bolted tearing off through the forest. I was far enough to outrun them but they were lightening fast. Huge.

I was tempting fate now. Too much.

I ran until I got to my motorcycle I had left and hopped on tearing off into the town, glancing behind me to see one of them pale platinum hair and another one with dark hair stopping, panting.

Not today.

I felt a smile tip my lips.

Like they would ever catch me?

I puffed out breaths as I rode to the town.

That was close.

I almost got caught.

CHAPTER 62
GABRIEL

"What the fuck was that?"

Killian came back to me angry mismatched eyes ready to fight someone. "She tore off."

I *knew*. I needed to tell Reed.

An eerie sensation ran down my spine at the blonde ghostly figure standing in my lawn. My wife's lawn.

Killian was pissy since I took him away from his girlfriend and he hadn't slept a wink since I had.

Never thought I'd see the day Killian O'Hara found someone like her. But I realized the toughest ones always found the softest counterparts.

Nisha Graham had him wrapped around her finger. Or his finger judging by the pink bandaid he wore. That was all her.

"Pretty sure that's our friend paying us a visit from the hospital." He had been too busy mooning over Nisha to notice her. But I had.

"I gotta tell Reed." I was already texting him. "I saw her when she first came in. I was following her the entire time..." I explained to Killian and a platinum blonde haired Alexei next to him.

Alexei was Aidan's right hand. And right now? With Lucas Devereaux under my fucking roof—I let Reed juggle him and Evie for once. I couldn't do it. She knew everything. She had come to me in the hospital crying. Leaning on me for support.

And I would always be there for her.

Right now? I couldn't do it.

I was lying to her face.

I couldn't watch her, be with her. It was painful.

Not when I needed to get this job done.

My throat worked as I spoke to the two guys in front of me as they nodded, taking orders from me came second nature to both of them who understood the important of following it.

"She was at the hospital, in front of Reed's room. I don't if she came to finish the job with Lucas—"

"Or if she came for someone else," Killian finished.

I dipped my head.

She didn't work there. Not with her hair color. I clocked everyone. Even the cleaning staff.

She was different. And she lingered. On top of the black uniform she had on?

She was...one of them. One of the people I'd been hunting. Blonde. Female. Was she? Talia Nash?

I didn't know I just know I clocked the surveillance footage at the hospital and the one here.

And I knew from Reed—he had assigned Liam to make sure nobody hacked it.

Liam didn't know what was going on—he took orders from Reed.

I hadn't spoken to him since he'd shown up to Titan.

But now?

Now I wanted to reach out to him. I just didn't even know where to fucking start.

Reed texted me.

I'll talk to Evie. Aidan's going to talk to Lucas about your plan.

I had been busy all night on Oracle. Earlier that night Evie had mentioned one solid thing.

There was a hacker in the city out of Cape Verde.

They had pinged in Cape Verde.

And then...they were in New York.

Now, there was a random blonde spooking out everyone?

Coincidences did not exist in intelligence.

Not a single fucking one.

Normal people always thought coincidences were so fortunate. They weren't.

There was no such thing.

Reed was babysitting my sister and her fucking *boyfriend*. Even if I wanted to murder Lucas in cold blood I couldn't.

Amor, he is a nice boy.

I know, baby. But I still hate him.

And every so often Alisha texted me. That was another thing.

Did I want Alisha?

Not...not the same way I wanted Isobel. No. It was something else. It was like a need for something else. I couldn't put my finger on it.

Seven long years of being ice and finally—I felt like I was... reacting. I didn't understand it.

You guy's are still awake?

> Yeah. No rest for the wicked.

Funny. I think I'll come tomorrow to see you guys.

I'm beginning to think nobody sleeps or eats there.

> Nah, we've been putting on our robes and chanting in Latin in my lair.

> Maybe doing rain dances on the roof.

Shall I bring a pitchfork for you?

I do hope your robes match with your shoes. It would be a crime if they didn't.

> I'll have Reed pick out the shoes.

> Right now I was debating lime green

I knew it.

You're a monster in disguise.

> Correction, I'm a monster in real life.

> In disguise I transform into a bat

399

A *were-bat*

What the fuck is a were-bat?

I don't know I must consult Avani

She's all things supernatural fantasy romance.

Right now she's reading a series about one of the
men being a shifter or something.

I do believe it's a were-bat.

Ah. Werewolf porn.

Just my cup of tea.

It is not werewolf porn.

It's fairy porn.

There's a difference.

One has wings. The other one has fangs.

And you don't drink tea.

I can totally drink tea.

I have fangs and wings.

Yes, in your night form.

You great big were-bear 🐻

That's were-bat to you.

I did manage to laugh. Even with the spooky business Alisha
and I had solid banter. Like nothing had changed.
Even though everything had.
I had resolved that I didn't imagine any of it.

I'm coming tomorrow morning.

Don't try to argue. You won't win.

I wasn't even thinking about it.

Lies. I had been thinking about her.

I waited a second.

Liar. You were totally thinking about it.

Very well then

I can hear you thinking from here. You're not even going to bother going to sleep.

Are you?

How is he?

He hasn't said a word. I'm worried he's on edge again.

Reed.

Of course she was concerned about Reed. I blew out a breath the twist in my gut becoming familiar. I didn't know what the fuck was wrong with me.

I was happy for Reed. I was.

You can ask him tomorrow.

All right.

Have fun being the other woman temporarily, I'll be there to steal your place tomorrow.

I smirked.

Alisha always joked about me being Reed's work wife.

I just rolled with it because it did make me laugh at the idea of it. I bitched and he handled it with a stoic expression giving me what I needed. It fit.

But...every single time Alisha said it—I was fucked up for imagining her with me right now. The memory of her. Her scent.

Was that even...possible? Could I fucking want her...with Reed together? I didn't know.

Asking my best friend to share his girlfriend with me?

Out of the fucking question.

I shook it off. Nope. Wasn't going there. She wasn't getting under my skin.

Not while I was picking data about Charles Devereaux selling his kids out to his buddy—*Marcus Hagen.*

Over the years I was figuring out that might be an overarching alias for something. Maybe it wasn't a person. Maybe it was a name given to a person.

Like a boss.

A leader.

I had seven years to dissect this.

And for once I felt like I was getting closer.

~

I WASN'T THERE WHEN ALISHA SWUNG BY THE MANOR. I TRIED NOT TO be. Maybe I was a coward.

I didn't know if Reed and her talked about my...or her...I didn't know.

The next morning I found Reed in the kitchen, shirtless, covered in scratches and hickies. My stomach twisted again as I pasted on a bland expression. I shouldn't feel anything. She wasn't mine.

I couldn't.

"Reed, there are kids in the house."

His smirk was one of laziness and satisfaction. More marks on his chest, his neck I tried to ignore.

Like she was his peace.

And then my attention found fucking Lucas sitting there in a hoodie and sweats looking too comfortable in my home. Under my roof. With my sister/daughter. How dare he?

I was miserable getting coffee.

Miserable pouring it with the hazelnut syrup Reed took with his coffee. "Can't just be a work wife around here..." I muttered.

"Never thought you two would be a couple," Lucas quipped in a lower voice. Before I could throw something at him, I heard a huskier laugh cut through the kitchen.

"Tell me about it."

My spine stiffened and I felt my entire being malfunction when I turned to find Alisha in the doorway, dark hair all around her in waves, eyes sparkling on Reed—in what had to be the tiniest robe plausible but on her it fit. It was her thing.

402

All delicate lace, dangerous curves slipping off one shoulder like an invitation. Not for me, of course. For Reed.

I could see the beard rash from Reed's stubble on her cheeks.

They'd been together. I swallowed hard. Dark and sexy. Seductive. Without even trying.

Now I saw why Lara was friends with her. Both girls had effortless grace to them.

The two of them got along well and I didn't even put it together I was so focused on myself.

If I had been a smarter man? I would've paid attention the last three years, Alisha had somehow been in my orbit.

But Reed had. Thats why she was his.

"Lish." Reed's smile was soft.

"I know you said you'd get food, but I felt weird staying in bed."

Reed moved to her and took her in his arms and I turned away focusing on my coffee and not flipping a chair.

That would not be civil.

I could always murder Lucas.

That would be a decent morning activity.

I heard Reed mutter. "Angel, I'll go back with you in a second."

Her eyes held concern up at him. "There's something wrong in the house."

"*Someone* was trying to get in the house." I couldn't resist. That was my two cents. I swore it was my two cents. But Alisha being Alisha would notice me.

"Gabe, maybe you should Palo Santo the house," she said innocently enough. "It may help remove the negative energy."

Would it? I blinked at the backyard. Perhaps. Would it remove Lucas?

Probably not.

"While we're at it, can we Palo Santo Gabriel?"

Oh, fuck you, Reed. I shot him the finger.

Alisha laughed low. "Reed, be nice to your wife." And before I could respond to it she gave me a heart attack as she said. "What's this?" And she pointed to the fucking card.

The black one.

With the gold claw marks.

On the kitchen table.

All three of us, me, Reed, and Lucas gaped as Alisha picked it up not knowing the level of poison it was.

"This is beautiful." She murmured. "Have I seen this before?"

"Lish—" Reed started.

"It's so shiny," she smiled at me. "Is this yours?" Alisha didn't even wait for a response. "When I was a little girl, my mum would hate the word claw because these are bird claw marks, so she called them talons."

Reed and I both double blinked. *Talons?*

Alisha nodded, smiling. "A bird talon, singular. *Talon.*" She pointed at Reed. "My accent is *not*—darling, will you—"

"Talon," Reed's accent wasn't English. So it came out clear. He shot me a look. *The Gold Claw?*

I felt heat creeping up my neck, as I shrugged. I had been throwing out potential names for whatever these fuckers were.

"I was just guessing. Now that Alisha said Talon, it sounds better."

"What are you two talking about?" Alisha looked between us.

And I moved in front of her suddenly aware of something creeping up my neck that wasn't embarassment.

"Have you seen that card before?"

I saw that tiny little notch in her brow as she frowned. "I think so…"

Reed who was leaning against the counter paled as I shot him a look. *Stay calm. She said she's seen it. Not that she got it.*

"I just can't remember where I saw it, but I'd remember the design." She looked at me and Reed. "I…I can't remember. That's so strange; it's like the thought was right there."

Ever since she'd been attacked weeks ago, she had some lapses in memory. I was tracking that. Privately. I wanted to know.

After William Santos had died from a head injury I was more aware of how severe they were.

And then of course, privately some part of me wondered if Isobel was alive…if she forgot about me…if she remembered me and hated me?

I couldn't think about my wife right now.

Reed watched her with soft concern in his eyes. I spoke up. "Let it go. It'll come back."

She looked embarrassed at me. "Drat, is that what Perla warned me would happen?"

"I've even blown up enough times to not have any memories either. I usually wake up in the hospital," Lucas said quietly. Sometimes I forgot he existed. Or I wished he didn't. I still didn't like him. Not for Evie. "My brain is shot."

I knew that.

I knew his entire medical record.

And privately, deep down—I knew why he loved Evie. I knew why he fought so hard. I watched the way he looked at her. Reed told me they were together last night.

Evie had made up with him. Which meant he was one step closer to being my brother-in-law.

That shifted my mindset on him.

Because I realized I was Liam. And I didn't want to do that to Lucas. Didn't mean I liked him.

I just didn't want to see anything happen to him for Evie's sake.

Alisha and Lucas talked and I didn't hear a thing. I just Reed watching her quietly.

Taking her in with a pain in his eyes I recognized. The last thing he wanted to see was her hurt. I still remembered that night.

Every night. Selena bleeding out on the floor. Alisha being carried out unconscious by Reed. Avani screaming into Kieran's neck.

And I had been in hell watching my team in the present relive in my hell.

I caught Alisha saying something to Lucas about her being happy for him and Evie.

Alisha was polite to everyone but I didn't like her smile on him. I didn't like her smile aimed at anyone but me and Reed.

And then Lucas said. "What's it like sharing them?" If I could choke on my coffee I would've. I felt Reed pause.

Both of us didn't breathe. One, Reed might've been aware I was attracted to her. Two, they thought I liked her because she looked like Isobel.

No.

I liked Alisha because she felt like a bridge to humanity and warmth. The cracks under my skin were surfacing again.

And three?

Lucas just asked how it felt like for Alisha to share us.

Me and Reed. In bed. In a relationship. I was going to strangle him. I would apologize to Evie after.

Alisha—being fucking Alisha—smiled at Lucas who watched her carefully and calmly.

Because he was friends with fucking deviants. I didn't need to know anything about Evie's sex life with this motherfucker. I would know. Because I certainly fucking thought about sharing Alisha.

I wasn't dumb enough to say it out loud.

"It's not that hard," Alisha said. "I want to come up more to see them both."

And then she turned that smile on me but I was watching Lucas who opened his fucking mouth.

Again.

"Do you guys go to *De Nuit*?"

The question out of his lips hung in the air like smoke. And before I could decide whether to throw my entire coffee cup at him, or just read across the table and just kill him right then Alisha moved.

Alisha turned to Lucas sharply. "I beg your pardon?"

The moment her accent turned sharp and proper I knew Lucas was about to be eviscerated.

"I fucking knew you were an idiot." So I asked him the one thing I knew would trip him up. "Who's the third DuPont?"

A couple of weeks ago, Reed had come and told me when he'd gone to see Matteo DuPont, his family member pulled a gun on him.

With a silencer.

Professional.

Except that particular member? Did not exist. Not on paper. Not in reality. Which meant he was dangerous and connected. And a ghost. In our world? We were tracking a few.

To me? What were the odds of ghost appearing at the same time as a black ops unit?

Lucas blinked wide blue eyes at me. "Wait, what?"

Reed caught on real fast, his eyes a stormy grey that I knew would go after Lucas regardless of his like of the guy.

And then Alisha got it.

"Did you just presume I was sleeping with both of them?" The three of us whipped our heads to her. Oh. Shit. Forget what I said. I forgot that Alisha was this cupcake. Until…she was pushed.

Lucas was about to get his ass handed to him.

She held her hand out to me. And I already knew. I quickly grabbed the first thing I saw. A ladle.

She had it in her hand a second later and she stood to her five-three like an angry pixie and I suppressed my laughter hunting for something that would hurt a little more.

"How could you be so daft? You arsehole! *He is my friend—*" Alisha thwacked Lucas and Reed winced a little.

"I'm sorry!"

I snorted. Was that all it took? I finally found the rolling pin. I was on her in a second right behind her switching it out for the weapon of choice.

He winced as he looked at it. And Reed teamed up with us advancing on Lucas's other side looking proud of Alisha.

"Answer Reed's questions." Alisha held out the rolling pin. And just like Lucas melted. Reed took notes and Alisha held her rolling pin out threateningly.

He gave us enough about Thierry DuPont—the mystery ghost. Another one to add to the fucking growing list of assassins apparently invading New York.

Did my day ever calm down?

Alisha cleared her throat at Lucas.

And he stumbled over an apology. He thought I was with Alisha.

No. I wasn't. Was I obvious? I felt my stomach turn. I barely heard what he said. I just inhaled the scent of her hair. The way she defended me then. Her fire. Her ability to handle things with grace and soft anger.

Rolling pin aside.

Lucas looked at Reed bemused. "Was I just...adopted?"

Reed smirked taking us in. He knew about our...'friendship.' Did he know...about me? I didn't even know how to ask.

But knowing Reed, the glint in his eyes he guessed it. He knew he held my leash.

Maybe not a work wife.

I was certainly a work demon.

I didn't hear shit. All I heard was Alisha saying she would spend some time with Lucas and Evie.

Absolutely not.

"He's not coming to brunch."

She smiled up at me with those eyes of hers. "No, that's just you and me."

And I fucking *melted.*

A knock on the door from Adam out of all people broke the spell.

Reed who was juggling the entire fucking world didn't have the mental capacity to handle his brother who was back in his life after a dozen years. I saw him stiffen.

Alisha and I knew privately? Reed wasn't happy about it. Not because he hated Adam.

I think Reed had come to terms with Adam.

I think he was struggling with his memories of his past.

Something I knew all too well.

When you went through the type of trauma that we did, it was hard to shake it off and move on and say well, it happened so what?

Adam took Lucas out of the room leaving Alisha to move over to Reed and hug him. She knew. Just like I knew. Reed was having a harder time now.

I knew that too.

And I felt sick knowing—the entire reason this was happening?

Was because of me.

CHAPTER 63
ISOBEL

I WAS LOSING MY MIND IN THE GREENWICH HOTEL.

The days began blending together, as I tried to make sense of what I just saw.

Heron Manor used to be my dream.

On my team, Bexley was still playing digital cat-and-mouse with Reed's team.

She could keep people on their toes which was exactly a good way to keep Reed off my back.

Lucas Devereaux was innocent, I figured as much when Bexley and I talked about his father selling him out—and her not seeing Lucy near him but the Titan's. He was with a Titan so it made sense.

Lucy was not innocent. She was working for Reed Whittaker—it had be the only thing that made sense. How else would she get passports? Evade other countries securities?

The only reason Reed Whittaker would take Lucas under his wing—is because he knew about us. He knew something he shouldn't have and he had my necklace. I don't know how I knew—but in my gut it made sense.

Reed Whittaker had power, money, resources, and connections our world valued.

Lucas Devereaux only loved his girlfriend.

Bexley had tracked Reed Whittaker with a woman. Alisha Malhotra. Influencer and model to K2. A building he owned.

He had gone there after leaving the manor. I didn't understand this back and forth. Why did he own so many properties? I was confused and my head hurt and the visit at the Heron Manor left me shaken up.

One day this will be mine.

Liam is working hard...at Titan Security?

I went back to the Primrose. I couldn't breathe through my own emotions. *My necklace...why would Reed take it there?*

Why did he have it? Who was he? *Who was Eva Monroe?*

Who were these people?

I didn't know *what* to do anymore.

I feel like they did mean something, but it was like trying to catch smoke with my hands.

And that's what was so frustrating about being back here, ever since I had left the island I thought it was jet lag, I thought it was me just adjusting to new people, but now I felt like something was off about me.

I felt more lost than ever. And my team?

Bexley was coming down with a cold from all the running around she wanted to do in the colder weather now.

I stopped by Samara's room and she answered uncharacteristically flustered. In her robe and hair askew. Loose, tumbling dark brunette locks as she bat her dark eyes on me.

I know it had been a few days since I checked in on my team, but she looked like she'd been mauled.

"What happened to you? Why do you look nervous?"

She didn't say a word.

"Samara," a deeper man's voice said from inside. "You didn't have to get it."

A man.

With Samara.

Dio Mio. I had seen it all.

"Dio Mio," I whispered feeling more stunned than I could've been. She winced like I'd discovered her secret. "This is what you've been doing?" Or who.

"I promise I explain later. I'm sorry!" She looked so unlike herself. *"Coming, Shane!"*

Shane?

"Babe, is everything okay? You didn't need to get up, I would've gotten it."

He was coming closer. But he couldn't see me. Shane was probably a civilian. Not a part of our world.

"I'm sorry" she whispered fiercely looking panicked. "CIV. I'll explain later."

"Wrong room!" I called out and quickly left shooting her a look.

She looked apologetic and embarrassed turning ten shades of red ducking back in.

What on Earth was happening to my team?

We were supposed to be elite. Strategic. Put-together.

I went back to my room and flopped onto my bed feeling out of it. Bexley was still trying to mess with Reed. But I would bet money she was watching cartoons.

I just had a feeling in my gut. She was nineteen going on nine.

I was nowhere near finding the necklace—in fact since I had gotten here? I had been in chaos. Samara was sleeping with a man. *Shane.*

And I was...flopped on my bed.

What was happening to us?

We were supposed to be put together. Handling business. Doing important things.

And all we had done is flop around.

Did Titan know we were a mess? Dio, I hoped not.

I needed to clean up, shower, take a hot bath and soak my scars. I ordered room service, I turned on my TV knowing Oracle would handle this mess.

I texted Bexley.

> You are doing okay?

Yeah. I automated Oracle to fuck with Reed instead of me.

> Why?

I wanna watch anime. It's nice.

They have so many here. So many cool ones. I go on VPN and I find all the nice ones. Did you know there's a section of anime that is just porn?

Anime.

Porn.

Anime.

Alma.

Yes I do understand this.

I found one about five girls who transform into animals with ears and tails.

Oh and they have wands

Magical

Wands

Like sex wands?

They transform during sex?

No. Like magical wands.

No, it's not an anime with porn.

This is a different anime.

Got it. No porn. Just five girls transforming into...

One is a cat. The other is a manatee.

What is a manatee

A sea animal

Like a beluga

But...bigger

They're friendly and she's green

Manatees are green? This one is brown in the picture.

Insert Manatee Picture

Yeah. But it's a cartoon.

She's green in the cartoon

In her fish form?

No. She's NOT A FISH.

SHE'S A MANATEE PRINCESS.

> If Talia could see me now she would wonder where I went wrong

> I am a manatee princess

Bwahahahahahaha

😂😂😂😂😂😂😂😂😂😂😂😂

No, the other animals are cat, bird, fox, and I think one of them is a monkey

> You are a monkey

> I can see you laughing too hard about this

> Meanwhile I am losing my mind

Back to the show!

They have wands Alma, I want a wand

> I'm sure that's what they're called 😊

Alma.

> Bex.

Alma come on, let's stay here forever.

I hope Reed thinks I'm sophisticated and strategic because I just used that auto function on Oracle so I can eat my pancakes and watch anime.

> You're making sure their network is under attack while eating pancakes?

Yeah? Like it's hard? Oracle's great.

I made her better.

Reed's so serious, his networks solid but every so often I get in there. I think.

> Just make sure you stay on top of it.

413

I don't need him finding out anything about us

YOU GOT IT BOSS LADY

I'm serious

I promise. Reed will never know.

I'm good.

I love American.

I never wanna leave.

They have room service.

All

The

Time

I know I saw the bill

No more pancakes

You're like a neurotic rabbit

Eat some veggies or I send you back to your cave in the island

Poo. Fine

You're no fun

You're not a manatee princess

LOL. No but I am in charge. Eat a vegetable or I can get Thierry to scare you into eating one

Jokes on you, I fucking love Thierry

I felt hysterical laughter bubble up even as a dim memory came to me. In all black.

Jer, stop talking about werewolves.

Sutton, you know better.

I paused in texting Bexley.

Who...

I couldn't think about it for too long since the memory blipped away.

One of my operatives had a man in her room after being celibate for so long I thought she was a nun.

A civilian no less who had no doubt been why she looked adorably messy.

The other eating her way to diabetes with Japanese animation.

And me?

I laid in bed watching a telenovela on the television from twenty years ago as ate ice cream. *This is my life.*

But I can't remember the last time I had a break.

The big bad leader of the black ops organization.

Turning into a hot mess because some gorgeous man stole my necklace.

Now I was here in America, in New York, eating ice cream in my robe day dreaming in my imagination about pale blue eyes. Blonde hair.

If that man found me now? He'd find me in a sad state of a woman.

I felt miserable. Like I brought shame to Talon.

I prayed deep down Titan did not know I was this.

I prayed to whatever was listening to me in the Universe they thought I was fierce. Deadly. Dangerous. And Titan thought we were sophisticated deadly organization and not three women in different directions all eating copious amounts of room service.

No. They would never find out my secrets.

"Deadly, my ass," I whispered at the television over my ice cream.

Not depressed over chocolate cookie dough.

Dio.

What is my life?

My phone beeped with a text from Samara.

> I met this cute guy at the gym. His name is Shane.

> He works for some IT company and goes to school part-time. But he stepped in when there was a creep…he fought him off.

>> You did not need him to fight for you. I know you have knives on you.

Shane didn't know that.

And you brought him home?

Technically it's a hotel...

Samara.

YES. He was SWEET. Normal. HE IS NORMAL.

He brought me flowers that night because he thought I was "shaken up" and hot chocolate, and he said he wanted to take care of me.

I'm so glad you cannot see my face.

"Shaken up." I'm cackling.

He does not know you can eat his soul yet?

No. He doesn't know who I am.

He thinks I'm a tourist visiting my family...

AND IT'S GONNA STAY THAT WAY. THIS IS TEMPORARY.

I need to live. I watched Bexley eat four dozen pancakes. I need TO LIVE.

I didn't know whether to laugh or cry as I flopped onto the bed. What was happening to my team?

Shane is sweet. He's so nerdy and funny. He's just a NORMAL man. When was the last time I got that?

Besides, when we go back to the island—I'll just murder the Kincaide's anyway, it's good...

A knock on the door came before I could respond.

Room service. Bexley was not wrong. This was great. I was having a blast.

"*Coming!*" I opened the door in my robe not thinking anything of it. "*Lo siento—did you come for the—*"

My brain went blank. The words died on my lips.

416

A pair of dark green eyes on the most familiar face to my own watched me. His eyes widened on me.

And I *knew* him. I knew him when he was twelve.

When he was fourteen and gangly and trying to protect me on my bike.

When he was seventeen and he laughed when our father got us dressed up to prom and he realized he liked the look on him.

When we went to college together and worked in IT for a few years building up Oracle.

I felt long nights, early mornings, and laughter when I looked at him.

At the gas station before we went to the CIA.

We never made it there.

"*Isobel?*" His voice cracked.

I took in all six-foot three inches of him looking leaner than I knew him. His eyes haunted. Face crumbling.

No. He couldn't be real. Talia said he died. Years ago.

"*Liam?*"

"*Shortcake, you're alive.*"

CHAPTER 64
ISOBEL

LIAM.

Liam was here, in front of me, his hands gripping my face, eyes wide. His hands shook as he fingered my platinum hair.

"Isa."

His voice broke as he held me like he was afraid I would vanish into the air if he didn't hold on tight enough.

"You...you are alive," I whispered. "You are here?"

He was real.

He was alive.

Why would Talia lie?

Did she even know? In the years that I knew her, she only kept secrets out of everybody else's good.

Every secret she never said, was to protect somebody else. To this day?

I didn't know some of the Talon members came from.

I knew Talia saved them.

Right now, I was shaking so hard, my knees were gonna give out. Liam's face crumbled as he drank me in.

"You're alive, you're alive," he kept repeating it as his lips brushed over my forehead, my cheeks, my lips. Over and over.

"Dio..." he was saying how much he missed me.

How much he needed me. How much he had known in his heart he couldn't live without me.

My vision blurred as my entire body shook. His arms crushing me into his body until I felt my spine would snap into pieces.

"How—how?" He wasn't dead. He was here. He was *real*.

Liam is alive.

"*I thought you were gone,*" his voice cracked and splintered. " I thought you were dead. How did you make it out? Did Kourtney not come after you? I thought she shot you!" His hands roamed over me.

"What?" What was he saying. "How did you find me?"

Liam's lips twisted. "I have Oracle. The original. The fucking powerhouse. Nobody knew. I did though."

"*You are alive.*"

I couldn't stop breaking down, and his eyes were so full of tears. They look like green glass.

"I promised—" he broke off crying. "I promised him. I promised your dad. I failed so fucking hard. I'm so sorry, shortcake."

Something in his eyes shifted as he stamped his lips over mine.

The moment Liam did? Pale blue eyes flashed in my vision.

Him.

I saw someone else.

The man in the mist.

In the years he had been in my life, I always thought he was gentle. He was really sweet. Caring.

Soft.

This was nothing like the Liam I had known.

It wasn't gentle or sweet but desperate. Like he was trying to breathe his soul into mine, inhale me whole. Like he could pour grief and sorrow and shock into this one moment.

"*I'm so sorry.*"

His bigger hands shut the door as he hauled me up to him and I tasted him. Something metallic.

His tongue piercing, the ball a strange sensation compared to— no. I didn't have a comparison.

I tasted salt and Liam. This wasn't my Liam.

Not this desperate and hungry man haunted.

His hands shook and so did mine holding onto him as I accepted it because maybe a part of me needed the human contact.

Something more than me.

Except I didn't feel Liam.

I felt someone else. Him.

Pale blue eyes.

Blonde hair.

I didn't understand it and I didn't know why I craved it. Not because it was him—I was starving for the contact.

Starving. Desperate. Hungry. Ravenous. For heat.

For something.

My heart was trying to pound its way out of my chest.

Pale blue eyes.

Blonde hair.

I can see you.

But not clearly. The man in the mist was there. Telling me to stay away from...Liam?

Why?

I was so confused. I felt the panic threatening to swallow me whole. It was endless.

Each breath was becoming shorter than the last one, and the edges of my vision were turning black.

Something about this moment did not feel right. It wasn't about him, it was about the fact that, even if I thought I wanted it, my body seemed to remember something.

I was hyper ventilating and Liam's eyes went wide on me again.

"Shit, shit shit, I'm sorry, I'm so sorry."

I was in his arms my knees giving out as nothing but blue filled my vision.

Amor?

Alma.

Gabrielle.

Monroe.

Wake up.

Wake the fuck up!

"Nonono, breathe for me. I'm sorry, that was my fault. I'm sorry. I'm sorry, Isobel. Isobel, breathe for me. Breathe, baby."

I was out.

~

I CAME TO SLOWLY. AWARE OF SOMEONE'S HANDS ON MY HAIR, threading their fingers through, rubbing my neck.

"There you are..." his voice was gruff and I blinked slowly to deep green eyes blinking back his emotions. "I'm sorry I freaked you out. I'm sorry." I glanced at him tucking the blanket around me. I was in my bed.

Liam...my Liam, was laying over the comforter, his jacket was also on me keeping me warm. He brushed my hair back.

"I'm sorry," he kept apologizing looking down at me as he wiped his eyes. "I missed you so much. Thought about you every single day. Every single fucking day of my life for the last seven years it was always about you."

His eyes moved to my collarbone. To my scars.

"I didn't know you were alive. I didn't know at all. I never thought I would see you again in this lifetime. I thought I let your family down. After you saved my life? I watched you lose yours."

I had never seen Liam like this.

But I didn't think I knew this Liam. He looked darker than the best friend I had.

"Were you looking for me?" I whispered. His expression turned pained. "How did you know?"

"I didn't know you existed. Not in my wildest dreams. Why are you here?" He brushed my hair back. "How are you here?" His fingers moved over my scars and I flinched away instinctively. "Sorry, I'm sorry I just..."

"It's okay..." Laying there, I broken, totally about waking up in Africa, all places. I saw his horrified expression as I told him. About Talia Nash. About Talon.

"She recruited you?" Liam's voice was a whisper. A horrified one. *"She's Marcus Hagen?"*

I shook my head. "I am now."

I motioned to myself lying there and Liam looked at me like I was an alien. Like I had come from the moon onto Earth.

"It's my company. Talon." I put my hand on my chest. "You are here too. In New York?"

He sputtered. "I have something here. I saw you...in security feeds. I work IT." He looked away shaking. I felt the bed trembling as he laid down next to me like he couldn't sit up anymore. "Holy shit...you're the head of...Malcolm Nash's unit. You're the new... Marcus Hagen..."

"Did you..." he knew about Talia? I saw his hand rubbing his eyes and I saw something there now that his jacket was off.

On his left wrist. It was my name. In large script. He'd gotten me tattooed on his body after he thought I was gone?

421

My heart wasn't going to make it through today.

"I saw you…I saw your uniform. I thought maybe—" he broke off. "I didn't know what to think. But I followed you. I missed you. Every single day. But…" he shook his head looking devastated. "I…have a girlfriend. She's…*wonderful*. Her name is Lara." He looked devastated at that. "I met her that night. That night I died."

Part of me was overjoyed that my best friend who ran away from everything, found a woman he loved enough.

"What do you know? Talia told me she thought you were dead that night? I thought at the gas station during the day. We were going somewhere. To the Agency? What happened?"

As I said it, Liam's face became confused. "What do you mean? Kourtney shot me and then—she said she was going after you—"

"Who is Kourtney?" I shook my head. "You say her name. Do I know her?"

Liam's entire expression blanked out as he followed me up, while I clutched the sheets to me and his jacket. "Isa…

He looked at me and then my eyes.

"What?"

What did he mean what?

"What do you mean what? What happened?"

Something happened then.

Because I had spent years with Talia, I was really good now at looking at people and seeing things that weren't there. At least not to the naked eye.

Something happened in his expression as he watched me.

"What do you mean what happened?" He was quiet now. "What…do you not…what do you remember?"

I told him. The gas station.

"I know you and Papi…Talia said…you were gone…" I shrugged lightly. "That's it. Sometimes I remember flashes or hazy things, but she said I died that night…in the hospital. When I woke up…I didn't know anyone."

I swallowed as his eyes searched mine. His mouth fell open.

"You don't remember *anyone*?" Liam slowly shook his head. "Just me and your father."

I nodded slowly. "Little things in between…like that girl who chased you in high school…"

His lips didn't tip up in a smile.

Instead, he held my face with his hand, his eyes searching mine desperate.

"Talia *knew* you lost your memories and kept you in Cape Verde for years because she said *she was keeping you safe?*" His eyes widened. "Holy *shit*, she's smarter than I ever gave her credit for. Crazy, but smart."

What was he saying?

He frowned then, his eyes going dark. "If you were in Cape Verde, why did you come back to the city? Your cards, your markers are all over the place."

I knew. "My necklace..."

I could tell Liam the truth.

It was Liam.

He was my best friend.

And his face fell slowly as I explained to him that when I woke up Talia, I put all my things aside in a bag. And the necklace was inside of it. I knew it was.

It fell out of me. Lucy. Reed Whittaker.

"He owns Titan Security..." I murmured. "I swear I thought I remembered you talking about it when we were younger. But he looks very young. I don't know the owner of a security company would want my necklace—why do you look like that?"

As I spoke? Liam had paled. More and more.

"All this time...it was the necklace..." he whispered. "All this time."

"I had it," I motioned to my throat. "I wear it. But they took it from me. I came back to find it."

He nodded. "You—you came back for the necklace?" His eyes searched mine again. "*Just* the necklace?"

"It's mine, but I...it has the name Monroe on the back. Do you know who that is? Why did I have it? Sometimes I think I see someone—but he isn't real. You were my best friend, you lived with me...did I have someone in my life? A man?"

As I said it, Liam shook his head closing his eyes. "No, shortcake."

I nodded feeling a little broken looking at my lap. I laid back down.

"I came back to find the necklace..."

Instead I had found my best friend. My adopted brother. Or *he had found me.*

Hang on.

"How—*You* used Oracle to find me?" I looked at him sitting up almost looking around the room. "Can you help me find it? Can you help me find my—"

"Why are you..." he looked around the room landing on my uniform. "You lead Talon now. You came for the necklace and then you leave? For Cape Verde?"

"This is temporary. Why?"

Did I want to stay with him?

The man in the mist. Who is he?

Is he going to find me?

His eyes turned to me desperate again with fire int hem.

"Wherever you go, I'm going. Whatever you need, I'll give you. I was always yours."

And even as he said it I felt the blue eye in my vision.

Amor? The word floated through my mind like smoke, gone before I could catch it.

Liam's mouth turned down. "I love you," he whispered, raw and desperate. "I never want to leave you. Ever. Not a single day in this world. Take me with you. Wherever you go. I'll tell Lara. We can go with you—"

"What?" I shook my head. "You would leave your entire life—you have a life—a woman—"

"*None of it matters.*" Liam looked scary then. Darkness in his eyes. "None of this life ever mattered without you. I tell Lara about you. She knows you were my whole soul. I lost you once. After I promised your father the day he died—I would stand by you. I would make you happy. I would be there for you until the end. Do you know what the fuck it did to me? To know that you were bleeding out—cold—without me? Without knowing anything?" His face crumbled. "I don't care what you need...I'll help you get whatever you want. Whatever you want. And then I'm going with you. I'm by your side. Forever."

He held out his pink. "You are my love. You are my entire world. I'm never losing you again. Remember? I *promise.*"

I nodded shaking unsure of what was in the room with me then. "Promise." I linked my pinky with his.

Amor...

He wiped his eyes and then held me tight to him.

I didn't find the necklace. But I found him.

That was a win in a way, right?

Except now I had more questions than answers. And more unease rippling through me when those blue eyes appeared in my sight again.

His words floated to the surface.

Amor?

I was his. I knew it.

Because Liam in all his desperation never called me those words.

Amor?

And privately...I wondered if Liam was protecting me like he always had.

Or if I was losing more of myself.

PART THREE | THE MOON GODDESS

CHAPTER 65
GABRIEL

"Liam is your brother-in-law. Isobel may be alive?"

"Thank fuck Koller is dead," Reed muttered looking away like he wanted to kill him for me. "I didn't know about Liam. I'm sorry. I didn't—"

"I know." I held out a hand my voice gruff as Alisha hands shook in her lap. She was crying quietly.

"Liam was in love with her," Reed's eyes were pained. "Jesus, he knows about the Talon card. The marker. I had to show him because I thought that if anything happened, he should know. You guys didn't talk so I didn't think anything of it. I didn't even know... Lucy...he told me was tracing her steps back."

He probably was. He was good at what he did.

"This company..." Reed looked at his hands. "I fixed Liam's blueprints."

I nodded.

My eyes drifted to the skyline of New York.

Half of Reed's living room overlooked the Hudson River.

Right now, the skyline was lit up, the pitch black night and lights glittering.

I focused on that in the feminine space that Alisha and Reed had created all around me with creme couches and so much color.

I focused on that.

"And you know it's the same unit who took Isobel."

Reed looked out the window looking like he was regretting every choice he made.

"I sent Lucy on a suicide mission. What the fuck am I supposed to do now? I thought it was another necklace..."

I nodded. "My fault too. It's all my fault. I didn't know how to let you in. I didn't know what to do."

Reed looked the and I saw his red his eyes were. "You didn't tell me? All these years...you looked for her? *I could've done something for you—*"

"No," I shook my head remembering those dead bodies Koller showed me. "These guys were good. Malcolm Nash was scary. He already knew about us. The more that people knew? The more dangerous it was."

Malcolm Nash would've butchered Reed.

Alisha made a noise as I said it and Reed's worried eyes landed on her.

"It's okay, Angel. Nothing's gonna happen to us."

Reed, unbeknownst to most people while kind? Was usually colder like me.

It explained why they worked.

I didn't say a word about her to Reed.

I told them about Selena, Evie, Isobel. Reed had moved next to us with curiosity and horror in his eyes as one word after another left me.

Until I was pouring it out. Desperately latching onto something.

"What would you have done had you not found her...at the end of your journey?" Alisha's eyes were on her lap. Her lower lip wobbled. She clutched the pillow to her.

She didn't look at me.

I didn't answer her.

And after a moment she nodded covering her face as she sniffled.

In that moment—I knew she was nothing like my wife.

Isobel was fire.

She would fight anything if she could, because she'd been raised by a family that believed in it.

She challenged, she met darkness head on, and she was a fighter at heart. I had loved that and valued that at twenty-four.

She matched me. At the time it was exactly what I needed.

Our love felt like a wildfire—uncontrollable, unstoppable, and ultimately killing everything in it's path.

By contrast? Alisha was nothing like that. She was a cupcake.

Warm honey. She didn't need to fight.

She didn't exist in a world where she had to. She just lit up a space with her laughter and food and warmth.

That's why Reed fell for her. Her warmth. It was like the sun.

Where Isobel challenged, Alisha soothed.

Where she fought back, Alisha met at the middle.

Where she wanted to help me, Alisha accepted me as I was—in all my forms.

And created a space for me to exist in her life.

I wasn't a moron. The only reason I was still in her life and Reed's? Was because of her. Reed had tried to kill men for looking at her?

Kissing her was a fucking felony to him and he hadn't raised a hand to me.

But right now? She didn't look at me she just looked devastated as she stood abruptly her hair covering her face.

"I need a second."

And she was up and off the couch with Reed staring after her. He looked away out the window as he sat back on the couch.

I was surprised he didn't go after her.

"Aren't you—"

"You know she tells me everything. Since the day I met her, she tells me everything. " His eyes focused on the window not me. Carefully neutral and composed. *"Everything."*

My heart dropped to my stomach.

"We talk about you a lot."

Shit.

"Reed—"

"She did tell me about that day in the car." Reed's jaw was clenched. "She cried a lot over you. She always cries over you. Says she feels like her heart is breaking when she interacts with you." He shook his head like he was processing it too. "And now Liam…"

My face fell.

"She's not Isobel."

"Oh, I know." His eyes widened like he was mock-surprised. "I know she isn't. They're not even remotely the same person. Besides the minor facial structure aside, I didn't think you were scummy enough to hang out with *my* girl daydreaming about *yours."*

"No." I shook my head. I wasn't scummy enough for that.

Reed's eyes looked at me. "So when Lucas thinks she's sleeping with you—it's because he sees what *I knew."* I paled.

"Reed, I'm sorry—"

"And so does she."

What?

Reed's intelligent eyes stayed on me his smile lethal.

"Imagine my surprise when Alisha realizes that relationships like that are real and normal?"

Reed said it casually.

"I already knew *what* kind of Dom Lucas was. He's friends with Matteo and Kieran. Those two are like fire and gasoline together. Lucas has a space in De Nuit—" A growl built in me. *"Not* that he uses it. Now that he's with Evie. I think he's good."

Reed looked a little amused at me.

"He's good. Breathe. You're turning red."

He sighed leaning back at my expression. I was quiet. I didn't know what was coming out of his mouth. I mean…maybe I did. But I wasn't about to fuck it up.

"So Lish talks to me about it. She realizes if you were attracted to her, and if *I* was cool with it—she realized in that moment she wouldn't be *opposed* to it."

He smirked at my expression as he let it sink in.

I was pretty sure my brain stopped working at what he said.

"Wuh."

I needed words. Any kind of word would be good. But nothing left my mouth.

Reed was grinning now at my discomfort.

"Most of what you said? Lish and I had already guessed it. Like I said, we talk about you a lot." He shrugged lightly. "But I realized on the way back from Greenwich, she told me about you. Again."

My stomach soured. Despite knowing what he said.

He wouldn't—she wouldn't be opposed to it.

"I realize that if anything were to happen to me in this entire process, there was only one person I trusted her and Avani with, and it was you. You love her as much as I love her. You could be a partner and not the enemy."

I would…wait what?

At my expression he laughed low now. "So we talked. I remember her saying clearly that if she saw something beyond you seeing Isobel—"

"I don't see Isobel in her."

"But Alisha didn't know that." He looked at me. "You stare at her like that, and she thinks all you see is your wife. Meanwhile, I know you're just a weirdo. You stare at anything like that. With your freaky ass eyes. Don't pout, you're weird as fuck."

I looked away offended. "I don't have freaky eyes—"

"They're a little scary. Have you seen yourself in the dark? No? You should try. You scare everyone." He chuckled looking amused and younger despite the stress.

"But when I realized what she said in the car, how you were with her, how you dropped by at the hospital all the time when *we both know* you'd rather shoot your own foot then be caught in public—"

This is true.

He leaned back again with a humorless smile on his face.

"She wants to talk to you about it. This was pre-mature."

I didn't know he knew the entire time.

He smiled softly. "She does tell me everything. Every. Single. Thing. And for that I'm always grateful. But she also wanted us to wait because she didn't want you to feel like we were taking you in at a vulnerable time. But I feel like this is the right time to tell you."

His eyes met mine.

"About…"

I felt like I understood what he was saying, but I thought he was speaking in tongues. My brain, refused to process what he was saying.

His eyes met mine. "She wants *you* to be with *us."*

He motioned between us.

"Me and her. *And* you. To heal. To move on. To calm down. To grow up. I'm telling you this as your best friend. Before you start to spiral listen to me—" he broke off motioning to himself all pretenses gone.

"If Isobel is alive, which she *might* be, she's not the same Isobel *you* lost. *She's gone.* Just like the version of you at twenty-four years old. *You are not the same man."*

His eyes were hard as he watched me.

432

"I know what you have been pining for *seven fucking years*. I am telling you right now—you need to let her go. For real."

He might as well have punched me.

"Look at me. The Isobel you might find at the end is not your wife. She is not your wife."

Reed and I sparred often. Enough for me to know he kept up with me somehow. But right now?

It felt like he was delivering blow after blow to my insides.

"Alisha and I have tried to brainstorm every single conceivable thought about *why* Isobel *might* be alive. What condition her head is in. Her body. Why did she stay away for this long? I know you thought about all of this too. And I know you've driven yourself and everyone around you to madness. I was worried about you. *That's why I didn't get angry when you kissed Alisha. I knew—*" he broke off shaking his head in frustration.

"Liam lost his legs, he lost his identity, his life, his car, his family, his father, *Isobel*," Reed listed it off on his fingers. "I can't even fucking hate Liam right now. I know *why* Liam's in the dark. Now it makes sense why he's with Lara."

"He doesn't love Lara," I nodded. "He loves the idea of her."

"I know."

He loved his past. The golden age when he was capable, loved—whole.

Lara was the woman he met the night he died.

Reed leaned back. "I won't stop that train. When it hits the fan, Liam's going to dig himself into his grave."

And we would take care of Lara.

I didn't like the idea of Lara finding that out.

"Isobel was Liam's savior," Reed whispered. "Now, his cane, his life—it's a *vortex* of trauma and hurt. He won't reach out to *anyone*. He doesn't know *how* to because he's never done it. Isobel found him. *You* need to realize Liam cannot form connections. *You can. You've always been able to. You might've called him your brother once? He isn't your family anymore."*

Reed was going to be hard on me.

I could tell.

He always was.

"Listen to me," Reed pointed at himself. "You lost *everything*. You lost your wife. You lost your baby. *I'm sorry*. But you did *something* about it. I know you have the capacity to grow. But over the last seven years you have lived in your *past*. Just like Liam."

That one hurt.

"When you find whatever is at the end of the journey, you cannot be the same man who *started* this journey. Best case? It's Isobel looking for the necklace. She still loves you. She remembers she lost her baby. And you. We *still* have to explain *why* she was gone for seven years Malcolm Nash aside. He's dead. If he was holding her hostage? Why hasn't she found you? So *worst case*, it's not *her*." He shook his head looking remorseful as he said it. "It was *never* her. It was Talia Nash playing some demented game. And Isobel is dead."

As he said it I swallowed because nobody spoke to me like Reed did.

My heart sank.

"No matter what, Lish and I agreed on one thing. The outcome of this might not be *anything* good—and you? Are not prepared for the outcome. You can't make it through a day without moping. Without existing in the past. You have to move on. I know it hurts. It's gonna fucking kill you—but I'd rather see you live for another day, when you wake up and realize that you might not get what you want. I don't wanna lose you. I won't."

I'd rather see you live another day.

You might not get what you want.

I don't want to lose you.

His words were knives shattering the ice in my soul, around my heart, around my body that was there from losing my old life.

I had been living in my past. I had been holding onto it so tight, I didn't know how to move on.

I was young. I had been a child. If it had been Evie, I never would've blamed her for anything. I would've told her she was really young, and she was put into an impossible situation.

But I never gave myself the same grace.

The same love.

I just hardened by heart, iced out, and lived in a world where I was dying slowly with my love for my wife. My dead wife.

Reed's eyes were softer now sympathetic and I knew he'd been emotional too.

"Alisha isn't the same woman I met three years ago, she changes all the time. So do I. Everything I learned was from her."

His eyes met mine hard and years of memories passed through me.

"We already knew when you found what you wanted to. If you found a shell or a body? I knew you were going with her. Alisha and I knew. We talked about it."

He leaned back watching me with colder eyes.

"Imagine my surprise when Lish says to me *'what if we gave him something to stick around for?' What if we gave him an option. A choice.*"

I felt like he was strangling me. "Jesus—"

"That's what I said," he looked unimpressed with me. "She was talking about it in *all* ways. As in you live with us, you become my family, and in return, we will help you look for your wife."

What...

If he kept punching me I wasn't going to live.

"However long it takes. *Whatever* it entails. Even if the person on the other end isn't your wife." He motioned to Alisha's spot. *"You* need to finish this conversation with Alisha—I know she wants to hear you say what I know—but Alisha and I are offering you a safety net. At the end of your road when you hit your wall, I don't wanna lose my brother. Alisha and I want to offer you a safe place. A home. A family. *A life.* A better life than the one you have been suffering through on purpose. We think you need love, to grow up, to move on, to find your peace—so when you find what you don't expect? You don't flip out. You come home. To her. To me. To us."

I thought I might explode. That was it.

"Lish and I are worried you're gonna blow your brains out if you don't find your wife remembers you."

Reed didn't mind his words.

"Lish and I also think whatever version of this woman you're going to find might not be the one you knew years ago. Whatever she is," Reed's voice was calmer now. "But it doesn't matter who she is now. What matters is at the end of the day—when you reach the end of your rope—"

"I don't cut it off."

"Exactly."

"I come home—"

To her. To me. To us.

As in—them. A family.

"And she—" I whispered it.

Alisha wanted this?

435

He nodded at my unasked question in my eyes.

All these years he knew things before I said it and I understood him at his core.

"When you kissed her all those months ago, I was gonna kill you. If you were anybody else you would be bleeding out in the basement of Midtown."

"But you let me walk—"

"Because I love you too," his eyes held mine. "You're my family. I would do *anything* for you. And you shut me out to save *my* life? Is that what you thought you were doing? Liam isn't your family anymore. I *am*."

He didn't hate Adam.

No. He just hated every single time he looked at Adam, he remembered the lowest points of his life.

Just like I did with Liam.

Reed understood it all as I spoke.

"I *respect* Liam's technical abilities. But he's as bad as Nate. Liam and Nate both wallow in their misery. As though it defines them. Nate never moved on from Gemma. I know he loves her. But his love for Gemma destroyed everything else in the process. Liam? He needed to let Isobel go. He needed to move on. When he hurts Lara, because you and I both know the only reason casualty for Liam is going to be Lara—I will make sure Killian is there to help her."

And that Aidan hunts Liam down and out.

Because whether Liam was aware of it or not—I was fully aware of the O'Hara's backing every single thing Lara did.

Whether the world knew or not.

Because it was inevitable if Liam hurt her? Everyone else would come after him. I wouldn't need to do a thing.

Reed nodded looking at me. I didn't even need to tell him anything, he knew me so well. He already knew what I was thinking.

"You started a company, saved her sister, buried her mother, kept her legacy, and his Legacy. You preserved their IT work, you protected *everyone*—for *both* of them."

Reed held my gaze.

"You did that. Liam is an idiot. You *saved* Evie, Selena, Nate, and me. None of Titan would be possible without *you*. And in turn, you saved every single O'Hara, you saved Lara—Liam has Lara because of you. *He's had Evie who is technically his baby sister more than yours.*

Something he couldn't do with all the powers of Oracle in the past, you took in Evie. You honored your wife by giving Evie Oracle. You honored her. Not Liam."

I never thought about it like that.

Not once.

Evie had no idea she was talking to technically her real sibling in Liam.

"Evie asked me if I would be friends with Liam—"

"She had no fucking clue who he was—"

"No." Liam wouldn't tell her. Because he couldn't even say Isobel's name. But I could. I could. I just didn't—do it.

Reed ticked it off with his fingers looking pissed off. "Liam has spent the last seven years as an alcoholic and drug-addict, selling software programs to the highest bidder and making cold cash. He's comfortable. He didn't need the job at Titan. I thought having him would help you and me. It has. He's been fucking fantastic. But *it's not the same. You loved her. She's your entire heart. Out there. Somewhere. He wanted her like a possession to prop up on his mantle. There's a difference."*

"Hypothetically if you found Isobel—*and she had no fucking clue who you were? It would gut you alive?* You look at your wife in the future, and you tell her you love her, you missed her, you kept her memory alive in your heart—and she says, *'I don't know you.'* Yeah that would gut me alive if Alisha lost her memories of me. I imagine it would do the same."

It would.

Reed delivering this seemed apt. It was tearing through my lungs as he said it. *"I know you. Alisha knows you."*

She wanted me a part of her home.

Her family.

"You have nothing to atone for. Not anymore. It's time you stop being a dead man. It's time you understand you turned thirty-*one.* You're not the same boy you were. Not even close. You didn't make a mistake. Liam convinced Isobel to join the CIA. You were six months older than Evie. If Evie fucked up in the Agency right now? Would you blame her?"

"No." I would *never.* "It's not her fault, she was too young—"

"Then why blame yourself?"

Reed kept going like he wasn't slicing me open.

"It's not—"

437

Alisha wasn't my wife. She never would be. And I would never love Alisha or any other woman the way I loved Isobel.

Ever.

The words that left me though were not the ones I expected.

"You didn't kill your wife, Gabriel. But *someone* did. Something took her that night, and whoever is in the city right now wants a piece of that necklace for some fucking reason they still have it. And whatever is inside of it—Lucy never got the key. So I know something's in there."

My wife's wedding ring.

"You have done the world for everyone. You never expect anything in return."

"Alisha—" I broke off. "She knows it's *not* about Isobel?"

"I think that's *why* you have to talk to her. I guessed but I didn't know until you said it. She might need that too. What are you going to do about Liam?"

He wasn't the only one putting off talking to his brother. Except now that Reed had hit me with all this?

I felt something more than guilty and shame.

I felt resentment. Reed sensed it.

"He didn't speak to you for seven years. He didn't ask if you were good. He's been here in the city for a while. And Alisha would argue sure, you could've gone to him—but you lost your wife. You lost your daughter. Who the fuck comforted you? You got up, and you left everything behind—"

"And I began Titan."

"And Liam became an alcoholic. His old girlfriend Sutton, Claire? She's married now to a nice normal man and she says she tried—"

"Claire's solid—"

"But she said he was getting worse when she left him—"

I swallowed.

I got that. Liam had been in the city for a while. I knew he was with Lara. She came to see me about him. She was worried and I didn't know how to tell her I was guilty for killing the guy's sister.

I didn't murder my wife—but some days some nights—it always felt like my fault.

Not only that, but Liam saw everything that I had done. And he didn't say a word to me. Because he was stuck in the past, in his own hatred of me, that he refused to see it.

I felt like…something exploded in my chest.

All the ice in me cracked open.

Revealing layers I had buried under me. I blinked rapidly like I just woke up from a deep sleep. I felt synapsis in my brain, snapping, like electricity crackling through my veins.

I felt like this conversation with Reed woke me up. It was exactly what I had needed for seven fucking years.

Because come hell or high water I was going to be with my wife.

And I was going to find Isobel no matter what.

CHAPTER 66
ISOBEL

"You look different now."

Liam had become a part of my life at the Primrose. He filled me in on Lara over dinners and he asked me careful questions about my life.

"You are different too," I murmured over the dinner table.

We had come downstairs. Me with my platinum hair. Liam, quieter and reserved as he took me in with his cane.

I had missed his cane.

He thought the woman who shot him wanted to make him suffer longer than death. So she'd shot his legs.

I had known cruelty. So had Talia.

I recognized Liam had sold his car because driving had hurt him. His car that he worked all summer to afford the downpayment on.

He couldn't ice-skate anymore. He couldn't do karate. Nothing.

This Liam spent twenty hours at his desk working and building himself up because disability didn't cover for all his expenses.

I cried a lot over this Liam, the same he cried when he saw my injuries.

"I think we both died in different ways," I spoke over the din of the cutlery against our plates and Liam met my eyes over his wineglass.

He drank a lot more now too. I remember when we were

younger Liam wouldn't go near alcohol. Now? He seemed to carry a flask, he drank wine all the time. Even for lunch.

But he seemed steady and stable to me.

Leaning on his cane when he needed to. He was still muscled so I knew it didn't hurt him. But it was painful watching it.

I hadn't spoken to my team in a few days. Not Samara. Not Bexley. I texted them but I didn't know how to look at them.

Not because I was angry with them or because I stopped searching for the necklace. But because after finding out Talia lied to me. For some fucking reason—I didn't even know what to say.

Some part of me shattered.

"You died," he said calmly. "I was awake the entire time." His eyes went darker than hunter green now. "I remember everything."

I did die. I nodded understanding that Talia hadn't been wrong. Losing my memories had been a blessing. I had come back a different person.

Liam noticed it. I wasn't the sister he had.

The girl who shared a room with him growing up. I didn't understand his jokes or tease him.

I kept to myself a lot for seven years and became someone different.

I was determined to heal.

I was determined to get better no matter what. I was going to crawl out of my own grave if I had to make it in this world. But I would.

"It's good you don't remember," he said softer than before, his eyes on mine filled with something unreadable. "It's good you forgot about your pain and started over from scratch. I can't even be mad. I missed you, but I'm glad you're here."

Because Liam had been alive, suffering, and struggling and so had I. My heart had been weaker so I couldn't go to him.

I had healed.

Part of me wondered if Talia knew or if his death was the only public information she had.

"I didn't know anything," I filled him in.

Talia hadn't had Oracle then.

But she had the power to shut off the grid. I didn't know if she knew. If she assumed. If she chose not to tell me.

If she believed if never looking back.

I was angry with Talia for keeping secrets from me.

And I needed to go talk to her but only when I cooled down.

Only when I had drank in enough of Liam to satiate the part of me that had missed him.

"Talia probably had an inkling," he said. "But it sounds like she disobeyed her father directly every single time. It sounds like she kept secrets. You said she was with Andrei DuPont and Malcolm threatened to kill him?"

Liam frowned as I nodded. "That's interesting because as of three years ago, Andrei DuPont doesn't have many photos of him and he keeps to himself. Nobody knows if he's with someone or not. If Natasha killed Malcolm because Talia was pregnant—"

"Talia was keeping secrets from everyone." I finished because it sounded like her. She had chosen to be with Andrei after her father threatened him. "To protect them?"

He shrugged lightly. "She didn't tell her father about the man she loved, I entertained that if her father ordered her to kill someone? And she kept them alive? He would never let her live it down. I don't know. I don't like her very much for keeping you from me." His lips twisted up wryly, his eyes amused on me. "I'm glad you're back in my life."

I smiled over at him. "You are drinking more now."

He nodded with a humorless smile. "I needed it." He changed the subject. "I haven't told Lara about you. But I want to. I want us both to come with you when you go. After I help you that necklace back from Reed."

He had told me he would. He would help me get it back and we would leave together.

As a family still. Even if I wasn't the same woman? I was his family.

"I would love to meet her, I never thought I'd see the day where you fell in love."

Come find me.

I've been waiting for you.

The words whispered into my ear and I looked over my shoulder. Nothing was there.

I was losing my mind. Liam's eyes softened.

A new emotion entering his eyes as he let out a shuddering breath.

"Yeah, me too," his voice was soft and somber. "Me too. Listen, I gotta get going."

Liam did his own IT thing he said. He didn't mind walking away from all of it.

"When will you tell Lara you want to come with me?" I asked him as he stood with his cane. The image of the boy that I used to know, with the man he became was jarring.

He shrugged lightly looking uneasily at me. "I'm figuring it out."

It was with that mindset, I checked on Bexley fighting a cold now with anime marathons and somehow a cleaner room. She coughed up at me, brushing her hair back.

"Thierry came by," she murmured, her eyes a little watery. "To see me. He took care of my room and got me veggies. Samara said she went looking for you too. She told me about her boyfriend."

I smiled softly. Bexley and Samara had been solid stable figures for me to focus my attention on.

They didn't even know my name.

Talia had protected me. I was still angry with her.

"Do you know where Talia lives?" I asked Bexley. She shook her head slowly.

"Talia never told anyone to protect Andrei. I can look up some of his properties and get you a list to check out. She's more private than anyone."

Because Malcolm had tried to kill Andrei.

Did Talia protect me from someone trying to kill me?

"Bex," I kept my voice low sitting at the edge of her bed. I knew it was wrong to reach out to her like this when she was sick but I had to know. "Where did Talia get you from?"

"A farm." Bexley murmured muting her anime shows her eyes a little softer and no doubt fuzzy from her flu. "I was twelve. I was on a holiday with my family. And this man picked me up and took me away from my Mom when she went to the restroom."

My heart clenched as she slowly said it.

"You were...kidnapped?"

I always thought Bexley was a part of Talon.

On the compound. One of us.

I sometimes forgot we all came from somewhere.

Bexley nodded slowly. "Not by Talia. She wouldn't hurt anyone if she could help it." Big blue eyes glanced at me. "Sometimes I think her father made her who she is, but deep down Talia is just..."

"A mother."

A mom to her kid. Andrei's wife.

Sometimes I wondered if the Talia I knew was who she was.

"Sometimes," Bexley smiled. "I don't remember much but I know that when Talia found me, I was in a farm. A barn. I was chained to the wall and the girl next to me was asleep. Talia was visiting with Duke, her old IT guy in South Africa. She found me there." Her eyes were downcast and sad. "Talia saved my life."

I swallowed at that thought. "She found you."

Bexley nodded. "She found Samara. All of us. I know things too. But she doesn't tell anyone anything so I don't know much about Samara. I know she's got scars on her back. I just know we all came from somewhere and she made us a home."

I didn't know how to feel about that.

"Do you think…" I broke off unsure of what to say.

I never went to Bexley like this but now? I needed something to lean on.

"Do you think Talia would lie to you about your past?"

"I know she did," Bexley wheezed out coughing a little, her South African accent unclear to my own words. Thicker. "Talia told me she found me in someone's house. She told me my parents were gone. But they weren't. I looked it up years ago. They had been searching for me and they found out I had been sold to traffickers. My parents couldn't handle that and my mom killed herself. Talia found me months later. She told me both of my parents died in an accident so I wouldn't know that."

I felt the words hit me sentence after sentence delivered with a physical blow to my chest over and over.

"Were you…" she blinked up at me. "Did Talia tell you something about your old life?"

I nodded dumbly. For nineteen years old she was wiser than I gave her credit for. Most of the time she was a silly girl but now her anime appreciation and love of pancakes…simple things took on a different meaning for me. I felt my eyes blur.

"Years ago, Talia told me not to go back to my past," Bexley whispered blinking her emotions back. "She taught me you might not like what you find when you go back."

I didn't know what to say.

Because the other half was—you might not like yourself when you find your past again.

Come find me.

There it was. That voice. I didn't know who he was.

Pale eyes. Blonde hair.

He was driving me insane. He came to me all the time.

I felt like my heart was seeking something.

And he was right there.

Right there.

And I—I couldn't see him.

"Some secrets aren't meant to be spoken," she whispered it now unable to talk normally wiping her eyes. "If Talia kept something from you? It's because she knows it would destroy you if you found out."

But at the same time...Talia was with Andrei.

Which meant she had still gone back to her past.

That didn't explain why she was keeping mine from me.

I needed answers.

"I'll look through the list of Andrei's homes whenever you're better."

CHAPTER 67
GABRIEL

"Well, that went like shit."

I was in K2 again slumped at the marble counter with Reed and Alisha's worried expressions.

Reed was putting out fires with Nathan's charge Gemma Marchand and now this bombshell dropped on us.

Alisha sat on Reed's lap, raven hair pulled up high into a bun and wisps framing her face, hazel eyes filled with worry. Reed kept working around her but I noticed lately, the last few days, they'd been all over each other.

I hadn't slept with her. No. I stayed in the guest room. As company.

Because my heart was always on Isobel. It was complicated. I loved my wife. Always.

But Reed was giving me something new. Another love. One that didn't burn into my skin. One that felt like coming home and peace.

One that didn't destroy me like mine had.

I wasn't sure what Isobel I would find.

Reed knew me better than I knew myself sometimes.

~

I did confront Adam about Lucy.

The meeting had already confirmed what we suspected.

He knew exactly where Lucy was and she was safe. With him.

I was annoyed. More than anything else.

Adam and Lucy were young. She was twenty-four. He was twenty-five. And together they made sense when I broke it down—two people focused on outrunning their past.

Lucas hadn't spoken to his sister in forever.

He just found out with Titan, Lucy had worked for Reed. He had no clue.

And Reed hadn't spoken to Adam since he hired Adam to Titan a few months ago letting Liam onboard the guy.

The comparison now was fitting.

Reed did empathize with Liam not being able to talk to me in some ways.

It didn't mean it wasn't annoying.

"I had a suspicion about her. She knows to contact you when she's not okay. I don't know why she didn't. She has everything possible to do so but I feel she's like Liam. She laments about her life, her past and she uses it as an excuse," I said this.

"You didn't like her family," Reed murmured looking upset with me too his stormy eyes brimming with emotion. "She *does* know to contact me. But she also has been alone a lot so she's probably scared."

"I saw her," Alisha admitted to me. "She didn't know what to do."

"But that's not your fault. That's hers. She's worked for Reed for three fucking years. She knew better. She didn't just ask Reed for help?" I held Alisha's gaze. "That's exactly why she's Liam. If she told us the truth that day? We could take action. Half of the reason why we are constantly in the dark, is because people use their trauma to hide the truth."

Alisha's stood so she would match my height then.

"Indeed, but it's safe to assume while Lucy may be fine, Adam is upset with us. Both of them might feel betrayed. Just like you did. You kept your secrets because you didn't feel safe. Is it possible Lucy did not feel safe?"

She held her ground with me her brows furrowed.

"Honey, she's a thief." I told Alisha's soft hazel eyes. "If she wanted safe she should've been librarian. If it's not Reed sending her into a dangerous job, then it's her landing herself in Colombian jail. Does everyone forget she's been *imprisoned* in foreign countries until Reed got her out?"

"He didn't know how to—" Alisha stood up to her full height glaring me down.

I held my ground with her. I couldn't spar physically with Alisha...I mean not like *that*. But she was hot even when she was pissed.

"Adam had lunch with you," I told her. "His brother runs a security firm, he could've asked—"

Alisha shot back fire in her eyes. "He's young, he's terrified—"

"He's *your* age—"

"He's not used to this life—"

"She sure as fuck is. She's always in danger, Lish. This isn't her first rodeo. Lucy Devereaux is a wanted convict in most countries under ninety aliases. Reed is the only reason she's alive and well today. And If Adam is dumb enough to believe that Reed is the enemy and he won't tell us? Then he's dumber than I thought he was."

Alisha growled at me until she was nose to nose. "Oh, would you get a load of yourself. They're young."

"Doesn't mean they're not dumb—"

"I thought better of you—"

"Honey, I'm still a demon. *You* might calm me down. But you put the right brand of idiot in front of me? Even the best of me would snap." I eyed my best friend who frowned at both of us. "I'm still me."

Alisha looked furious with both of us and her lips twitched.

She knew I was right.

Lucy Devereaux might think Reed put her in danger, but her entire job was danger.

If not for Reed? I had no doubt Lucy would've died a long time ago. In a Cambodian jail. Starving.

Miserable.

"I hate that you're right about everything you said," she whispered. "I feel for Adam."

I know. But she loved me. "That's why Reed and I love you."

And I loved verbal sparring with Alisha.

I held out my arm and tugged her into them, letting her sit on my lap as Reed sighed.

Reed looked at us with a dry expression while I brushed Alisha's hair back.

"Liam tracked a woman with Adam everywhere she went. Everywhere he went. And that's how he found out it might've been her. Which means he has some idea. You said it yourself—he wasn't shocked by anything you said."

"No," I shook my head as Alisha frowned at me. "Don't look at me like that, Lish."

"It's just cruel," she softened. "He's been nothing but sweet to me. I know he wants to connect with Reed." I saw Reed stiffen visibly at that. "He was just a boy too. I feel for him. I do."

When I confronted Adam at Midtown, he didn't confirm it but his body language did. I knew Adam had been abused by his father too. Not just Reed.

I felt for Adam. But I also knew when he was being protective of his girl over nothing.

"Adam is probably heartbroken." Her eyes looked at Reed. "Darling, I know you're tired but you really cannot keep up this."

Reed said looking grim as his stormy eyes met mine and then hers. "I don't know what to say to him. What if he blames me for his girlfriend? It is my fault."

"No, it's not," I shook my head. "If she stole from the crown prince of a nation or she stole from Talon? Her life was always at risk. Lish, I know you adore Adam, I know how much he tugs at your heart. I know he reminds you of Avani. But he is not Avani. He's dating a woman who is probably wanted in twenty-five countries and has nineteen passports. If he wanted safe he should've found someone else. *Not a wanted criminal.*"

Alisha looked dejected at that but I just cuddled her closer.

"She put herself in danger every single job she did."

I explained that Lucy Devereaux was an heiress on paper.

As in—she didn't have to steal anything. She chose to. She chose it for excitement, to belong, for the thrills.

Not because she had *no* choice.

"You were wrong," I looked at Reed. "I didn't take her in as a Titan because she was a Devereaux, no, that's beside the point. I never took her in because I only took in people with no choice."

"That's not true," Alisha countered. "You took in Kellan."

"Kellan would *die* for Selena, he's got a good track record. He's a team player. That's why Reed trusted him with you. He would've taken a bullet for you." I explained calmly feeling calmer the longer she snuggled into me. "He's been loyal to Reed before. He was vetted. Lucy is loyal to no one. She never has been. She's a solo operative. She's not a team-mate. And I can't have liabilities on my team."

"I *did* think about taking Lucy into my team. I thought about making her Shane's partner. And then I kept imagining Shane dead because Lucy likes to risk it all. I can't have that in a Titan. None of my guys are like that."

I looked at Reed who looked confused. "You debated taking Lucy onto the team?"

Reed explained. "I'm not a fucking moron. I knew you were watching her. I found Isobel's necklace from her random Africa visits. I'm not saying she's an idiot. But she's a billionaire on paper. She doesn't need to steal."

"Lucy is a billionaire?" Alisha blinked. "Why was that never mentioned."

"Probably because her wealth comes from everyone else who doesn't know she took it," Reed murmured. "Lucy's been stealing for years."

I added in the net worth the Devereaux's had while trying to get to her skin. Combined with Lucy's money in off-shore accounts. Combined with their old money assets.

Lucy was more than comfortable.

"Like I said, Lish. She steals for fun. Not because she has to. She can quit whenever she wants." Which led me to my next point. "I think she's a liability."

I watched Reed take me in then all amusement gone. "You think Lucy or Talon will try and break into K2?"

"I do. I don't know who. But I know they won't see me coming."

Reed tipped his head. "For the necklace they think is here."

"The fake." I added. I wore the real one on occasion. "Which means you're vulnerable." I looked down at Alisha turning progressively red.

"But I think *someone's* going to try something in K2."

Reed frowned. "Stephanie reported a woman trying to rent the apartment below ours."

Alisha's jaw dropped. "Lucy?"

"I fucking told you guys. She's busy," I finally found the damn zipper. Why was everything hidden on her?

Reed shook his head. "Let it play out. I'd like to see what she does and how she does it. It's on the left, G. It's the left side."

Ah, found it.

Alisha blinked at both of us bemused. "You two are going to toy with Adam? Gabriel, don't rip that."

"I'm trying not to," I muttered.

"Angel, if it get's us the answers we need?" Reed eyed us more entertained than anything else. "I think we're down to let them think we don't know anything. As of right now? I think I found who Thierry DuPont is. It leads us closer to finding out what he's doing in the city. My gut tells me he's important. Not Lucy. My priority isn't keeping her safe. She's done a solid job so far. The sooner we find out where Talon is hiding?"

"The sooner we get to the bottom of this."

You could never make somebody do something they didn't want.

Like Liam talking to me. Or Reed overcoming his fear of seeing his step-father who tried to kill him years ago.

I knew why Alisha was worried Reed and Adam would fight each other. I knew already they would.

Because if I got my hands on Liam right now?

I would kill him.

CHAPTER 68
ISOBEL

Ever since I got to New York my dreams were driving me insane.

Talia always said, because of my head injury and dying, she wasn't surprised I was more in touch with the in between of two worlds.

Over the years I did my research.

I wasn't insane.

But I felt insane.

Because I felt like I saw life through two filters, one in the physical world, and the other like…I saw…things. Not there. I had dreams that felt like they could happen or had happened.

I couldn't tell the difference between past and present.

I would drop in my head into spaces of time that stretched out where I was different people, in different bodies—traveling through time.

And he was there. In every single one.

Pale eyes. Blonde hair.

Waiting. Watching me. Protecting me.

Come find me.

I woke up with a yell in my hotel room bed scrambling for my phone. 2:06am.

Again.

I didn't get help for what was wrong with me. Instead I laid there breathing harder seeing nothing but water. A body of water. Pale eyes.

His voice coasting over me.

I was looking for you.

Forever.

LIAM AND I SPENT ALL OUR TIME TOGETHER.

I felt like I was drinking in moments with him.

It felt really good to be back with him. Memories of us growing up, him always carrying me on his back, protecting me, being family?

It was healing something in me I didn't know I needed.

Sometimes I still saw that boy who my father put into karate, the one whose bruises healed living with us—but his temper flared every so often.

I saw the boy who tried to get me to go ice skating with him all the time or me pulling him to dance classes grudgingly.

He felt familiar and foreign at the same time.

We sat together outside at a cafe he liked he said he brought Lara to sometimes.

"What is it like for you?" I motioned to his legs, his cane. He never talked about it. "Do you still…" I trailed off. Unsure how to approach something like this for him. I knew how it felt, but my legs were fine.

I could move.

"I swim now," he murmured over his coffee. "I don't do anything I used to do." A bittersweet smile touched his lips. "Lara says it's for the best. She says running is overrated anyway."

"Your Lara is good to you?"

He nodded tipping his head forward. "Too good. She's got a sense of humor, she's playful. You'd like her. I met her in my old life and…" he trailed off a host of emotions playing on his face. "And now we're together." He seemed to check himself from saying anything else as he sipped his coffee.

It was awkward now.

I never remembered it being awkward between us.

He was careful with me. But I felt careful with him.

"What's it like in Cape Verde?" He asked softly.

453

I smiled telling him about the island, the compound, our lives. And how much had changed. As I spoke his eyes softened.

"You like it there."

A statement not a question.

I nodded. "It is warm and nice."

Liam snorted like it was surprising. "Never thought Malcolm Nash's paradise would be something you'd like."

"You know him?" I had never met him.

Liam shook his head. "I heard of him in the past but no, never met the guy." His expression shuttered. "Say, you got any plans today?"

"I never have plans." Not since I came to New York.

I didn't know how to get my necklace back anymore.

"Do you know how to get the necklace back from Reed?"

His expression became unreadable. "Yeah, I'm brainstorming a few things."

He quickly changed the subject. "What do you say I give you a tour around the city?"

That sounded good, but as we both got up, I noted the way Liam leaned heavily on his cane.

"You know," I said softly. "Talia put me through physical therapy—"

"Physical therapy isn't gonna fix me, Isa." His voice was clipped and colder. Firm. His eyes turning dark. "I'm not fixable."

I frowned behind him as he pressed down on his cane.

"I promise I'm good," he said but he grimaced as he stood to his full height.

"Liam, you are not good," I cut in feeling something in my chest ache at his pain. He used to fight and move and live his life. And now?

"Come on." I linked my arm with his. "I'm still hungry. Coffee and croissants is not going to fill me up. Let's go get pizza. I don't want to walk all over the city—it's cold."

He smirked. "Fine, but at the minimum I'm paying."

I let him think he was. Liam didn't know how much I made over the years and I hadn't told him.

We talked about everything and nothing in between and sometimes he made jokes, I didn't remember or understand.

But I told myself I had something important in my life again and I would drink it in.

454

CHAPTER 69
GABRIEL

IT WAS TOO EARLY IN THE MORNING AND THE THING ABOUT CIVILIANS was no matter how much danger they were in? The body had muscle memory.

When the doorbell rang? They went to get it.

In this case though? That civilian was Alisha.

Lucy did try and rob K2. Sort of.

It was early. Reed and I had kept her up all night. I knew she was tired and not thinking, and I was reviewing security footage.

The moment Reed and I got the alert?

I was all over it.

I had never felt that kind of fear at the idea of something happening to Alisha because of me. Reed losing her.

Because.

Of.

Me.

I felt something off the entire morning, my stomach was off, and Alisha was asleep. That was when I heard the alarm, the ping on my phone. Reed.

Iris is in the building.

Lish is up?

No. But I am.

455

I grabbed my gun the moment I heard the door click open. It took me a second to process Lucy mother-fucking Devereaux. Even in disguise I knew her. Of her.

Reed had been annoyed with her lately for not coming to him.

But I saw her raising something to Lish's neck. I lost it.

I saw Alisha duck and I raced after her. Not. Giving. A. Shit.

It wasn't even in the cards for me to be chasing Lucy fucking Devereaux up to the roof of K2, but by the time I got there—I took another shot. Irritated. Annoyed. Pissed-off beyond measure that I was dealing with this and not hunting for my wife.

"Motherfucker. I warned Reed about you."

"I'm sorry! I didn't have a choice!" She did have a choice.

She just chose wrong.

"You tried to hurt Alisha!" I shot back.

"I didn't mean to!" I broke off feeling trapped. "You shouldn't have slept with Natasha—"

"Who?" Natasha? Nash?

"Malcolm Nash?"

And then she dropped a few surprises on me letting me know just how much she knew.

"Natasha Nash is in the city looking for that necklace. Because of you. *You* did this. You started a war for who?"

"What the fuck are you talking about? Who the fuck is Natasha Nash?"

My mind was swirling. Reed and I weren't tracking that.

I needed to though judging by the way Lucy was watching me.

"What do you mean who the fuck is Natasha Nash? Isn't she your girlfriend?"

"What the fuck is your problem?"

I fucking hated Lucy Devereaux.

For a moment, my heart was pounding and my blood ran cold at the site of someone else standing there that was an authorized to be there.

But Reed and I left Lucy's key card untouched on purpose.

I fucking knew it.

"She jumped off the fucking roof, Reed." I called him. "But it's her. I shot her mask off."

"I'm going to Adam. Now."

Alisha was in my arms, shaking wildly in her slip. I tore off my hoodie and put it on her.

"I-I thought it was Avani," she whispered terrified. "Was that Lucy?"

I nodded, guilt churning in my gut. "Reed's going to kill Adam."

"Oh dear."

～

WHEN REED DID SHOW UP, HIS NOSE WAS BLEEDING.

"Did you kill him?" Alisha and I muttered at the same time sitting in the bedroom.

Reed strode on holding an ice pack to his nose. "No." His eyes were wounded though. He looked like shit. "But he got a few hits in. I need to bandage my nose. I'm fine though."

"Fine?" Alisha gingerly walked to him. "You look terrible. I knew you'd fight."

"His girlfriend's an idiot," I muttered. "Sorry, Lish. It's true. He could've just talked to us." I went and got ice for Reed who groaned taking off his shirt. "Is Shane outside?"

"No, but Lucy didn't take anything. She would have to look inside the apartment," Reed groaned as Alisha cleaned him up with alcohol pads.

"Darling, hospital—"

"Not now, Angel. I think Lucy broke in as a decoy." He winced as he said it. "I think something else is happening. She wasn't going to get anything. What was the point?"

"Exposing a weakness?" I offered. His eyes met mine. "Exposing a strength." I finished. "Me."

Reed nodded. "Lucy thought Alisha might be alone. She just found out she wasn't, but she wouldn't know why you're here."

"You don't think Lucy is working for Talon, do you?" Alisha caught on quickly.

Reed and I didn't say a word.

"No," Alisha shook her head. "Absolutely not."

"Angel," Reed looked at her with a bruised eyebrow. "All the cameras are down within a five mile radius from here. Every single one. The last time that happened? It was Talon's hacker keeping me on my toes."

Or trying to at least. Reed subverted her fairly reasonably.

"But they were after her, why would they trust her to work for them," Alisha countered. "You two both said Talon was sophisticated. This doesn't sound like Talon. Plus, she failed. This sounds like her working alone. Like she always has."

That was a valid point.

"So why would Lucy fake a break-in?" I asked. "Why now?"

"We're missing something," Alisha muttered. "But first he needs a doctor. And we need to breathe. We saw this coming. Now we have to figure out why. In the meantime, Sonya texted me about Aidan coming to see her…"

Because we had ninety other things going on aside from a false break-in.

$$\sim$$

A WEEK AND A HALF, REED AND I HAD A SUSPICION OF A FEW THINGS.

We were piecing it together day by day. With Lucy's additional information?

I was set.

Nash.

As in Malcolm fucking Nash. Marcus Hagen. That motherfucker had haunted me for years.

Especially when Selena called Reed telling him, the night she had been injured months ago—she had seen someone with our blonde friend who hadn't appeared since Lucas's near death experience.

One, Lucy Devereaux failed in stealing the necklace.

And Two? She wasn't working with Talon.

BUT WE KNEW WHO WAS.

"THE DUPONT'S ARE TALON." I REPEATED. "I FUCKING KNEW Matteo was too clever for his own good."

"I DON'T THINK IT'S MATTEO. BUT I DO THINK MATTEO KNOWS exactly what's going on. His youngest brother's name is Thierry Mattison," Reed announced in his office in K2. "He's the third DuPont brother. And you'll never believe who he was with."

. . .

"THE BLONDE." ALISHA MUTTERED. "GOOD LORD, HE WAS WITH HER that night and they talked about taking a Whittaker?"

Reed tipped his head. "Now I know why Lucy tried to break in. She's not working with Talon—"

"She's saving Adam," I finished.

"No," Alisha shook her head with warmth in her eyes. "She did it for both of you. I still think Lucy adored you," she nodded to Reed. "I do. She wouldn't stick around for three years if she didn't. I still think even if you both find her immature—I think she's misunderstood."

Alisha would put the benefit of the doubt in people.

"That may be true. But Kellan and Selena are going to be here in forty-eight hours. Selena decided to come back," Reed smiled at me and Alisha. "Well, it worked. He won her back and we got back two operatives."

I smirked. "*I fucking told you guys.*"

Alisha cleared her throat. "*We* told you." She motioned between her and Reed. "You cannot lose Kellan. He's wonderful."

"Killian did say he's really good as an operative," Reed added. "And speaking of Killian. The O'Hara's are handling their own fucking crisis..."

Reed filled us in about Killian and his girlfriend's problems he was juggling, Nathan's assignment, and everything else in between.

But now? We were one step closer to Talon.

"Thierry Mattison is being hidden by his brother's," Reed looked at me with a grim smile. "Do you want to know who his oldest brother is married to?"

He held out his phone. "Recognize this woman? Her alias is her mother's name Tatiana Minamoto. Japanese passport. *She* flew into New York City the same day on the same flight as Thierry or Theo. He's got ninety-two different alias's."

Reed threw down a passport on the table. On it listed under Hero Minamoto, as the baby brother of Tatiana.

Dark inky hair falling over DuPont's infamous eyes, aqua blue alien bright, black rimmed pupils.

His smile was wide in his photo making him look wicked. And barely seventeen.

"Lee Minamoto..." I murmured. "Minamoto means origin in Japanese. Jeremy Bradford was a fanatic about this anime shit with Vincent, I remember this..."

I explained to Reed and Alisha that Minamoto was associated with the clan known as the Genji. They were one of four clans dominating Japanese politics during the Heian period.

"In the year 794?" Alisha blinked. "Tatiana Minamoto."

"She's Talia Nash's alias, but she's also Talia Nash's mother's name. Tatiana Hiromi Minamoto. She was in Hong Kong when she met Malcolm Nash who was visiting. They had Talia, but she died in childbirth in the States..." Reed filled me in on the tiny bits of clues he had about Talia. "And you'll never fucking believe this... Talia was pregnant when she came *back* to the States."

Alisha covered her mouth. "Good lord. With...Andrei DuPont. Hang on—Talia Nash is in the States?"

"She's his wife," Reed murmured looking gleeful. "He tried to hide it but she's married to the motherfucker. According to Lucas who was friends with Andrei and Talia? Talia has been his wife for years."

I frowned down at the woman with dark hair and green eyes, sharper features. "Don't fucking tell me—"

"Talia is in New York. And we can go get her."

And we could get one step closer to finding out why she took my wife?

CHAPTER 70
ISOBEL

"*THIERRY GOT MY NECKLACE BACK?*"

I sat in my hotel room as Bexley who had a fever had gotten me my necklace back.

On paper? I would've believed her.

But the moment she gave it to me—I knew it was a fake. Seven years of metal. I knew it. I knew the moment she gingerly gave it to me sniffling, that it wasn't real.

It didn't make the sound.

Not the sound I knew. The little clink was gone.

I hadn't been able to open it for seven years. Unless the person who had it? Had a way to open it?

I knew it wasn't my necklace.

The only question was—why was Bexley lying to me? Why did Thierry give her a fake?

"Thierry and Teo got someone to break into K2 for you," she said a little more than nervously. "That's what he told me. He said he had it and he wanted you to have it back so we can go home together. As a family."

She shrugged a little looking younger than nineteen. "Can we go home now?"

Rage filled my chest a little even on her.

Bexley had never lied to me. She had always been loyal. Almost fanatically so since Talia saved her.

I didn't know what was going on.

Bexley's voice wobbled. "Is everything okay? You don't look happy?" She looked down. "Is that not the right necklace?"

And just like that my anger faded.

"What?" I blinked. "What do you mean?"

She shrugged again. "Thierry just said he worked with Teo. But he wouldn't give me anymore information."

Thierry. And Talia. And the DuPont's were playing me.

Why?

The fake was burning into my palm now.

I needed to talk to Liam.

"Go lay down, it's fine." I forced myself to speak. "You did a good job. And yeah, we'll go home soon. Tell Samara to get our flight out of town ready."

She nodded looking grateful. "I'm gonna miss this place. Maybe we can come back and stay here again and not have to deal with the Titans."

I smiled nodding a little.

I would never come back to New York.

"I KNOW THE DUPONT'S ARE LYING TO ME." I TOLD LIAM. IT HAD been weeks since he'd come into my life and I went to see him in his apartment.

I couldn't wait for him to show up.

"My team is lying to me. Everyone is lying to me." But Liam.

Liam would tell me the truth. But as I said it, his darker green eyes clouded over. The same way they had for weeks.

His inky black hair fell over his forehead, and he leaned onto his cane, even though he was sitting down.

Seeing him like this was always a constant reminder of everything that he had lost. He always wore longer sweats.

His white T-shirt contrasting with all of the tattoos all over his arms. They hadn't been there when I died. He'd gotten them over the years.

"Why are you looking at me like that?" Something was off.

"Like what?" His words were softer. Careful.

Like he was afraid to spook me.

"Like I'm not real." I shook my head. "Ever since I've been in your life you look at me like this." I motioned to him. "What is going on?"

Liam looked like he was biting back a reply as he motioned to the necklace.

"Why does it matter so much to you?"

"What?" I shook my head. "I told you—it's the only thing in my past I have."

"No," he looked upset me and annoyed almost. At me. "You have me. You have a future. You have a life in Cape Verde. Not here. I told you I would go with you—"

Confusion swirled in my body like wisps of smoke and pale blue eyes were in my vision.

"What?"

Liam continued like I hadn't looked stunned. "You have me back. I'm your family. Why do you need answers—"

"Because it's my life!" I was in disbelief. "What is wrong with you? Since I've been back in your life, you keep living like it's the past. Like we are twenty. Not hitting thirty—"

"Because you're my life!" Liam snapped his cane hitting the floor. And then I realized something.

"You are drunk."

"No," he shook his head. "For fucks sake, everyone thinks I'm a fucking alcoholic. I'm not drunk. I'm pretty fucking sober. I'm not living in the past. You've been holding onto that fucking necklace for seven years—"

"What is wrong with you?" I stood up with him matching him as he looked angrier now.

"I have lived without you thinking you were gone!" He was erupting and snapping at me now. *"Did you think about me once?"*

"Of course—" Why was he being like this?

"Then why did you hold onto something when you don't even know what it is! You don't him! You remember Monroe! But I'm here. You know me. You remembered me! Doesn't that mean anything to you?"

As he said it something flickered in his eyes when he said Monroe. I caught it.

An eerie sensation skated down my spine.

Something I only felt when my team was in danger.

This entire time, I didn't understand why everybody was lying to me. But I knew when they were. It's something that I realized, that when I saw Liam for the first time, I was so happy to see him. I wasn't analyzing him. I was just taking him in as my family. Now?

I didn't see him as Liam.

I saw him as a threat.

Something I never thought I would say.

The anxiety churned in my stomach as I forced myself to whisper. *"What do you know?"*

And I was right.

"You know who he is." My heart began to pound erratically in my chest and I felt the panic attack descend. "You know who Monroe is. Who is he?"

Liam looked away from me like he was livid with me. With me.

"Liam. You know who Monroe is."

He did know.

But he wasn't going to tell me.

"If you don't tell me, I'll find out. I'll find him. I am done with you—"

"What? You would walk away from me?" He sounded like he swallowed glass. *"For a man you don't know! You don't remember?"*

"You lied to me!"

"I did!"

"You know who he is! Why won't you say it?"

"BECAUSE HE'S THE REASON WHY YOU'RE DEAD!"

I froze. Liam closed his eyes blowing out a breath looking like he was in pain.

Neither one of us spoke, but I heard him.

I heard him loud and clear.

"I'm alive," I whispered.

"No, you're not." His eyes opened and they were unrecognizable. My Liam was gone. My family. Gone.

In his place was an empty shell behind those eyes.

"You're not my sister. I don't know who you are. You don't act like her. You don't make jokes. You barely smile. You don't look happy—" he broke off looking like he was in disbelief. With me. "I don't recognize you anymore. And you come to me and tell me after seven years the only thing that brought you back to New York —the place we both died—was because of the one man who did it."

I swallowed feeling sick to my stomach. "You lied to me."

"I did! And I would do it every single fucking day it meant keeping him away from you?"

Fury like no other lit up my insides.

"You are not my family!" I shouted. "Family does not do this."

"Listen to yourself! I just told you Gabriel got you killed—"

His name is Gabriel?

Amor?

"—and all you can say is I'm not who you thought I was!"

"You are a monster." I whispered. I wasn't shocked. I was furious with Liam. "You are a horrible person. His name is Gabriel Monroe?" Why did that sound so familiar? "Is he related to Eva Monroe?" Was that his sister?

Liam swallowed looking nauseous then. "You don't remember Eva either?"

"Who are they?" And then I didn't even think. Sometimes I forgot who I was. I whipped out my gun. I didn't even think and Liam's eyes went wide.

Something other than calm or anger on his face.

He closed his eyes as he held his hands up. I saw his expression break.

"Tell me who Gabriel and Eva are." I growled. "I'm not your anything anymore. I'm the head of Talon. My entire life you kept secrets, you made choices without me. I know why Talia gave me this life. Because she was protecting me. From everything. But I don't want to be protected anymore. I want the fucking truth."

I cocked my gun on the last person I ever wanted to do it now.

My vision blurred.

"Tell. Me. Everything." I growled through my teeth feeling my eyes spill over on Liam. Liam. My Liam. "Starting with Gabriel Monroe..."

465

CHAPTER 71
GABRIEL

"TALIA NASH BOOKED A PRIVATE CHARTER AND IS NO LONGER IN THE city."

Reed's voice was grim. Dark. His eyes clouded over with concern for me.

"No," I felt defeat in my chest. "Is she onto us? We have to get to her!"

Reed shook his head. "I don't think it's real. Over the last few weeks I've been tracking the anomalies separate from Liam. Once you told me who he was...I let him go back to doing his normal job..." Reed explained it to me as me and Alisha and him sat in his private office in K2.

"I noticed the camera hot spots around one block. One building." He pulled up the map on the giant screens to—

"The Primrose?" Alisha frowned. "You think Talon is operating out of the Primrose Hotel?"

She frowned as Reed explained. "Angel, you remember when you stayed there? That's when I noticed these weird glitches in the hotel lobby. When Gabriel came to see you? He didn't appear. They wiped it."

I felt my heart roaring in my chest. "What? Like a blank screen?"

And then before Reed could respond Alisha's jaw dropped and her eyes went wider like she'd seen a ghost. "Oh. My. God."

Both of us looked at her as she whipped her head up. "I know where I saw the black card. The markers with the gold claws?" She held up the black card with the gold marks. "I saw this! I saw this at the hotel!" She turned to me. "The day we were there. The *blonde girl. Pancakes.* She was eating a stack off them. But the woman sitting across her, the gothic looking sister? She had the card in her hand. This card. I saw it."

Alisha looked at Reed. "I went to the restroom, Gabriel was sitting with his back to them in the booth. When I passed by her, I saw the card in her hand. The dark-haired woman? She's Talon. I think I walked by them."

Reed and I shared a look of stunned amazement. "We need to find that footage."

"Wait—" Alisha stopped us. "When you made the reservation at the Primrose, I don't know why I didn't ask this earlier. Who did you make the reservation under?"

I motioned to Reed. "Whittaker."

Alisha's yes grew wide and she looked at me and an eerie expression was on her face like she'd seen a ghost again.

"*Whittaker.*"

I nodded.

"When I went to the restroom, a staff member washing her hands confused me and called me *Mrs. Monroe.*"

I swore I stopped breathing.

Her eyes were wider. "I said no, I was here with Mr. Monroe. Not realizing I forgot in that moment I met you as *Gabriel.* Not Raphael. So I never thought twice about it. But now that I remember the card was there in her hand?"

Reed said it. "*Holy fuck—*"

I was on it. "Call the Primrose. Get their descriptions. Tell them we're working with the police or something. The blonde. And the brunette." I told Reed.

"And hopefully Isobel," Alisha whispered. "My god what are the chances she would go under Monroe."

None.

But I could only hope.

It took Reed thirty minutes of back and forth.

"I got them," he said. "I spoke to the GM. He says the blonde is a Beatrice Carrigan. The brunette is a Sasha Kincaide." He paused. "The woman who checked in with them?" His throat worked. "*Adrianna* Monroe."

I closed my eyes. "Her mom's name."

Reed's eyes held a wicked glint. "Forget Talia Nash. She's a decoy. I think this is the Talon team in the city. The blonde, the brunette, and—"

"Whoever Adrianna is." I finished. *My wife.*

∿

We made it to the Primrose with a small team and waiting in the SUV, we got a clipped response from the team lead.

Landon used to work with Killian O'Hara on his team.

But Killian had taken a sabbatical once I found out his girlfriend Nisha was pregnant.

Now? Landon was leading the team at the Primrose. Garrett was on Beatrice, the blonde. And Landon was on Sasha the dark haired woman.

Alisha, Reed, and I would take Adrianna Monroe.

Just saying it made my stomach turn. So close. She was so close.

"We got all the floors occupied." Landon's voice was firm. "The hotel let us bring two staff members so it looks solid. We're in the stairwell."

"Copy that," Reed muttered as an anxious Alisha rubbed her face into his trying to eavesdrop. She looked ready to absorb the call through his skin as she climbed on him. She was tiny now in his arms as she chewed her lip.

If I wasn't in the SUV with them trying to find my wife? I would've laughed at her dressed in all black. Workout sneakers.

"I feel like a criminal," she whispered as he hung up.

"Baby, you don't gotta whisper," Reed looked like he was fighting back his laughter.

"I'm on a mission, Reed," she shot back in a whisper, her eyes fierce. "I have to whisper otherwise I might explode with excitement. How do you do this for a living?"

I knew the feeling as I bit back laughter. I felt the same. She was so close. I felt off, in my chest I didn't feel her. But I knew—I fucking knew.

Reed grinned then unable to stop. "Whenever you're ready. Landon has the go ahead to get Beatrice and Sasha. Whatever their real fucking names are—" And we would go for Adrianna. Isobel. I blew out a breath.

"No more alias's after this," Alisha frowned. "I'm losing my mind."

Reed snorted as the three of us went to the room that was marked for her.

Reed's phone rang again. He frowned at it.

"One sec," Reed picked up. "Landon, what's wrong?"

This time Reed put him on speaker.

"Boss, we got a problem—" Landon broke off.

"Mr. Whittaker—"

Reed and I frowned on the elevator exchanging a look at the familiar voice. *"Shane?"*

"I was with Samara. Her name isn't Sasha—she's my girlfriend. I didn't know she was Talon!"

I heard the sounds of someone in the background fighting.

Shane swore. "Reed—Mr. Whittaker—call them off. She's gonna kill them—"

"What the fuck—" Reed swore. I gaped as Alisha covered her mouth.

"Boss," Landon came back over the line. "Garrett got the blonde, Beatrice—but we got a bigger problem there—"

"God help me—" Reed swore fiercely.

The elevator dinged on Adrianna Monroe's floor.

Reed motioned for us to get out and we moved quickly. "What is it?"

"We got someone named *Avani*—" Landon broke off. Next to us Alisha looked like she hit a wall. *"She* was with the blonde and a man—he's a DuPont. She says they're together. Says his name's Thierry."

And just like that all three of us froze.

"What did he just say?" Alisha squeaked.

Alisha hit a wall.

Avani was dating the third DuPont brother?

Alisha's eyes met mine. "I need to go."

"I got her Angel," Reed's face was a mask of fury as he took in Alisha's distress. "Gabriel. Go without us. You got this? Good." He tossed me the keys. "I gotta go make sure nobody dies."

I took the keys from him and he and Alisha were tearing down the hallway to the stairs.

Leaving me standing there gaping as I realized I was two doors away from my…

My world.
My soul.

CHAPTER 72
ISOBEL

I was numb.

I walked back to the Primrose in a blur.

He's your husband. You guys got married...I was there...I watched him fall for you.

His name is Gabriel Monroe...but I don't think so anymore. He goes by an alias. His middle name and your old name.

Santos. Raphael Santos.

He's your husband.

He's your husband.

He's your husband.

Deep down I knew. I knew that necklace held meaning.

It held value. Now I held the fake in my hands feeling my eyes blur like Liam had shot me even though I held the gun. Because now I didn't just have the fake.

In my other hand? I held the key.

Liam said the key had been around Gabriel's neck the night he had gotten shot. Gabriel had bent down to check on him and when Liam grabbed his shirt collar—it had snapped.

Liam had kept it all these years for some reason.

Now I knew.

I had the key.

Reed Whittaker had my necklace. Because he was best friend's with Gabriel.

It wasn't a necklace.

It was my engagement ring. It was my wedding vows. It was my world. It was a symbol of him. And somehow Talia let me keep it.

It was proof of my old life.

My new one.

A man I couldn't even remember loving but I knew I loved him. I had to have loved him.

You stay away from me. I had told him.

I never hated Liam so much in my life.

Or anyone. I numbly walked to the Primrose all the way from Liam's place. Across the city.

I couldn't breathe properly when I made it to the Primrose. I numbly took the elevator up to my floor. I didn't see or notice anyone as I felt myself breaking.

Shattering to pieces.

A husband.

A husband I didn't know.

A husband who was...somewhere. Liam had said he was alive but he didn't know where he stayed.

Liam's words were still filtering through my brain after I left him looking broken in his apartment as I told him I never wanted to speak to him ever again.

Ever.

I think he stays at the manor but nobody's seen him in weeks. I think he might be with Reed Whittaker.

Reed Whittaker is Gabriel's Monroe's partner. I think they're best friends. Brother's.

Reed Whittaker wasn't the enemy. He was never the enemy.

I had to tell Bexley and Samara to call it all off.

No wonder we had been off since we'd gotten here.

Lucy Devereaux worked for Reed Whittaker because she was the one assigned to steal this necklace.

Gabriel thought I was dead.

He was hunting for pieces of me. The way I had been searching for seven years for him.

He had Reed steal the necklace for him to keep himself out of it? I didn't know. I didn't know but now? The pieces were falling together.

Why Lucy took it. Why Gabriel was looking. Why Reed was involved.

And Liam. Of course Liam knew.

He was a Titan.

And I never in my life wanted to see him ever again.

Because Liam lying had been the greatest betrayal of them all. It didn't explain why I had a fake from Bexley and Thierry. I would soon find out when I got to my room.

I would call them.

The moment I got to the door, I reached for my key card, and I felt to shiver run down my spine. I felt a blast of nothing but ice coming from the room. Which was strange.

Room service didn't come by this late.

I frowned at the doorknob as it turned green. I palmed my gun with the silencer on it.

Someone is inside my room.

And I was already in a bad mood. I was going to fucking kill them. I stepped into the room quickly and found it was dark. Of course it was dark.

I felt them before I saw them.

Hands.

Reaching for me. I growled instantly leaping into it. It was in a nano-second of time that I processed it. But I knew what to do.

Instinct and anger took over as my body moved.

Years of combat training with Talia intercepted my reflexes and my body knew what to do.

He was big. Strong.

Too bad I was fast, driving my elbow into his side. A growl left him as he caught it crashing together in the dark. I couldn't see him or feel him until he lifted me up.

A shout left me in the scuffle I dropped the gun.

Dio, how big was this man?

"Jesus, fucking christ, where the fuck is the goddamn light—" he swore as he slammed me not too gently into the wall and a click sounded in the room

The lights came on like a flood of color and I squeezed my eyes shut for a second before opening them.

My heart thundered in my chest at the wide eyes watching me then, widening in shock and awe.

Pale.

Ice.

Blue.

Eyes that haunted my dreams for seven years.

"Fuck." His voice was a whisper.

Pale blue blinked slowly as he watched me holding me up off the floor.

Amor.

The word floated through my mind like smoke, and suddenly I knew—my body had recognized him before my mind could catch up.

Seven years of searching, and here we were—me trapped between him and the wall.

Both of us breathing hard, neither of us willing to look away.

Afraid the other might disappear if we blinked. If we breathed wrong.

The hands pinning me to the wall weren't a stranger's.

They were my husband's.

CHAPTER 73
GABRIEL

Amor.

That was my wife.

Dark hair. Dark eyes.

Reed was right. She's not her. But she was my wife. I always knew her and who she was. I would always know my wife.

No. But I did know her. She had been at the hospital the night Lucas had been shot. She had been outside the manor like a ghost scaring Evie.

Evie…did she know her sister was alive? And well?

God, I never told Evie...

This woman in my arms had my wife's face, older and sharper. Haunted in ways that made my chest tighten, my throat catch.

I swallowed and it felt like nails.

But the eyes were wrong. Snuffed of all her light. Her hair was platinum blonde. Isobel's was beautiful raven.

And she was Isobel.

She was.

But she wasn't.

"H—how?"

I took her in as she let out a shuddering breath, her throat worked and she took me in. I did want to kiss her. I did.

But I also held back.

Because seven years had done their number on me.

Every cell in my body should have been screaming. I should've been shaking her.

My hands were trembling, but I heard Reed's voice in my head.

Breathe.

When you see her, you're going to lose it. Like you've lost it this entire time. Look at me. You can never lose it again.

Not with her.

Breathe. At the end of the day you go in there. You get your answers. And you go with it. You GO. WITH. IT.

The woman in my arms was wearing my wife's face. But that was it.

She was searching my face like I was a stranger from a memory.

"Do you—do you know...me?"

She shrugged a little, nodding with a dip of her head. "I think so."

I closed my eyes. It did hurt more than thinking she was dead. It did in a different way. Because all of my memories, every single thing I found in her—obliterated. Shattered. Like glass fragments all over the floor.

It was painful.

I opened my eyes to find her watching me.

"How..." I let her go slowly trailing off and setting her down on the floor. "How?" I motioned to her.

She blinked several times. "You are...Gabriel..."

I closed my eyes and inhaled her into my lungs. I couldn't even hold her.

Gabri-el.

At least some things never changed.

I tipped my head down. She had changed. I could already see the light in her snuffed out completely.

I was grateful she was there.

It was her, and not Talia Nash fucking with my head.

But she...*she* wasn't...she wasn't...mine anymore.

"Prove it." She whispered. "Prove it to me."

I drew out her necklace from around my throat. Her eyes lit up at the sight.

"Your mother's ring is inside of it. The one she left you, with William. When he died, he gave it to Liam. He asked Liam to marry you. You were in love with me. So he gave me this." I held it out to her. "This is yours."

I saw her process the shock.

If she felt stunned—I wish I could tell her how agonizing it felt to look at your wife and know she remembered nothing.

Not a *single* thing.

Not her wedding.

Not my love.

Not *our* daughter.

Nothing.

My ache was hollow from the inside out like someone took an ice cream scooper to me.

And then I remembered Reed and Alisha. I held onto them. I slowly passed it to her like she was a wild animal. Like I should've been afraid of her.

And then to my fucking surprise she took out something from her neck.

I gaped. "You had the fucking key?"

She shook her head. "No. Liam...I just...I just left him..." Her eyes flashed. "He lied to me." Her throat worked. "He told me he didn't know you."

As soon as she said his name? As soon as I fucking heard it? My grief transformed into pure hell fire rage.

I buried every single emotion deep in me. Every bit of my body was screaming.

"You knew about Liam?" I sounded like a fucking demon. I cleared my throat. "He knew about you?"

She nodded slowly like she was piecing it together.

Something's wrong with her head. I was experienced enough to see her. She reacted slower.

The red flickered burning deeper until it turned into a forrest fire.

The war of relief and grief and rage waged inside of me.

He lied to her about me. He lied to me.

Oh.

Fuck.

I'm going to kill Liam. Slowly.

Painfully.

He knew. How long did he know?

I would bide my time carefully. Reed could break the news to Lara we buried him alive in a ditch.

Part of me was burning to touch her as her eyes widened on me glancing warily between me and the necklace.

Screaming for me to hug her, to kiss her, to tell her she was my love. But another part of me felt the lick of rage fueling me.

"How long did he know about you?"

"Weeks," she gingerly snapped the lock into place and just like that it clicked open, Adrianna's ring falling onto into her hand and just like her eyes watered. "This is my mother's."

I blinked overhand over until my eyes cleared.

"Do you...what do you know?" Her throat worked as I said it again. "*How* are you alive?"

Slowly, she opened her mouth.

And it was the one thing I didn't suspect as she slowly talked. I blinked at her. *"Talia saved you?"*

Isobel...Adrianna...whoever she was now nodded and slowly explained some of it. I listened taking a step back until I was sitting down because my knees were shaking. It wasn't every single day your wife came back from the dead where she had in fact died.

She did die. She did wake up.

And she only remembered her life from twelve to twenty-two in fragments. Barely.

As in her brain completely shut down. She probably had brain damage, memory loss, PTSD, her scar tissues from Kourtney. I had to explain why Kourtney had tried to kill her.

What Claire Sutton did. What Vincent Grant did. What Jim Koller did. As I spoke it was like I was twenty-four again and gut-wrenching violent pain wracked through me.

She held her mother's ring staring at it with shock on her face as she spoke. "You—you took this from me..."

"To be fair," I forced myself to keep my voice calm. But I failed. I heard it come out as a croak. "I didn't even know if it was you, but I *suspected*. Talia Nash playing the good guy was not what I saw coming."

She slowly sat back playing with the ring and her necklace and the key.

"You searched for me?"

I tipped my head. "I never stopped." Not once. "When did Liam find about you? Did he know the entire time?"

She shook her head and explained to me what happened between her and Liam.

How he had found her...*a few weeks ago*...My mind was already working.

"Liam was in charge of finding Lucy Devereaux," I kept my voice low to not freak her out. "Adam stayed here for a few days when Lucas was shot."

"That was an accident," she filled me in slowly as well. The more she spoke the more the pieces filled in.

She held up the fake necklace. "Thierry gave me this. I think he might be working with someone—"

Lucy. It could only be Lucy.

"Lucy. Thierry is working with Lucy somehow...or he was."

We were both filling it in. Lucy had cut a deal with Thierry, and he had returned a fake to Isobel through Bexley.

"For Avani," I whispered. "He did it for her. Because he thought—"

"I was going to kill Reed."

"Thierry is dating Avani—"

I needed to check on that. Because for a nanosecond I thought he was Talon and he was working Avani. But now?

Hearing Isobel say he gave her the fake necklace? My mind was working overtime.

"Thierry gave you a fake," I shook my head. "He wasn't Talon, was he?"

She shook her head. "He left when Talia was pregnant..." she explained it all to me and as she did my jaw dropped a little.

And the secrets unraveled.

Thierry had been dating Avani for real.

Just like Lucy had been dating Adam.

They were doing what they did—to protect their love.

Of fucking course.

A hysterical laugh bubbled up inside of me at the idea that all of us?

We'd been running circles around each other.

Lucas wasn't in danger like I originally thought. I'd have to talk to him about this.

Selena had seen Thierry with Isobel, but they'd just been talking. Thierry wasn't a villain.

He was trying to set Avani's family free with the information he had.

"And it's been you..." I whispered. "This entire time." My heart cracked open. "No wonder I could never figure it out."

"How did you? How did you find me?"

I explained Alisha was Reed's girlfriend and she had remembered the black card in Samara's hand.

Isobel's smile was harmless. "I was given away by pancakes?"

The hysterical laughter bubble up in me now, in my throat.

My vision blurred. "Yeah."

I looked at my wife and she watched me warily. "We were married." She held up Adrianna's ring.

"We were."

Her throat worked. "I am the head of Talon."

"I got that." I smirked. "Reed's technically the head of Titan—"

"No, it's you."

I shook my head feeling my bitter smile tug at my lips. "My name isn't Gabriel Monroe anymore. I took Raphael Santos after you. Raphael's my middle name and Santos is well...yours." Speaking of. "Adrianna Monroe isn't your real name now, is it?"

She shook her head. "I picked Alma."

I froze. Cold spreading through my veins like frost. My smile dropped. She didn't...she couldn't...

"Why?"

I kept my face neutral fighting my emotion as I looked at my lap. "Why'd you pick it?"

Thank fuck I had weeks of Reed yelling at me to stay calm.

Otherwise I'd flip a chair.

She shrugged lightly and didn't that gut me alive. "It felt right."

I blinked looking down at my hands trying not to shatter. She didn't even know about our kid.

She didn't remember. Some part of me wanted to shake her. Make her remember me.

And I remembered the last few weeks of living at K2 and how Alisha and Reed warned me day in and day out—how they were my rocks. Both of them.

She isn't your wife. Not anymore.

Let her find her way back to you.

If it's meant to be it will.

It will.

It will.

She's yours.

480

Both of them had held me through it.

Isobel didn't know.

Nothing could've prepared me for knowing that she had unknowingly taken our daughter's name holding onto it.

Just like the necklace.

Isobel's mind had always been razor sharp. It shouldn't have surprised me she held onto me and our girl.

Small mercies she doesn't know. But I wouldn't lie to her. I'd tell her after the shock of finding her wore off.

Her curtains were drawn so I didn't even know what time it was anymore.

"Who is she?" Isobel whispered. "Alma. Do I know her too?"

It was fascinating what the brain held onto.

"No," I shook my head. "We can bookmark Alma for now. Your team was taken in by Titan. Garrett took Bexley to the hospital for her fever. Just to make sure she's solid," I added quickly at Isobel's expression. "Did you know Samara was accidentally dating one of my operatives?"

She blinked and for a moment I noted her eyes were still soft and curious on me like I was sitting in an exhibit. Those eyes that used to flash with unholy fire not calmer. Cooler.

"Shane is yours?"

"Yeah, and he had no idea she was Talon. And she had no idea he was a Titan."

Isobel looked more amused than shocked. "We have always been around each other."

I knew it.

"You were at the hospital. Outside the manor…"

She nodded and it burned. It burned because my wife had been there all along. Right in front of me.

I wiped my eyes feeling my vision blur. "Fuck."

She didn't say a word. Seven years of silence stretched between us. What the fuck did I say to my wife?

I didn't have this in my playbook.

"What are you going to do now? You got your necklace. Your team isn't from here, are they? You lived in Cape Verde."

She nodded. But her eyes never left mine.

"Are you going back?"

I had to ask.

This wasn't my wife. Every word ripped out of my throat.

She isn't mine.

Reed was right.

When I saw Isobel, who this version was—it was going to kill me. She didn't say a word. She just watched me.

"Cabo Verde…"

"Is home…" I trailed off. Her eyes darted to anywhere but me then. The awkwardness evident in the room.

"I don't know," she answered. "I spent years looking for you. I don't think I want to leave right now."

Don't leave at all.

Stay.

Let me get to know you.

I didn't say any of that. Instead I said. "Do you remember…Evie? Sorry, Eva."

"Your sister?" She frowned. No. I blinked rapidly.

Reed's voice was in my head. *Do not breathe wrong. She isn't your wife. Breathe. She doesn't know.*

"Your sister," my voice was gruff as I told her everything. Her eyed widened. "She's married now to Lucas Devereaux. She's also pregnant with a little girl."

I bit back a noise that was trapped in my throat at the sound of that. I had found out when Alisha broke the news gently to me.

She knew what it had done to my brain.

Isobel sat up like an eager child as I told her about Evie.

"You raised her?"

She wiped her eyes as I spoke.

"We have to fill you in on a lot, but if you'd like," I looked around the room. "I know you stay here. You can come back with me. My family. Reed and his girlfriend Alisha are here—"

Eventually I'd have to tell her about that arrangement. I had always been honest with her.

"You should come back with us. Have dinner…" Like it was mundane.

"Talk." She added.

"Yeah," I wiped my eyes. Talk. Meet my new family.

I was still going to kill Liam.

Forget wildfire. I was a volcano waiting to erupt the moment I laid my hands on him.

I had no doubt I'd take him out.

For good.

I held out my hand standing slowly. "What do you say?"

She stood and then, just then, she looked like an eager little girl who was hungry. In more ways than one.

For information.

For family.

For affection.

I knew her still.

Alisha's whisper was there too.

She's still yours in some ways. Honor what you do see. She's just a little different.

But so are you.

She might've not been the same woman who died that night but this girl? I knew bits and pieces of her.

I cataloged those things.

"Yes."

"I'm sorry," the words were a croak now. "I am sorry."

"Why?"

But we were both emotional now.

I wiped my eyes not knowing where to look. "I led you into that assignment. I should've quit. Given you your dance studio. A normal wife. A normal life."

Those words haunted me for seven years.

She let out a breath.

For a moment neither one of us said anything.

"I don't know what happened," she said softly after an eternity. "But if you did…we would not be here…" she motioned to us. "Or any of this."

I tipped my head. Reed wasn't wrong.

I realized now that on the hunt for Isobel's necklace and my lost love?

I had expedited several love stories.

No. I had expedited *all* of them without even trying to.

It would make for one funny story one day. Some day.

"I am sorry for driving your team crazy."

I smirked then easily.

"You can apologize to Reed who probably is losing his mind his entire system got played by a teenager who thinks pancakes are a food group."

At that her laughter bubbled up and it was the same laughter that used to fill my old apartment.

My old life.

My old wife.

I felt myself smiling and then laughter bubbled up in my throat at the idea of Reed finally meeting the devious little hacker downstairs.

"You wanna come and meet them?"

"Yes."

CHAPTER 74
ISOBEL / GABRIEL

"Nice to finally meet you."

Reed Whittaker was huge.

As big as Gabriel in person.

In the winter wind, he looked frightening as it whipped around us.

Unforgiving and colder for me than Cape Verde, I burrowed deeper into my coat as a woman next to him with black hair did the same.

She smiled at me. "Hi, I'm Lish. Nice to finally meet you."

Both of them were smiling equally warm down at me. Despite everything I had done.

Hours ago, I had held a gun to my old brother's face. And then I met my long lost husband. And now I was going to his family's apartment. At K2. With Reed Whittaker. The man who had robbed me.

It was safe to say—I was done adapting. I was just going with it at this point.

Reed was friendly to me as he and Alisha talked about Thierry and Avani going back home to his place after making sure Bexley was safe and sound.

"I'm still adjusting to the fact that he doesn't work for you," Reed added. "I'm still coming to terms with him not being a serial killer."

"He is a serial killer," I said quietly. "But a good one."

Gabriel snorted next to me as he ducked his head rubbing his neck and turning red in the passenger seat.

"Let's go home." He wheezed casting me an amused look, the streetlights glittering off his eyes.

My husband was handsome. Very handsome.

Too handsome. Chiseled jawline. Wheat colored hair. Those pale eyes were a little terrifying in real life. I didn't even hear what he said to Reed who frowned at him.

They were all acting like…I was…just a friend. Like Gabriel had gone to the Primrose to pick me up for their movie date or something. Like this was normal.

Like I was not…Isobel Santos…or Alma…or whoever I was.

Next to me Alisha smiled in the car. "I love your hair, do you bleach it often?"

I shook my head aware I saw Gabriel sit up straighter.

"No. Just for this trip."

"I'm turning on the heated seat, baby." Reed muttered. "It's fucking freezing all the time now."

"New York winter's are terrible," Alisha murmured. "I'm sure it's worse in other places but the wind chill is low. Are you comfortable?"

I blinked drowsily like I was underwater. What was wrong with these people? Why did they act like I was on vacation?

As Reed drove he filled me in.

Samara was still with Shane and clearly upset according to Reed who still looked stunned his operative had been dating mine.

"They met at the gym," he explained shrugging. "Who the fuck does that?"

Gabriel smirked over him lazily. "You met Lish at a club—"

"That's different."

"Why?"

"Lish isn't an operative."

"I was today," she chipped in.

"That's true, Angel. You did a great job."

Alisha sat back beaming at Reed's praise and I found myself smiling with her.

I wanted to go see Bexley but Alisha assured me Garrett was the nicest Titan.

"He sent me photos of her and her donuts…" Reed showed me a photo of Bexley in a hospital bed looking adorably angry but the bed was covered in boxes. "He says, she can be angry all she wants but she's taken a bite out of all of them. Your little hacker is feral." Another text popped up of Garrett saying Bexley had almost bit a nurse.

"Yes, she is. But she is good, no? She keeps you on your toes."

"How did she do that?" Reed asked conversationally.

I told him about Oracle and he almost braked the car. "You redesigned Oracle for Talon?"

I blinked. "Yes."

Why was he so shocked?

Instead of him answering Alisha looked at me carefully.

"Do you think maybe you'd want to do your hair sometime with me?" Alisha blinked all sweet with her hazel eyes on me. "I could help you condition it or something."

"Don't say no to her, Isobel. She'll hunt you down in your sleep." Reed said driving us out of the Primrose.

Gabriel sat in the passenger side next to him with a smirk on his face again. He was quiet. Ever since we spoke in the hotel room we'd walked downstairs like were roommate or something and he'd been quiet.

This was nothing I had prepared for.

Finding a husband was not on my list of to-do things in New York.

"Okay," I agreed to Alisha who watched me.

And then for the entire ride back to wherever we were going? Alisha talked to me.

Like a normal girl.

Like…she was not aware I had died.

Like she was not aware of the last few months at all. Of chess games and psychological warfare. No, like I was just a girl.

Did I ever have female friends? What were they like? I couldn't remember it.

And I didn't know I could feel so grateful for it.

"Your ring is in your hand, do you want me to put it into your necklace?"

She motioned to my cold fingers clutching my ring tightly.

I didn't know if I nodded or not but Alisha helped me put it together. Her warm hands slowly reaching for me, she took out a pair of blue gloves and slipped my fingers into them.

And then she took the necklace and put it over my neck.

She fixed the key next and I thought she would give it to me as well.

Instead, she twisted and handed it to Gabriel.

"This half is yours," she smiled up at him. I saw Gabriel's surprise as he took it.

And then she sat back and looked at me with another smile.

"So, did you like brunch at the Primrose? We never saw you. Otherwise I guess the last few weeks wouldn't have happened..."

~

Gabriel

"I can't fucking believe Avani was dating Thierry," Reed muttered sitting in his office on his computer.

I left Isobel with Alisha as we both talked about one thing—Liam. I did have her in fucking K2. She could stay here tonight.

Right now, everything that I had held back in the hotel room, every single hint of motion and ounce of control was threatening to explode inside of me. The only reason I had an open my mouth is because the only thing that was gonna come out of my mouth was sheer violence.

Alisha had held onto Isobel like they were girlfriends sensing something was wrong as she walked into K2. She showed Isobel around slowly and brought her to the kitchen.

When Reed and I left them, I could smell cinnamon rolls and hot chai being brewed. For dinner.

One of these days Reed and I were going to eventually teach Alisha to eat dinner like a normal person.

"Thierry was working with Lucy somehow," I explained. "How?"

Reed shook his head. "I can't even...I gotta think about that one. For now, I tracked Liam. He's in his apartment still."

"Liam knew about her." I looked at Reed and his entire face paled then. "He knew."

Stormy eyes narrowed on me. "You wanna kill him tonight or tomorrow morning?"

My grin was feral.

And *this* is why I loved Reed. No questions. No hesitations. I simply passed him a shovel and he help me bury the body.

This was seven years careful control that were about to become minutes of vengeance.

I couldn't wait.

I couldn't hold back anymore.

Seven years. He had lost her.

But so had I.

And I loved her.

She chose me.

Not him. And he couldn't live with it.

"Let's go."

I didn't even see anything on the drive to his apartment. Reed didn't say a word. He knew how I felt. For all the training that they had given me the time that I had lived with them, all of the conversations I had, all of the long nights were the three of us stayed up, agonizing over every detail—nothing prepared me for this.

Nothing.

I was moving through like a machine.

"You sure he was here?"

Reed nodded. "His cell phone is."

"And if he isn't?" I asked him. "If he caught on?"

Reed shook his head with a wicked grin. "Before we left I just cut him off the system. He has no access to anything. Evie had given it to him without knowing he was the creator of Oracle. But what Liam didn't know…"

Reed went onto explain that, the copy of the drive I had given him all those years ago? The base of our Oracle AI?

Was Evie's thoughts and her feelings and her emotions.

As in all of the data that Liam had put into the original was his. Not Evie's. It was the same with the one that Isobel had done for Talon.

That's why they had been so good at keeping up with us and staying off the grid.

The one Titan had? Had been perfected by Evie—and so ours ran differently. It had different functions. Based off the creator.

"But because it was Evie's," Reed smirked. "I could go in there and mess around with it easily and her password is Lucas's middle name—Hunter—so I ended up putting that in and boom—Liam's out. He's got no access to our stuff." We made it to his floor. "We really got stop making our passwords so obvious."

I snorted. "Nobody is going to guess Lucas's middle name is Hunter."

Reed motioned. "I'll be out here. Unless you kill him. Then I'll help but you got this."

I should've felt guilty. In a way I did. I did.

Just enough.

But then I remembered her lost look on me.

I remembered she had died bleeding out losing herself and Alma in the process.

She had died not knowing if I was alive or who I was.

And he found her.

He found her on the same cameras he found Lucy.

And he hadn't been planning on telling a soul.

And suddenly the fire was back.

"I got it."

I shot the lock on the door and kicked it open.

CHAPTER 75
ISOBEL / GABRIEL

ALISHA GAVE ME A PAIR OF SOFT PAJAMAS.

The sensation wasn't foreign but Alisha was.

She was foreign to me.

She fed me dinner, moving around the kitchen with comfort and familiarity. Reed Whittaker's penthouse. I was finally here. And as his guest out of all things.

Alisha's hazel eyes were warm and soft on me, her English accent soft and husky and everything about her made me feel like I had known her for years. Alisha had very mothering energy. My girls would like her.

Talia would like her.

The space was unfamiliar. I wasn't used to this. Even Talia did not fuss about me.

She cranked up the heat and then let me shower in a guest room with some pink items she said belonged to Avani.

"You two are about the same size, but she's an inch or two taller, it shouldn't be too bad."

She passed me everything I needed as I did clean up and crawl into the bed feeling more exhausted than I had in forever.

"Gabriel…" I said his name slowly. Testing it out on my tongue.

"He should be back eventually," but Alisha chewed her lip. "Do you want to see photos of Bexley perhaps? My sister went to see her with your…friend Thierry." Alisha's eyes were a little wet as she said it. I didn't know what was happening.

"She stopped biting Garrett finally and he got her to eat. You didn't tell us she was scared of people and hospitals..and food..."

I didn't know. She was raised in Talon. I told Alisha that.

Alisha smiled reassuringly at me. "Well, rest assured I'm pretty sure Garrett has adopted her now. She's in good hands. He wouldn't hurt a fly."

I just wanted Gabriel for some reason.

Pale eyes...my...person?

Ask him more questions.

Find out who Alma was.

"He is honest," I said openly.

Alisha smiled softly at me. "He is. You can ask him anything and he'll talk to you openly. I promise."

I didn't catch a hint of deception in her. "You don't have to go to bed either, if you're not tired you can stay up with me until they come home. But as she said I felt myself ready to pass out.

"My girls are safe?"

She nodded with another warm smile. "I think your Samara wants to murder Shane but he's got her safe and sound. I promise. Nobody would hurt your team..." she trailed off. "Did Gabriel tell you about Evie?"

I nodded. My sister.

"You know her?"

Alisha looked almost embarrassed. "We talk. I know she doesn't know about you and Gabriel held back because of her pregnancy..." She looked more nervous. "Did he tell you what she's naming her daughter?"

"He did not."

Alisha's eyes were softer on me. "She's naming her after you. Isobel Alina Devereaux. But Lucas already calls her Belle for short." I felt my heart thud in my chest. "I think she'll be really happy to see you again. You have no idea how much she's wanted you."

My chest tightened. I didn't even know her and she was... honoring me?

"She...remembers me?"

"She knows Gabriel loves you very much. And I think that's enough until you meet her. And the good news is, things will always get better. No matter what. I know he's very excited to get to know the new you."

492

~

Gabriel

LIAM STOOD FROM HIS COUCH THE MOMENT THE DOOR SLAMMED IN.

Seven years. I hadn't seen him in seven fucking years.

And the first moment of seeing him it was because he took advantage of my wife.

I saw his face fall as he took me in. I saw it in real time. He looked like a ghost of himself. The Liam I knew—the Liam I remembered, was this grinning strong playful man his inky black hair wild and the brightest green eyes. As bright as Selena's.

But right now? They were so dark they were almost black. His hair was matted to his forehead.

The old Liam had died that night.

"You took my necklace," I hissed closing the distance between me and him and his face contorted.

"You killed my sister."

He was unrecognizable.

He wasn't my family.

No, my family was standing outside right now.

When I moved at Liam he seemed to know what was coming.

The rage and fury exploded in me ignoring the bottles of alcohol, the mess, that he was—that he made me.

I didn't feel anything but fury as I moved.

Years of training kicked in and I launched forward. We crashed like animals, a vicious growl leaving his lips—he didn't have his cane and I was glad. I'd kill him either way.

My fist connected not with his face. No. I went for his ribs, his solar plexus. Like a dirty fighter.

And then I went for his face.

Liam's lips were barred. *"You did this to me! You killed my family."*

"You kept my family from me."

Somehow he rolled me over and his fist snapped into my face. "Still got it, motherfucker."

No. I had blind rage. And some part of me knew, for the first time in my life of fighting Liam—I was going to win this time.

I lost it. He was flying off me a second later slamming into the coffee table, spitting up blood. I felt the glass under my sheets and palms as I scrambled to him.

"You were my brother!" I roared. *"You kept her from me!"*

"You killed her!"

"I didn't kill anyone!"

I wasn't sparring. I was going to take him out.

This was about my wife. My daughter.

He broke my family.

I didn't even think, didn't speak. I just lunged myself as Liam and fists went flying. The two of us went at it, I saw him struggling.

He was out of practice. His legs were weaker. I used to think I wasn't that dirty. But I was.

I was a demon.

I went straight for his knees. Sinking to the ground and taking him out. An animal noise left Liam then and I saw him gasping. I didn't give a fuck. Two hits into his face later he groaned.

The first thing my hand found on the ground was the bottle, and I shattered it, the glass was light, and I could smell the alcohol and the blood. I pressed it to his throat, watching red well on the edges.

"Do it," he spat blood out. "Fucking do it. You always wanted to."

"No," I growled. "I never wanted to. I wanted you to be family." I saw it and I felt my voice breaking. *"You knew she was alive. She was alive. She didn't know me. You knew."*

He laughed then outright, blood in his teeth as he practically shoved himself into the glass. "That was her second chance, you son of a bitch. You know how stupid you have to be to drag her into—"

I growled pressing the glass further until Liam's blood was over my hands. "Listen to me, you motherfucker. I didn't drag her into anything. *She is my wife.* She is the mother of my fucking daughter that I lost that night—" Liam stilled. "You think you lost your sister? *I lost my family. I lost. My. Girls.* I lost them both! *And you stayed the victim.* I saved Evie. *I buried Adrianna.* I saved everyone. *You* stayed the victim." His eyes dark as night met mine wilder.

"I lost my world. Over and over and over. I reached out to you. I looked for you. I asked Claire Sutton where you went. She said you left her and you turned into your fucking parents!"

I looked around the place and saw how he lived exactly like how he lived in Quantico. Exactly like that.

Nothing had changed.

No.

He had stayed the same.

And I hadn't.

"All this time, I thought that I had fucked up and I was wrong. I thought I did something to you. And then I realized, that you were never a good person. You were always a piece of shit. She wasn't just your family. She was the only good thing about you. You're a scum bag Liam *Sullivan."*

I sneered watching him grimace at me.

"You're a piece of shit. And you deserve everything that's coming for you. I will never forgive you for keeping my injured wife from me. I will never forget it." I threw the glass on the ground as he bled. "And neither will you."

I stood to my full height and looked down at Liam.

My old brother. On the floor.

I saw him teaching me how to ice skate, I saw him laughing with him when Isobel caught us doing something stupid, I saw him introducing new music to me. I remembered how he made me feel in the past, how he made me laugh, how he and Isobel broke me out of my comfort zones.

Flashes of brothers. Flashes of family.

"Neither will you," I repeated.

I wasn't going to kill Liam.

He was already dead.

He had been for a long time.

And now he was bleeding among all his broken. Not a trace of life anywhere. Not even a plant.

I wiped my chin and walked out. Only to freeze as I closed the door.

I had left Reed alone.

He wasn't alone now. A red-faced Lara looked up at me from the circle of Reed's arms. Alisha's best friend. Now at least.

Her eyes were watering as Reed quietly said. "She came here because he broke up with her to leave her for Isobel. She wanted to talk to him…"

I closed my eyes breathing out. "I didn't kill him, but I can."

Reed shook his head looking down at Lara with soft eyes. Reed always said Lara was the stroke of luck he needed to be with Alisha. She always told him when Alisha was there at Teasers where they met.

"No, I already called Killian, Lara's gonna spend some time with him and Nisha…" Reed trailed off as Lara wiped her eyes shaking.

And then I hated Liam even more.

I hated him the most then.

I had saved her life too.

I couldn't...I couldn't process my emotions for Liam.

I couldn't ever forgive him for keeping her from me.

For putting Lucy in danger by jumping off a building. For letting all of this happen.

If Liam had told me she was my wife and she was alive and she had no fucking clue who I was—I couldn't feel sorry for Liam anymore.

He was too blind to see everything in front of him.

And I wasn't able to let it go.

My fucking wife.

It was her.

This entire time—she had always been mine.

Reed's phone pinged. "Killian's outside in a cab." He motioned to me. "Let's go home. Our girls are waiting. And Alisha made dinner...she says she wants to celebrate."

A new beginning.

A new chapter.

Without the past at my heels.

CHAPTER 76
ISOBEL

I DIDN'T KNOW WHAT TO DO AROUND HIM. BUT I WANTED TO BE around him all the time.

Gabriel did come back that night but I could tell he changed his clothes and cleaned up. A lot.

But I was in the kitchen and when I walked out he was coming in. Without Reed.

"You're bleeding."

I don't know why I felt awkward around him, when I should've felt comfortable. I should've.

But it was hard. He paused at the door, eyes softer watching me as he came in.

"Did you fight Liam?"

He blinked wide and innocently like he was surprised I spoke to him and amused at the same time. His eyes were eerie pale and brighter than usual. But I knew when Thierry got out of a fight and I knew

My heart ached at what I did to Liam. I didn't hate him. I knew why he did what he did. But I was so angry with Liam.

But every single time I thought about Liam—I thought about the little boy who had grown up with me. My brother. Not the Liam he had become.

The Liam life had made him.

Reed Whittaker kept passing me food through the night and feeding me plenty.

Gabriel was doing the same with me.

They seemed to be handling us both, trading places and Reed kept feeding me and asking me questions about my time in New York.

He was really calm when I spoke to him and I wasn't expecting that at all.

"How long do you plan on staying?" Reed asked me his voice lowered. "And can you tell me about Talia?" Reed wanted to know things. Information.

I told him since Renata had been running Cape Verde, I didn't have to go back anytime soon or anywhere. Since I'd come to New York I seemed to have taken a step back.

He listened to me nodding with a delicate frown. "Talon isn't struggling is it?"

I shook my head. "No, we have grown a lot..." I explained our operations to him as he nodded impressed.

"You think if you had a reason to come back you would?" Without me asking Reed kept passing me more pita bread and meats. My plate was overflowing as I ate now.

I shrugged lightly aware he was asking me with his intelligent gray eyes for his best friend.

"I would."

He nodded again like he was considering something. He didn't ask me anything again and thankfully, he put on a movie as the four of us ate. Like we did this all the time.

I did not know how Reed and Alisha were so calm.

But in a way they kept us together.

"Do you want the rest of your lamb?" Gabriel asked me quietly even though there was a plate full of it in front of him. Was he trying to make conversation?

I shook my head. I didn't like it too much.

As Gabriel took from my plate, Reed shot a look over at Alisha who smiled at him. If there was one person he softened around the most it was hers.

Throughout the night I was just catered to and taken care of.

I didn't remember when it hit me but I was slowly passing out. I didn't remember being moved or adjusted but I felt Gabriel sitting by my side my head resting on his shoulders as my eyes drifted.

I was out moments later.

I WENT BACK TO THE PRIMROSE TO CHECK OUT OF MY HOTEL WITH Alisha who insisted on giving me a makeover.

"This might help you reconnect with yourself," she murmured. It took her several hours of a salon visit, and some new clothes for me to look in the mirror and see my hair. "Hmmmm, is this more cherry chocolate or cherry cola?" She said to the stylist.

The woman frowned over it. "Let me go add the gloss."

I had no idea what they were even saying. I did my hair myself. Hours later I was cleaned up and my eyes looked bright as I looked at myself in the mirror. I was getting older, but Alisha had done her magic.

Now? I felt...more like myself. Less than an imposter.

"Selena is going to love meeting you," Alisha said conversationally checking out of the salon using her card. "I thought I'd invite her and Lucy and Avani one day so you can finally meet Lucy. She's technically your sister-in-law. I hope you're not upset about her stealing from you still, now that it all worked out."

Alisha mentioned Lucy and Adam were on a vacation but Selena was in physical therapy with Kellan her boyfriend today.

"I know Gabriel spoke to Lucas..." Alisha looked nervous as we headed to Heron Manor. Now I was a guest. "Safe to say I think given that he's about to be a father he reacted as well as he could." She muttered under her breath. "Which is to say not at all."

I was nervous.

"Samara did not mean to shoot him."

Alisha chewed her lip. "You must forgive Lucas, he wasn't expecting to almost die several times. But he's a bit protective of your sister. Extremely so since then. I know he thinks Talon was after him. Evie's pregnancy for him has definitely driven him over an edge. But Reed and I think it's understandable. Lucas has lost a lot..." she told me all about Lucas and Evie as Selena finished her side and cleaned me up.

Alisha and her let me sit and Selena listened avidly to everything.

Out of everyone there I expected Alisha's sister but she insisted Avani had finals which she was juggling at the end of her term. And Selena was willing to help Gabriel since she was his loyal operative.

Even if it meant this.

I looked different as Alisha finished with me.

I looked more like me.

Alisha beamed at my new raven blue-black hair. It made my eyes brighter. Selena blinked several times looking at me with her emerald eyes.

"Ready to meet your sister?"

I was.

ALISHA TOOK ME TO GREENWICH. THE TITAN MANOR.

Heron Manor...

I was shaking as Alisha led me to the room I knew this place. I dreamed of this home.

I wanted this home.

This was mine. Echoes of my dreams filled me. I held onto Alisha's hand the entire way.

"We were going to have kids..." I whispered. "I wanted to fill the halls with them."

Alisha looked away for a moment as I said it. "Evie will be thrilled to hear that."

She was polite. Proper. And her spine ramrod straight as she opened large French doors into an enormous sunroom.

For a moment had to process all the plants there before I could respond to Alisha.

And then at the end sat my husband.

Gabriel.

With another blonde man who sat with...

"Evie," her name was breath from my lungs.

She was pregnant. On her husband's lap his arms wrapped around her. She looked like she had been crying.

Gabriel looked resigned and Lucas Devereaux...he was my sister's *husband*. No wonder he was familiar. He was family...I met him once sneaking into his office.

As a blonde. With my contacts on. Now? I was me again.

If Evie felt me through the bushes and trees inside she looked up then. Her eyes locked with mine and they widened. How had I missed it?

I had lost myself so much...I didn't see her.

I saw right through her.

500

She looks like Mama.

Her eyes watered as she took me in and stood on weak legs.

Lucas stood with her, blue eyes eyeing me with a wary look his hands on her hips as he pressed his lips to her hair.

Alisha had explained it to me on the way here.

He was especially acute of my sister. She had saved his life in many ways. If he felt like I threatened her—it wouldn't matter who I was.

"Isa..." she whispered her lower lip wobbling.

I felt my eyes blur and water then as Alisha faded way in the background and Gabriel stood next to her while I slowly walked to my sister.

"You're so big now..." I whispered. "You were this big when Mama brought you home." I didn't know how I knew that. I held out my hands to show her.

She smiled her bottom lip wobbling as she nodded.

"You look...you look...like...your p-photos..." Evie wiped her eyes. "Is it...Gabriel says you have head injuries...can I...can I hug you?"

I nodded. And then she was in my arms gingerly, slowly, gently like Alisha had. I didn't move I inhaled her scent. She smelled like... familiar. Like home. Like candy. Lucas moved back letting her go moving to go to Alisha too.

The three of them far away from us now giving us space.

"I didn't know..." Evie whispered. "Gabriel said he didn't know what condition you were in...I'm just happy you're alive..."

I didn't understand. I didn't think Evie knew...I was a robot now. I didn't know what to say.

And that somehow made it worse.

"Will you tell me all bout you?" Evie whispered. "I want to...I want you in my life..."

I nodded unable to speak. I felt...I felt like I hated myself in that moment for not being able to connect with Evie.

I felt for her.

I just couldn't feel her. I felt like I was connecting with people through layers of frost that was slowly thawing out. Alisha told me things took time. Healing wasn't linear. Especially not after what I had been through.

She had seen my scars and told me Adam didn't mind working with me on them. He worked at a place called Haven and Alisha thought I might like her friend Sonya who owned the place.

Alisha came with connections, a network of people who wanted to help me.

And I was healing. Even if it felt glacially slow.

Like I summoned her from a spell Alisha was there. "Isobel wants you two to know she's sorry about the misunderstandings and everything calmed down, isn't that right?" I nodded unable to formulate words right now.

No amount of practice could've prepared me for the moment.

I looked at Lucas. "I am sorry." He looked just as emotional as us.

"It's all good," he whispered like he couldn't formulate words either.

Evie laughed a little in my arms. "Lucy's going to flip out when she meets you but I think you'll like her. She's your sister-in-law too. Technically we're all family now."

Alisha laughed lightly. "This is true. You two catch up a little..." Alisha motioned to us wiping her eyes. "I'll go make tea and cake with Lucas."

She eyed him with the universal sign of *follow me.* As reluctant as Lucas looked eyeing Evie, he went with Alisha.

I saw Gabriel watching after them before turning to us. I could see how much he held back in those moments.

Evie wiped her hands saying something to me about Gabriel and adopting her, but I also saw him moving around us coming closer until he could sit by a few of the plants.

He had done all this. My husband.

Over the week I was getting to know him and he had been polite. Reed insisted I stay at K2 during my stay here. I had prolonged it.

I had stuck around.

As Evie and I talked I was aware of Gabriel fiddling with the plants and hanging out until Evie smiled over at him.

"I'm still angry with you..." she trailed off. "But now our family is complete. Gabriel said your team is staying at the manor..."

They were?

Gabriel filled me in. "Bex is out of the hospital. She's still a little pissed, but Garrett stays here so he brought her over. Samara and

Shane..." he drifted off. "They'll work it out. You can go visit Bexley whenever. Pretty sure she keeps getting lost."

Evie laughed beaming at us her cheeks rosier now between us. "I can't wait to meet Bexley, I can't believe she's a hacker too...It's good to have you back."

"How far along are you?" I asked her quietly motioning to her belly. My sister was having a baby. And for some reason I couldn't quite name it I felt my own stomach hollow out.

"Six months," she flushed. "Lucas is more nervous than I am though." Gabriel smirked at that. "He says he just wants to have the baby at home where he can control all the variables instead of leaving it up to doctors. He hired a mid-wife and a doctor on call so I can have her...we named her after you and Selena. You haven't met her yet but..."

As Evie talked I saw Gabriel's eyes meet mine over her head. He was rubbing her back and holding her on the other side.

Evie rambled happily about her plans and I realized Gabriel had been her support system for so long and he still was.

A family.

And I realized the more I met my new family—the less I wanted to leave.

Later that evening the rays of sunlight hit the sunroom and I was walking out alone in the pathway leading to a swing Gabriel had put up for Evie.

I didn't feel good seeing my sister.

Instead I felt this impending sense of having done everything wrong in my life.

I felt like a failure of a big sister or a person all the time.

It was something Talia and I had spoken about. Life always went on without me and Talia and I always felt like we were juggling too much or struggling. For once I felt like I wasn't.

But I was struggling with other emotions.

I felt out of place comforting a sister I had never known that was rescued by my husband I forgot.

But I liked Evie. I had a hard time connecting with people. And so for a majority of dinner I spent it watching Evie and Gabriel interact. Like a weird outsider engaging conversation where I didn't belong.

"You do belong."

His voice cut through my thoughts like soft butter.

"You okay?"

I didn't whip around.

No. He was too pretty to ignore, but it was an adjustment being around my husband.

Initially I stayed in a separate room in K2 with Reed Whittaker. It wasn't as awkward as I thought it would've been after I saw Bexley in the hospital. Samara was staying with Shane and I found myself at K2.

Gabriel stayed there and eventually wanted me to move into Greenwich. To Heron Manor.

I didn't know what kind of reception I thought I'd get at finding my long lost husband but both of us were just adapting and adjusting daily.

I didn't know how to say yes.

"Yes, I'm good."

"You always say that," his half-smile told me he knew I was lying.

"I am," I wrapped the sweater around myself I was wearing. Earlier on Lucy Devereaux dropped by to grab her brother and Evie and I got to confront the woman who stole my necklace.

My husband hadn't exactly hired her. But I had to forgive her and move on from finding it.

Gabriel gave it back. He did.

But once I knew what it was I had more questions than not.

"Did you go to Talia?"

I did. I had.

"I went, but her and Drew her husband weren't available. Something about the baby—" I explained it to him. Gabriel frowned.

"I didn't know the DuPont's had a new baby."

I talked to him for a bit about the DuPont's but in all reality I sat on the swing killing time. Gabriel ended up sitting next to me and talking like a friend.

I laughed when he rolled his eyes. Easy-going was not the word I associated with him.

"How long are you staying with Reed?"

He was deceptively casual when it came to asking me questions.

"Not sure. I do not need to go back to Cape Verde for a few more weeks."

"Is it difficult now being in the States for your work?"

No. It wasn't.

It was difficult realizing I had a husband. And then I had to adapt to the rest of the things that had happened to me in the last few years.

"Do you wanna move into the manor?"

That question came out of nowhere but I should have seen it coming. I should've.

I did not either way.

Alisha warned me he would want me closer. She told me to say yes if he did because he never let anyone live there but Evie. And guests.

The idea of him being with a woman made my stomach churn but then again, what did I know?

I thought about it.

What did I have to lose?

After a lifetime of moving and running and pushing, I realized that I had to give in a tiny bit like I did with Talia.

I thought about it quietly.

And more.

I swung my feet back and I felt him getting up. Since I'd met him we hadn't really done anything. Not a kiss. Barely a hug. He was polite about keeping his distance, but I realized discreetly how playful my husband was.

A burst of laughter left me when I felt him pulling the swing back a little.

I couldn't stop my laughter from bubbling over when he grinned.

"I haven't done this to you in years."

"Did we do things like this a lot?"

"We did. You were my best friend."

"We did?"

"Mhm, we went out to local diners, restaurants, and you picked out strange furniture—"

"It's not strange—"

"It's eclectic—"

"It is—"

He chuckled and I felt a burst of heat blossom in my gut. Lower. Places I didn't think even worked anymore.

My husband was beautiful in a way I couldn't even explain anymore. And he got along with everyone.

And he was pushing me on a swing set he built for my sister.

Out of nowhere the emotions bubbled up in me and I couldn't hold it back. But I did my best.

"Did you want to move in? Or do you plan on staying at the Primrose?"

"I was planning on staying at the Primrose..."

But not with Reed.

It's not that I felt uncomfortable with them, but I felt like I was always intruding until I was alone.

But with Gabriel I didn't feel like that at all. I didn't.

But I didn't know how I felt.

I just knew I didn't know Gabriel. But I knew myself. Right?

"If you want you can stay here..."

What?

I paused swinging my feet. "But this is your home."

"It is, but if you wanted a place to stay that wasn't K2."

Gabriel paused for a second, his face held no expression.

Sometimes when he sat like that he was a stone statue.

He sat like that at K2 sometimes over coffee, pouring over his laptop and notes about everything he did for Titan.

Whenever I walked by him, I wanted to stop and ask him questions, but he let me live. He left me alone.

And after spending seven years searching, I was surprised by how calm he was.

I wanted to say ninety different things to him. But instead all I could manage was a numbed out hello.

Most of the time I didn't know what to do around him.

"You stay here with Evie?"

I knew he didn't. I don't know why I asked a question I already knew the answer to. I don't know why I said anything at all sometimes. I just felt uncomfortable and maybe he knew that.

"No, I used to—"

He told me about how years ago after my death he adopted my sister. We sat and talked until the sun slowly went down and Gabriel didn't pressure me for an answer.

I don't know why I thought he would.

"Will you stay?"

I thought about it for a second because the wind rushed in and everything in me leaned towards him not away from him.

"Yes."

TEN YEARS LATER

GABRIEL

"...BUT I WANTED TO SNUGGLE MAMA..."
  "I know, but I get to snuggle Mama first—"
  "But you always snuggle her..."
  "I do not—"
  "Roman—"
  "Thierry—"
  "Both of you be quiet or we're going to wake up Mom—"
  "Thierry—"
  "No—"
  "I wanna wake him up—"
  "No, don't—"
  "I wanna snuggle Mom—"
  "No—"
  "Yes—"
I felt the bundle hit the bed before I could stop it.
Roman.
Here we go. I love my life, but my kids were gonna kill me.
I was already awake.
Even if I felt like I went to sleep ten minutes ago.
Nobody ever said having kids was easy.
Especially not my offspring.
  I rolled over to find three identical pair of blue eyes batting up at me. They were brighter than mine and one of them was grinning ear to ear as I looked. All three of them, had their mom's smile.

Mischievous and playful, dark blue eyes bat up at me.

Roman.

"Dad—"

Thierry shot me a shy smile as Adam launched himself into my arms.

"Dad," my oldest Roman looked remorseful as Isobel rolled over slightly. Every single molecule in my body froze.

Roman raised a brow over at her first and slowly inched over until he was snuggled up in her.

Isobel unconsciously moved to snuggle him like it was a second nature. At this point, it was. Roman was her baby, but he was our second.

Thierry was our first. And he was quiet like me.

"What are you guys doing?" My voice was gruff, but I should've been used to them sneaking in all the time.

But I wasn't.

Not when I knew my wife snuck in, passed out, and I was trading shifts to care for our toddler. She was supposed to be sleeping next to us in a bassinet by the bed, but she snuck out to her sisters all the time.

Roman mumbled something but Isobel unconsciously smoothed his hair back and he quieted down.

He always broke in and I'd wake up with him wrapped around her. I wasn't saying I was jealous, but I was. Now with kids I got less of my wife in general. And it wasn't the same.

Our marriage had changed over the years after so many kids, but I remembered being the kid who met her and fell in love all those years ago.

After months and months of fighting for her, fighting for everything—I had her. And now?

The least of all my problems was lying in bed doing absolutely nothing, but snuggling my sons. But I always felt like I didn't get enough of my wife anymore.

But Thierry slid closer to me and snuggled under the covers.

"Can we have pancakes today?" Adam whispered. And then he hit me with the—"I ordered some."

Adam was the responsible one out of my kids. Reasonably.

Roman was super responsible but I swore he was thirty before he was three.

All of my boys were on top of everything letting their sisters breathe a lot more and I was grateful.

I didn't want my daughters turning out like my wife, hyper-vigilant and on guard all the time after everything.

No, they got to relax a lot more.

Reed had given them phones for Christmas early on and they'd lost their minds.

"Chocolate chip?"

"Chocolate chip pancakes sounds good," I snuggled them closer. "Your sisters agreed?"

"All of them are asleep, Dad."

I grinned.

That's because whenever Isobel would go to the other girls rooms, they'd all snuggle up together and they'd never wake up.

In the last ten years, we had six kids. Three daughters Sarielle and Serafina and Seraphim. And three sons.

It had been ten years since my wife came into my life. She did move in. We got engaged a year after we started dating.

I was expecting even a tiny bit of a fuss, but Isobel had changed.

I had changed.

Life happened to both of us.

And rather than being that hot-headed idiot I had been losing my wife, I learned to change and think more like her.

And once we started having kids?

Instead of silence in my house, there was the patter of footsteps all along the halls. And it was more than I could've ever asked for.

I was forty-one. And she was forty.

And we were celebrating my youngest birthday, Seraphim was turning two and she was fast asleep. After keeping Isobel up all night.

I never thought once I'd make it past thirty. And there I was looking forward to a lifetime with my wife.

But first—I had a bunch of new recruits to greet, a few handful of errands to run, babies to feed, and my wife to love.

Being a Dad meant adapting to everyone else's schedules in the house even if you wanted to make love to your wife all day and all night.

Because that's all I wanted to do sometimes is be wrapped around my wife the way Roman was. But we were a busy couple.

She was the head of Talon.

I was the head of Titan.

And together we merged them together to have Thierry lead the teams.

And that was my life now.

And I couldn't have asked for better. But I would be lying if I said I didn't want to be with my wife.

But with six kids?

It was impossible.

I leaned back to find Isobel sleeping soundly and Roman snuggling into Isobel soundly. He didn't move after he got comfortable.

And what was I supposed to do?

I hid my grin in Adam's hair.

"What are you up to so early?"

"I called the catering team."

I burst into quiet laughter in his hair. "Did you?"

"They texted your phone so I went to the kitchen and called them and told them what kind of cakes we wanted."

That was my son.

That was definitely my son.

"And what was that?"

He murmured about the flavors of cake. My wife stirred and I rolled over to watch over her and Roman. That was my only new hobby. Along with managing Titan? I loved my wife too much to be anything else.

I stayed in bed for hours. Eventually Adam and Thierry started murmuring to me and Roman fell asleep in her arms.

"Do you guys wanna head to the kitchen without me? I'll meet you there?"

"Okay," Adam murmured. "But I want to snuggle too."

"Me too."

I cuddled them closer fully aware of myself processing emotions just like Isobel was always doing.

Both of us had changed after the seven years of searching for each other.

Life hadn't quieted down but my life had gone from running around all the time to settling down with kids—finally at Heron Manor. Finally.

My wife.

She was my wife.

And I had her. The kids. The life. Titan.

Everything had worked out.

Everything.

Everything.

"Roman."

"Yes, Daddy."

I sighed snuggling closer to them, drawing Adam and Thierry into my arms.

"Daddy, do you have work today?"

"Roman, come here."

"I'm coming, Daddy. Do you have work?"

I did. For a brief moment. I had to go to Titan Midtown, something I could easily assign to Thierry.

I held him closer to me.

"What are you gonna tell them when you see them? The people who work for you?"

I thought about it for a second.

Just a second.

"Do you want to do it with me?"

He beamed ear to ear. "Yes."

We went through the entire day wrangling the kids in who were the most well-behaved kids I could've had. I would've thought they'd take after Liam, but he had a daughter—Luna.

And Luna was a sweetheart attached to Adam.

Adam sat with Luna during the brief and I started it never feeling more proud of who I was.

"Welcome to Titan..."

ABOUT THE AUTHOR

Lilah Lance writes for every girl who just wants to be loved for who she is.

When Lilah isn't writing she likes to travel and spend her downtime on the beach.

For more info, check out www.lilahlance.com where you can subscribe to her newsletter for all things exclusively Titan.

www.ingramcontent.com/pod-product-compliance
Lightning Source LLC
Chambersburg PA
CBHW072011020726
47501CB00006B/1765